Amy Elman Doesn't Feel Sexy

Mary Newnham grew up in Didcot with a view of the power stations. Her love for filmmaking led her to a degree in Film Production. She has worked in an advertising agency in London, as a producer in Australia, and as a tour guide in Oxford. She found her passion for writing in her early twenties, when she started blogging about Bloody Marys. In 2022, she gained an MA in Creative Writing at Oxford Brookes. When she's not writing fiction, she writes and records The Quack, which features humorous stories and muddled observations about being a millennial woman. *Amy Elman Doesn't Feel Sexy* is her debut novel.

Amy Elman Doesn't Feel *Sexy*

MARY NEWNHAM

HODDER &
STOUGHTON

First published in Great Britain in 2026 by Hodder & Stoughton Limited
An Hachette UK company

The authorised representative in the EEA is Hachette Ireland,
8 Castlecourt Centre, Dublin 15, D15 XTP3, Ireland (email: info@hbgi.ie)

1

Copyright © Mary Newnham 2026

The right of Mary Newnham to be identified as the Author of the
Work has been asserted by her in accordance with
the Copyright, Designs and Patents Act 1988.

All rights reserved. No part of this publication may be reproduced, stored
in a retrieval system, or transmitted, in any form or by any means without
the prior written permission of the publisher, nor be otherwise circulated
in any form of binding or cover other than that in which it is published and
without a similar condition being imposed on the subsequent purchaser.

All characters in this publication are fictitious and any resemblance
to real persons, living or dead, is purely coincidental.

A CIP catalogue record for this title is available from the British Library

Paperback ISBN 9781399751841
ebook ISBN 9781399751858

Typeset in Plantin Light by Manipal Technologies Limited

Printed and bound in Great Britain by Clays Ltd, Elcograf S.p.A.

Hodder & Stoughton policy is to use papers that are natural, renewable
and recyclable products and made from wood grown in sustainable forests.
The logging and manufacturing processes are expected to conform
to the environmental regulations of the country of origin.

Hodder & Stoughton Limited
Carmelite House
50 Victoria Embankment
London EC4Y 0DZ

www.hodder.co.uk

To the ones who felt they weren't enough.

Skogsfräken

180 Nights

Josh's back is a hairless white wall with seven moles – four on the left shoulder and three down the spine. If you stare at it long enough, you can make out the Big Dipper or a square-bodied sperm. He's spooning his Swedish lover, Skogsfräken. When we bought the easy-care IKEA pillow last summer, I didn't expect it would be something I had to compete with, but mornings like these make me feel jealous of the machine-washable Scandinavian.

It hasn't always been this way. When we were two scrappy students, we'd wake up and find each other under the thin duvet, and I'd get so close to him that his skin became blurry. I guess it's only natural after 10 years for the novelty of my body to wear off.

Josh's alarm goes off, which means it's six on the dot. There isn't a sound on earth that I hate more than Apple's Radar alarm. He wriggles, stretches and flips over.

'How's the head, Lab Rat?' he asks. His smile is too big for this time of morning.

'Why didn't you stop me?' My voice comes out like a fuzzy radio. It was meant to be a quiet local New Year's Eve in Clapham Junction with Pete and Nina, but cheap Prosecco and other forces (sambuca) ended that. I can sort of remember Nina and me singing Aretha Franklin's 'Respect' into wine bottles and Pete challenging Josh to a press-up competition in the middle of Northcote Records. The rest is a little hazy.

Josh jumps out of bed, picks up a pair of boxers from the folded pile on the drawers and gives them a big, long sniff.

'They're clean,' I groan.

'Clean boxers, what a beautiful start to the year.' He pulls them up, then puts his gym shorts on and tightens them around his branchy hips.

'Are you *actually* going to the gym on *New Year's Day*?' I ask in disgust.

'It's Chest Day,' he says, offended. 'Muscles don't read calendars, Amy.'

I roll my eyes at the ceiling. It began with the Joe Rogan podcast, followed by a gym membership, and now I'm living with a man who seems to be training for war. I've never heard so many motivational quotes in my life. At any given opportunity, he will slip one into a conversation, even when not requested (they are never requested). Another element of this new lifestyle is that the days of the week are now named after body parts. Today is Monday, which means Chest Day. Tomorrow will be Back Day, Wednesday is Leg Day, and so forth. I didn't want this gym routine to be burnt into my brain, taking up space, but that's where we are.

Josh begins lunging in the middle of our bedroom floor.

'Mum's going to ask us a favour today,' he says.

'If it's to look after Gary again, then please, please, please, can we not say yes?'

'What's wrong with Gary?' he says, frowning.

'Don't you remember? He barked at everything all day, every day.'

'Gary is great.'

I bite my lip. I refuse to spend the first morning of 2025 listing reasons why Gary, the chaotic Springer Spaniel, is not great. 'So, you think that's the favour, dog sitting?'

He shrugs mid-lunge and gives me that dimpled smile that has escorted him through life. Josh is blessed with the elements of a good-looking man; he has the dark hair, the watery blue eyes, the thick beard. His only insecurity is that he wishes he was six foot, not five foot ten. It doesn't bother me in the slightest as he's still way taller than me, but men are funny about those things.

'Right, let the gains begin,' he shouts, bouncing up into the air. He kisses me on the forehead and dashes off like he's late for a train.

I'm left with his grubby grey imprint next to me. We really need to buy new sheets this year. On his bedside table is a photo of us, gifted by me and put there by me. It was taken in the Alps during an après-ski session almost two years ago to the day. We are puffed out in skiwear with his arm over my shoulder and we have identical grins. He had proposed only an hour before in a cable car that we were sharing with a couple from Ohio. '*Oh my Ghad!*', '*Oh my Ghad!*', '*Oh my Ghad!*' was the background noise to that intimate moment.

I get my notebook (*not* journal) from the drawer in my bedside table. It was bought so I could plan our wedding in it. On the first page, I've written, 'Amy and Josh's Wedding'; beneath it is a long list with nothing checked off. We quickly realised that if we wanted to save for a deposit for our dream countryside cottage life *and* afford our dream wedding venue, which is one of those rustic barns (I know, it's cliché), we would need some time to save. So that's what we're doing now – saving. I flick to the back of the notebook, where the page is filled with tally marks. I draw a diagonal stick to make another set of five. That makes 180 sexless nights in a row.

There are prison sentences shorter than this.

I sort myself out. Porn is too on the nose for me. Instead, I have Graham Moores, the astrophysicist podcaster, who talks about the universe in a husky, Southern drawl. The cover is of him staring up at the night sky. He's on a horse wearing a black cowboy hat, his thick thighs are bursting out of his jeans.

I pop in my earbuds and take off my star-patterned pyjama bottoms. Graham's voice goes into my ears and down my body. '*The mean orbit velocity which is the average speed of an entire orbit of Pluto is around 10,444 mph. Y'all know this is a snail's pace compared to Earth, which orbits at 66,622 mph ...*'

Under the covers, I let out a tiny moan as I climax. I lie there, arms spread out, enjoying that blissful minute as my body recovers. Graham. What a man.

Right. *Now*, I can start the new year.

I get to the bathroom before Fifi gets there first. Fifi is our flatmate who hibernates in her bedroom, only appearing to heat up bowls of Heinz Cream of Tomato soup. When our paths do cross, the conversation is staggered and awkward, and neither of us enjoys the interaction. However, she pays her rent, she's tidy and she doesn't throw drug parties. That's all anyone needs from a London flatmate.

I rinse off the hangover and then try to make myself presentable for the world.

Unlike Josh, there isn't anything gravitating about my appearance. I am that mousey-haired pale British woman you see on every Tube ride. Over the years, people have told me I've got nice eyes. They are brown with a hint of gold. Can't complain. Josh likes my eyes too. He has also said that I have good skin and a cute nose. Like a lot of men, he's sparing with his compliments. I could do more with what I've got; learn how to do make-up properly, maybe get manicures, and I really should go to the gym. Now and again, I get inspired to buy something on-trend, like high-waisted flared jeans. Everyone seems to be wearing high-waisted flared jeans. So, I'll try them on, only to look like Humpty-Dumpty at a disco. At 29, I'm resigning to the fact I'm just not that woman, and that's okay. I bring other qualities to the table.

I towel-dry my hair and put on my trusty black jumper dress. Done.

By the time I'm ready, Josh is back from the gym and in the kitchen, whisking a post-workout protein shake, a bright pink goo that matches the colour of his cheeks.

'Ready for The Big Butterses' New Year's Day Lunch?' he says. No, I'm not ready to force leftover beef and stale mince pies into my mouth to please your mum. I don't say this.

'After coffee,' I murmur as I reach for the kettle.

'Caffeine.' He tuts and shakes his head. This is the same man who survived on flat whites for most of our relationship, but since he's been sucked into the fitness cult, he believes caffeine is on par with heroin.

'Your ring is here, by the way.' He holds up my engagement ring, aka his dead Grandma's engagement ring. It's a battered silver band with a humongous amethyst gem. When he opened the velvet box in the cable car that day, a tiny voice in my mind screamed, WHAT ON EARTH IS THAT? Then he asked me the question, and I cried as he slipped it on. Happy tears, of course.

'Oh! I must have taken it off to wash up . . . again,' I say, putting the bright purple diamond back on.

Gramps

No matter what is happening in the world, you can always rely on The Butters Family to be consistent.

Josh always parks behind his dad's white van in the driveway. Gary goes berserk as soon as the engine is cut, and then the red door of the terrace house opens, and Josh's parents appear arm in arm. His dad, Jason Butters, is bald with a surprisingly gentle face. He lives for Man United, Saturday fry-ups and his kids. Linda Butters was born to be a mother. She is cuddly, floral and likes her tea milky with three sugars. She may have had wild nights in the eighties, but there are no signs of them now.

'I hope you guys are hungry,' Linda calls out from the doorstep. And I get that feeling that I always get when I see Josh's family, of being wrapped in a crochet blanket.

Their home is a shrine to the Butters Family. As you walk in, you are met with the hall of fame of family moments from the last three decades. There is a framed photo of 16-year-old Josh eating a burger at a family BBQ, and another of his older sister Laura sitting in a tree as a toddler. Then there are more typical photos, like Josh's graduation and Laura and Ray's wedding. Laura is almost reaching Ray's height with her hair in a huge up-do, whilst Ray is staring intensely into the camera through his glasses as if he's there against his will. Linda and Jason are next to Laura and look so proud that they could burst into a thousand confetti pieces. I am next to Josh – sunburnt and distracted by something off-camera. There is also a photo of Josh and me at his dad's sixtieth birthday. His arm is over my shoulder, and this time I'm looking at the camera and smiling. I remember when I first saw it hanging there and felt warmed that the family didn't mind seeing my face every day on their wall.

I wasn't used to seeing myself in a frame. My parents were never the type to capture and cherish memories. The family photos we did have were kept in a photo album on a shelf in the dining room, next to the encyclopaedia set. The walls of our house were used to display The Elmans' achievements. Mum's dentistry certificate was in the lounge. Dad's Gynaecologist certificate was awkwardly placed in our kitchen. Where there wasn't a certificate, there was an oil painting of a landscape. Dad would find them in antique stores and charity shops and prided himself on having a 'good eye'. Mum silently disagreed, and when they broke up, she found great joy in throwing all the landscapes away.

I go into the kitchen and, as always, it's alive and kicking. Empty New Year's Eve Prosecco bottles line the bench and gold confetti pieces in the shape of 2025 are sprinkled across the floor. The Christmas tree is struggling in the corner, and Robbie Willims is playing. Jason believes nineties pop was the best era of music. I don't fully disagree with him.

'Hot! Hot! Hot!' Laura's husband, Ray, shouts as he rushes past me. He squeezes a tray of brown balls onto the kitchen table, which is already full of food. There are different-sized sausages, a half-eaten classic dip selection, a plate of bashed-in mince pies, slices of dried-up beef, broken-up pieces of bread and a bowl of Pringles. On every place mat, there is a Christmas cracker ready to be cracked.

'What's that?' Laura asks, gesturing towards the cabbage in Josh's hand. She is sitting at the end of the table on her phone. Laura likes nothing more than scrolling through videos on Instagram, most likely titled things like, 'POV: You're Married' or 'POV: You Hate Your Job'. She met Ray on a dating app and moved him from Kent to Maidenhead so she could be close to her parents. He paints Warhammer figures and earns a heck of a lot of money in IT. Laura works as an HR person for a pharmaceutical company. She hates every second of it but is staying for the maternity leave package. Recently, she dyed her hair blonde and cut it into a bob, turning her straight into her mum.

'Our contribution to the lunch,' Josh says, proudly lifting the cabbage. It was the only thing we had other than protein bars.

'A cabbage? You are useless. My stuff is from M&S,' she says and looks back down at her phone.

Linda takes my arm. 'I need your help, Amy. It was Jason's job, but the football seems to have taken him again.' She pulls me to the cooker, where there is a tower of M&S boxes. She takes one from the top and squints. 'Prawns . . . in . . . blankets. What is this world coming to?' She examines the cooking instructions for a second and then gets flustered. 'Oh, I don't know.'

'Leave it with me,' I say. It's not that Linda is incapable of heating canapés, she just can't be bothered.

She pulls me into one of her peach-potpourri-scented hugs.

'You're a star. What would we do without you?'

'Mum. What do you want to do with the cabbage?' Josh says, demanding her attention.

'Just put it on the side, dear. We'll erm . . .' She stares into space. 'Actually, Joshy, can you use your new big muscles to mash the potatoes?'

Josh hesitates for a second. 'I . . . was about to catch the end of the match, if that's okay?' He gives her his dimpled smile.

Linda puts her hands on her hips and sighs warmly at her son. 'Oh, go on then.'

Josh escapes the kitchen. A moment later, I hear him with his dad in the living room, shouting profanities at the referee. Classic.

I begin sliding the trays into the oven in order of duration. Ray has been given the potatoes to mash, along with opening the wine and putting the dishwasher on. An animal cheer comes from the lounge; Man United must have scored. Is it bad that my fiancé makes more noise while watching football than in our bed?

'Where's Ellie?' a croaky, small voice says. I turn to see Gramps staring vacantly around the kitchen. Gramps hasn't been 'with it' since Grandma Ellie died five years ago. He looks about 105. There's a white crust around his mouth, a ring of cloudy hair from ear to ear, and he is practically blue from all the veins poking out from his skin. He always wears a suit and tie, and today his tie has a dancing penguin on it.

'I hope you like M&S food, Gramps,' Laura says. Gramps squints like he can't detect where the voice has come from.

'Where's Ellie?' he repeats.

'Let's sit you down, Dad.' Linda parks him at the end of the table. I open the oven door to put the chicken doughnuts in.

'Who's that girl over there, the one with the big bottom?' Gramps yells.

'Dad, don't say things like that,' Linda loudly whispers.

'Who is it, though?'

'That's Amy, Josh's fiancée.' Still loudly whispering. 'You're not allowed to say things like that anymore.' I carry on as if I haven't heard anything, but turn away so that my bum is out of Gramp's eyeline. Josh and Jason pile back into the kitchen on a high. Man United won. Good for them. Josh comes over, peers at what I'm doing, and picks up one of the M&S canapé boxes.

'Did you know there are 200 calories in that chicken doughnut?' he says.

'Joshy! Please, I do not want to hear a word about calories or carbs or that macro malarky,' Linda says, pointing at her son with a spoon. 'And you, Mr . . .' She turns to Jason, who is taking a can of Budweiser out of the fridge. 'Slow down. We don't want a dizzy Butters on our hands.'

There is a loud bang. I jump, Linda yelps and Gary barks. Gramps is unpacking his now-cracked cracker. He inspects a tiny pack of cards with dissatisfaction and then places a purple paper crown on his head.

'I want to eat now,' he says.

Ray's OCD doesn't let us sit until all the food has been arranged properly. Eventually, after a lot of slotting here and there, everything just about fits. Just. Linda digs in first, poking a podgy cocktail sausage with her fork.

'Diet starts tomorrow,' she announces to everybody. The smell of experimental canapés wafts up my nose and stirs up the warm puddle of last night's Prosecco in my stomach.

'Beef?' Josh asks, hovering a slightly grey slice over my plate. I shake my head, feeling sick, and then tear off a chunk of stale baguette.

'Where's the turkey?' Gramps asks.

'Dad, we ate the turkey,' Linda replies.

Gramps chuckles in disbelief. 'What kind of woman doesn't have a turkey at Christmas?'

Linda sighs and puts her knife and fork down to explain. 'We had Christmas, Dad. I got you that penguin tie you're wearing right now. This is The New Year's Leftover Lunch. Mum used to do it, remember?' She picks up her fork again and stabs another sausage.

Gramps looks down at his plate like it's a puzzle. To be fair to him, considering there is a pile of mash, two balls of stuffing, a prawn-in-blanket and a couple of Ferrero Rochers, I would be confused too.

'Why don't you try an M&S blue cheese ball?' Linda says and puts one on his plate. Gramps tries to scoop it up with his fork, but instead, he pushes it off the plate and it rolls onto the floor. Gary eats it.

'What was that favour you wanted to ask, Mum?' Josh says.

Gramps slams his fist on the table. 'Where's the turkey?'

'Dad,' Linda moans. Gramps stands up. 'Dad. Dad. Sit down. Here, have a chicken doughnut.'

'No.' He shuffles out of the kitchen and continues his rant down the hallway. 'I won't have this family going without a turkey this Christmas.'

Josh gets up.

'Leave him,' Linda says, waving her son down. 'He usually goes to the end of the road and comes back.' The front door slams, and the only noise left is Robbie singing 'Old Before I Die'.

The song ends. A pause, and then 'Angels' starts to play. Jason gets up. 'I'll go find him,' he says. Josh stands again but is waved down once more. 'Stay, Josh. Your mum needs to talk to you.' Jason pats Linda on the shoulder before leaving the kitchen. 'Ray, come,' he demands from the hallway. Ray's only protest is a small sigh before he leaves the table. As soon as the front door closes, Linda bursts into tears.

'Mum, are you okay? What's wrong?' Josh asks. It's as if it's the first time he has seen his mum cry, which is odd because she cries at everything: a royal parade, *The Bake Off* final, or having to parallel park on a busy street.

'Sorry. Sorry. Oh dear. This is not how we want to start the new year now, is it?' She wipes her cheeks, but then begins sobbing again.

'Mum, I think you should just ask them,' Laura says.

'Ask what?' Josh says.

'Go for it, Mum,' Laura says encouragingly. Linda takes a long, shaky inhale through her nose. I stare at the torn-up piece of bread on my plate, mentally preparing myself for whatever this may be.

Linda sniffs. 'I have one wish, and that is to see Dad . . . see my son . . . get married.'

'We are getting married,' Josh says, confused. We give each other a sideways glance, and he adds, 'Eventually.' This seems to infuriate Laura.

'When is "*eventually*", though?' she says, waving her hands about. I didn't realise this was such an emotional topic.

Josh shrugs. 'Like next year or the year after.' Linda starts crying even more. Josh and I look at each other, alarmed. 'Why? What's happening? Is something wrong?'

Laura looks pained as she rubs her mum's back. I have a bad, bad feeling about this.

'Gramps is getting worse by the day. This morning, he thought Ray was our cleaner,' she says. I want to say that this is an easy assumption to make because Ray is always either tidying things up or cooking, so it's not fair to judge Gramps for making this mistake. 'We all think the wedding needs to be sooner.'

'How soon?' Josh asks, but I jump in before Laura can answer. I've already explained this a few times to The Butters Family, but here we go again.

'We would get married sooner, but like we've said before, we really want our wedding in The Chipping Barn, and we also need to save for our dream home in the country. We *both* think it's more important to get on the property ladder before we spend money on our wedding. If we stick to my budget . . .' I eyeball Josh, because he's not been very good at this. 'We'll move next year, and the wedding will be a year after that. Right, Josh?'

He nods.

To my surprise, Laura breathes out a sigh of relief. 'Phew, we were hoping it was only the financial issues.' She smiles at her mum and back at us. 'To speed things along, we are going to pay for The Chipping Barn. Mum, Dad, Ray and I.'

Josh's mouth falls open.

'You're going to pay for the venue?' he says, excited as a child on Christmas Day. He shakes my arm, but I am too suspicious to share his excitement. The Butters Family are excellent at together time and TV quizzes. They are not so good at forward thinking. The year after university, when I was in teacher training and Josh was still figuring out what to do, we all went on a family holiday to Cornwall . . . in January. Josh had toyed with becoming a surfing barista, so Linda surprised us with a surf lesson. We spent an hour falling off surfboards into ice-cold Cornish seas. Consequently, we both got sick, and spent the rest of the holiday snuggled under a duvet, having snotty sex. That was far better than the original itinerary of crab fishing with his parents. It also, thankfully, put a pin in Josh's surfer dream.

'Ray's boss has given him a huge bonus, and Mum and Dad are happy to help,' Laura says.

'Gosh. That's so kind,' I say, careful not to sound patronising. 'But it's more expensive than what people think. Not crazy expensive, but not the amount you would expect.'

Laura smiles. 'We know how expensive it is, because we popped in and spoke to them.'

'You *popped* in and *spoke* to them?'

'It's only down the road . . .' Laura adds, as if the distance was my biggest concern.

'Okay,' I say, trying to make sense of this in my head. 'But, even if we had all the money in the world, it's an 18-month waiting list.' They shift when I say this, suddenly looking uncomfortable. Linda watches her hands intensely as her fingers dance around each other.

'What is it, Mum?' Josh says.

Linda opens her mouth and says, slowly, 'Yes . . . they are completely booked up . . . But there is a cancellation on the 22nd February.'

'Next year? That's doable. I guess. Although, we kind of wanted a summer wed—'

'This year,' Laura interrupts.

'This year?' I blurt out. 'As in seven weeks? You want us to have a wedding in seven weeks? In February?' Josh squeezes my thigh to shut me up. Linda begins to sob, really sob.

'I knew it – I knew it would be too much to ask,' she wails.

'No, Mum, we can get married—' Josh goes to say, but I cut him off before he says anything detrimental. I go for a softer approach.

'Look, we would get married then, we would. But it's almost impossible for my family to make it with such short notice. Dad and Jean-Ivy will likely be busy on holiday, and Mum will be cruising in the Adriatic Sea.'

Laura jumps in. 'Well, we thought about that, so we called them, and your mum said she'll cancel her cruise if needed, and your dad and his wife can make it, so . . .'

'Wow. Isn't that great, Amy?' Josh says, shaking my leg. I realise then that I'm a one-man army rapidly running out of ammo.

'Okay, well, my family may be able to make it, but what about my bridesmaids? Rebecca has a baby now, and Abi is busy with her lab experiments. Nina is a workaholic. They're busy women.'

Laura flashes a victory smile, and my heart drops. I already know what she's going to say. 'They all said yes. The good thing about having a wedding in February is that everybody is free.' She claps to herself.

'Everybody is free because nobody plans anything in February . . . because it's February,' I say bluntly. I feel Josh's arm around my shoulder.

'February is not a bad month, Amy. With global warming, we'll probably have a heatwave.' The family laughs. They all have the same tone of laughter, like a cartoon family—a bubbly titter. He then adds, 'Come on, Ames. Why not?'

'Why not? Because . . .' They wait for me to finish my sentence. Linda has her hands clasped like she's begging for her life. This is absurd. I can't fast-track my wedding for next month.

There is so much to do, that's why people give themselves at least a year to plan it. More importantly, I'm not sure if getting married in the middle of our 'dry spell' is appropriate. I was hoping our 'situation' would be solved and long forgotten by the time I was walking down the aisle. What happens if we don't have sex on our wedding night? I'm sure I read somewhere that that's bad luck. The front door slams. Gramps comes into the kitchen holding a humongous uncooked turkey.

'I have saved Christmas,' he announces, and Linda begins to sob again.

*

Cheers, Gramps, you frail blue twit. Josh is waving frantically from the car at his family. They're all standing on the doorstep, grinning and waving in sync. He beeps the horn and speeds away.

'That was fun, wasn't it?' he says. I twist away to face the window with my arms crossed. 'I ate too much beef, though. I'd better burn that off tomorrow.' My arms tighten. He continues, oblivious to the woman about to explode in his car. 'Still, it's good for protein. Did you know, 100 grams of beef is like eating three eggs? So that means I've had—'

'Josh, our wedding is in seven weeks.'

He turns to me, then turns back to the road, back to me again, and back to the road. 'You said it was fine. You said . . .' I throw my arms up.

'In what world would our wedding in seven weeks be *fine*?' We stay silent as the information processes in his brain. I carry on. 'Are we even ready for this?' Again, there is a silence.

'Why wouldn't we be ready?' he laughs. 'The venue is going to be booked, they're sorting the food . . .'

'But are we ready, considering . . .?' I start waving my hand around my lap, so I don't have to say the words. *Are we ready to marry if we're not having sex?* I want to say, but instead, I go for something more vague. 'Considering the state we're in?'

Josh turns down the air conditioning. 'I'm glad you've said something, because I was worried about that too.' He sounds serious. I can't look at him. The air feels heavy now. We've never spoken about our situation before; we've just left it as an elephant in the room. I swallow.

'Right. What can we do about it?' I ask, my throat feels tight, scared of what he may say.

'Well,' Josh exhales. 'If we want to be in the best shape for our wedding, we will have to do an extreme health kick. No booze. No carbs. Gym every day, but we can do it.'

I twist to look at him.

'Wait. What?'

'Our wedding bodies,' he says, as if it's obvious that's what we're talking about.

'I'm sorry. Are you saying *I* need a health kick?'

'No. No. No,' he says quickly, realising we're not on the same page. 'But you're welcome to join me if you want to. I'll call it "The Seven-Week Wedding Body Blitz"!'

I don't know what to say. I am here, petrified that our sex life is dead, whilst he's concerned about the title for a gym routine. Maybe he doesn't think it's a big deal that we haven't had sex since last summer. Josh doesn't spend a second worrying about life, because he believes everything will work itself out. This can be infuriating, today being a top example, but other times, it's comforting. So, maybe that's how he sees our dry spell – something that will work itself out. I hope so.

'So, you think *we'll* be okay?' I inspect his face for clues.

'Why wouldn't we be?'

'I don't know.'

'Is Lab Rat overthinking again?'

'Mmm.' I change my tone. 'On the bright side, if The Chipping Barn is being paid for, we can move to the country quicker, right?' I say, convincing myself that this fast-track wedding isn't the craziest idea in the world. Josh hits the indicator and moves into the fast lane.

'Yeah. Right.'

The great countryside migration! We have always agreed to do London while we're young, and then move to the countryside to settle down. I'm aware it's not the most unique life plan, but we're not trying to reinvent the wheel here. We know exactly what we want. We want to live in a cottage made of stone, which has a log fire in the lounge and jars full of seeds in the kitchen. Josh wants to mimic his dad and have an outdoor space with a BBQ so we can host summer parties. We'll have a king-sized bed and wake up to a view of cornfields. (This may be too much to ask for.) There will be a guest bedroom and another room for, hopefully, a baby or two. We don't know precisely where this cottage will be in the countryside, but Josh wants to stay as close to London as possible and be close to his family in Maidenhead, so ideally, a village in Berkshire. I just want to be far away from a flatshare in London.

'But is it possible to make a wedding happen in seven weeks?' I say, backtracking.

'We've got everything pretty much sorted. Don't we?' Josh asks.

'Sorted?' I raise my voice. This is exasperating. I am exasperated. 'What about the cake? Hen party. Or . . . or . . . my dress?'

Josh shrugs as if these are simple things to be solved. 'We can choose a cake in a matter of seconds. We can get one from that bakery you love in Clapham Junction.'

'Clapcake.'

'Right. Make it a Victoria sponge, three tiers, white icing, with a bride and groom on top. Cake done.' I whimper at his casualness. 'And I thought the plan was that you were wearing your mum's dress?'

'Okay. Yeah, I am. But what about the invitations? I was going to make handmade ones, but now I don't have time, do I? Now, we'll have to do those email ones.'

'Amy, you were never going to do *handmade* invitations. You can't even put a stamp on straight.' He affectionately shakes my leg. I brush him off and then make a show of getting out my phone.

'I suppose I'd better text my bridesmaids then. How's this? Thanks for the heads-up that I'm getting married next month. Can't wait. Kiss. Kiss. Kiss. Kiss.' There is a pause between us, the only sound is the engine rumbling. I peer over to Josh. He looks deflated. 'Josh?'

'You do want to get married still, don't you?' He bites his lip, and glances at me.

'Of course I do. I just don't want a shit wedding, that's all. Like, remember Rebecca and Tight Tim's wedding? Everyone remembers it being shit. I would hate that.'

Rebecca, my best friend from school, fell in love with the tightest man in England (affectionately named Tight Tim). The stingy wedding budget had us painting ceramics in Barnet for the hen party. The worst part was the wedding day;

we drank cava instead of champagne, and she arrived at her reception in a Ford Fiesta.

'For starters, you're not Rebecca, *thank God*. And I'm not Tight Tim, *thank God*. It's us, so it won't be shit. Just as long as you don't do handmade invitations, Lab Rat.' He laughs and shakes my leg again.

We arrive home to the usual sound of Fifi, our flatmate, hurrying down the hallway and shutting her bedroom door. Josh flops on the sofa and sets up the next episode of *Making a Murderer*. We didn't watch it when everyone else did, so now we're furiously catching up. I settle on my side of the sofa with my notebook.

'Why have you got your journal out?' Josh asks.

'It's not my journal. It's my notebook. I'm starting our wedding to-do list.'

'Good plan,' he says, and presses play. 'Let me know if you want me to do anything.'

Josh and Amy's Wedding 2025

To Do:

Let your bridesmaids and parents know you're aware of your surprise wedding.
Design and email invitations to guests.
Visit The Chipping Barn.
Talk to Rebecca about bridesmaids' dresses.
Talk to Rebecca about the hen party.
Talk to Rebecca about wedding flowers.
Give Josh the job of finding the band.
Taste wedding cakes at Clapcake.
Try on Mum's wedding dress.

First things first, I send a (not sarcastic) text to my bridesmaids and family.

> Hello!!! Josh's family announced the surprise today! 📣
> All confirmed for 22ⁿᵈ February. Can't wait!!! 👰 🤵 ♥

Nina
> Bring on 2025! See you tomorrow 🏛. Still on for the pub quiz?

Rebecca
> FINALLY!!!! Let's plan the hen party! Are you free Saturday?
> Will bring Benny 🐶

Abi
> Yaaaaay xxxxx

Mum
> OK. Will call when in Salvador. x

Dad
> Jean-Ivy and I have a surprise. We'll tell you on her birthday.
> Shui, Berkeley Square, Mayfair, 7 pm. C U then.

Oh, please, no more surprises.

Satsuma

181 Nights

The first workday of the year. The country is united in one big groan as they plod out from the holidays. My first task – attach a papier mâché Mars onto a bike trailer. I've been trying to do this for the last 10 minutes on the pavement outside the flat. It's frickin' freezing. Office workers are giving dirty looks as they manoeuvre around me. I try to explain to them that it's Mars, but that doesn't seem to help. I try attaching it again, pulling the elastic high and stretching it over the red ball. It pings back and catches my finger.

'Fuck!' My finger turns the same colour as the Red Planet. Josh appears above me, sweaty from his workout.

'I got it,' he says, and pulls the elastic across the ball in one motion. He stands back and stares at it for a long time.

'What? What is it?' I say, sensing his judgment.

'Nothing. I'm just wondering why you're bringing a satsuma to work.'

'Satsuma?' I say with exasperation. 'It's Mars. See.' Josh squints as if he's trying to see what I see. I give him a small push and he laughs. 'Go get ready! We need to leave soon! This thing will slow me down, and we really, really, REALLY, can't be late for the staff meeting.'

'We won't be late,' he says. His relaxed tone makes me more nervous. There are many upsides to teaching in the same school as Josh, but a downside is trying to leave the house together at the same time every morning. Our problem lies in the fact that he's a time optimist and I am not.

'Twenty minutes and we need to be gone!'

'It's fine . . .'

'You're not even showered yet!'

'Amy, if it doesn't challenge you, it doesn't change you.' He rubs my hair affectionately and runs inside. I am left staring at my YouTube project strapped up in its trailer. Eight hours . . . and I made a giant piece of fruit. Great. When I chose to be a physics teacher, I had visions of myself in a sparkly white lab coat, surrounded by wide-eyed teenagers fascinated by the wonders of science. It hasn't quite worked out like that.

Surprise, surprise . . . we are going to be late. Josh couldn't find his Year 9 workbooks, so we both had to turn the house upside down to search for them. Well, I say both. Josh walked into each room and immediately concluded that the books were not there. I eventually found them by the sofa under a *Men's Health* magazine. We get on our bikes, and he reassures me again that we won't be late, then cycles off, leaving me wobbling behind with my planet.

'Wha' the fuck is that?' I'm stuck behind a red light, and a group of teenage boys are pointing at my trailer. 'Is it an infected bollock? Lady? Oi, Lady?' The lights turn green, and I pedal as fast as I can, leaving them laughing behind. After receiving a middle finger from a tradesman who thought I was going too slow and upsetting a collie dog on The Common, I finally see the white sign for Clapham High for Girls.

It's known for being one of the more friendly independent girls schools in Southwest London. History, Drama and English are the top subjects. Science still has a way to go, but we're slowly getting there. Yvonne Thompson got accepted into Cambridge last year. She was the first pupil at Clapham High ever to do a science at Oxbridge, and guess whose pupil she was? Mine. Not that this was acknowledged by the headmistress, Dr Therone. This would be almost bearable if she hadn't made such a song and dance about Josh's volcano display. She even gave him a book voucher as an award. Did *I* get a book voucher when Yvonne got into Cambridge? Did I hell. Don't get me wrong, it was a good display, and Josh deserved his book voucher (I spent it in the end), but the favouritism is shocking.

I wheel my bike to the shed, where Josh is hopping from one foot to another.

'What happened to *you*?' he asks. I stop and give him daggers. 'Oh,' he says, only just realising he left me behind. 'Here, let me . . .' He unclips Mars from the trailer and hands it over.

We open the staffroom door and Dr Therone is in mid-speech. Nina, my work bestie, waves at the back and points to the seats she has saved for us.

'Miss Elman, what do you think?' Dr Therone says. I freeze halfway between the door and the safety of my chair.

Josh begins to speak. 'Sorry, Dr Therone . . .'

'Mr Butters, please sit. I was asking Miss Elman,' she says in a sweeter voice, then tilts her head at me like an unhinged doll. After a moment of hesitation, Josh does as he's told and goes to sit next to Nina. This is the favouritism I am talking about. I'm sure it can't be legal. 'Miss Elman?'

'Sorry. I don't know,' I say sheepishly.

'You don't know because you were three minutes late. Why?'

I hold up Mars. 'I had to cycle with this, and it slowed me down.'

Dr Therone glares at Mars like it's a bag of manure.

'What *is* it?'

'It's Mars.'

'It's like something I've seen in my fruit bowl.'

'It's for my space display. It's—'

'Just sit down, Miss Elman.'

I stumble over the feet of other staff members to get to the chair in-between Josh and Nina. Nina squeezes my arm, and Josh mouths an apology.

Dr Therone is pacing up and down with a deep frown. There is nothing soft about her. Her dyed black hair is sliced into a sharp pixie cut, and her eyeliner shapes her eyes to make them look almost cat-like. Every day, she wears a different-coloured suit tailored to her toned 6ft frame. Today, it's lemon sherbet-coloured, designed to make you think she's a happy-go-lucky woman. She is not. She came fresh out of the Ministry of Defence, goodness knows why she decided to teach at an all-girls school, considering she doesn't seem to like women very much.

She begins to speak again. 'My goal is to improve the performance of this school, and I am determined to achieve it. We need higher grades, and we need to win. Mrs Redson, could you tell me why we didn't win a single netball game last term?'

'B-bad luck?' Mrs Redson, the PE teacher, says.

'Bad luck or a bad coach?' Dr Therone says and walks away. Mrs Redson shrinks in her chair. 'Miss Elman, maybe you'll have better chances in science. Your job is to win this competition.' She drops a flyer onto my lap.

Imperial College and Science for Teens
Presents:
The Great Science Awareness Contest 2025
WHAT'S WRONG WITH THE WORLD?
Come and present your topic to a panel of Imperial College researchers.
7th February 2025.
The winning school will receive:

> **£5,000** for their science department.
> **£5,000** fund towards researching the winning topic.
> **Year 10 Only.**
> **Please visit www.ScienceForTeensLondon.co.uk
> for more information.**

My heart sinks. I sense Nina reading it over my shoulder. She makes an excited squeak in my ear. She loves extracurricular activities like this, but that's because the pupils enjoy history and adore her as a teacher. Whereas, I discovered early on in my career, that teenage girls rarely get excited about physics and firmly believe that I'm a bitch for trying to teach it to them. I swear my Year 10 class want to cut me up and stuff me into a test tube. This is going to be torturous.

'Speaking of competition,' Dr Therone continues, 'Our Head of Humanities, Mr Grim, and our Head of Science, Mrs Lector, are leaving us at the end of the academic year, which means there will be an internal promotion opportunity for both departments. If you would like to be considered for the role, book in your interview by the end of the week.' A promotion? I could almost dance. Almost. Mrs Lector, nice lady, but it's time for her to go. She has been sitting as head of science like a goose guarding the golden egg since the early 2000s. I already know how I could instantly improve the department, and let's not forget the money, a £10,000 pay rise at least. That will go straight into the deposit pot, which means our countryside life can begin even sooner, especially now we don't have to fork out a load for our wedding.

I look at Nina, who is buzzing just as much as I am. She will definitely get the promotion to Head of Humanities, so we will be heads of departments together. #HeadofDepartmentGirls.

Josh whispers in my ear. 'Can you imagine if we both get it?'

I smile and pat his leg.

Obviously, it would be ideal if Josh were promoted to Head of Humanities, as this would mean more money, but he's up against Nina, who lives and breathes her job. Josh has great rapport with the pupils because he makes geography fun and, let's face it, he's the only good-looking man around. But he does what he needs to do and goes home, and that's fine, but it's never going to get him a promotion. I'm surprised he's even going to give it a shot.

'Any announcements?' Dr Therone asks the room. Nina shoots up her hand, and Dr Therone acknowledges her with a groan. 'Miss Pascoe?'

Nina opens her notebook. 'As always, I will be taking my sixth formers to the Million Women Rise march on Saturday 8th March, where we will be protesting against men's violence towards women. I look forward to seeing many of you there. What else? Oh, Harriett Boldman, the sweet redhead in Year 9, is having some issues at home, so please be kind to her, and . . .' She flips over the page. 'I'm still collecting clothes for the homeless women's shelter. Keep donating! You do not need all the clothes you have in your wardrobe. And . . . that's it.' Nina closes her notebook and smiles at the room. Dr Therone rolls her eyes.

'Anyone else? No? Good. I look forward to seeing your applications in my inbox.' She heads towards the door.

'Dr Therone,' I say, catching up with her. She turns, reluctantly. 'I need to, if you wouldn't mind, I need to talk about this science contest.'

'Yes?' she says.

'Well, I noticed that the presentation is only four weeks away.' I wait for her to realise how ridiculous this deadline is.

'And?' she says.

'And this gives me no time to organise my Year 10 class. They are already behind on their grades, so I would love to use the time to focus on that. And although my private life shouldn't interfere with my career, I have a wedding to organise in seven weeks' time.'

'Whose wedding?'

'Mine and Josh's.'

She stares at me for a long second and then snaps back, 'You're right, Miss Elman. Your personal life shouldn't interfere with your career. I'll be checking in to see how the science contest is progressing.' And she's off down the hallway.

'Here comes the bride. Here comes the bride,' Nina sings from behind. She looks terribly cool as always, with her wide linen trousers and braids flowing down one shoulder to her waist. She's got her coffee in one hand and a pile of American history textbooks under her arm.

'Oh God, don't.'

'Woah. Come on, it's the new year! You're getting married, you have a science contest, a potential promotion . . . 2025 is full of possibilities. It's going to be grand.'

'Hopefully.'

'Not hopefully. Say it, 2025 is going to be grand.'

'2025 is going to be grand,' I repeat in a monotone voice.

'Smashing. We need all that positive energy if we're going for the full 30 tonight.' She paces off. Josh comes over with his mug of hot water and lemon.

'If we both get promoted, that's £20,000 at least,' he says.

'So, you're going to apply?' I ask, not meaning to sound so surprised. He laughs and frowns at the same time.

'Why wouldn't I apply?'

'Oh, just Nina, you know. She's very passionate, and you're . . . you know,' I say. He seems confused.

'Are *you* going to apply?' he asks.

'Course. I'm up against Mr Rawlinson . . .' I gesture towards Mr Rawlinson, who is currently sleeping in the corner of the staffroom. He is a gentle elderly man but comes across as if he has sniffed far too many lab chemicals in his career. I add, 'It's a done deal.'

'We could squeeze an extra ski trip in if we both get it,' Josh says.

'Or move to the country sooner,' I say.

'Or that,' Josh says, less enthused. He finds saving for adult stuff boring. If it weren't for me, he wouldn't have a penny to his name, but if it weren't for him, we wouldn't do fun things like skiing. Yin and Yang and all that. 'I'll see you at lunch, Lab Rat.' He wanders down the hallway, high-fiving the pupils as he goes.

*

I've hung Mars in the space display. I hoped it would make more sense with the solar system poster next to it, but the lab lighting makes it look even more like a satsuma. I feed my neon tetras and wish them a Happy New Year. They dart up the tank and suck each flake into their wiggly silvery bodies. Then the bell goes, and I feel the weight of the next hour crashing on my shoulders.

'Wish me luck,' I say to the fish.

Year 10 comes straggling in, dumping their bags and screeching their stools. They really do have a way of dampening the atmosphere of my lab. As always, Beatrice sits at the front with her two plaits that dangle down like hound dog ears. She smiles at me and wishes me a Happy New Year. She's all I have in the world during this hour. I take a big breath and begin the class.

'Right, Year 10s, I have an exciting announcement.' I'm interrupted by Arabella Hartford's late arrival. She waltzes in with her tote bag and manicure. Last summer, she went viral on TikTok, which means she's basically a celebrity.

'You're late,' I say, but she's not paying attention to me. Instead, she's scowling at my space display.

'Why is there a piece of fruit hanging from the ceiling?' she asks.

'It's not a piece of fruit.'

'Wait. Wait. Wait. Is that Mars?' She begins to giggle, and like a contagious virus, the whole class begins giggling too.

'Why are you late?' I ask in my most stern voice.

'Mr Butters wanted to catch up. I told him I would be late, but he kept talking and talking.' This is the game she plays, the one where she likes to make me think that my fiancé is crushing on her. I'm a grown woman, so her games do not get to me. (Although, I have the occasional thought of dipping her head into my fish tank.)

I turn back to the class. 'Now, who wants to win this department £5,000?' I raise my hand and say in a high-pitched voice, 'I do.' Twelve zombie faces stare at me. I clear my throat. 'So, we're entering a science contest. We will pick a scientific issue that needs more awareness and pitch it to a panel of judges from Imperial College. If we win, they'll fund the research and give this school £5,000. Exciting, right?' Ashwini shoots up her hand, and I know what she is going to ask. 'Yes, it's compulsory.' She drops her hand, and the class lets out a gigantic moan. 'As it's so soon, we will have to work during our Wednesday lunch breaks.' Another moan erupts. 'What's really fun, though, is that you get to decide what topic you're passionate about. I'm assuming something about the environment, like plastic in the ocean, saving the turtles from straws. That kind of thing?' Beatrice is the only one nodding; the rest seem dead. Ophelia puts up her hand. 'Yes?'

'I am interested in how the Pill affects the brain,' she says. The class suddenly comes alive, backing her up with a chorus of 'Yeaaaaahs'.

'No,' I say as I massage my temples.

'Why not?' Someone yells. I'm already getting a headache, and it hasn't even been 15 minutes of the first class of the first year.

'We can't do a presentation on contraception because we're representing this school.'

Ophelia argues back. 'It's not contraception. It's the woman's body, it's the menstrual cycle. It's basically biology.'

'It's not basically biology . . . it *is* biology. We're not doing it. We'll do plastic and how it kills turtles.' The class is silent and miserable again. 'Right, space time.' I hit the space bar to play my slideshow. The letters 'Expanding Universe' bounce across the screen. The only good thing about teaching Year 10 is that I get to talk about space. I open my mouth to begin, but then I hear Arabella giggling in the back. 'What is it?' I say through a big exhale. She can't talk through her giggles. 'Come on,' I snap. She doesn't stop. I march over and see a white note under her hand. 'Give it,' I say.

'It's nothing,' she mutters, stuffing it in her sleeve.

'Give it,' I yell.

She nervously hands it over, and I unravel it just enough to see what it says.

> Bet she only does missionary
> Poor Mr Butters ☹

The words cut through me like a knife on a frog's belly. I scrunch the note up, throw it into the bin and go back to the front of my lab.

'The expanding universe . . .'

Petey and the Brains

What's wrong with missionary? It's the default for a reason. If Arabella really wants to know, we had a step-by-step routine. One of us would start getting touchy, we did a bit of foreplay, and then I'd get on top, and Mr Butters would stay on his back until he was done, and then I would roll onto my back, and he'd lie beside me in a post-orgasmic daze as I finished myself off. We did that twice a week, and then once a week, and then once a month, until we stopped doing it altogether. So, no, Arabella, not poor Mr Butters. Poor Miss Elman. But I can't worry about that now, I have a quiz to win.

Our arena is The Cock and Bull in Kennington, a humble pub that is longer than it is wide. It smells of stale beer, vinegar and wee, and offers knobbly nuts and pints in murky glasses. It's not the pub I would choose to spend my Tuesday evenings in, but we've been on a winning streak here since December, so we can't leave now.

I know we're still in our twenties and shouldn't be stuck in a pub quiz routine, but it's our thing. Some couples run together, others dance, we do quizzes.

The other team members are Nina and Pete – Josh's recruitment friend, who he met at golf. He is, on all counts, a bit of a dick, but surprisingly remarkable at trivia knowledge.

'And the answer to number 30 is . . . true, the American President Jimmy Carter was indeed a peanut farmer,' says Daz, the quiz master. A 40-something man who likes his Carlsberg and makes the effort to wear a gold sequin blazer every week. 'Swap your papers back, and let's see if we can get a *different* winner this week.' I go to North London Invasion's table to return their quiz.

'You did better this time,' I say encouragingly. It's 18/30. Embarrassing, but I admire their efforts. 'You did well on the sports round. It's just the history you guys need to improve on. Nina, over there, is a history teacher, and I'm sure she'd be happy to recommend a few books.' They glare at me, and then one of them snatches the paper out of my hands. Rude.

Daz is back on the mic. 'Did anyone get 30? . . . 29? . . . 28?'

'We've got 28,' Nina shouts out.

Daz visibly deflates. 'Did anyone else get 28? Anyone?' His long sigh crackles in the speaker. 'Petey and the Brains win again. You know where the Prosecco is.' He turns off the mic and slumps down onto the bar to get his Carlsberg. He was way more optimistic the first time we won.

'Can I bring Tess to this shotgun wedding of yours?' Pete says.

'It's not a shotgun wedding, so no,' I say tightly. 'And who's Tess?' I don't know why I even bother entertaining the idea. I know Tess won't be coming. It's nothing personal towards this Tess girl. It's just that Pete's girls have as much lifespan as a loaf of bread.

'Why not? She's fucking hot,' Pete says, pretending to be offended. He takes out his phone and shows a photo of a stunning young (too young) woman in a yellow bikini. The hardest my brain works on these nights is figuring out how Pete manages to pull these women. 'Come on, Josh, you know you want her at your wedding.'

'He doesn't, Pete,' I say with a smile, so everyone knows I'm half joking.

'Oh, answering for him now, are we? Married life is already starting, Joshy,' Pete says, nudging him. 'Before you know it, there will be a mortgage, kids, and the sex will be a distant memory.'

The elephant bursts into The Cock and Bull and plonks itself between Josh and me, like it always does whenever sex is brought up in conversation or whenever a sex scene appears on TV. This happens a lot because when you're not getting any, sex is EVERYWHERE. I've also developed a paranoia that people can sense that Josh and I haven't had sex for 181 nights. Of course, nobody can know. Neither of us would tell anybody. I certainly wouldn't breathe a word of it, and I'm sure Josh isn't broadcasting it to his friends. After all, it's humiliating.

'Shall we get that bottle?' I suggest.

'You're disgusting. These are our friends,' Nina snaps at Pete. He has the skill of repulsing Nina every time he sees her. If it weren't for their shared competitiveness over general knowledge, they wouldn't spend a second with each other. Pete puts his hand on Nina's arm.

'I'm joking Nina. These guys will be having sex, even when they're crumbly and old in a stinking care home with those scratchy yellow blankets.' He's the only one laughing.

'I'll get the bottle,' Josh says. He goes to the bar, taking the elephant with him. Nina shakes her head at Pete.

'You're broken,' she says to him. Pete puts his hands up like he's under arrest, then laughs, and Nina laughs. Peace is restored for now. I zone out and watch Josh, leaning on the bar, waiting for the bottle of Prosecco he won't drink. He's frowning into the air, clearly in his head. He catches me staring and gives me a goofy wave. I give him a goofy wave back.

Gigantic Baby
185 Nights

Saturday morning, and I'm pushing the biro back and forth on the one hundred and eighty-fifth tally line.

Couples don't have sex on weekdays because they're too busy adulting, right? I'm pretty sure if we were deserted on an island, we'd sort this pickle out, but we live in London. There is rent to pay, books to mark, an Instagram feed to scroll through, and *Making a Murderer* to watch. Weekends are the windows of opportunity for intimacy, but they seem to fly by. Before I know it, it's Sunday night, and I'm flapping around the flat, preparing stuff for work. There simply isn't time to be seductive.

I doubt this weekend will be any different. Rebecca is coming over to do Maid of Honour stuff. Josh is golfing all day. This evening is the stepmother's birthday dinner. Back-to-back football is on tomorrow, so that's where Josh will be. I'll be spending the day attempting to design a virtual wedding invitation. God help us. At least when they're sent out, that will be one less thing on the to-do list. I have given Josh *one* job, and that is to sort the wedding band. He's been to Glastonbury a couple of times, so he knows better than I do about that stuff. The rest of the list I'll sort. This suits me fine – we are most productive when I do it myself.

Josh walks in fresh out of the shower. He rubs the towel over his hair, and his willy dances about.

I've seen two willies in my life. The first one was when I was 17, and I laughed at it. It was Rebecca's fault. Throughout school, Rebecca and I would listen from a distance as the girls obsessively talked about their boyfriends. They had stories about going to first, second and third base, all of which sounded disgusting and terrifying back then. *He licked what?!* We avoided all of that, creating men on *The Sims* rather than meeting real ones. But then, Rebecca lost her virginity and told me that the ball sack looked like Jabba the Hutt from Star Wars. A few weeks later, feeling left behind, I attempted to lose my virginity too, but when Hugo pulled his boxers down, all I saw was the Bloated One. I couldn't stop laughing. Hugo shouted at me, saying I was frigid and immature, and then ordered me to leave his parents' games room. So that was Willy One.

Willy Two belongs to Josh, and he took my virginity with it. On the fourth Saturday after he called me his girlfriend, we went to Pizza Express and shared a Sloppy Giuseppe and then went back to his room in student halls. As he was setting up the music, I got into bed with my clothes on. Flo Rida began to play. He joined me under the covers and put his spicy beef-flavoured tongue in my mouth. I was very aware that his boner, which was digging into my stomach, would soon be digging elsewhere. He took down my jeans, so I took down his. A Durex condom appeared in his hand. He must have sensed my nerves because he asked if I was sure I wanted to do it. I wasn't sure. I was scared of doing something wrong. But I gave him the go-ahead. I needed to lose my virginity, and I wanted to lose it with Josh. He told me it would be fine, then made a bad joke about pizza, and then said he loved me. I told him I loved him back. And then it happened. It was fast, painless and surprisingly uneventful.

The doorbell goes.

'Who's that?' Josh asks.

'Rebecca . . .' I sigh. He never listens. 'Remember, we're doing wedding planning stuff? Like the hen party and flowers.'

'Wasn't her hen party rubbish? Didn't you end up painting mugs or something?'

'I'm going to manage her,' I say. Josh doesn't look convinced. We both know that Rebecca wears the trousers in our friendship. I'm about to leave the bedroom when I ask, 'What will you do for your stag do?'

'Not sure. Pete's got it all in hand,' he says.

'Pete?'

'Yeah, he's in charge of the stag.'

'Pete's in charge of the stag?' I repeat back. I can see it now . . . a seedy strip club with Pete cackling whilst flinging his cash at some poor semi-naked woman.

'Don't worry, I'll *manage* him,' Josh says, as if reading my mind.

Rebecca stands at the door looking frazzled with a bag of baby equipment and her colossal-sized baby, Benson, in his pram. He's the biggest-smallest human in the world.

'Say hello to Amy, Benny,' she says. I don't know what has happened to my longest, oldest friend, but she is the most mummy-mum-mum I have ever met. She's always been the more maternal one, but since she had Benson it's been like hanging out with a children's TV presenter. She pushes Benson through the doorway and down the hall.

'Weeeeeee,' she squeals as she goes, before parking him next to the sofa. She then proceeds to ask him again and again if that was fun. He does not reply, obviously, just kicks furiously as if he's trying to escape.

'So, this hen party,' I say, trying to get her attention.

'Hen party, Benny. What noise does a hen make? Cluck. Cluck. Cluck. Cluck.' She mimics chicken wings with her arms. She finally looks up at me and turns her voice back to normal. 'Yes, hen party. Sorry. What are we talking? Magic Mike? Drinking from penis straws?' We both begin giggling, knowing that neither one of us would know what to do with a thrusting man in Speedos *or* penis merchandise.

'There is this thing I saw in *Time Out* where you can have afternoon tea on a bus. That looks fun,' I say. Josh comes into the kitchen dressed in his golf wear. He looks like a 77-year-old. He sees Benson and jumps out of his skin.

'He's massive,' he blurts out, looking at me alarmed. I try not to laugh.

'He's within average,' Rebecca says defensively and then goes back to her baby voice. 'Is Uncle Joshy body shaming you?'

'Well, I'm off to play golf,' he says, miming a golf swing in the middle of the kitchen.

'Don't you think you should be planning your wedding, considering it is seven weeks away?' Rebecca says, but Josh is not listening to her. 'Josh? Josh?' He keeps swinging the invisible club.

'Josh,' I shout. He stops.

'Sorry, did you say something?' He grins mockingly. Rebecca shakes her head in the way that women do when men are being boyish. 'Don't worry, Bex. Wedding stuff is all in hand.'

'Rebecca,' Rebecca corrects him tightly.

'Yeah, yeah. Anyway, I'm off. When's the big dinner party again?' he asks me.

'Seven p.m. Please don't be late.'

'Me? I'm never late.'

Josh waves at a vacant Benson as he leaves the kitchen. When the front door shuts, Benson lets out a moan and pushes his belly out like something is going to burst from it. (Perhaps a normal-sized baby?)

'Can I ask you something?' Rebecca leans in. Before I can say yes or no, she is already asking it. 'Are you rushing this wedding because of . . .' She points to my stomach and raises her eyebrows.

'I'm getting fat?'

'No, Amy, because you may be pregnant.'

I panic. 'Do I look pregnant?'

'No.' Rebecca rolls her eyes. 'I just assumed, because it seemed a more likely reason than the demented grandad one.'

Oh, Rebecca, pregnancy would be a miracle, because we will need sexual intercourse for that to happen . . . I wanted to say, but I don't because that would open a whole can of worms, which I can't do with Rebecca. Her opinion about my sex life – or lack of it – is not going to help the situation. It's not like she's a sex therapist, so there's not much she can say or do that will help. And honestly, I don't want her to know that my fiancé doesn't want to have sex with me. Especially because I am (unfortunately) very aware of Tim's ferocious bedroom antics. So instead, I say, 'No, Rebecca, I'm not pregnant.'

'So, the demented grandad story is real?'

'Unfortunately, yes.'

'That's—'

'Ridiculous, I know.'

'Oh well, Benny, you'll have to keep waiting for a friend. Won't you? Won't you?' He kicks his chunky legs and the whole pram shakes violently. She suddenly twists her head at me. 'You're still going to have kids, right?'

I force a smile. 'That's the plan.'

'Good. You can't leave me in motherhood alone.'

'Ha.'

'Oh!' she yelps. 'Can you have one this year?'

'Ha. Maybe not this year . . .'

'You better not let Josh's golf dictate your family plans . . .'

'Josh wants a family. That's one of the main reasons we want to move out of London.'

'Yes, the dream cottage life, I know,' she says dismissively. Have I banged on about it that much? 'Now, are you going to show me this dress?'

I go to my room and pull the old cardboard box down from the top shelf of the wardrobe. I dust off the lid and open it. The dress seems a little less white than I remembered. Still, that can be sorted by the dry cleaners. I put it on, buttoning it up at the back as far as I can. I'm the shape and size Mum was, so it fits me well . . . though perhaps slightly on the tight side. The wide taffeta skirt hides my stubby legs, pinches in at the waist and has a heart-shaped neckline that enhances the good stuff. I'll admit it smells a little like one of those second-hand clothes stores in Camden, and the puffed-out sleeves are a bit extra, but that's the charm of wearing vintage. I turn one way in the mirror and spot the tear in the sleeve that I had forgotten about. I can get that fixed.

You have a postcard image in your mind when you do your first wedding dress reveal. Perhaps a posh shop on the high street with sofas and pink carpets, and all the women in your life sobbing with pride at the sight of you. But when I go into my living room to reveal my dress to Rebecca, I find Benson having a suck on her nipple. It takes her a second to concentrate on me. The only way to describe her face is – sceptical.

'It's quite . . . yellowish,' she says.

'Because it's vintage,' I explain.

'Hmm.' The noise of the suckling takes over. 'Maybe a dry cleaner can sort it out.'

'That is what I was thinking, and they can fix this hole too.' I turn and point to the sleeve.

'Hmm . . .'

'You hate it, don't you?'

'I never said that.' Suckling . . . suckling . . . suckling. 'It's sweet you're wearing your mum's dress.'

'But?'

'No, but. But . . .'

'Yeah?'

'You deserve a new dress for your wedding day.' Benson suddenly detaches himself from the boob and begins wailing, which turns Rebecca back into a Tweenie. 'Oh, Benny . . . Oh, Benny . . . Oh, Benny.'

I have to shout over Benson's wails. 'I don't want a new dress!'

Rebecca doesn't hear me. 'Oh, Benny. Benny. Come on now . . .'

'I'm going to take this off then,' I shout again, then shuffle out of the living room. As I go past Fifi's door, it swings open, and my mysterious flatmate appears with one eye open and matted black hair. She's never been a morning person.

'Who's making that baby noise?' she croaks.

'Benson, the baby,' I reply. She scans me up and down and frowns.

'What's with the fairy princess dress?'

'It's my wedding dress. Well, it's my mum's . . .'

'Didn't your parents, like, divorce?'

'Well, yeah, but it wasn't because of the dress.'

'Mmm . . .' She gives me one last look over and then shuts her bedroom door.

Gnome

The first time I heard the name Jean-Ivy Brown, I was 19 and sitting in a Homebase car park.

It was the Easter break of my first year at university, and I was back at my parents' house in Henley. I had just switched on my desk lamp to start my day of revision when Dad came barging into my bedroom, insisting that I go with him to 'get some things'. This would usually be something Mum would do with him, but she had randomly gone to visit Aunt Ruth that morning.

The need to fill the car journey with a conversation was saved by LBC. A man from Doncaster was arguing that we should legalise all drugs. Dad, who is usually overly vocal about these things, stared ahead at the road with his hands at 10 and 2. We got to Homebase without a word.

I followed him around the store as he dithered from aisle to aisle, inspecting a tool here and a wallpaper sample there.

'Er, Dad,' I said. 'What are you looking for?'

'What? Oh, I er . . .' He headed into the garden section where he picked up a gnome in a bright green suit with a matching hat. It was holding a red mushroom and around its neck was a label, *Howard the Fun-gi*. 'I've never got into gnomes,' he mumbled. The next thing I know, Howard was being carried to the car under Dad's arm. It cost £15.99. I don't know why I remember that.

I waited for Dad to start the engine, but instead, he placed Howard on the dashboard and admired him.

'He's a smart old chap, isn't he?' he said. I looked at the overpriced gnome who was staring through us and felt instantly frustrated.

'We came here to buy a *gnome*? Dad, I have so much revision to do!'

Dad cleared his throat. 'Um . . . No, we didn't come here to buy a gnome.' He put his hands on the steering wheel and took them off again. 'Your mother and I are . . . not together, no longer.'

'Yeah, I know. She's at Aunt Ruth's and I'm here at Homebase with you.'

'No!' He let out a breath to calm himself down. The next part he said coldly, as if stating facts of war. 'We're not going to *be together*. We're not going to be married anymore. We're going to separate. Divorcing, almost certainly.'

I laughed. It was a strange reaction I am aware, but if you had known my parents back then, then you would have known how stupid this sounded to me. Their relationship was a well-oiled machine. They had their places at the kitchen table. They had their friends Karen and Mark to have Malbecs with. They had a holiday house in the Lake District and a Christmas Day routine. Sure, they weren't all over each other like other couples, and there had been a lot of arguing recently, but I never thought they would ever be so scandalous as to divorce. 'Dad, do you even know what you're saying?'

'Yes, Amy, I know what I'm saying.' He breathed out again. 'I, er . . . I'm leaving her . . . for . . . er . . . someone . . . er . . . Jean-Ivy . . . Jean-Ivy Brown.'

'Jean . . . Ivy . . . Brown?' I repeated back. It was the most ridiculous name I had ever heard.

There was a knock and we both jumped. A lemon-shaped head man was standing at Dad's window with his face up to the pane. Dad moved to open the door. 'Dad, don't. Dad . . .' He opened the door.

'Hello. How can I help you?' he asked the lemon-shaped head man.

'Nice car, mate.'

Dad seemed very happy with himself suddenly. 'Thanks, *mate*, it's a Bentley Continental GT.'

'I can see that, mate. Good goin'.' The man stuck his thumb up before walking away. Dad stuck up his thumb back and it looked strange. He then shut the door, and we were back in our world of silence. I noticed Howard's drawn-on smile; it was a tilted, simple, black line, and it made my eyes sting. I sniffed back my tears.

'Shall we go home then?' Dad mumbled. Dealing with emotions had never been in the Elman family guidebook. The engine turned on and Shelagh Fogarty's voice filled the car. I took Howard off the dashboard and held on to him for the drive back.

The morning after gnome day, Jean-Ivy Brown was in our kitchen offering me a cup of tea. She navigated her way around our cupboards without any question as to where things were. She told me (whilst pouring coffee into one of my mum's mugs) that she was one of dad's patients.

'One minute he's looking at your fanny, the next you're sharing a bottle of Gavi with the man,' she said, like it was something out of her control. She told me that she was a punk singer in the seventies and asked if I had heard of her. I had not. It explained the leather trousers and the skull-themed jewellery. She bragged about her one-hit record in 1978, 'Choke! Choke! Choke!' I didn't know it at the time, but I was going to hear 'Choke! Choke! Choke!' being performed at every possible occasion – Grandad's funeral was a particular favourite gig of mine.

Before I knew it there was a gold-themed wedding, and Jean-Ivy Brown became my stepmum. It was the kind of wedding where every guest put on their best act. It would have been the day from hell if Josh hadn't been there.

He had been my boyfriend for over a year by then. I had come back to university after that Easter holiday, feeling bamboozled by my parents' break-up. Josh noticed how down I was at our pub quiz and became a shoulder to cry on. One day, when I was crying on his shoulder, we began making out. It went from there. I don't want to say that the death of my parents' marriage was what brought my love life to life, but it kind of was.

Josh wore a deep blue suit at the wedding, and I felt so proud he was mine. He held my hand when the vows were being read. And when Dad said something about Jean-Ivy being the first woman he had ever truly loved, I squeezed Josh's hand so hard that he let out a loud yelp. A few guests turned around to see what all the commotion was. I couldn't stop giggling, and for a moment, it made me forget that I was in the process of getting a stepmum.

At the wedding reception, my new stepbrother, Woodstock, who is as eccentric as his mother, gave a speech in a gold bow tie. He told everyone that this was the best day of his life, which was funny because it was one of my worst. He said that his mum deserved to be in love, and that he was *ecstatic* to have a new dad and sister. His actual words were, 'The twinkly stars have finally aligned to bring our families together as one big bang.' I was so furious I could have cried right there on the top table. How could he say that this mess was fate? Mum had rang me that morning, crying on the bathroom floor. Okay, it was the bathroom floor of a luxury cruise liner heading towards Lisbon. But still, she was a broken woman. Was that part of fate's plan, too?

When the room stopped applauding Woodstock, Josh took me outside to the hotel garden. He opened his blazer and took out a bottle of champagne. We drank it by the swimming pool and then jumped in with our wedding clothes on. We splashed and we kissed.

'Would you ever get married?' I asked, as our heads bobbed just above the water.

'Probably,' he said.

'Would you have it in a place like this?'

'I don't know. Don't care. It's about you.'

'Me?' My heart thumped under the water. 'You would marry me?'

'Of course, Lab Rat,' he said, splashing me.

'Lab Rat? What kind of name is that!' I splashed back.

'Ha! It's your name, because you're cute and smart.'

'I'm not a lab rat!' I jumped and pushed down on his shoulders, dunking him underwater for a second.

We didn't go back to the reception. We missed the cutting of the cake and the first dance, which I feel bad about, because Dad always talks about it as if I were there.

Dim Sum

I try to avoid spending time with Dad and Jean-Ivy as it only winds me up. Unfortunately, Jean-Ivy's birthday dinner is mandatory, and she gets to choose the restaurant. Last year, it was Provocative Cow, a steak restaurant with leather-padded walls and topless male waiters with cow-patterned trousers. Nobody knew where to look, apart from Woodstock, who ended up getting our waiter's number. The year before that was a tapas restaurant, where we were surrounded by flamenco dancers who clicked and clicked as we tried to eat our patatas bravas. The year before that, the restaurant was pitch black which created a lot of issues, including Josh accidentally elbowing Dad throughout the meal.

Josh and I are on the Victoria line heading towards Green Park. A hen party of 10 tipsy women wearing 'Beth's Hen Party' sashes are dancing to (the now vintage song) The Pussycat Dolls' 'Don't Cha (Wish Your Girlfriend Was Hot Like Me)?' Beth makes her friend hold the giant inflatable penis and then gets everyone's attention in the carriage.

'I'm going to dance on this!' she announces, and holds on to the centre pole, prances around it, and then, without a worry in the world, grips the pole with her leg and lifts herself up and tries to spin. The train jolts, Beth falls onto the carriage floor, and we all, including Beth, start laughing. It's always a special moment when you can unite a carriage on the London Underground.

'Your turn,' Josh jokes. He knows I couldn't do anything like that in a million years, but I wonder if he wishes I were more carefree about those things. A little more Beth, a little less me.

The restaurant is on the corner of Berkeley Square. Shui is spelt out in giant pink neon lights, and two models are dressed as butterflies dancing in front of the doors.

'It doesn't look *that* bad,' Josh says.

I squirm. 'Why can't we just go to a normal Italian restaurant like most families?'

We are ushered in by the butterflies and led down a candle-lit hallway. A woman in a tight black dress demands our name and leads us into the restaurant. A concrete Buddha sits cross-legged in the centre and is surrounded by candlelit tables, where people are posing with the food, more so than eating it. We are shown to Jean-Ivy and Dad's table. Couples are meant to mould into each other over time, they usually start dressing in a similar style and using the same vocabulary, but Dad and Jean-Ivy have never moulded, with her gold dress and him in his knitted jumper, they look like guests at a murder mystery party.

'Oh, look who we have here, the future bride and groom, coming to celebrating my little birthday,' Jean-Ivy squeals. She stands and wraps her arms around Josh for an awkward amount of time. Then it's my turn.

Dad stays sitting as he fiercely concentrates on the menu. After being squeezed to death by his wife, I sit down next to him.

'Hello, Amy,' he says, glancing up.

'Hi, Dad.'

'Congratulations on your wedding' he says, ticking that box.

'Thanks.'

'How's work?'

'Great. I'm probably going to be promoted to head of department.'

'I didn't know teachers could get promoted,' he says. His eyes don't look up from the menu. (When I decided to be a teacher and not a doctor, I also signed up for a lifetime subscription to degrading comments about my career.)

'Well, they do. They get a pay rise and have control over how their department is run. I'll be the youngest head of department the school has ever had.'

Dad, still looking at the menu, nods in a way that I can tell he's listening and is (a little bit) impressed. He whips the page over. 'So, you've got this promotion?'

'It's in the bag.'

I wait for him to say something encouraging, but instead, he says, 'Should we order the chicken *and* the pork dumplings?'

'Order everything Bobby, we've got a growing man here,' Jean-Ivy says as she feels Josh's bicep.

'I'm off the carbs right now, so if there is some steamed veg perhaps?' Josh says.

'Steamed veg?' Dad says, and scowls around the table. He's about to launch into a 'what kind of man are you' rant, but then my stepbrother Woodstock arrives in his red sequin jumpsuit.

'Mummy! Mummy! Mummy!' he squeals with animated jazz hands. The mother and son wriggle their fingers together like squid tentacles.

Growing up as an only child of academic parents, I was used to hearing the clock ticking at dinner. I would dream of having a sibling to fill the silence, but since Woodstock came parading into my family, I have longed to hear the clock ticking again.

'You look gorgeous baby. That outfit is to die for,' Jean-Ivy says and encourages Woodstock to spin around to display how tight the jumpsuit is in certain areas, and once that is done, he leaps over and begins hugging each of us from behind.

'Sissy!' he says, squeezing me. This is the most annoying thing about Woody, he insists on calling me Sissy, even though the only thing we have in common is our parents share a bed . . . (Let's not think about that, though.) He moves on to Josh. 'Joshy Bosh. And Doctor Daddy.' Dad freezes as a grown man wraps his arms around him. 'Love the jumper, Daddy. Very Sylvanian Families.' He takes a dramatic breath. 'And family, without further ado, please meet my Moon.' A gaunt, transparent man appears from nowhere. There is silence as we ponder whether to call an ambulance or not. 'He's a little shy. Aren't you, baba?' Woodstock pinches Moon's cheek. The ill-looking man manages a half smile. He sits down next to Jean-Ivy, who starts complimenting his buzz cut, but then she gets distracted by the arrival of the Laurent-Perrier rosé.

'Bubble time.' She claps.

'I love bubble time,' Woody squeals.

'I'm not drinking until the wedding,' Josh says.

'But it's Jean-Ivy's birthday,' Dad snaps.

'I know Robert, but you've got to sacrifice today for a better tomorrow,' Josh says with a straight face. This is not going to go down well. Dad turns to me.

'What in God's name is he talking about?' I give him a leave-it-alone look. Dad points at Moon. 'What about you? Are you going to have some champagne?'

'Moon doesn't drink because it disturbs his natural energy,' Woodstock explains with a sympathetic head tilt as if it's Moon's disability.

'Natural energy? What is happening to men?' Dad exhales impatiently. 'Right, let's toast anyway. Cheers to Jean-Ivy, my beautiful wife, on her birthday, you are my whole world.'

He leans into Jean-Ivy for a kiss, but instead, he gets a slap on the arm.

'Bobby, give it a rest and order this food, we're starving.'

Dad smiles off his rejection, then clicks the air, and the waitress with her flying high ponytail comes over with her iPad.

'Yes. We'll have the wagyu beef yakitori, shrimp tempura, black rice, crispy rice, fried rice, tipsy lobster pad Thai, honey glazed salmon and petals, a chow fun, petal pad Thai, chicken dim sums and a whole Peking duck.'

'Daddy, we would like some tofu,' Woody says.

'Toe . . . *what*?' Dad frowns.

'Moon doesn't sacrifice animals.'

'Some toe-poo then. And . . .' He sighs at my fiancé. 'Some steamed vegetables.' He then looks across at Moon, who now has his eyes closed. 'Make that two steamed vegetables. That's all. Thanks.' He hands the menu over without looking up.

'Bobby, I need to tell Amy about this surprise. I'm bursting,' Jean-Ivy squeals. Dad looks at his watch and gives her the go-ahead nod. She crawls her bony, ring-filled fingers across the table towards me. I slowly put my hand near hers, and she grabs it like a spider on a fly. 'Dad and I want to treat you on your very special day, so we have paid for a luxurious dressmaker to make you a bespoke wedding dress.' Her eyes crinkle and her mouth makes the shape of a cat's bum. I try to free my hand, but she keeps a firm grip. This is a disaster.

I stumble through my words. 'Tha-that's kind. It is. But I'm planning on wearing my mum's dress.' Both Jean-Ivy and Woodstock cackle at the same time.

'Oh, Sissy, you don't want to wear that old thing. It's not like it brought much luck.'

'It did until—' Josh squeezes my knee to stop me from finishing the sentence.

'What do you think, Josh, don't you think she deserves a nice wedding dress?' Jean-Ivy asks.

'I think that would be nice,' he says and squeezes my knee again. 'Won't it?' He asks me the question, unsure if he's right or wrong. He is very wrong. Woodstock starts clapping like a wound-up toy. I push Josh's hand off my knee.

'My friend Lace is going to make it. You're going to love her, Sissy. She made this fabulous jumpsuit.' He stands up, and we all flinch from the view at eye level.

'But I've got Mum's dress.' I protest. 'What we really need help with is the music. Josh has been looking at bands, and the hiring fees are insane. If you could contribute towards that instead . . .'

'I have a better idea,' Dad interrupts. 'Jean-Ivy could get the band back. Couldn't you, darling?' Her face lights up, and Woodstock claps again. No. No. No.

'No, please. I—'

Suddenly, five humming waitresses surround our table and place bamboo steamers in front of us.

'Namaste,' the waitresses say in sync. And then throw a handful of pink petals over our heads. Josh picks a petal from my hair and flicks it to the ground.

Amy & Josh

Invite you to celebrate their marriage
on
Saturday, February 22nd 2025
2 p.m.
The Chipping Barn, Berkshire

RSVP
Amy_Elman95@gmail.com

Twerk

189 Nights

It's 13:35 and the only pupil who has turned up for the first science contest prep session is Beatrice. She has a folder containing 53 pages about plastic in the ocean and is talking me through it, line by line. I nod and say, 'mmm' now and again so she knows I'm listening. I glance at my phone under the desk and silently groan. Woodstock has texted me the details of the dressmaker.

> **SISSY! ♥ ♥ ♥**
> **Lace will meet you 2 pm Sat 💁**
> **Beanie Coffee. Redchurch Street.**
> **Tiny, brunette, STUNNING, Impossible to miss.**
> **HAVE FUN!!!!!!!**

Geez. The last time I went to Shoreditch was when Nina invited us to an art show called Blobs, where artists had created their interpretations of boobs. Josh and I went around the gallery in lightning speed. There were clay boobies, watercolour boobies, red boobies, striped boobies. I tried to be a good sport and mimic the behaviour of people in galleries. I'd go close to the art, step back and tilt my head to the side, but really, I had no clue what I was supposed to be taking from the abstract boobs. Unlike Dad with his landscape paintings, I am aware of my limitations when it comes to art. After 15 minutes of pretending, Josh and I left and got a burger with a shiny bun, which cost £18 each because they were 'gourmet'. That's Shoreditch for you.

'Miss Elman, what do you think about microplastics?' Beatrice says, bringing me back into the room. I have no idea what I think about microplastics.

'Where is everyone?' I stand up.

Beatrice shrinks on her stool. She reminds me of how I was when I was her age; sensitive as a baby hamster. 'They're doing a dance session in the classroom,' she stutters. She's also a good snitch. Great to have on side.

'Thank you, Beatrice,' I say and march out of the lab.

Sabrina Carpenter is blasting out from the Year 10 classroom and can be heard from down the hallway. I burst through the door to show the class that I mean business, but they're too busy cheering Arabella dancing. Ashwini is filming her, no doubt for another TikTok. Arabella bends down in front of the phone.

'YEAR 10,' I shout above the music. 'YEAR 10.' Someone finally notices me, and the music is cut off. Arabella straightens up from a bent-over position.

'Oh gosh, is your little science thing today?' she says.

'To my lab, now,' I demand.

They grudgingly follow me back down the hallway as if I'm leading them to their deaths.

Josh comes towards us in his tiny nylon shorts and with his sixth-form football team bouncing around him. We nod at each other. I like to keep things professional during work hours. (The first week he started at Clapham High, he came into my lab and tried it on. I told him not to be an idiot and sent him on his way. He never tried it again. Not to be a bore, but work is work.)

'I'd save his balls,' I hear Arabella whisper from behind.

'Quickly,' I shout.

We get to the lab, and the girls flop onto their stools. We only have 10 minutes left, so I spend it dictating the roles of each student as they stare on like they want my blood. Ophelia raises her hand.

'Miss Elman?'

'Yes, Ophelia.'

'Do we *have* to do plastic in the ocean?'

'Yes.'

'But we want to do something that we give a shit about.'

'Language!'

'Care about ...' She corrects herself and continues. 'Plastic in the ocean is so abstract to us, whereas contraception is something we all have to think about in this room. Apparently, the Pill can change who you are attracted to. Isn't that crazy? Wouldn't it be so much more relevant for us girls to talk about?' The class backs her up with a chorus of '*Yeah*' and '*Please*'.

'Like I said before, it's inappropriate for us to talk about contraception.' They begin protesting why it's not inappropriate, that we should stop making women topics so taboo. 'Do you want me to lose my job?' I ask. Their silence tells me everything. The 2 p.m. bell goes, and they shoot up. 'Next week, be on time, please.'

The class leaves, and I have an urge to run out of work and hide in a wine bar all afternoon. Instead, I reach for some motivation by scrolling through the countryside homes I have saved recently. My favourite is a cottage called Pebble Corner. Adorable name. It has a kitchen island, a thatched roof and a herb garden, and is far away from Southwest London. I never understood why people in my generation are so obsessed with living here. I would never have moved here if I hadn't got this job. At least when this promotion happens, I can escape to the country. I can already see myself sipping a drink at that kitchen island.

'Do you think I'll get that promotion?' I ask the neon tetras. They dart around the tank as if they are cheering me on.

'*Yes, Amy! You're the best, Amy!*'

Josh and Amy's Wedding 2025

To Do:

Visit The Chipping Barn.
Ask Josh how he's getting on with the band.
Taste wedding cakes at Clapcake.
Tell Mum you're not going to be wearing her wedding dress.
Meet Lace.

Brendan Dassey
191 Nights

Another evening, another episode of *Making a Murderer*.

Brendan Dassey, the accused nephew, is hunched on the sofa in a box room at the police station. He's wearing those practical zip-off jeans that can be turned into shorts. Two outfits in one. On the left of him is the time stamp of the tape, the date 3-01-06 WED. A hint of the detective's shoe is visible in the far bottom corner. One of the detectives tells him that he needs to be honest with them. Brendan plays with his hands as he begins to mumble through the day of the murder . . .

'I was working on his car . . .' he begins.

My phone starts to ring. I jump off the sofa.

'Pause it, pause it, pause it,' I say to Josh, running out of the living room and answering the call. 'Hey, Mum.' I go into our bedroom and throw myself onto the bed. We haven't spoken since the wedding announcement. 'Are you in Salvador now?'

'I am. It's beautiful. Look.' Mum requests a video call. I accept and see a pixelated magic hour; the buildings glowing, the sky pink and orange. It's a contrast from my grey bedroom in grey England.

'Very nice,' I say.

'Yes, well.' She turns the camera, and her nostrils fill the screen.

'Camera,' I remind her.

She pulls it back so I can see her whole face. The sea air and living off à la carte cruise menus are doing wonders for Mum. She has let her hair grow out from the tight, bleached bob she had for decades, to a flowing silver mane that makes her look like she could be a character in a fantasy novel. Her face has a natural sun-kissed glow, which goes well with her dangling turquoise earrings. The old Charlotte wouldn't be caught dead in plastic turquoise earrings, but that Charlotte is long gone.

'Better?' she says.

'Better.' I smile.

'You look a tad tired, darling,' she says.

'I am tired.'

'Could that be something to do with planning a wedding?' she says. 'Just so you know, I did try to say something, but bloody Linda kept crying about her demented dad. I can't believe you agreed to it.'

Mum has met Linda twice. The first time was at my and Josh's graduation. The second was at Jason's sixtieth BBQ party that Linda insisted on inviting Mum to. For the entirety of the afternoon, Mum was stuck to my side, whispering things in my ear about the brown food and football-patterned paper napkins. I had to keep telling her to be kind and to stop being a snob. Linda stopped bothering after that BBQ. I know she would have wanted my mum to be like her, a family woman who would have met her for cups of tea in a Costa so they could talk about their children. Unfortunately, Charlotte Dennis is not that woman. I can't imagine she's ever sat in a Costa before.

'It will save us a lot of money,' I say to Mum. 'And we'll be able to buy a house quicker, so it makes sense. We're signing off the venue this weekend. Rebecca is getting the brides-maids' dresses sorted . . .'

'And you've got my dress, so that's one less thing,' she says. She remembers then. I must have been 15 or so when

I blurted out that I would love to wear her wedding dress one day. I thought the divorce would put her off the idea, but she gave the dress to me and told me that if I ever made the mistake of walking down the aisle, then at least do it in her wedding dress.

'So, I need to tell you something,' I say.

'Okay . . .'

'D-Dad has bought me a wedding dress to be tailor-made.'

'Course he has. Bastard.'

I had my answer ready for this very predictable reaction of hers.

'I thought it would be really special if I remodelled the dress on your dress, Mum.'

'Right.' She doesn't sound satisfied. This is not about me not wearing her dress, it's about her ex-husband bulldozing her plans once again. First, he left her for another woman. Now, her only daughter is not wearing her ragged wedding dress.

'If I'm honest, your dress may have had its day. It's like . . . yellow, and there is a hole in the sleeve,' I say. I get it and show her the hole.

'That hole was your father's fault. It was the first dance, and he . . .' I put her wedding dress back in the box as she tells the story. I've already heard a million times how Dad pulled her by the sleeve because she was too busy talking to friends to realise their first dance was happening. It's another one of the many occasions that is brought up from the archives of, *'The times Robert Elman was a dickhead to me'*. In fairness to Dad, Mum is infuriatingly late for everything.

'I suppose it's karma that he's having to fork out to pay for a new one,' Mum says, justifying it to herself. She laughs in that strained way she does whenever Dad has a misfortune. I hate it. When Mum was married to Dad, she didn't say a bad word against him, but when he broke her heart, she let rip. It was like venomous bats being released from a box after being trapped for 20 years. Now, the man can't do anything right. For the initial years after the divorce, I put it down to heartbreak, but it's been almost a decade, and we still can't have a conversation where she doesn't have a dig at Dad or Jean-Ivy. The bitterness is exhausting.

'I think Dad wants to pay. It's a gift,' I say.

'Mmm. I'm sure,' Mum says dismissively. The camera shakes briefly as she sits up against her bed frame. 'Well, financial practicalities aside, I want to make sure you know what you're doing.' She suddenly sounds formal, like we're work colleagues in a business meeting.

'Yes, I have a checklist.' I grab my notebook from the bedside table and wave it to the camera.

'No. I mean. Is this what you want, Amy? Marriage?' The door opens, and Josh comes bumbling in. Thank God for that. I can't be bothered to have to convince Mum, the anti-marriage officer, that I'm doing the right thing. Josh and I have been together since we were 19, lived together for five years, and been engaged for two. We have our plan to move to the country, start a family and build a deck for our BBQ parties. Of course it's what I want.

'Josh is here,' I tell Mum. Josh throws himself on the bed and waves at the camera.

'Hello, Charlotte.'

'Hello, pet,' Mum says in her forced, enthusiastic voice.

'How's cruise life?' he asks.

She looks away from the screen as if distracted by something. 'Good. How's work?'

'Stressful. Can't wait for the term to end.'

'Oh, you can't be that stressed. It's only teaching after all,' Mum replies, rather cuttingly. The one thing Mum and Dad would still agree on is that teaching is not a hard job. Performing a hysterectomy on a young woman is stressful.

Going on school trips with a bunch of kids to count rocks on a beach is not stressful. Mum gets up from her bed, and I can sense she's going to make an excuse to end the call. 'Well, I'd better be off. Captain's dinner tonight.' There you go.

'The captain, eh? Behave yourself, Charlotte,' Josh says and laughs alone. A flicker of irritation crosses Mum's face. It baffles me that, still, after all these years, Josh doesn't know how to manage my mother.

'Good luck with the wedding plans,' Mum says, ignoring him. 'Amy, let's talk when I get back. Properly.'

'When are you back?' I ask. I need to talk to her too. Well, I need to plead with her not to start World War Three at my wedding against Dad and Jean-Ivy. It's not going to be an easy request, so I will have to do it when she's had a glass or two or three.

'First weekend of February,' she says. 'We'll do dinner.'

'Bye, Charlotte,' Josh shouts. She hangs up. Josh grabs my arm. 'Let's go, let's go, let's go. I want to see if Brendan confesses.' He runs out of the room.

Lace

192 Nights

Beanie is squashed between The Owl and the Pussycat pub and a vintage shop called Thread. It's everything you expect from a Shoreditch coffee shop. It's painted white and has enough plants to save the ozone layer. The menu is on a peg board, and there's a display of Polaroid pictures of the baristas. As a millennial, I am programmed to love these types of places. So far, nobody here fits Woodstock's brief of a stunning, tiny brunette who is impossible to miss, which means 'Lace' is officially late. Not very professional.

'Regular latte for Amy,' the barista yells out. He has one of those long, wiry beards a bird could happily nest in. I take the coffee and squeeze onto a crate between two guys tapping furiously on their laptops.

It's 14:17. Lace is 17 minutes late.

'Excuse me. Can I take this seat?' A pretty woman with brunette hair is in front of me, holding a mug. This must be her.

'Are you Lace?' I ask. She looks clueless. Maybe not. 'Sorry, I'm waiting for someone. I need the chair. Sorry.' The woman rolls her eyes and leaves. I understand her frustration, finding a seat in this city is no joke. Lace is now 21 minutes late.

'She's upstairs,' says the man on the laptop beside me.

'Excuse me?' I ask.

'Lace. I just heard you say her name. Her door is on the outside to the left, the black one. Make sure to press the buzzer five times. She won't answer otherwise.' He reads the confusion on my face. 'She's an oddball. Hot, but an oddball.'

With a groan, I leave the crate and go to the black door. The intercom has a single worn button. I hover my finger over it for a moment, and then press it five times. I wait and wait. I go to press it again, but then it clicks.

'Hello?' says a childlike voice.

'It's Amy. I was waiting for you in Beanie.'

There is a long pause. 'Amy, did you say?'

'Yes,' I say, exasperated. 'I'm here to have a wedding dress made. I'm Woodstock Brown's stepsister, Amy Elman. My dad, Robert Elman, paid in full over the phone.'

'Woodstock . . . Woodstock . . . Oh . . . Woody. Right . . .'

'Sh-shall I come in then? Hello? Hello?' I try the door, but it's still locked. I press the buzzer again and again.

'Stop pressing that bloody buzzer!' yells a plummy male voice from the other side. A second later, the door swings open, and a 30-something man with pokey eyes and thick blond hair that flops up and over his head stands in front of me. He looks pained. 'God. Are you trying to torture us with that thing?' he says, rubbing his ear. Despite his deep voice, he is very angelic. I can imagine he would have been chosen as the angel in the school nativity when he was a kid.

'Um. Sorry. Is Lace . . .?'

'Yes. Yes. Come in,' he says, making it clear I'm an inconvenience. Does he know I'm a paying customer? I step under his arm and wait for further instructions. He tuts impatiently. 'Go right to the top. Her room is the one with Lace written on it.' He walks out the door and lets it slam behind him. I stomp up the stairs. I need to get this over and done with so I can get back to the comfort of my home. As promised, on the door, in huge red curly font, is the word 'Lace'. I shut my eyes and knock.

'Yes, doll. Come in,' the dainty voice says.

I put my head around and then step inside. The first thing I notice is the sweet, artificial rose scent and the opera music playing softly in the background. The second thing is the mess. The room is packed full of dressed-up mannequins, and fabric scraps are all over the floor. A tiny brunette is in the corner with her back to me, sticking pins into a pink-tie-dye medieval dress.

'Can you believe it?' she says, without turning from the mannequin. 'Seventies Robin Hood, you couldn't write it. Well, you could. He did, but you shouldn't.' She plays with the netted skirt in her fingers. 'Don't get me wrong, he's a real sweetie, but drowning in acid. So sad. Now . . .' She turns around, and I step back. Lace is beautiful. Her mouth and honey-coloured eyes are oversized in an almost cartoon way. Her thick, dark hair drapes down the back of her tiny frame. She is chewing on her full lip, and I realise that she is examining me as much as I am examining her. She suddenly swirls one finger and says, 'Do a 360, please.'

'What?'

'Turn,' she orders. I turn slowly with all my muscles clenched. She then approaches me, and I see the faint freckles hidden beneath a thin layer of foundation. 'What's the costume again?' I let her lift my arms to a 'T' shape.

'It's not a costume. It's my wedding dress.'

'Oh, doll, a wedding dress is the ultimate costume.' She slips a measuring tape out of her back pocket. 'Now, do stand tall.' She measures me from head to toe, then wraps the tape around my chest. 'Relax, won't you?' I breathe out and she is around my hips with the tape. 'Who's the husband-to-be?'

'Erm, Josh.'

'Josh . . .?'

'Butters.'

'Amy Butters. Amy Butters.' She repeats it as if she is learning a new word. 'Amy Butters, you're as tense as they come.' She scans me up and down and smiles. 'Yes. High neck, fine lace and a long trail. The brightest of white, of course.' She walks over to the cabinet of drawers and lifts a half-empty bottle of wine from a pile of magazines. 'Drink?'

'Actually,' I say, 'I was going to wear my mum's wedding dress, but my dad has obviously paid you to make me one, which is great. But I had an idea that we could recreate my mum's original dress. You know, keep them both happy. I can show you what I mean.' I take out my phone.

'Bitterly divorced parents?' Lace asks.

'How do you know?'

'Just a hunch. Here.' She holds up a huge glass of red for me to take. I'm not a red wine drinker at the best of times, let alone early afternoon on its own without cheese or steak.

'Sorry, I'm not much of a day drinker.'

'Please hold it. My hand is tired,' she moans. So, I mindlessly do. She sits on the tatty red velvet seat by the window, crossing one sparrow leg over the other. 'Why don't you relax, Amy Butters?' She points to the French daybed. It has a swirly, rusty frame and is covered in different pieces of denim. I perch on the edge, and there is a loud screech.

'What the fu—!' I shout, jumping up.

A giant grey cat dashes out from underneath me.

'Oh, poor Pep,' Lace says. 'I forgot about Peppy.'

'You *forgot* you had a *cat*?'

'Technically, he or she is not mine.' She looks sad. The cat sits under a mannequin and gives me daggers. I check for any more hidden animals before settling back down.

'Whose cat is it then?'

'Nobody important,' Lace says, brushing the question away. 'Anyway, how long have you been with Josh then?'

'Erm, like . . . 10 years I think.'

'Ten years,' she shrieks. 'Why ever for?'

'Because we haven't broken up.' She giggles condescendingly, and it grinds on me a tad. 'Shall I show you the photos of Mum's dress then?'

'No.'

'No?'

'You're going to have your own dress, Amy.'

'But I want my mum's.'

'Perhaps that's what you want, but not what you need.'

'But I am paying—'

'Shh.' She stands straight to attention. I then hear that the buzzer is being rung from downstairs. I can see why the preppy man was so tense with me. It's an awful sound from the inside. Lace is counting something on her fingers, and I realise it's the number of buzzes. '3 . . . 4 . . . 5 . . . 6 . . . 7 . . . 8 . . . 9 . . . 10 . . . 11 . . . 12.' She closes her eyes. 'Oh, the bastard.'

'What's happening?' I ask. She scutters towards me and cups her hand over my ear like we're friends in primary school.

She begins to whisper. 'You need to tell the gentleman downstairs that I'm not here. Tell him I'm not going to be back for a long time. Tell him I'm in Hawaii or Newfoundland or the North Pole. Wherever. I'm just not here, okay?' The buzzer stops and then starts again.

'What? Newfoundland?'

'It's in Canada.'

'I know that. Who is he? What does he want?' She begins to usher me up from the bed. 'Is he dangerous?'

Lace giggles. 'No, poor Ian. No, now, please.' She looks at me pleadingly. I open my mouth to say something. 'Please.' She clasps her hands in prayer. The last time I saw someone look so desperate was Linda Butters when she was emotionally blackmailing me to do this wedding. I breathe out in surrender and go to the studio door. 'Thank you. Thank you. Thank you. And, oh, before I forget, you've never seen a cat, okay?' she says.

'But I have seen a cat!' I argue. She clasps her hands in prayer again.

'Please, Amy. I won't ask you for any more favours after this.'

As I make my way downstairs, the buzzer carries on in sets of 12. Am I being set up here? Am I going to be on one of those Candid Camera shows to give the nation a jolly good laugh? I hope not. But what if this is real? What if this Ian is dangerous? What happens if he has a knife? The buzzer starts again. The sound of it by the front door is horrendous. BUZZ . . . BUZZ . . . BUZZ. Oh, here goes nothing. I open the door a smidge. On the other side is a balding, 40-something-year-old man with watery, dark eyes. He's in a creased grey suit and has ungroomed stubble across his face. The man is quite obviously having a bad time of it.

'Is she here?' he cries. 'Say she's here.'

I hesitate and then say, 'She's away. Newfoundland.'

'Newfoundland?'

'It's in Canada.'

'I know where Newfoundland is,' he huffs. 'When will she be back? Will she be back soon? I need her. Tell her Ian needs to see her.'

'No. She's going to be gone for a while,' I say, but I'm a terrible liar. I don't think he's buying it. There is a moment of stillness where I think he's about to go, but then he lurches towards the door, and I have to block him.

'Lace! Lace! Lace!' he's yelling over my head. People on the street behind are beginning to stare as they walk by. This is excruciating.

'She's not here,' I say. 'Stop yelling, please. Please stop yelling. Please.' He groans and rubs his face.

'Just tell her that she needs to bring Peppy back. I need him back now.' He starts walking backwards and yelling up at Lace's window. 'I need Peppy back now.' He loses his footing and tumbles in the middle of the street.

'Are you okay?' I shout. 'Sir?' He looks at me as if it's my fault, dusts off his hands and walks away.

When I return to Lace's room, she is in her faded red velvet chair, and Peppy is asleep on her lap. She is stroking him and mumbling something into his fur.

'Ian wants his cat back,' I say. Lace doesn't look up. 'Lace? . . . Lace? . . . LACE?'

'It's not his cat. It's his wife's,' she finally says. I cross my arms and give her my best teacher stare. 'What? Oh gosh, please don't feel sorry for that sleazebag.'

'I think you need to give him back. Oh, and Peppy is a boy, by the way,' I say. Lace lifts the cat, waking him up. His legs stiffen, making him look like a possessed Simba.

'I knew you were a boy,' she mutters proudly, and kisses him on his head.

Why couldn't I have a normal dressmaker, who works in a legit shop and doesn't steal cats? Woody, that's why. This is all Woody's fault.

'What do you do, Amy Butters?' Lace asks and gestures to the French daybed once again. I sit down and take a big gulp of red wine.

'I teach physics.'

'And him, what does he do?'

'Geography. At the same school.'

She pulls a face as if she has tasted something disgusting. 'Do you not get sick of one another?'

'No. Not really.'

'Don't be silly. Of course you do,' Lace says.

I don't argue back. I sometimes get sick of Josh at work, but that is only because everything seems too easy for him.

I am tirelessly trying everything to earn an ounce of respect from Dr Therone or to get one of my pupils to smile at me. Whereas, Josh is loved and respected by everyone just for being himself.

Lace suddenly puts the kidnapped cat on the floor and stands. 'Sorry, Peppy, I must go somewhere now.'

'What? Where are you going?' My head is beginning to hurt.

'I must take something to someone.' She picks up a covered red garment hanging on one of the rails.

'Okay. How about I text you what I want?' I say. She dashes around me like she is trying to find something. She puts on a brown leather coat with a fur collar. She looks like a rockstar from the 1970s.

'I was hoping you would accompany me to drop this garment off,' she says. I frown. What is this woman on?

'I really would, but I can't.' I can see Lace pull a bemused face in the mirror, and it makes me feel extremely lame.

'Amy.' She turns around and comes close to me. Suddenly, she slides her fingers between my left hand and stares at my engagement ring with disdain. 'Is that the engagement ring?'

'Yes.'

'Interesting.' She looks away and continues. 'I hope you don't mind me saying this, but I believe we're both on the late side of our twenties, right?' I nod. 'Yes, thought so. I think you owe it to yourself to live a little, don't you think?' She slides her fingers back out, and my hand falls like a dead weight. 'Coming?' she asks.

I think of my afternoon ahead. I had planned to do head of department interview prep on the sofa. Josh said he'll do some too, but he probably won't. He'll more likely doom scroll fitness Reels on Instagram. At 16:30, he will make his late afternoon protein shake and sip away at it until dinner time. I'll have pasta, he'll have eggs, we'll watch some *Making a Murderer*, and then around 10 we'll go to bed.

It was different when we weren't living and working in the same place. We would dress up nicely, meet in a mid-range restaurant, and have lots to say. Josh hated the first school he taught in, so he would come equipped with unflattering, but hilarious, impressions of his colleagues. And as the night went on, we'd get drunker and closer, until we stumbled back to one of our houses. We would have only been apart two or three days, but I missed him, and it felt like home when I was wrapped up in him again. We moved in together during the lockdown, and by then Josh had started at Clapham High. We would spend the weekdays teaching on Zoom in separate rooms. Sometimes, we would sneak a fumble between classes. On Saturday nights, we would order in from our favourite Thai, light a candle, and dress up like we were at a restaurant. That stopped after a while, and the sex began to slow down too, which I suppose was bound to happen when you see each other every second of every day.

We've now made a habit of ordering from the same Thai restaurant on Saturday nights and watching Netflix. We talk about trying out a new restaurant, but when it comes to it, we can't be bothered. Why put up with the Tubes when you can be cosy on your sofa? The only difference tonight is that we won't order in Thai as that will break Josh's Seven-Week Wedding Body Blitz. God forbid.

I look at Lace, who is halfway out the door.

'Yeah, I'll come. Why not?'

Pink Latex Jumpsuit

Lace and I walk through Shoreditch. The winter sun has just gone down, and the shops are closing and the pubs are filling up. I follow Lace into a brick warehouse where an awful techno track with a robotic voice is blaring out. *We dance. We blow. We dance. We blow.* Inside is chaos. There are cameras, theatre lights and people running around like they're on a countdown to save the world. At the centre of the commotion is a band of grown men in different-coloured latex jumpsuits. The guitarist is in blue, the keyboard player is in yellow, and there is one in white shaking a tambourine. The only person in plain clothes is the lead singer, and it's . . .

'Sissy and Lacey,' Woody squeals into the mic. Geez. He runs towards us with his hands waving in the air. His band is shouting after him to come back. 'Sorry, chicks, my costume has arrived!' He comes and does his usual theatrical hugging and kissing. 'Sissy, what a gorgeous surprise. Why are you here?'

'I don't know,' I say. 'What is this?'

Woody looks offended. 'It's our first music video, Sissy.'

'I thought you were an actor?'

'I am. Actor, slash singer, slash director, slash model.' He seems oddly proud for a man who has three failing careers going at the same time. He hasn't modelled since he was 18, and that was for an off-brand Abercrombie & Fitch. One of the photos hangs in Dad and Jean-Ivy's bathroom. I have to endure Woodstock in a field, topless, giving me a sex face whenever I use their loo. His last acting gig consisted of a small, unpaid role in a student film where he played an alien butler.

'Right . . .' I say, unconvinced.

'Woody is a very talented soul,' Lace interrupts. 'And a talented soul needs the right costume.' She gives me the hanger to hold. Woodstock claps excitedly as she unzips the red-covered garment. He does a dramatic gasp and then takes the thing out of the cover, revealing it's a pink latex jumpsuit, hanging like a piece of rubbery skin. Woodstock wipes his eyes. 'You're . . . a genius,' he says to Lace. 'Isn't she just wonderful, Amy?'

I don't know if anyone here is *wonderful* or plain bat-shit crazy. I nod anyway.

'Did I tell you how we met? Brighton Pride! She made these *wonderful* sequin costumes for the karaoke float. I told her she had to make me one too, otherwise, I'd die. Then, out of nowhere, I get this text saying that she has a gift for me. OOOOH! So, I got to this pub in Shoreditch. *Oh God!* I was *so* trollied! *So* sorry about that, Lace. Anyway, can you believe it? She's there with the red sequin suit.' He claps furiously again. 'It was so magical!' The band are irritably calling Woodstock back. 'I'm coming, chicks. Keep your skins on!' I'm not sure how long this rockstar career will last for Woody, but his band seem to be regretting their decision to let him in already. 'Showbiz is calling, ladies. Sorry. So sorry.' He kisses us both and scuttles off with his new latex suit over his shoulder.

'Exhausting,' I say.

Lace takes hold of my arm. 'Let's loosen you up.'

The Owl and the Pussycat

I feel like a toad hopping beside Lace. I wonder if she knows how good-looking she is. Surely, she notices how many people check her out, or perhaps it's happened her whole life, so she thinks it's the norm for people to stare.

She seems to be genuinely interested in who I am. She's asked me questions about my parents and my love for astronomy, and I can tell she's listening because she asks follow-up questions. I end up telling her about the science contest drama.

'What's so inappropriate about the Pill?' she asks.

'It's like . . . sex,' I say, and feel stupid as I say it.

She lets out a dramatic gasp. 'Not sex,' she says and giggles. She moves on to ask me about the arts and quickly finds out I don't have an arty bone in my body. She names painters, fashion designers and operas, and they all go over my head.

'What music do you listen to then?'

I hate this question. People usually say a bit of everything, but that's a cop-out. I certainly won't listen to death metal, classical, or whatever Woody's band was playing back there.

'A bit of Ed Sheeran, Taylor Swift. I'm more of a podcast type woman; true crime, space and science and stuff. What do you listen to?'

'I love the opera. It's the school of passion,' Lace says.

'Mmm,' I say. I have no idea what she means.

We go into the pub next to her studio, The Owl and the Pussycat, and Lace tells me to save the high table as she goes to the bar. Young day drinkers are yelling over each other, and at the bar, a frail man sits on a stool. It looks like he's been there for a while. Lace stands on the foot rail and leans over to give the order to the bartender. He seems very happy to see her. I gaze around and read the verse on the wall next to me.

> *O lovely Pussy! O Pussy, my love,*
> *What a beautiful Pussy you are,*
> *You are,*
> *You are!*
> *What a beautiful Pussy you are!*

Lace comes over with a glass of red in each hand. More red. Great. She sits down and flicks out her thick chocolate hair. I wish my hair flicked about like that. Instead, I have this mousey shoulder-length cut that is flat and forgettable.

'To the dress,' she says and clinks my glass.

'Yes, about that,' I say. 'I don't like diamonds or anything too big, and I hate extra-long veils on people who aren't royalty.' She is staring at me like I have something on my face. 'What is it?' I say as I rub both cheeks.

'The sex must be good,' she says.

'What?' I ask quietly. I feel my cheeks warming up. Does she know about Josh and me? How? No, don't be stupid. That's impossible.

'The sex. It must be spectacular for you to want to stay with him for the rest of your life,' she says. I laugh nervously. 'What's funny?'

'Nothing,' I say, then resort to old tactics of changing the subject. 'What wine is this?' I inspect the glass.

'Merlot. House. Wait. Please tell me the sex is good?' She is staring right at me. It's moments like these that I wish I were a good liar.

'Yeah. Yeah. Yeah. The sex is great. Top notch.' I frown. Top notch? Where did that come from?

'What specifically is so "*top notch*" about it?' she asks. She's on to me.

'Oh . . .' My mind goes blank. 'All of it.'

Lace suddenly leans across the high table with a Cheshire Cat smile.

'Why are you lying?'

'I'm not!'

'Amy! What is it? Are you faking it? Is it too thin? Too small? Is he selfish?'

I go to defend myself again, but then I remember I don't have to explain my private life to anyone, especially to a stranger. Who the hell does she think she is?

'I'm not going to tell you.'

'So, there is something then.' She smiles proudly at her achievement. A second later, her smile drops. 'Oh God,' she whispers.

'What?' I whisper back.

'Now it all makes sense.' Her eyes widen. 'You aren't having sex *at all*.'

I feel myself go bright red. Busted.

'No. We have sex. Loads of it.'

'Why are you not having sex?' she yells. It's loud enough to catch everyone's attention in the pub.

'What? Shh. What? I am.'

'You're a bad liar.'

'But I am having sex.'

'Oh, really?' she says, unconvinced. 'If that's the case, then what do you like?'

'I like?' I ask, confused. She nods. 'Erm . . . planets, escape rooms, skiing . . .'

'No. What do you like in the *bedroom*?'

In the bedroom. I hate that phrase. It makes it sound like a sport. I suppose it is in a way. Just as some people can catch a ball and others can't, some people are good in bed, others are bad in bed. As someone who is struggling to keep their own fiancé turned on, I am pretty sure I would be in the latter category.

'In the bedroom, hmm . . .' I say, pretending I'm mulling over the many options. 'Oh, you know. Same old. A chair. I like a chair.' (I haven't had sex in a chair for about four years.)

She rolls her eyes. 'More. Come on. How does he turn you on?' I lean back on the bar stool, disgusted. Does she have to be so graphic? 'Don't pull that face. It's natural.'

'I don't want to talk about this stuff. If you don't mind.'

'It's just sex. We can solve this.'

'I should get going,' I say, but before I stand, she grabs my wrist.

'A marriage is a long time, Amy.'

'Good. I like Josh.'

'Do you want tips?'

'Tips?'

'For better sex?'

'No, thank you,' I lie.

'I'm going to tell you anyway,' she says. I groan and twist away so I'm not facing her, but I'm listening. I'm listening *very* closely. 'Okay, phones need to be far, far away from your pillow. Those things are the devil when it comes to sex. That's point one. Point two, men are visual creatures. The beauty industry is worth billions because we all subconsciously want to get laid. You don't have to do much, a little goes a long way.' She puts her hands near my face and adjusts my fringe. I feel marginally offended by this comment. 'An easy fix is lingerie. Red or black never fails. The more obvious the better, but make sure you are comfortable in it. A shy woman is a dry woman. And then, are you listening?' She grabs my wrist again, and I nod. 'This is important. You need to make him feel like *the man*. He's not going to be *the man*, of course. At the end of the day, he's a geography teacher who can't satisfy his fiancé, so you're just going to have to *pretend* he's the man. Or you can do what the masses do . . .' She gives me a look as if I should know the answer. I don't.

'And what's that?'

'Close your eyes and think of someone else.' She closes her eyes and smiles to herself as if she's thinking of that someone.

'Isn't that cheating?' I ask.

'No. It's what you do so you *don't* cheat. Go on, who would you think of?'

'I'm not telling you that.'

'Go on, we're friends.'

'We are?'

'Go on.'

'Fine!' I huff. 'There's a man called Graham.'

'Ooooh, Graham.' She leans in with her head in her hands. 'Who's Graham?'

'Ummm. He's this astrophysics guy who does a podcast, Graham's Universe,' I say. She looks confused, so I carry on explaining. 'He's from Texas and has this Southern accent. He talks about the planets so passionately . . . I don't know, it does things.'

Lace blinks and then says slowly. 'That's your sex life? Masturbating to some science podcast?'

I cross my arms. Mortified. 'I knew I shouldn't have said anything.'

'No, you should. It just makes me sad, that's all.'

'Could we make this dress and not talk about the sex thing, please?'

'I want to help, though.'

'Please drop it,' I say firmly.

'Final *tiny* word.'

I sigh. 'Go on.'

'At the very least, Josh should be making you feel like the sexiest woman that ever lived. It's a big reason why you're willing to commit to him for the rest of your life.'

'Well, that's terrifying,' I say. 'Thanks for the advice and the wine, but I do need to go now. Next week?'

Lace gives me a half smile. 'You deserve the best, Amy Elman.'

I laugh. 'I could be skinning cats or trolling teenagers on the internet.'

'Are you?'

'No, but . . .' I shrug. 'Could be. See you next Saturday, Lace.'

I leave her at the high table with her empty glass of wine and her perfect hair, face and body. Lace can give all the advice she wants, but at the end of the day, she never has to worry about getting laid.

The Tubes are severely delayed, so I go to the H bus stop on Old Street. When the bus arrives, I sit near the back and lean my head against the window.

Josh and I used to have lots of sex. Okay, it wasn't the crazy, animal passionate sex that some claim to have, but I felt really good and so did he. Naturally, we fell into a routine and the sex became less frequent, but it has been 10 years, so what can you do?

The last time we had sex was at the beginning of summer, 192 nights ago. I was enjoying an early night, reading Brian Cox's *Human Universe*. At around nine, Josh stumbled into the bedroom and crawled onto the bed with his dimples. He had been drinking at The Ship in Wandsworth with his gym friends. I pretended to be too into the book to notice the drunk man straddling my legs. He started tapping the back of my book. I told him to stop. He fidgeted like a schoolboy on a carpet, and then his fingers pulled on my pyjamas. I wasn't in the mood, but it had been a few months since he had come onto me that way. So, I shut my book. He gave a childish cheer before pulling down his boxers and getting on his back. I lathered some strawberry lube on and climbed on top. Even though I wasn't feeling it, I gave it my all, with the right moans, groans and occasional weary 'Josh'. I moved up and down, up and down, up and down, and felt my bloated body jiggle as I did. (I had treated myself to a delicious chicken pesto pasta with lots of cheese only hours before.) I caught him eyeing my jiggling belly . . . and that's when his face changed. Suddenly, there was space where there wasn't before. And I realised he had gone soft . . . again. It's not a big deal for men to lose their mojo during sex; we are just bags of chemicals after all, but this was the fourth time in a row he had gone soft on me. He blamed the drink on this occasion. It wasn't the drink though – it was me.

So, after that, I didn't want to be the one to initiate, in case I was right, and my body had turned him off. I waited a month, and that's when I started doing tally marks. Now we're at 192 nights. Waiting for him is clearly not working. Lace was right to look at me like I'm insane; this is insanity. Here I am, worrying about invitations, cake and dresses, when what I need to be doing is getting my fiancé to have sex with me again before we say, "Til death do us part.'

First things first, I text Lace.

What were those tips again?
Thanks. Amy.

A moment later, she replied.

1. **No phones in the bedroom.**
2. **Make him feel like the man (even when he's not).**
3. **Lingerie. THAT YOU FEEL GOOD IN!**
   If all else fails, close your eyes and think of Dennis.
   See you next week doll!
   Xxxxxx

Bigger

193 Nights

Josh and I have been driving for an hour, and I have spent most of the journey talking about my day with Lace. I can't remember the last time I had a spontaneous day like that, and it's made me feel marginally more exciting as a person. Josh is half listening to me and half listening to the Man U vs Newcastle match on Radio 5 Live. Now and again, he'll make a 'Uh-huh' or a 'Hmm' to let me know he can still hear me.

'Oh, you should see her studio. It's chaos, but in a good way. She has all these mannequins and materials everywhere. I reckon she must sleep on the French daybed . . . although that can't be very comfortable.'

'No . . .' Josh turns up the radio a smidge.

'Still, there is something quite freeing about living that way.'

'Ha. You would hate to live like that.'

'I know, *I* would, but it's great to see a woman doing exactly what she wants, even if that's living above a coffee shop, making dresses and drinking red wine like water . . .'

Someone is running up to the goal, and the commentators are going apeshit. Josh is on the edge of his car seat, looking like he's about to sneeze. Whoever it is, scores.

'YEEEESS!' he screams.

We turn right at the sign for The Chipping Barn and drive up the familiar hill. The barn appears in the windscreen and grows and grows.

We spent the first few months of the engagement looking for anything but a barn (everyone was getting married in them at the time). We began in London, looking at quirky places like old breweries and rickety pubs, but then we got annoyed at the cost, so we went against London altogether. We would drive past The Chipping Barn to his family's house and ignore it purely *because* it was a barn – plus it was way out of our budget. On the way back from one of Linda's Sunday lunches, we decided to have a peep at it for fun and then accidentally fell in love with it. As a result, we ended up pushing the wedding back a year to save, but the savings didn't go quite as I expected (the landlord raised the rent, and Josh bought a new car), so we pushed it back again.

Emily, the owner of The Chipping Barn, is waiting for us in the car park with her hands behind her back and a huge grin on her face. We met Emily the first time we visited, and she hasn't changed a bit. She's still head to toe in tweed and has the enthusiasm of someone who works at Disneyland. Nobody loves their job more than Emily Prize. She greets me and Josh by calling us 'lovebirds' and begins another tour of the place.

The first stop is the little brick chapel. It's the kind of place you imagine fairy-tale creatures would hang out. It's surrounded by trees and has a dusty path leading to its creaky wooden door. The inside glows orange from a stained-glass sunrise, and there are rows of wooden chairs for the family and friends. I saw one wedding on Instagram where the couple had filled the space with candles. I thought this was slightly overkill – it's a wedding, not a sacrifice to the gods. We will keep it simple with flowers, a few candles and perhaps some loose petals sprinkled on the aisle.

'Isn't it amazing?' Emily is standing at the altar with a toothpaste commercial grin on her face. 'Do you guys have any questions so far?'

'How many chairs are in here?' I ask.

'Sixty-two,' Emily says without a beat. 'Same as last time.'

I count them just to make sure. 'Yup, sixty-two,' I say, and Emily smiles again. Josh starts playing random keys on the piano.

'You can hire our pianist if you like. He's amazing,' Emily says.

'Thanks, but we have our music. Ed Sheeran. Can't go wrong,' I say. We spent an evening in the first month of our engagement going through wedding playlists on Spotify. We decided that I was going to come down the aisle to an instrumental version of 'A Thousand Years' (Josh doesn't know that it was on the *Twilight* soundtrack). And then we'll leave together to Ed Sheeran's 'Perfect'. Predictable, but it will do.

'As the *band manager* of the wedding, I reckon we should get a pianist,' Josh says in a low voice.

'It would be better spent on the house deposit, don't you think?' I say. Josh shrugs, leaves the piano, and fiddles with the lights instead.

'Would you two like to practise walking up the aisle, perhaps?' Emily suggests, eyeballing the lights as they go dim and bright over and over again.

'No. It's fine, we'll figure it out closer to the time. Right, Josh?' I say.

Josh turns the lights off completely. 'Yeah, right.'

'Alrighty then. Shall we move to the barn, lovebirds?' Emily says, still holding her grin. Josh and I shrug and nod at her. 'Amazing.'

One of the best things about the venue is that it's on top of a hill, so all you see are fields and fields. When we visited it the first time, it was a blue-sky day in June, and all those fields were bright green and golden.

Now the fields are mud.

'Looks like you have company,' Emily says.

Next to the barn doors is a familiar-shaped woman in a bright floral coat.

'Josh, why is your mum here?'

He slaps his head. 'Ah, I completely forgot I mentioned it to her. Poor Mum, standing out in the cold. Why didn't she phone me?' He calls out, 'Mum,' and runs ahead. Oh, fantastic.

The four of us go into the barn together.

'Isn't it just amazing,' Emily says. Linda whimpers into a tissue.

Emily starts on what to expect on the day. She tells us how the food will be served, where the dance floor will be, and where she suggests we put the cake.

'Yes, I agree. The cake should be there,' Linda says. 'What flavour are you two having? Have you decided?'

'A vanilla sponge, three tiers,' I say.

'Shame. Dad loves carrot cake. And it will go with your orange theme.'

'The theme is rustic,' I correct her gently.

'Bagsy this seat,' Josh shouts and sits at the top table.

'Amy, go sit with him, and I'll take your photo,' Linda says.

I laugh it off. 'There is plenty of time for photos on the day.'

'Go on.' She insists. Josh taps the seat next to him. I go over and sit down. Emily and Linda make an 'Aww' sound. 'Put your arm around your bride, Joshy.' Josh does as he's told, popping his arm across my shoulder and letting it rest there. It feels awkward. 'Amy, smile. Oh, Gramps will love this.' Gramps won't even know who we are, I want to say. Linda takes a million photos of us. Emily stands next to her with her hand on her heart. 'Okay, done. You're free.' Josh and I get up.

'I was thinking about your colour theme, orange,' Linda says.

'Rustic.'

'Perhaps a little gold would make it a little fancier? Less low-key?'

'It's meant to be low-key,' I say.

'I feel a touch of gold would be nice.' Linda persists. 'Just a splash.' I need Josh for support, but he's too busy doing pull-ups on a beam.

'We'll think about it,' I say.

'Oh, but please, don't take any notice of me. It's your day. I'm just the finance department.' Linda chuckles.

'Are we happy?' Emily asks.

'Yep,' Josh says, dropping dramatically to the floor from the beam.

Emily claps. 'Amazing. The last thing is to decide the catering for the day. So, if you follow me . . .' Linda and Emily leave together. I stand in the middle of the barn.

'Are you coming, Ames?' Josh asks. 'Amy?'

'Doesn't it seem bigger?' I say, gazing up at the high beams.

'Maybe a little bigger,' Josh adds as he gazes up with me. We stare in silence as if we are inspecting the night sky. The door opens, and Linda pokes her head in and hurries us up.

'Come on, guys. Emily is waiting.'

Josh and Amy's Wedding 2025

To Do:

Email final numbers to The Chipping Barn.
Find out all dietary requirements from guests.
Go to Lace's first fitting of the wedding dress.
Send band suggestions to Josh.
Taste wedding cakes at Clapcake.
Remove phones from the bedroom.
Make Josh feel like *the man*.
Buy <u>sexy</u> lingerie.

Sex Tip 1: No Phones in the Bedroom
194 Nights

Our bedroom is not the homeliest place on earth, but I don't see the point in spending money on a room that we're renting. I'd rather save it for our actual home. The walls are a dull custard, and the carpet is a scratchy beige with unidentified splodges. There is a pile of books on the chest of drawers, some geography-themed ones that I have bought for Josh over the years, but most are my astronomy books. Our only attempt to make the space more inviting was by adding Herbert, the Peace Lily. Unfortunately, Herbert is now dead. We probably should throw him out, but neither of us has the heart to. The only artwork is a photo canvas of the London skyline that belongs to the landlord. I did buy a world map in a frame for Josh a year ago. It's leaning on the wall, ready to be put up.

'Do not, I repeat, do not beg your students. Do not be aggressive. If you want to motivate them, then you must praise them.' @DrLabby's thick-framed glasses are taking up most of the screen. I don't tend to follow many people on Instagram, but @DrLabby has proven to be very useful for teaching tips. Below, the caption reads, 'Top tips for motivating your students! #TeacherTips #TeacherGram #HighSchoolTeacher'. I like and save the video and scroll down. An advert for lube fills the screen. (I had investigated buying a teeny-tiny vibrator a month ago, and I've been stuck in a sex algorithm since. I didn't even buy the teeny-tiny vibrator.) The advert is a black and white photo of a woman holding down the wrists of a man in bed. The caption reads, 'Take Control of Your Pleasure.' I look over at Josh, squinting at his phone with his tongue out. Here it goes. I flip on my side to face him.

'What's up?' he asks, flicking his eyes to me and then back at the screen.

'I don't think we should have phones in the bedroom anymore.'

'How would we wake up?'

'We can set an alarm on a clock like they used to do in the nineties. It's healthier.'

'Healthier?' He scoffs. '*This* is healthy. Look at the muscles on his chest.' He turns his phone to show a video of a humongous man flipping a tyre. 'Tony and I are going to try and get a tyre for the gym.'

Tony is Josh's gym buddy, who is partially responsible for Josh's obsession with trying to look like an inflated human. I can imagine Tony has a topknot, tattoos and wears tight tank tops. He also must be the size of a silverback gorilla, because last November, he beat Josh at a squat challenge with over 100 more squats a day. I had to count Josh's squats every evening, which was painfully boring, so I was super happy when that challenge was over.

I move closer and put my hand on Josh's bare, hairless chest. (He only wears boxers to bed. Tonight, he's in his baby blue ones from a multipack that Linda bought him two Christmases ago.) 'Your chest is so ripped,' I flirt.

Josh laughs. 'Hardly. I need to add four inches at least.' He turns away and puts his phone on the bedside table, I get ready for him to turn back to me. 'Night, Lab Rat.' He takes hold of Skogsfräken and stays facing away. I turn off the light. Hmm.

Eggplant, Peach, Waterdrop
195 Nights

I went to school alone this morning to do some prep work before the promotion interview on Friday. I'm feeling pretty confident about it, but I still want to make sure I'm watertight. Especially now that I've told Dad that I have it in the bag.

Josh is having a tyre meeting at the gym. He has been overly calm about his upcoming interview. I think he's playing it cool to save face, knowing that Nina will get it. That or he's doing that Josh thing where he's too optimistic about his ability. (Not that he's not capable, but he does have a booster seat of confidence beneath his skill set.) Usually, I would help him prepare for things like this, but with the wedding, the science contest and my own interview to prep, I don't have time. My only hope is that when I do get promoted, he won't get chippy about the pay gap.

Only Rosie Bibbly, the timid maths teacher, and I are in the staffroom. Despite working at this school for two years, Rosie has not looked any of us in the eye for more than two seconds. We have a mutual understanding that we don't need to converse any further than a polite 'good morning'. She is sitting at the end of the communal desk, trying to mark, but every time she starts typing something on her laptop, her phone vibrates, and she sighs and starts texting. She then goes back to her laptop, her phone vibrates, and the cycle begins again.

As part of my interview prep, I've made a document outlining every possible question that Dr Therone may ask me. Why do you think you're the best teacher for the job? How will you develop the department over the next three years? What challenges do you think you will face? Under each question, I've written a paragraph of what I will say, which I'm trying to learn by heart. It's overkill, but as @DrLabby says, 'There is no such thing as overpreparing'.

A pile of books slam down next to me on the table, and before I even look up, I know it's Nina because of the titles. *Women Saving Women!*, *How Women Fought Back*, *The Suffragettes Suffering*.

'Assembly prep,' she says.

'Careful,' I say. Nina likes to use her morning assembly slots to express her political views, which does Dr Therone's head in.

She shrugs. 'I've got to do what I've got to do. Is Josh coming in today?'

I look around and see that all the staff are here, but there is no sign of Josh.

'He's late,' I say through a sigh.

'I suppose I would be late too if I could get away with it,' Nina says back.

She sits down next to me just as Dr Therone comes strutting in. Every staff member scatters and finds a seat. Dr Therone stops. She scans the room and gives me daggers.

'Where's Mr Butters?' I panic trying to think of the best excuse. I can't exactly tell her Josh is late because he's having a meeting about a tyre. I open my mouth just as Josh bursts into the room, breathless and pink-cheeked. Thank God. 'Mr Butters, nice of you to join us.'

'Sorry, roadworks,' he says.

Dr Therone flashes a rare smile and says, 'You didn't miss anything.'

Amy Elman Doesn't Feel Sexy

Nina tuts as Josh settles down next to me. He gives me a thumbs up, which means the gym has agreed to the tyre.

Dr Therone goes to speak, but her eyes are suddenly fixed on the back of the room. The staff turn to see what she's glaring at. It's Rosie Bibbly; she is texting with a huge grin on her face, completely unaware that everyone is looking at her. Poor Rosie.

'Miss Bibbly,' Dr Therone says. Rosie's head shoots up.

'Sorry!'

'Whoever you're texting must be extremely entertaining. Please would you share with us the conversation that you're having in my meeting?'

'No, I-I can't,' Rosie stutters.

'Would you prefer if I read it?' Dr Therone threatens.

'This is against privacy laws,' Nina shouts. Dr Therone makes her way towards Rosie with her hand out ready to receive the phone.

'I'll read it,' Rosie blurts out. Dr Therone gestures for her to start.

'You don't have to read it,' Nina says.

'Shh, Miss Pascoe,' Dr Therone snaps.

Rosie takes a deep breath and begins to read with a shaky voice. 'I wish you were here . . . right now . . . so you can . . . fuck me . . . in this meeting . . . Eggplant emoji. Peach emoji. Waterdrop emoji.' Rosie puts her phone down and squeezes her eyes shut.

For the first time, Dr Therone is speechless. I can hear Josh quietly sniggering next to me. I bite my lip hard. There is a scatter of forced coughs throughout the room. When I look up, everyone is staring at the floor to avoid eye contact. I glance at Rosie, who is bright red and playing with her floral cardigan sleeve. Am I the *only* woman who hasn't got a raging sex life around here?

Dr Therone clears her throat.

'As you are aware,' she says with a raised voice, and noticeably not looking at Rosie, 'interviews for the Head of Science and Head of Humanities will happen on Friday. You have had your slots emailed to you. Come prepared and on time. I will pick the successful candidates over the weekend and announce them next week. Now, are there any *appropriate* announcements?' Nina puts up her hand. Dr Therone scans the room. 'No? Good.' She leaves. I look across at Nina.

'That woman is out of control,' she says. She gets up and goes to comfort Rosie.

Sex Tip 2: Make Him Feel Like *The Man*
(Even when he's not)

Josh writes *Kevin Keegan* in his childlike handwriting on the pub quiz paper.

'You're so smart, Josh,' I say and rub his bicep. 'Gosh, your muscles have got so big.'

He laughs, but I can tell he's uncomfortable. 'Erm, okay, Amy. Thanks.'

After the failure of Sex Tip 1 of getting phones out of the bedroom, I'm moving on to Sex Tip 2: Make Josh feel like *The Man*. I have started tonight in The Cock and Bull during our pub quiz.

I didn't think it would be hard, but it's becoming apparent that I'm not very good at compliments. I have given out five so far, from his muscles to his hair to his brain, all of which have fallen flat.

'I'm being serious, they're huge,' I add with an extra squeeze. He frowns as if he can't quite recognise me. I keep going. 'How do you make them so—'

'Concentrate, Amy,' Nina interrupts. She slaps the table and then points to Daz, who is asking the next question. Nina was already wound up after this morning's staff meeting, and now Pete has brought his office manager, Tiff, to the pub quiz. She's a sweet girl, but is not taking the quiz seriously enough for our liking. Nina hasn't said anything yet, but every time Tiff giggles at a question she doesn't know (which has been all the questions so far), she scowls and makes a tight fist.

'I repeat, where is Niagara Falls?' Daz says into the mic.

Tiff giggles (again) and says, 'I'm far too dumb for this.'

Nina blurts out. 'How do you not know where Niagara Falls is?'

Tiff giggles and shrugs.

'Not everyone knows where it is,' Pete chimes in, which is ironic because he's the first to lose his head over famous landmarks. 'Tiff is pop culture anyway, right, Twinkles?' Tiff replies with another unnecessary giggle. Nina rolls her head and mumbles something mean under her breath.

'Guys, Josh has already written it down,' I announce proudly, pointing at the answer he has written: *Border New York and Ontario, Canada*. I turn to him. 'It's so admirable how much you know about geography.'

'Well, I hope he does know about geography; it is what he teaches after all,' Nina says. She's not helping with my campaign.

'Next question,' Daz says. 'In what year was *The Godfather* released?'

'Pop culture. Tiff?' Nina says.

Tiff giggles again and twists a strand of loose hair with her finger. Something tells me that when she said pop culture, she meant *Love Island*, not movies that came out before she was born.

'I know it, I know it,' Josh says, and he writes *1970* on the paper.

'I think it's 1972,' I whisper. 'Dad loves *The Godfather*. I remember him saying—'

'No, it's definitely 1970,' Josh insists. I go to argue back, but I stop myself.

'You're probably right,' I say, touching his back.

Daz begins the next question. 'In what year—' He stops abruptly. He's smirking at us. 'Petey and the Brains are immediately disqualified.'

We all fly up from our seats, protesting. 'What? Why? What?'

Daz points. 'Phone. You know there is a no-tolerance rule.'

'We haven't used any . . .' Nina's voice dies out as we notice Tiff sitting with guilt written all over her face and, in her hand, a phone.

'Baby, we spoke about this . . .' Pete whines.

'I-I was taking a selfie,' Tiff whispers.

'She was taking a selfie, Daz,' Pete shouts across the pub.

'Mate, you're out,' Daz says. The rest of the pub starts cheering, and we all slowly drop to our chairs.

'This is why we don't invite dates to a quiz night,' Nina hisses to Pete.

'Why do you have to take it so seriously?' Pete hisses back.

'My Year 7 class knows more than her.'

Josh and I sink back and glance at each other like kids whose parents are arguing.

Tiff looks down at her hand and mutters. 'Sorry, I wasn't thinking.'

'That's precisely the problem,' Nina says sharply.

Tiff's face crumples. She gets up, apologises again and leaves.

'Call yourself a feminist,' Pete shouts, then screeches his chair back and storms out.

'Guys, please, we're trying to do a pub quiz here,' Daz shouts into the mic. This is mortifying.

A moment passes, and then Nina growls and stomps out. Josh throws the pen across the table and slumps back in his chair. I put my hand back on his thigh and try to think of my next compliment.

'You're such a patient man.'
'You're being so weird tonight, Lab Rat.'

*

Fifi clearly did not expect us to come home so early. We find her standing in the kitchen in a teeny pink transparent nightdress and holding a knife (*my knife*). On the bench in front of her is a (*my*) chopping board, where there is a pile of perfectly cut onion slices. This would have been *almost* normal if she wasn't filming herself on her phone. I don't know what to say, nor does Josh, and nor does Fifi.

Eventually, she mumbles something. 'I thought it was pub quiz night.'

'It finished early,' Josh says, gazing up at the ceiling.

'I'll wash the knife. Promise.'

'Don't worry. We'll stick it in the dishwasher, won't we, Amy? Amy?'

'Dishwasher, yeah,' I reply, tearing my eyes away from her. I must admit she looks sickeningly good in lingerie. I didn't realise a diet of Heinz soup could create abs . . . Note to self: try the Heinz tomato soup diet.

'Dishwasher, gotcha,' Fifi says. 'I have, er, people, er, waiting,' she whispers and points to the phone.

'Sure, okay, we'll, erm, go. Come on, Amy,' Josh says, dragging me out of the kitchen. We hear her address her viewers, apologising for the minor interruption.

Josh closes the door.

'I can't believe she is filming porn in our home,' I whisper.

'She's hardly filming porn,' Josh says. 'Come on, it's funny.'

'Funny? What happens if she attracts some weirdo to our home, who then murders us all whilst we're sleeping? And they then turn our murder into one of those true crime documentaries.'

'You won't get murdered. So many people are doing OnlyFans videos, so it would be highly unlikely they would target Fifi.'

'OnlyFans? Is that what she's doing?'

'Looks like it. I don't blame her. I heard one girl gets £1,000 a minute just to wiggle her toes for a man in Florida.'

'That's porn,' I snap. He scoffs as if I have no idea what porn is. 'Did you see what she was wearing?'

'I did see what she was wearing,' Josh says, clearly pleased about what he saw. 'I need the loo.'

He goes to the toilet for a while. I go to the toilet after him, and then we are in bed. He's on his phone, so I go on my phone and watch another @DrLabby reel about career development.

'When you're interviewing for a promotion, make sure you keep eye contact with the interviewer; this shows real confidence in yourself. A good tip is to examine their eye colour,' @DrLabby says. I save it and look over at Josh, who is watching a reel of a man doing press-ups. I sigh and look down at my full-length star-patterned pyjamas. I feel stupid. What woman in their late-twenties wears astronomy-themed nightwear? No wonder Josh is not turned on. I wonder where Fifi got her lingerie from . . . I turn off the light.

'*The Godfather* was 1972, by the way,' I say in the dark.

'Are you sure?'

'Yup. I googled it on the toilet.'

Scones in Reading

196 Nights

The calendar invite came in this morning before work. An 8 p.m. phone call with Rebecca labelled **'UPDATE: HEN PARTY!!!!!!'** I had accepted it this morning when I had optimism, but now I am sitting on my bed with heavy eyes and a headache, and Rebecca is calling. It takes every bit of me to pick up.

'Why are you speaking like a crow?' she asks.

'It's been a long day,' I croak back.

The day began with a broken box of test tubes in my Year 7 class. Lilly cut her finger. Joanne fainted from the blood. Year 10 had done no research on plastic in the ocean. Surprise, surprise. My day ended with Dr Therone wanting an update about the science contest. I told her everything was going *really* well. She asked me what the topic was, but luckily, she got distracted by Mrs Redson, who had just lost another netball game, so I made a dash for it.

'So, how are the wedding plans?' Rebecca asks. I search my brain.

'Fine. The venue is paid for. Invites all sent. Dress is terrifying,' I say.

'Is that girl still making it?'

'Lace. Yeah. I think I'll end up wearing a white sequin jumpsuit down the aisle.'

'Gosh. And Josh, is he doing anything?' I can hear the judgment in her voice.

'Yes. He's in charge of the band, although he keeps showing me musicians that are way out of budget, which is not helpful.'

'MEN! Anyway. Hen party,' she says, shifting her tone. I put the phone on loudspeaker and lie on the bed, resting my eyes. 'I know you said afternoon tea in London, but they are an absolute rip-off. You wouldn't believe how much they charge people for a little crummy sandwich and a cake – £69 per head in sketch London! I thought your tea on the bus would be better, but trust me, you don't want to do it, it's a greedy tourist trap. Anyway, I managed to do some research during Benson's nap times and . . . well, you know *Reading*?'

I open my eyes at the ceiling. I don't like where this is going. 'As in, the city we grew up near?'

'Yup. Forty minutes on the train and the afternoon teas are *three-quarters* of the price. I've booked a sweet place near the river. You're going to love it.' She says *three-quarters* like this surprises her.

'But it's *Reading*,' I say.

'A scone is a scone,' she says. 'Besides, it's not about where we are, it's about who we're with. Everyone can come. Nina's very excited. Something about an old prison and Oscar Wilde. I don't know, she lost me. I've got a booth at Be At One for happy hour. They have a dance floor, so we won't need to move from there. The last train is at 00:30, but we'll aim for 23:45. The dress code is purple. What do you think?'

I rub my eyes. I think I'd rather paint ceramics.

'What was wrong with the afternoon tea bus?' I ask.

'Daylight robbery – or should I say, afternoon robbery!' She laughs. 'I am going to email you the invitation with all the details, but I just wanted to run it by you first in case you hated it.' I'm about to say yes, I do hate it, but she interrupts. 'Oh, Benny is crying. Better go. I'll send you the invite.' She hangs up.

I guess I'll be eating scones in Reading then.

Sex Tip 3: Lingerie (That you feel good in)
197 Nights

I'll admit my underwear collection isn't the most thrilling. I usually stick to cotton Brazilian pants with a lace seam. Marks & Spencer do excellent multipacks of these. I have patterned ones in yellow, purple and black. I don't worry about matching my bra; life is too short for that. I usually stick to a 34C black wired cotton number (also from M&S) on weekdays and coloured bras on weekends. I do have a couple of more risqué pieces. Well, I thought they were risqué, but after seeing Fifi's pink number, they seem pretty granny-ish. So here I am in Thrills & Frills on Oxford Street. It's colourful like a sweet shop, but instead of trays of gummy bears and gobstoppers, it's lingerie and sex toys.

The front of the shop is not so bad: pink and blue bras with rainbow straps and glitter for the outgoing teenagers. It gets progressively darker and more aggressive towards the back of the shop, where there are black leather bras and chain straps for the medieval torturers amongst us. The far corner seems particularly lethal with its whips and chains. There is a couple in that corner who look like they belong in a bingo hall. The woman holds up a pair of handcuffs. He gives her a shy nod, and she puts it in the basket. I wonder if men like him were ready for the *Fifty Shades of Grey* movement, their once quiet wives suddenly requesting to be whipped about in their cul-de-sac homes. Pete had a woman asking to be strangled and whipped once. We asked him if he did it, and he said something disgusting, like 'I'd do anything if she licks my balls.'

Right. Concentrate. What is sexy? Nothing with tassels or diamonds; I don't think dressing like a spoilt chihuahua is the key to all of this. Lace said that red or black never fails, so I go to the collection of red lingerie next to the dildo section. I pick up a frilly bra and thong, check around me, and then swiftly hold them in front of me in the mirror while hoping nobody is looking.

'You should get a suspender belt with that set.' A bleached-haired shop assistant with a thick East London accent appears out of nowhere. 'It's half price if you get it with the thong and bra.' She waves the suspender belt in the air. 'Really will get him going.' I am about to say no, as I feel it's too much, but I suppose that's the point. I must be obviously sexy for this to work.

'Sure.' I take it from Gemma. (That's the name on her badge.)

'That's an... interesting engagement ring,' she says, staring at my hand with a baffled expression. I'm still waiting for the day that someone compliments the ring. 'Have you seen our wild wedding night collection?' She points behind, where there is a section filled with white lingerie. 'We're having a sale today; 10 per cent off.'

I hadn't thought to dress up for the wedding night. It's not like the olden days when we were losing our virginities to each other. Nowadays, the bride and groom get so wasted during the reception that it's probably a fumbling mess at best.

'Do women still get stuff like that for their weddings?'

Gemma looks gobsmacked. 'Of course. He's put a ring on it, the least you can do is put out.' She pulls out three white lingerie sets that she thinks are the best (conveniently the most expensive). "This one will look stunning on you.' She holds up a white lace all-in-one job. 'It's crotchless too.' She has a very loud voice. 'So, you know, when you've had one too many fizzes, you don't worry about taking it all off. You simply pop the crotch and . . .'

'Yeah, yeah, yeah,' I say quickly, taking it from her. 'Cool. Thanks.'

'And don't forget your garter.'

'Is that necessary?'

'Yes,' she says. 'It goes round your thigh, and he takes it off with his teeth and throws it to his single lads. Don't look so scared, love, it's a tradition. So, do you want it?'

I thought that was more of an American thing, and I can't think of anything worse than Josh using his teeth to take a scrunchie off my thigh in front of my dad. I nod anyway.

I go to pay. Gemma takes out a Thrills & Frills bag, but I tell her I don't need one. I don't want to publicise to the whole Victoria line that I've just bought lingerie.

'That will be £76.99,' Gemma says. Geez. Who said sex was free? I go to tap my card and stop.

'Do you think it will work?' I'm not sure why I am asking her this. I just assume she's around underwear all day, so she must be an expert.

'What will work?'

'Like, do you think he will like me in this stuff? Me?'

Gemma puts her hand on her heart. 'Aww, sweetie. He's got a pulse, doesn't he?' I nod. 'Well, there you go, it will work.'

'Okay,' I say, and tap my card. I stuff the underwear into my backpack, along with my book on dark matter and my yoghurt pot.

'But remember, if it doesn't work, we don't offer refunds or exchanges.' She smiles. I leave Thrills & Frills thinking of all the women who have attempted to return used underwear in the history of underwear.

Now, all I have to do is find an appropriate occasion for my new red lingerie set. You can't just whack it out on a Thursday night after *Making a Murderer*. Josh turns 30 next week, the perfect occasion.

Stuffed Snowy Owl

198 Nights

'I have been a dedicated teacher at this school for six years. I have been a dedicated teacher at this school for six years . . .' I repeat my mantra to myself as I wait outside Dr Therone's office. I close my eyes to visualise myself after I've got the job. This is another @DrLabby interview tip. She said, 'You will make it happen if you see it happening'. I think of Dad's face when I tell him I'm officially Head of Science for Clapham Girls. Even though it's not quite the same as, 'Hey, Dad, I'm a brain surgeon,' I still think I will get a reaction from him, even if it's just a twitch of his mouth to show that he's (a little) proud.

Mr Rawlinson's interview is currently happening on the other side of the door, and from what I can hear, he's doing terribly. Goody. Dr Therone, who sounds like she is on her last tether, has asked him three times what he would bring to the role. 'No, Mr Rawlinson, what would you bring to the role of Head of *Science*?' Goodness knows what his answer was before. I don't know what she expected from this interview – the man has clearly lost his marbles. Even Gramps could do a better job than him. 'Mr Rawlinson, thank you for your time,' Dr Therone shouts. 'Yes, the interview has ended. Yes, please leave through that only door.' I sit up straight in the chair, ready for the door to open. 'I will be announcing the results next week, Mr Rawlinson. Next week. Yes.' Mr Rawlinson comes hobbling out. He has a black smudge on the top of his bald head, and his glasses are on a wonk. It takes him a second to see me and then a second more to compute who I am.

'Good luck, Alice,' he says and mumbles to himself as he shuffles off. Good God, get that man a blanket.

Dr Therone shouts my (correct) name from her office. I get up and dust off my pencil skirt, the one saved for major professional occasions and funerals. I think of @DrLabby's tips about showing confidence in meetings. She said that you should walk in slowly to portray that you're in control of yourself. So that's what I do, taking each step deliberately.

'In your own time,' Dr Therone says. Her white leather chair creaks as she adjusts herself in it. Dr Therone's office is not a typical headmistress's office. When she got the job, she insisted on having it redecorated. There is a moss green statement wall, and the rest of the walls are a mute grey. There is a floor-length mirror and a collection of certificates, including her PhD certificate from King's College in War Studies. I'm assuming this is where she learnt how to be a tyrant. On her desk is a vase full of fresh lilies and a taxidermy snowy owl who is staring at me.

My chair is significantly lower than Dr Therone's chair. I assume she does this on purpose as some sort of power play. I won't let this trick me though. @DrLabby advised me to 'Stay tall and steady', so I stretch my spine as much as possible, making all my back muscles complain. I consciously lock eyes with Dr Therone, inspecting her eye colour like @DrLabby said to do. I had always thought Dr Therone's eyes were dark brown, but on closer inspection, it seems that they're almost black – like the pupils of her stuffed owl.

'Why are you looking at me like that?'

'Sorry,' I look away. Dr Therone sighs heavily, making it clear she doesn't want to be here. She takes hold of a biro and roughly scribbles circles onto a blank piece of lined paper until the ink starts coming out. She sighs again.

'Amy Elman, why should you be the Head of Science at Clapham Girls?' She has her pen ready to write down my answer. I sit up. I've got this.

'I have been a dedicated teacher at this school for six years now, and—'

'Six years?' Dr Therone cuts in. 'Are you sure about that?'

'Yes, I started in September 2018.' I wait for her to respond to this, but she's too occupied scribbling notes. I continue. 'Since I started teaching physics here, there has been a 10 per cent rise of students taking it at A level. And the grades for A Levels have increased year on year. Last year, Yvonne Thompson got into Cambridge University. She's the first pupil ever in this school to get accepted into Cambridge for sci—'

'Her parents were both scientists,' Dr Therone cuts in again.

I stumble. 'S-still, um, she got almost 100 per cent in her exam.'

'As I said, her parents were scientists.'

I readjust myself in the chair. It takes a lot more effort to be 'tall and steady' than I had anticipated. I continue, 'I have a passionate, youthful approach to science that appeals to the girls, and being so young—' Dr Therone points her pen in my face, making me stop in my tracks.

'How old are you?'

'Erm, 29.'

'Not that young,' she says, smirking.

'Young, considering the role, and doesn't that say a lot about my dedication?'

'So, you're saying . . .' she says, tapping her pen on her chin. 'You may be a little inexperienced for such a responsibility?'

'No, I'm saying I have a youthful approach to science that appeals to the girls.'

She glances at her watch. 'Right, time is running out.' I spot the clock behind her head. It's only been five minutes.

'I thought these were 20-minute interviews?'

'So, Miss Elman, how would you want to see the science department developing in the next five years?' I pause to try to remember what I wrote down on my interview prep document. After a split second, Dr Therone raises her eyebrows. 'Do you not know?' she asks.

I clear my throat and smile.

'All science comes down to is having the courage to ask questions and the confidence to work those questions out. For some reason, many girls lose that confidence during their school days, and I want to do my best to stop this. When I hear our pupils say that they don't like science, it confuses me because there is something for everyone, be that aerospace in physics, nutrition in chemistry, or . . . women's health in biology. It's our job as teachers to show this to the pupils and to feed whatever hint of passion they have. If, in the next five years, there is an increase in our girls who have gone on to have a career in science, because we have given them the encouragement, the tools and the confidence during their most curious years, then that will be the kind of department I would be proud to be leading . . .'

'Time's up,' Dr Therone says as if she hasn't listened to a single thing I just said. I frown at the clock.

'But there's 10 minutes left,' I protest. She puts out her hand for me to shake, and I reluctantly do.

'We will be announcing the new head of the department next week. Thank you, Miss Elman.' She gestures towards the door. I open my mouth, but she shouts over me before I can say a word. 'Thank you, Miss Elman.'

I leave the office in a blur. What just happened? One minute, I'm giving the best answer of my life, and the next, I'm being shown the door. It doesn't add up. I see Josh sitting in a chair outside, waiting for his interview.

'All okay?' he asks, obviously reading the dazed look on my face.

'I don't know,' I say. Seeing that I'm on the verge of tears, Josh stands up and hugs me, which makes me feel even more emotional.

'I'm sure it went fine, Lab Rat,' he says into my hair. I pull away from him and sniff away a tear.

'Don't worry, please. Concentrate on your interview.' I flatten a crease on his shirt. He could have at least ironed it, especially now that he may be our only hope. Dr Therone calls out his name from her desk. I do one last pat-down of his shirt and wish him luck. He strolls into the office and says Dr Therone's name like she's an old friend. As the door shuts, I hear Dr Therone offer tea or coffee.

What on earth, I never got offered tea or coffee.

Poached Breast

It's past seven, and when I get home from work, I find Josh at the kitchen table with his earbuds in. He's eating something that looks like a ball of skin. I nudge his arm, and he takes one earbud out. I hear the distinct voice of Joe Rogan coming out from the tiny speaker.

'What *are* you eating?' I ask.

'Poached chicken breast.' He slices a piece off and puts it in his mouth. 'Protein, protein, protein.' I gag, fill a pan with water, and put it on the stove.

'So, your interview went well then?' I say. I texted him in the afternoon asking how it went, and he replied with five thumbs up and five grinning faces. I remain cautious that this is Josh being overly optimistic, like when he was certain he'd got a first-class honours degree, but he got an upper second-class honours degree instead. And then there was that time he applied to be a geography teacher at Eton. He was so sure that he'd got the role that he told his whole family, but a few days later, the rejection letter came. It's not necessarily a bad trait, but I do take his positivity with a pinch of salt.

'Yes, very well,' he says with his usual conviction.

'How long was it exactly?'

'Like 20 minutes. Why?'

'I only had 10 minutes before she asked me to leave,' I mumble. I reach up to take the box of penne pasta from my shelf.

'Maybe she already knows you've got it,' Josh says. I had never thought about it like that. It would make sense why she didn't seem to be listening to me throughout the interview – I already have it in the bag. Yes. That's it. 'Also,' Josh continues, 'I kind of invited Dr Therone to our wedding. Hope that's okay.'

I drop the box of pasta, and the tubes scatter all over the floor.

'Please tell me you're joking?' I shriek, but I can already see from his face that he definitely isn't. 'Josh, why?'

Josh, for some reason, seems surprised by my reaction.

'We were talking about it in the interview, and well, I thought it would be a nice thing to do.' I can't find the words. I open the cupboard under the sink with unnecessary force and start unpacking each cleaning bottle, dropping them on the floor with a bang. Windex, Vanish, Fairy Liquid. BANG, BANG, BANG.

'If you're looking for the dustpan and brush, it broke yesterday,' Josh says. I stop and begin reversing my actions, banging the cleaning products back into the cupboard. 'Why are you mad?' he asks.

'I don't want her at my wedding, Josh.' I hiss his name.

'We won't even notice she's there.'

'She's the devil in a power suit, of course we'll know she's there.' I sweep the pasta up with my foot until it makes a little penne pile on the tiles.

'She *is* our boss. I think it's only *polite*. Amy? Please don't be mad.' Josh begs. I count to five in my head, then return to the pasta situation, scooping up the penne pile and putting it in the bin. 'Amy, come on. She probably won't even come.'

'Hopefully not,' I say. I feel suddenly exhausted with Dr Therone. I'm sick of talking about her, I'm sick of thinking about her, so I change the subject to something that makes me happy. 'Did you see the cottage I sent you today?' I say, with a calmer tone.

'Haven't had time,' Josh says.

'You'll love it. See.' I come over and put my phone in front of him. 'It only has two bedrooms, but it has a huge garden to make up for it. Look, you can BBQ just there.' Josh zooms into the garden.

'Yeah, it's huge,' he says, stating the fact.

'Maybe we should go view it for fun?' I push. Josh hands the phone back.

'You know I feel bad about wasting the estate agent's time,' he says.

'It's their job . . .'

'Shall we just get this wedding done first?'

'Fine,' I say. I put the phone down and pour a new load of pasta into the bubbling pan of water. 'The wedding . . . now with Dr Therone,' I say, staring into the pan.

'Maybe she can be your bridesmaid,' Josh says in his jokey way. I turn with my wooden spoon in the air.

'Too soon. Too bloody soon.'

Natalie

The only time Josh and I nearly broke up was six months into our relationship. I could say it was the booze's fault, but really it was mine.

It was Friday night in the Leeds student bar, and we all thought it would be fun to try every single flavoured vodka shot. I came back from the toilet and saw Natalie Jones and Josh grinding on each other. It was bad enough that he was doing this with a girl, but the fact that it was Natalie made it worse, because she had flirted with Josh ever since the foam party in Freshers' Week. I was as surprised as everyone else when Josh picked me over her. She could pull off crop tops and was doing a sexy degree in Fine Art, which had her painting her naked body bright red. Who wouldn't want Natalie?

I caught Josh's eye when Natalie was at a 90-degree angle against him, and he panicked and stepped away from the scene of the crime. I stormed out of the bar, and he followed me out.

'I knew you liked her,' I yelled. We were now in the university courtyard lit by streetlights and surrounded by smokers. Our friends began appearing from the bar, creating an audience for the fight that was about to unfold.

'Amy, we were only messing about,' he said with a laugh, and that laugh was like throwing petrol onto a fire.

'Why don't you just go out with her then?' I shouted.

'Amy, come on. You are drunk and being very dramatic.'

'Fuck off, pug penis,' I shouted. I could hear my friend Abi's distinctive giggle amongst the sniggering behind us. Josh's face dropped. My words, cutting right into the sorest part of a man. I had gone far over the line. He ran off, so I ran off after him. Well, I tried to. I got to the corner of Cromer Terrace, and then it was my turn to be at a 90-degree angle, and not in a Natalie-sexy-way, but just because I was trying to get my breath back. Even before his gym obsession, Josh was a speedy guy. I walked to his house and knocked on the door again and again until his flatmate came out and told me to go away.

Josh ignored my calls and texts for three days after, and it was torture. I felt disgusted in myself, and I looked disgusting too. I lived on instant noodles and only left my room for a lecture on density, which I ended up crying in and had to leave. The nights were the worst. It had been a while since I had slept alone, and the bed felt huge and cold. All I kept thinking was, if I could go back to that split second before I said *'pug penis'* and slap, gag, kick myself, to stop the words from coming out, then he would probably be here now. Lying in my student bed, I was terrified I had fucked it up. Dad had left Mum that year for Jean-Ivy. Mum, broken, was offloading on me every day, wiping out my memories and replacing them with stories of 'what *actually* happened'. Turns out Mum had been miserable being Robert Elman's wife. My whole life felt like an illusion. The only person who was real was Josh. He was the one who held me through it all. He was my rock, and I had smashed him apart, publicly, in the most humiliating way.

On the evening of the fourth day, I was in bed, crying on the phone to Mum. Her advice was to forget all men, as they will always disappoint you in the end. But as she talked, a text came through. Josh wanted me to come over to his. I immediately ended the call and made myself look the best

I could. I was certain he would finish it, so I thought if I got dressed up, then he would have a change of heart. At every stage of getting to his house, I made a mental note of all the things I did that would be the last as his girlfriend. This is the last time I'm leaving the house as Josh's girlfriend. This is the last time I am cycling as Josh's girlfriend. This is the last time I will walk towards Josh's door.

We sat far apart on the bed, surrounded by his laundry and plates. I was cross-legged, pulling my shortest skirt down to hide my thighs. My heels were on the floor. My new look didn't get the reaction I had hoped for. The high ponytail and red lips seemed to puzzle him more than turn him on. Josh was leaning against the wall with his knees up. He was twisting and turning his striped blue and yellow football sock that needed a wash. The silence was killing me, so I made the first move.

'If you're going to finish it—'

He cut me off. 'I heard that The George and Dragon is starting a pub quiz next Tuesday.'

'We could . . . Could we do that?' He pinged the sock across the room, and it flew and landed sloppily on his Xbox.

'Yeah, we could.'

And that was that. We never mentioned the 'pug penis' incident again, but we did have our first dry spell. It was three weeks, and I felt so terrible that what I had said had knocked Josh's confidence. If he had called me flappy fanny or puffy pussy, I wouldn't want to take my pants down in front of him again. The dry patch was broken, thanks to a night of tequila.

As for Natalie, Josh continued to be friends with her like he was friends with everyone, and she carried on shamelessly flirting with him. I kept all my thoughts about that to myself, only ranting to my lab partner Abi about it. I was scared to rock the boat again, because I couldn't think of anything worse than losing Josh. It was a relief once we graduated, knowing I didn't have to put up with Natalie. But as it turns out, there is always a Natalie in some form. After university, there was Caz, the other bartender at the pub Josh worked in briefly. She had a tattoo of a tiger on her belly and could open bottles with her teeth. And then there was Tara on his teaching training course who was, in Josh's words, 'fucking hilarious'. Then there was Jude the English teacher in his first job, who used to ski for Great Britain. Whenever Josh told me anything about them in his oblivious way, I wanted to shout WHY DON'T YOU JUST GO OUT WITH HER THEN? But I kept my mouth shut – forever scared of rocking the boat.

The Gherkin

199 Nights

I'm perched on the French daybed, waiting for Lace to be ready for me. She is sitting in her red velvet chair by the window, sewing a button on a man's worn black denim jacket. Apart from the usual greetings and telling me to sit on the bed, the only thing she has said to me is that men are rubbish at sewing buttons.

Today, she is dressed like a Parisian artist in a thin black turtleneck. Her hair is up high in a floppy, messy bun that keeps dropping down as she sews. I don't know how she can look scruffy and elegant at the same time.

Peppy suddenly emerges from the corner. He seems a little plumper than the last time I saw him. I call him over with a kissing sound, but he snubs me and goes to Lace instead. Knobhead. He jumps on her.

'Oh,' she shrieks. 'Get off, fluffy swine.' She drops the bemused cat onto the floor and then glances up at me. 'We're not getting on today,' she says, returning to her sewing.

'Why don't you give him back to that man? He seemed pretty distraught.'

She shakes her head aggressively. 'No, not yet. Sleazy bastard.'

'What did he do exactly?' I ask.

'He had a wife and tried it on with me. That's what.' She folds the jacket neatly into a brown parcel and gets up. 'Right, Amy Butters' wedding dress.' She goes across the room and takes an oat-coloured cotton dress from the rail by the wall. 'Try this on. It's the pattern of your wedding dress, so if you don't like the shape of it, tell me now or forever hold your peace.' She sits down in the chair as I stand holding the dress. 'Well, what are you waiting for? Put it on.'

'Is there a toilet I can get changed in?' I ask.

'A toilet? Why? Just change here,' she says. 'What's wrong?'

'Um, I know some women can walk around changing rooms with it all hanging out, but I am not one of those women,' I say.

'Amy, it's me. Don't be ridiculous.' I whimper, then hold the dress under my chin and unzip my zipper. I struggle to keep the dress there as I pull my trousers down. She rolls her head. 'Doll, what are you doing?' I stop.

'I'm taking off my clothes so I can try on the dress.'

'I suggest it would be a lot easier if you put the dress down,' she says. I whimper again as I realise that I'm just going to have to reveal my pink-spotty-full-bum-pants to Lace. I turn away and take off my jeans, purple hoodie and H&M t-shirt. Then, finally, my socks. What makes the pink spotty pants worse is the yellow patterned bra. In a rush to cover up, I quickly put one foot into the dress and nearly trip on it.

'Careful,' Lace cries.

I pull it up slowly, and Lace comes over and starts making the adjustments, pinning up the bottom and pinching the back of the dress so it sits tighter around my waist.

'Go stand in front of the mirror,' she orders. So, I do. Well, the dress isn't Mum's – that's for sure. It has a high neckline and sleeves that sit above my wrists. It pinches tightly around my waist, and the skirt floats to my ankles. 'Thoughts?' she asks. I hesitate, worried about her reaction. 'Tell me.'

'It's lovely. It's just different from Mum's.'

'Never mind your mum. This is *your* wedding dress for *your* wedding day. Do you like the shape of it? Because if you don't, I'll have to return to the drawing board.'

I look at it properly. I turn one way and notice how my bum does that peachy thing that I didn't know it could do. My waist has shrunk, and the high neckline is enhancing my boobs. In a million years, I would have never picked this shape for me, but it's already a hell of a lot more flattering than Mum's dress.

'Yes,' I say.

'Good, because there is no time to go back to the drawing board,' she says, as she continues to fiddle with the dress. Her fingertips brush my skin, and it makes my spine tingle. She goes away and comes back a second later with a hairbrush.

'What are you doing with that?' I panic.

'Your hair needs volume,' she explains and then begins to pull the brush through my dull, greasy hair.

'Sorry, it needs washing,' I say.

'You should go blonde,' she says.

I laugh. 'Blonde? I don't think I can pull off blonde.'

'Of course you can. If I had your colouring, I would go blonde.'

'Your colouring is the best,' I say. 'You're so lucky.'

'Everyone is lucky, and they are also unlucky,' she says. I try to make sense of yet another one of her riddles. 'Don't frown, Amy, just know that you're lucky too. Luckier in some ways.'

'How do you mean luckier?' I ask. She gives my hair one last brush and walks away.

'Right, get out of that thing. Let's go somewhere,' she says. I inspect my reflection one last time; me, standing there, in my soon-to-be-wedding dress. How surreal. Lace, noticing I'm having a moment, says, 'I'll meet you outside.'

We end up in one of those shipping containers that have been turned into a clothes shop. It's called Brown Duck and sells brown hoodies with cartoon rubber ducks on the back and front. I don't get it. The drum and bass is playing so loud that the man at the till doesn't realise we are in his shop until Lace is leaning over his counter. He drops his Spider-Man comic book.

'Can I help you?' he says.

'Duck Duck Goose,' Lace replies with a straight face. I think she's going nuts, but then the man springs into action. He gets up, checks the door and then pulls a load of hoodies across the back rail to reveal a wooden door.

'All yours,' he says.

Lace doesn't explain the secret door – she goes through it and expects me to follow her. It leads to a brick wall with a fire escape door, and through that is a bar. It's dark with a smell of leather and cigars. There is low mumbling of conversation and a light jazz piano playing. In the centre is a lit-up U-shaped bar. The bartender glances up at us and then goes back to stirring a drink. Very attractive people are dotted around in oversized armchairs and cracked leather sofas. A waitress walks past and serves whisky to three men in baseball caps who are too engrossed in their conversation to notice she has been and gone.

'Is this Soho House?' I ask.

'Don't insult me,' she says. She sounds like I had asked her if this was a Wetherspoon's, which is confusing because I thought Soho House was the cool place to be. We sit on art deco chairs that are not comfortable in the slightest. The waitress comes, puts napkins on the table between us, and offers us a drink. Lace orders two Merlots before I can say otherwise. I gaze around the room and spot a very glamorous couple in the corner, she in a pink jumpsuit and him in a denim shirt.

'Are they famous?' I ask, whispering.

Lace looks at them. 'Barely.'

'What is this place?'

'It's Frankie's. Oh, there he is now.' She waves at the tall blond man who is walking through the place like it's his lounge. I recognise him as the guy who opened the door for me last weekend. Lace and him would make a very good-looking couple. The kind you see in films. He sits next to me.

'It's you from last week. Who are you?' he asks, not politely. Lace jumps in and introduces me as her client. I give a little wave. '*You* are making a wedding dress for someone? Well, I never.' Lace slaps his arm flirtatiously, and he tells her that he's joking. Still, it's not the most reassuring thing I've heard.

'Is that your ring then?' Frankie asks, as he takes my hand and inspects it. He gives Lace a mocking look, as if he's about to burst out laughing. She hits him in the same way and tells him to be kind. He pinches his lips together in a smile, obviously enjoying any kind of physical contact from her. These two *must* be doing it.

'It's his grandma's. That's why it looks a little worn,' I say, defending the ring. Frankie laughs again. It's not a gentle laugh like Josh has, but high-pitched and mean.

'What a genius. He didn't have to spend a penny. Do you like it?'

'Yes, I like it,' I say too quickly. Frankie raises his eyebrows, making it clear that he's not convinced. I keep talking. 'I mean, maybe I wouldn't have chosen a purple diamond. But hey! It means something, and that's *obviously* worth more than any old silver diamond ring from . . . Tiffany's.'

'*Obviously*,' Frankie says sarcastically.

'Is Wera's still happening, Frankie?' Lace asks. She is slouched in her chair, looking very bored.

'You said you didn't fancy it yesterday.'

'That was yesterday. Shall we?'

'Okay, but we're bringing your friend and her old grandma's ring with us.'

'Don't worry about me,' I say. 'Josh will be coming back from golf soon, and we're planning on watching . . .' Lace covers my mouth with her hand.

'No, you're coming with us,' she says and pulls me up from the chair.

*

Wera's party is in a penthouse off Liverpool Street next to The Gherkin. It's her going-away party before she does the Camino de Santiago. I've been here for 30 minutes, and not one person has spoken to me. Lace disappeared into the crowd the second we arrived. Frankie has been pulled from one person to the next, each calling his name like they haven't seen him in years. I hold a glass of sangria whilst standing awkwardly by a statue of a naked woman in a very compromising position. This is easily the wildest party I have ever been to.

Everyone here looks like they could be a fashion influencer. A woman is rocking some yellow leather trousers, whilst a man is in a Spice Girls crop-top with his skinny, hairy midriff on display. I want to say they all look ridiculous, but they don't. The most creative I've been with an outfit was my one-hour emo stage when I was 14. I wore a skull t-shirt, black drainpipes, a studded belt and a fake nose ring. I came downstairs with my new look, and Dad immediately told me to go back upstairs and take it off. That was the end of the emo stage.

'If you could be any dinosaur in the world, which one would you be?' A man appears close to my face. He could be good-looking, but he needs some sleep. 'I think you would make a wonderful *Dilophosaurus*. They're the ones with . . .' He uses his hands to gesture the neck frills.

'Yeah, I know the one,' I say.

He stands back, surprised. 'Do you?' he slurs. 'My old lover didn't know anything about dinosaurs.' He leans in. I lean out. 'She was a real . . . real . . . heart cracker.' He puts his hand on his heart and appears comically sad like a clown, and then whispers, 'We shall kill her.'

I step back, frightened.

'I need to go to the bathroom,' I say and dash out of the living room. It's not a lie. After sinking three sangrias, I need the bathroom quite badly. I've been too nervous to leave my spot, but now it's been invaded by a whisky-stinking-murderer, I have no choice. I pass a small huddle of people in the corridor. A woman with red hair and a matching red kimono is talking loudly at a group of eccentrically-styled women. Her mouth expands across her face with every word.

'I *literally* found my identity at Everest Base Camp. *Seriously*, I came down from that mountain a *very* different lady. You – in the purple hoodie.' I'm wearing a purple hoodie. That's me. The red kimono woman is talking to me. 'Why are you staring at me like that?' She's smiling with her big mouth. Everyone is waiting for me to say something.

'Oh, nothing.'

'You have this look on your face. I'm *intrigued* to know what's in your mind. Please share.' She seems sincere, so I go ahead.

'I've just always wanted to go to Everest Base Camp. Either that or go see the Northern Lights in Iceland. A lot less climbing involved.'

'You could literally do both,' Kimono girl says, and all her friends nod at me.

'Ha! How much do you think teachers earn?' I blurt out. She narrows her eyes. 'I don't think I know any teachers.'

Yes. That's right. I'm not meant to be at this party.

'I need to pee,' I say and run away.

I find a very pink bathroom, lock the door, and pinch a spray of Chanel No. 5 perfume. I'm not sure if it's me wobbling or the room. I listen to the party. The muffled beat of the music and the confident laughter of the guests; one man has a particularly distinctive laugh, like a hiccuping sheep.

Wera's sangria has got me good.

There's a knock on the door. 'In a minute,' I yell, splashing my face with water. When I woke up this morning, I would never have predicted I would be here. Drunk, and locked in a pink bathroom next to The Gherkin.

I should probably call my soon-to-be-husband and tell him where I am. You would think he'd be slightly concerned, considering I left the house nine hours ago for my wedding dress fitting, but there are no missed calls or messages. I ring him. It rings and rings and rings . . . voicemail. I call him again. Voicemail.

We have always taken pride in how chilled we are about each other going out. Rebecca doesn't get it, because Tim is constantly ringing and texting her. I would find that annoying. Josh and I were like that at the start, but now we're secure. We're sensible adults, after all. And it's not like I'm a woman who needs saving. But right now, I wish more than anything he would text me in a panic, asking where I am, and then come charging across the city to get me – Disney prince style. I ring again. Voicemail. I scrunch my face, trying not to cry. *Don't cry at a party, Amy*. I ring again.

Voicemail. I'm weeks away from my wedding day, and I'm drunk at a party with a bunch of strangers. And my fiancé has no clue where I am. Maybe it's not about us being secure, maybe the man I'm going to marry just doesn't care. No, Amy, that's the sangria talking. The door knocks again.

'Hurry the fuck up,' someone yells from the other side.

I take a tissue from a mirrored tissue box and wipe my eyes. 'I'm coming,' I say as I unlock it. I didn't think I had been long, so it's surprising to see the queue outside. A man pushes past and slams the door. The queue is booing me.

'Sissy it was *you* hogging the bathroom.' Woodstock comes out of nowhere. 'Guys, it's my baby sister.' The booing turns into cheering. Despite his out-there leather outfit, I've never been so happy to see him. In fact, in the whole time he's been my step-brother, I've never been so delighted to see him.

'Why are you here?' I ask.

'No, why are *you* here?'

He has a point. These are probably his friends.

*

We're dancing to 'Toxic' in the middle of the living room. We've had a shot of vodka and now back on the sangria. Woodstock is the coolest person ever. I can't believe I've never given him a chance. He's going to take me shopping soon, because my H&M wardrobe makes him depressed, apparently.

'Slut drop,' he shouts. We drop down and come back up. 'Where's Josh?' he asks again. I do a little twirl. I feel like I'm dancing *really* well.

'I told you, he's at home, getting an early night for his gym session tomorrow.'

'Ew. Why is he so boring?'

'Hey!' I hit his arm. 'He's not boring. He's disciplined,' I say. Even though I do agree, the gym routine is boring as hell.

'You're both a yawn. You're living like you're 49.'

'I'm not a yawn!'

He mimics my voice. 'We have to save money for the countryside.'

I laugh, even though I'm marginally offended. 'It's called growing up, Woody!'

'You should explore the world, be naughty for once. You shouldn't be saving pennies and counting press-ups. Shit. Aren't you scared life is just fluttering away?'

I pause. 'Um, geez. I've never thought about it.'

'Well think about it! Slut drop!' We're down and up again. The music changes to a Miley Cyrus song. He stops dancing.

'Come on,' I shout, swinging his arms from side to side. He backs away.

'I need to find my lover now, Sissy. You keep dancing. I'll be back.' He kisses me on both cheeks. 'Be free, my H&M bird.'

'Woody, you can't leave. Woody!' He's gone. Whatever. I can dance alone. I see a group of women twerking, so I try to twerk but instantly realise that I can't, so instead wander off to look for Lace. I find the kitchen and plonk myself on a spinning stool at the marble island. There is a pile of self-help books and a bunch of candles in front of me. I open one of the books titled, *How to Glow for the Rest of Your Life*. The page has a photo of a green smoothie with a recipe next to it.

'What a load of shit,' I say and push it away. I'll never be one of life's glowers, no matter how many green smoothies I consume. You're either born to glow, or you are dim so others can glow. Lace, she glows. *Where is Lace?*

'Sissy, there you are.' Woody is in the kitchen. He grabs my face with his hands and looks me in the eye. 'Good God, Dr Daddy would be mad if he saw you now.' He goes to the fridge and takes out a bunch of food and starts making something on the chopping board. The next thing I know, he's placing a giant baguette in front of me and demanding that I eat it. I pick it up and inspect it.

'You haven't put something in here, have you? You know, like when you're hiding medicine from a dog,' I ask.

'I'm not trying to date rape you, Sissy, if that's what you're implying.' He sits down next to me with a bright red drink. I take a big bite. It's the best thing I have ever tasted.

'I didn't know you could cook,' I say with a mouthful.

'It's a baguette. Any idiot can stuff something inside something.' It makes me laugh so hard that I have to find a gap to be able to breathe. Woody is so funny.

'Did you find your lover?' I ask.

He lets out a sigh and leans his head on his palm. 'Yes, Moon, he's sleeping. He's adorable.'

'And Lace? Where is she?'

'Doing her thing, I suppose.'

'What if someone has done something to her?'

'Do you know who is at this party?' he asks. I shake my head. 'Right. Let's see. The founder of Shop-Ship, Lady Stanley, some Liverpool football player. Sorry to break it to you, but the most suspicious person in this place is you.'

'Me?' I say, and a bit of bread flies out of my mouth. Woody grimaces.

'Yes, you, spitty.'

'A man asked if I could kill his ex-girlfriend with him. He's the most aggressive person here.'

'Charles is the biggest joke that has ever left a man's sack. He is harmless. You, on the other hand, ran away from the host of the party.' I scrunch my face. I have no idea what he's talking about.

'I heard someone say something about a mystery girl in a purple hoodie.' He tilts his head and looks me up and down.

'Oh no!' I said, covering my mouth. 'Was that Wera, the Everest Base Camp girl?'

'Can't take you anywhere.' He takes a mouthful of my baguette and leans in. 'Riddle me this. Why did you agree to this bizarre wedding plan?'

I take the baguette back and have another mouthful.

'So Josh's grandad could remember it.'

'Aaah, that's right. *The Notebook* grandad thing.'

'Woody! He has dementia!'

Woody shrugs. 'Look, I will never get married, but fuck me, if I did, it would be on my own terms. I don't care how deep the man's dimples are.'

'Josh does have great dimples . . .'

'He does, but you have great things too. Don't forget that.'

'Aww, Woody. That's so kind.'

'I mean it. Don't let him have it *all* his way.'

'It's not him, it's his mum. She is surprisingly forceful behind that floral, *Great British Bake Off* persona of hers.' I then quickly add, 'Besides, I want to get married.'

Woody raises his hand. 'Sissy, this man should be putting you before his mama. No excuses.'

I pick off a piece of crust and play with it as I think of a response. I can see where Woody is coming from, but he has no idea what it's like to be in a serious, long-term relationship. There are compromises and sacrifices, and, sure, I am doing this for Josh, like he's done stuff for me – like support me through my parents' divorce. I steer the conversation away from us.

'Why don't you want to get married?'

'Sixty years of the same person. Passionless sex. Irritating habits. Chained to somebody's mistakes. Even when you're dead, you have to share your grave. No, thank you.' He rips off another bit of my baguette.

'There's nice stuff too,' I say. 'Like . . . cuddling on the sofa on boring Sundays, travelling to places, sharing secrets. And yeah, you may have to live with their mistakes, but there is someone there for you when you screw up too.' I look down at my wedding ring. 'Frankie doesn't like my ring. Do you like it?'

'God no,' he says. 'It should be six feet under with his grandma.' We're laughing so much that we don't notice Lace until she stands in front of us. She looks, well, she's glowing.

'Lace, you're glowing.' I am still giggling. She doesn't look amused.

'I'm going to leave the party,' she says.

I stand. 'Well, if you're going, I'm going too.'

Woody stands. 'I'm going too, but before we go, a toast to *moi*.' He raises his glass. 'For it was I who found the wonderful Lace amongst the gays in Brighton that day, which means my Sissy will be wearing a spectacular dress, when she's making a spectacular mistake. Cheers.'

I raise the remains of my baguette, laughing. My ribs hurt. This has been a great night.

Carrot

200 Nights

'Why am I here?' Gramps asks.

I don't know why you're here, Gramps. I don't know why Linda is here either, but hey, here we are, without Josh, in my favourite bakery, Clapcake. (Unfortunate name, but they have the fluffiest cakes in Southwest London.)

Josh and I had planned to do our wedding cake tasting together, as a normal couple would, but when I was trying to call him in the bathroom at around 10 last night, Josh was on the phone to his mum. He was concerned that eating sugary cakes would interfere with his wedding diet, so they devised a genius idea – Linda and I would go to the tasting together, and Gramps would come too. Why not? After this phone call with his mum, he saw 10 missed calls from me and tried to call me back. But by then, I was on the dance floor, and my phone was dead.

Last night is a little bit of a blur. I remember slut dropping with Woody and then being put into a taxi by Frankie and Lace. They were waving from the pavement, and I thought they looked like such a cute couple that I drew a love heart around them in the window condensation. The taxi driver told me off for making his window mucky, and this made me cry. Josh was awake in bed when I came stumbling in. I remember asking him a few times if he was mad, and he kept saying no. I wanted him to say yes. *Yes, Amy, you should have told me where you were, I was so worried. Why are you so drunk? You could get yourself into trouble* . . . Josh would never speak like this. If he's mad, he'll sulk.

'I told you, Dad, on the way here, remember? We're choosing the flavours for Josh and Amy's wedding cake. Isn't that exciting?' Linda says. Gramps looks as excited as I feel. I don't blame the guy either. The 88-year-old has been dragged out of his bed on a miserable Sunday morning, put on a train, and now is in London so he can have a mouthful of wedding cake, and he doesn't even know why. It must suck being old.

The Clapcake baker comes from the kitchen with four slices of different flavoured cake: vanilla, carrot, lemon and elderflower and red velvet. She hands us our forks, and Linda goes straight for the lemon and elderflower. She makes an awkward, pleasurable *'mmm'* sound whilst closing her eyes. I can't imagine Linda and Jason's sex life being too wild, but they do have 'Datey Wednesday', and I think I'm getting a preview of it now. 'Dad, you must try this one.'

Gramps tries the cake and then scrunches his face.

'Eurgh! Tastes like washing-up liquid,' he says loud enough for the baker to hear. Linda tries to shush him, but he carries on insulting each cake, yelling out across the bakery that Ellie's cake is far better than this flavourless rubbish.

'I think carrot,' Linda says, taking another bite. She closes her eyes and swallows and then confirms. 'Yes, carrot.'

'Carrot is nice, but I'm going to go for vanilla,' I say.

'The orange one,' Gramps shouts.

'I like the vanilla one,' I repeat. As much as I appreciate their support, their opinions are neither here nor there. It's my wedding and I like the vanilla one.

'Did you? I found it a little bland,' Linda says. She takes another mouthful of the vanilla. 'Boring, isn't it? Dad, what did you think of the vanilla?' Gramps has wandered away and is fingering all the bread on the shelf. 'Dad, did you like the vanilla cake?' Linda raises her voice across the customers.

'What vanilla cake?' he calls back.

'Exactly. Forgettable,' Linda says. I find this very unfair, considering Gramps's condition. I go for another try of the carrot cake. It's *not bad*. I just assumed I'd have vanilla at my wedding. Carrot doesn't seem classic enough. 'Let's get Joshy's opinion. Come here.' Linda takes out her phone and puts him on a video call. I stand close to Linda, and she puts her arm around me, and we wave to Josh down the phone.

'How's the wedding cake tasting going?' Josh asks, as if he's the big boss checking in on his workers. I open my mouth to explain, but Linda beats me to it.

'You see, we've tried all the cakes,' Linda yells, disturbing all the customers as they have their quiet Sunday coffee and cake. 'Amy likes vanilla, but I like the carrot, and so does Gramps.' Josh looks away. I work out he's on our sofa watching football. That's the real reason why he's not here – football is on, this has nothing to do with diets. Look, I've grown up in this country, I'm used to the Beautiful Game dominating my weekends. But for GOD'S SAKE, it's our wedding cake tasting.

'Are you watching football?' I ask.

Josh sits up. 'Erm . . . I'm catching the end of the game.'

'Right.'

'Bloody football,' Linda tuts, and then goes back to cakegate. 'So, what do you think Josh, vanilla or carrot?'

'Amy, what do you think?' he asks.

'Vanilla.'

'Cool, so vanilla it is.'

'Carrot is probably healthier,' Linda sneaks in.

'Erm,' Josh says, as he glances at the match. 'I suppose. And carrot will go with our orange theme, right, Amy?'

'It's rustic!' I say a little too loudly.

'So, carrot?' Linda says.

Josh is distracted again, gripping his head with one hand.

'Carrot, Josh, yeah?' Linda pushes.

'Yeah, carrot,' Josh says quickly.

'Josh?' I say.

'Oh, good, thanks, Joshy.' Linda hangs up the phone, smug as a cat. 'So, Josh thinks carrot.'

I feel I should carry on fighting for vanilla, considering I'm the bride, but I have lost my passion. If Josh doesn't care what our wedding cake should taste like, then why should I? We also need to go before Gramps gets us permanently banned from Clapcake. He has cornered the baker and is mansplaining how to make 'proper' cakes. I wouldn't know what to do without my weekly buttery flapjacks.

'Yeah, carrot, why not?' I say. Linda gives me a big hug.

'I knew you would come round, pet.'

We leave with an order for one three-tier carrot cake with 'semi-naked icing'. I'm showing Linda where Debenhams is, and then I'm off home to die on the sofa. We're walking across Clapham Junction, and Linda is describing the wedding outfit she will wear. A bright yellow dress with a wide yellow hat. Good, so she's coming as the sun.

'Oh, that reminds me, I need some magic tights to suck all this in.' She taps her stomach a couple of times. 'I don't know where Josh gets all his discipline from. He must be so exhausting to live with.'

I can't believe what I'm hearing. It's a miracle. The first time Linda is half insulting her son. She laughs and then says, 'I would hate it if Jason, bless his heart, were the good-looking one out of us two. I mean, I'm not saying you're not pretty, pet, but you know. You know.'

Yes, Linda, I do.

I drop them off at Debenhams, with Gramps as confused as ever. I walk home to burn off my anger and the teaspoons of cake. I don't know why Linda's comment has bothered me so much. She is only saying what I already know.

I am a six. Josh is a nine. You can't drown in the Red Sea. The universe is growing every second. Josh is hotter than me. Fact. Fact. Fact. And this is not me spiralling in self-pity and insecurity, the world also backs me up.

We were in a restaurant in France earlier this year when the waiter came over to collect the plates. I remember how he looked at me, then at Josh, and the surprised expression that followed. 'You've managed to get him? You must be a good cook,' he said. We laughed about it at the time, so funny. So, so funny. It ruined my holiday. And it's not just the French waiter. Our friends at Leeds University thought it. Arabella and every other pupil at Clapham High says it. I see baffled looks as we pass people on the streets. Now, his mum is joining in too.

Josh, though, always seemed oblivious to the gap between us. That is, until he started listening to Joe Rogan and his gym obsession began. The last time we had *decent* sex was the morning of his twenty-ninth birthday, nearly a year ago. After that, Josh began to go to the gym religiously in the morning, so the only time we had was when we could be bothered in the evenings, which wasn't very often. Meanwhile, he was becoming more ripped, and I was staying my dumpy self. I tried to seduce him on Valentine's Day, but he told me he was too tired from the gym. That hurt. How undesirable could I be that he doesn't want me on the day of love? We did it once or twice in the spring, and then he stopped being able to get hard, and it's because he's no longer oblivious to the fact that I'm a six and he's a nine.

After my long walk back from Debenhams, I find Josh watching a documentary about wall climbing. I flop on my side of the sofa and curl up.

'Lab Rat not good?' he asks.

'Lab Rat down.' I curl up tighter and feel every roll in my stomach squish up. On the telly, a man is almost running up a vertical rock without a pea of fat on him. I sigh, feeling sad for my plump, hungover self.

'What's wrong?' Josh asks and rubs my hair.

'Nothing. Just feel rough.'

I am not going to tell him what his mum said. It won't help. He'd either tell me that she didn't mean it or, worse, suggest that I go to the gym with him, confirming that he now agrees with his mum, the waiter in France and the rest of the world.

Head
202 Nights

Today is the day we find out who will be promoted as the head of the department. I put on my lucky purple pants for the occasion.

By the time Josh and I get to the staffroom, Nina is already there – marking papers and surrounded by half-empty coffee mugs. Everyone knows not to disturb her when she's in marking mode. She will either ignore you or bite your head off.

'Right, announcement time,' Dr Therone says as she struts into the staffroom. Josh and I sit in our usual place next to Nina, who puts down her pen and wishes us luck. 'I will be announcing the promotion for the humanities first. This person will lead the history and geography subjects full-time from September onwards and begin the training immediately. This role goes to someone dedicated, passionate and enthusiastic. After a very successful interview, I believe it was a no-brainer. The Head of Humanities goes to Josh Butters.' Dr Therone begins clapping, and a slow, painful round of applause follows, either because it's an early Tuesday morning or because everyone is as stunned as I am. Josh does a fist pump in the air. It's so clumsy of him that I have to squeeze my eyes shut.

'I did it!' he says in my ear. I turn and see his wide eyes and little dimples. He's so happy that I can't help but smile.

'Congratulations,' I say. Behind him, I catch Nina's eye. She looks away, crossing her arms. She's furious and she has every right to be. There is no way Josh deserves the promotion over her. Dr Therone silences the room with a one-arm sweep. 'And the Head of Science will be Mr Rawlinson,' she says. The air in the room goes, and the steady clapping begins again. This must be a mistake. I feel something on my arm – Josh giving me a sympathy rub. I shake him off. No. No. No. This must be a joke.

'You didn't even give me a proper interview,' I yell over the applause. The room goes silent, and my words are somehow echoing. Dr Therone comes over and towers over me.

'I don't believe we finished our conversation the other day, Miss Elman. How's my science contest ticking along?'

'F-fine. But for the interview, you only gave me a few minutes, and . . .' I stop. She leans so close that her head is now an inch away from mine.

'*Fine*, did you say?' She cups her hand around one ear.

Fine is an exaggeration – considering all we have is Beatrice's research folder on plastic in the ocean and a very rough script that I spent yesterday evening writing. I have emailed it to the girls with a personalised note about each of their responsibilities. I am yet to have a reply, but I'm hoping that's because they are so engrossed in the project that they have forgotten to. Stranger things have happened. Still, script or no script, I am certainly more qualified than Mr Rawlinson, who is currently in the corner of the staffroom ASLEEP. AGAIN!

'No offence to Mr Rawlinson. He's an established staff member at this school, but perhaps I may be more *capable* of such responsibility.' Josh squeezes my leg to stop me, but I carry on. 'I mean, he's not even awake right now . . .' The whole staffroom glances over to the sleeping Mr Rawlinson, slouched in his chair, and his mouth partly open. Dr Therone gives him a glance before setting her eyes back on me.

'What is the topic of my science contest?'

'Erm, plastic in the ocean. Look, I think if we have another interview, I can—'

She cuts me off. 'Plastic in the ocean.' She performs a comical yawn. 'How original. Well, we can say goodbye to *that* prize money.' She chuckles and shakes her head.

'It's a relevant topic . . .' I drift off as she walks away from me and towards Miss Green, who shrinks in her chair.

'Now, Miss Green, tell me how your *Midsummer Night's Dream* is getting on?'

I tune out as Miss Green bumbles through the costume issues she is having. I feel my arm being touched again – another sympathy rub from Josh. It takes every part of me not to snap at him. Without *me*, he would've never become a teacher in the first place. It was *me* who got him onto the teacher training course. It was *me* who got him an interview at Clapham Girls. It's *me* who marks his books when he's about to miss a deadline. And it was *me* who thought of doing that damn volcano display that got him that book voucher. And now he gets a promotion, and I don't. He must see how unfair that is.

As soon as the meeting ends, I get up before Josh can say anything sympathetic that will make me explode. Dr Therone sees me coming after her.

'Busy,' she shouts, then marches out of the room. A few of the staff members like Mrs Redson and Miss Bibbly, are congratulating Josh. On the other side of the room is Nina, stacking up her books, slamming each one on the other. I go over without knowing what to say. Should I apologise on Josh's behalf?

Before I even open my mouth, she's already speaking. 'I'm not going to the pub quiz tonight, I'm afraid,' she says and leaves the staffroom with her books towering up to her chin.

Fishy

I don't go to lunch. I'm not sulking per se, but I want to keep away from Josh in case he says something clumsy that will make me explode in the lunch hall in front of all the staff and pupils. So, I stay in my lab with a bag of Maltesers and start to search for a new job.

It turns out physics teachers are in demand. There's a job going at an all-boys school in Ealing that has particularly caught my eye. The science department has an excellent reputation, and Ealing would be far easier to get to once we move to the country. Sure, teenage boys come with their own set of problems, but I can't take any more of Dr Therone's blatant favouritism. I begin the application. This is exciting. A new chapter. My own world. And this could be a positive thing for Josh and me. It will be like the old days, before lockdown, when we were working in separate schools. I will have my stories about my job, and he will have his. Heck, even our sex may go back to how it used to be. I am typing the answer to the first question when my lab door opens. It's Josh.

'Why is nobody at lunch?' he says, in a jokey way. He spots the Maltesers packet on my desk and shakes his head. 'Oh, Amy. You're not eating chocolate for lunch, are you?'

I swallow a Malteser.

'I have a lot of work to do,' I say, with one eye on the job application. Josh wanders to the tank with his hands in his pockets and observes the fish as they dart about.

'I reckon we should go for the full 30 tonight,' he says.

'I don't think that will be possible,' I say.

'Why not?'

'Nina isn't coming.'

'What?' His cluelessness is extraordinary. I envy it, really. Can you imagine walking through life thinking everything is fine? To get the job you hardly wanted, to have your wedding planned for you by your fiancée, to have that same fiancée quietly sort herself out to a science podcast. How easy it would be to be a man like Josh.

'Well, she's disappointed about the promotion,' I say. I see it hit him – the realisation that Nina may be upset that he got the role over her. He rubs his eyes and groans.

'That's why she wasn't at lunch,' he says.

'Yeah, so maybe limit the fist-pumping.'

He exhales at the tank, then says, 'Fish have it so easy, don't you think? Just floating around without upsetting anyone.'

'They upset Jenny Wilson. She cries every lesson. Terrified of them. Ichthyophobia.'

'Ich . . . what?'

'Fear of fish.'

'Oh, that's why she screamed at that picture of a salmon in the ocean textbook.' We share a smile for a moment. Then he says, 'I don't understand why Dr Therone didn't promote you.' I want to say something about Dr Therone being a female misogynist, which is why she would rather promote men, even though they are less capable, but I bite my tongue.

'She hates me like Jenny hates fish, that's why.'

He shakes his head. 'Mr Rawlinson will mess it up in the first term; either that, or he'll accidentally burn the school down, and then nobody will be head of the department.'

I smile. 'Yeah, true.' He heads towards the door.

'Shall I swing by at five and then we can head to The Cock and Bull?' he says with his hand on the door handle. The application for Ealing Boys is glaring at me.

'I'll meet you there. I have some marking to do,' I say.

'Okay. Let's smash them tonight, Lab Rat,' he says and leaves. I pop another Malteser in and go back to the application. *'I would like to apply for the role of physics teacher at Ealing Boys because ...'*

I stop typing and think of Josh. If I get this job, Josh will no longer be able to pop into my lab like he just did, brightening my bad day. We couldn't pull faces across the assembly hall when Mrs Lector does one of her painfully slow announcements, or I will no longer see a spare seat at the lunch table and know Josh was saving it just for me. Who would I sit next to at lunch in Ealing?

'I would like to apply for the role of physics teacher at Ealing Boys because I'm pissed off and think my boss is a misogynist ...'

I close my laptop, grip my head and let out a groan over the school bell. The door opens, and Year 8 shuffles in. I flatten my hair and try to remember what I'm meant to teach them today. Ah yes. I go to the cupboard and take out 14 foam apples.

'Right, Year 8, gravity.'

Fur Coat

I'm not at the pub quiz. I'm in a car with Lace. I had every intention of going, but Lace was waiting for me by my bike in the school's bike shed. At first, all I could see was a figure in the dark.

'Hi, doll,' was the next thing I heard. She stepped out into the security light, dressed in a black fur coat and high heels, her hair in a tight bun like a ballerina.

'Lace, what are you doing here? At my school?' I laughed nervously.

'I'm surprising you,' she says in a matter-of-fact tone.

'Surprising me? What? How did you know where I worked?'

'I'll explain in the car.'

'In the car?'

'We can't be late.' We walked towards the school gate.

'What do you mean in the car?' I persisted. 'I can't go with you. I have a pub quiz.' I stopped talking when I saw the black Mercedes and the driver in a suit standing outside of it. 'What the hell is going on?' By this point, I felt a little scared. How much did I really know Lace, after all?

'Like I said, Amy, it's a surprise,' she says, before pulling me closer to the car.

'I have a pub quiz to get to,' I protested. 'I go every week, I'm part of this team with Josh, Nina and Pete. We're called Petey and the Brains. We were on a winning streak, but last week we were disqualified, and this week Nina can't go. So, I really need to be there or else there will be no chance of the team redeeming the crown . . .' We were standing in front of the black car.

'What a depressing little story,' Lace said, as the driver opened the back-seat door for us. 'You won't want to miss this for anything, especially for a pub quiz.' She ducked down into the car and waved her hand from inside. 'Get in, Amy.'

'This feels like a kidnapping,' I joked.

'It's not a kidnapping, it's a rescue,' she says. 'Get in.' I looked around to see if anyone was there to witness my last known sighting, but everyone had gone home. Oh well, I thought, and got into the car.

*

We are driving out of Clapham and have just passed The Cock and Bull. The quiz starts in five minutes. There is classical music blaring out from the car's radio. I ask the driver to turn it down because I can't think of how to word my text to Josh with all those violins making a racket. The driver mutes it, but Lace carries on humming the tune. I recognise the song but don't know who it's by. Mozart is always my guess, but I'm no good at naming the living artists, let alone the dead ones. When was Mozart even alive?

Sorry!! Not going to be at the pub quiz. Lace is surprising me. Sorry! Good luck!

'Please, can you tell me where we're going?' I ask as soon as the message is sent.

Lace carries on humming the tune and then says, 'Isn't life more exciting when you don't know where you are going?'

'No, not at all. I like to know exactly where I am going.'

We drive over Blackfriars Bridge and my phone buzzes. It's Josh.

???????

It's a fair response. I would be livid if he had done this to me.

Sorry. Will explain later. Xxx.

The car heads down The Strand, making a right towards Covent Garden and stops outside the Royal Opera House.

'Ready for some *Tosca*?' Lace says, unbuckling her belt.

'Toss . . . *what*?' I ask.

She ignores my question and gets out of the car, so I get out of the car. There is a swarm of people dressed up and heading inside. Lace's fur coat suddenly makes sense.

'I can't go in there,' I shriek. The driver gets a red-covered garment from the boot and hands it to Lace. 'What's that? Lace, if you think I'm going in there . . .' I call out to her as she walks towards the doors.

'Come on, doll,' she says.

'But I'm rubbish at musicals.'

'It's not a musical. It's op-er-a.' She spaces out the word as if I'm stupid.

'I didn't even like *Les Misérables*. And, and . . . look how I'm dressed' I pull on my black wool knee-length dress that has bobbled over the years. She shakes the covered garment.

'What do you think this is?'

'I don't want to know.'

'Amy Elman!' It's the first time I've heard her raise her voice, and it makes me jump. 'Trust me. You need this right now,' she says.

I search around as if there will be something, anything to save me, but even the car has driven off.

*

'How does it look?' Lace says from the other side of the cubicle door.

I look down at the long, figure-hugging red dress. *Red*. The last time I wore red was when I dressed as Red Riding Hood for my sixth birthday party. As glamorous as the dress is, there is no way I can pull off something so bold, so sensual, so not me.

'Come on, doll, I want some champagne,' Lace says. I look up at the ceiling panel above, wondering how possible it would be to escape. 'Amy?' she knocks again. I unlock the door and take half a step out. I'm wearing heels that feel like stilts. A step wrong, and I will be face-planting the toilet floor of the Royal Opéra House. Lace makes a dramatic orgasmic sound.

'Isn't she marvellous?' she says, tightening one of the spaghetti straps. 'I found her in the King's Road Oxfam. Only needed a few pinches. Come.'

I grip her hand, and she walks me to the mirror. I see myself. Red from head to toe, cleavage on display, my curves being shown off. There is no way I can hide in it. The dress is screaming for attention. I can't decide whether I look incredible in it or like a dog in a tutu. I hold my elbow across my body like a safety belt. Lace pulls my arms apart.

'Please can you just *pretend* to like yourself?' she says.

'I do like myself,' I say faintly at my reflection.

'One day, you'll believe it, but it's a start,' she says. 'Now, let's get some fizz.'

I'm feeling a little better about my surprise because of the champagne. The bar in the Opera House is a giant classy conservatory. With the men in their tuxes and women in their dresses, it's as if we're at a James Bond-themed party. Lace has taken her fur coat off and is in a black silk dress that sits like oil on her skin. Her tight hair is making her wide eyes even wider and her plump lips, plumper. A man at the bar is blatantly staring at us, and he's not the only one. They're all looking at Lace, no doubt, probably thinking that we're an odd pair. Pete talks about this a lot. He says hot girls always have an ugly friend with them to make them look even better. The ugly girl is called 'a tug'. They come into the bar first, 'tugging' along the hot one. I'm the tug.

A bell goes, and everyone starts putting their glasses down and vacating the conservatory. Lace tells me to leave my champagne because nobody is allowed to drink in the theatre, which sabotages the only thing about seeing this opera that I was looking forward to. The wine in my plastic cup was what got me through *Les Misérables*, so goodness knows how I'm going to survive a two-and-a-half-hour opera without alcohol. We go up the red-carpeted stairway. I'm aware I'm being dead slow, but these heels are a death trap waiting to happen. Once I (finally) get to the top, we go away from the crowds and down a corridor to the last door on the right. It's an actual opera box. I thought only royalty could sit in these.

'How much did this cost?' I ask.

'Ask Frankie the next time you see him,' Lace says as she sits down and peers over the edge.

'Frankie? Why would Frankie pay for me to be in a box?'

'He didn't. He paid for me,' Lace says, and then gets me to sit down next to her. Below us is a sea of grey hair sitting in red velvet chairs. Random instruments are playing odd notes above the chatter of the audience. I can just about see the drummer in the corner of the orchestra, standing above a big bass drum. She's beating it rapidly with sticks that look like campfire marshmallows.

'What does *Tosca* even mean?' I ask, but as soon as I do, the lights dim, the audience applauds and the velvet curtain rises. Lace takes my hand, and we sit with our fingers intertwined.

Stars

'I'm not saying I didn't feel anything,' I say. Lace shakes her head at me. Her eyes are pink, raw and wet. She gets up as fresh tears come out of her eyes, and she storms out of the box. I don't know what I've done wrong.

'I don't understand how you're not crying?' Lace says. We're back in the car, and she has finally started talking to me again. 'You do realise they're both dead, right? They were in love, and now they're dead.'

I shrug. 'It's not real, though.'

'The love is real. That passion between Tosca and Cavaradossi is real. That's why these stories are timeless — because people can relate to them. If it was me and . . .' She stops and looks out the window.

'You . . . and Frankie?'

'If it was you and Josh . . .' she says, ignoring the Frankie comment. 'If Josh was shot in the head by a firing squad . . .'

'I would be devastated,' I say. 'But that's not going to happen. Josh and I are teachers living in Southwest London who enjoy pub quizzes and Netflix. Yes, passion exists, but not as it does on stage or in film. That's why I can never get into the arts. It's too dramatic. Life isn't an opera.'

Lace unclips her seat belt and slides close to me.

'Amy, passion is real. Even that kind of passion you see in the opera. You just haven't . . .' She doesn't want to finish the sentence, and I don't want her to either. She leans so close to me that I feel the air grow static around us. I see the smudges around her eyes where her tears have made her mascara run. She takes my hand again, and then her head falls on my shoulder.

'Lace, the dress, the car, the opera . . . the lessons on passion. Why are you doing all of this?' I ask.

'*Pretty Woman* is my favourite film. I wanted to live it.'

'I did wonder.'

'No, Julia.' She yawns. 'Frankie gave me tickets, and I wanted to take you because you need to get out of the box you have made for yourself.'

'What box?' I ask. Lace doesn't reply. 'What box?' I ask again. I think she's asleep or pretending to be.

I look at the city as it passes the window. Tower Bridge is all lit up and The Shard is white and poking the sky. Josh loves crossing the bridges at night and seeing the city glow. I don't get it myself – it's just concrete blocks which are blocking the stars.

Once we get to Stockwell, I direct the driver to my door. Lace half wakes up as I detangle myself from her and say goodnight. She then settles back into her sleep again.

All the lights are off at home, so I quietly go to the bedroom. I find Josh in bed with his mouth open a smidge, making a whistle noise every time he exhales. He's not holding Skogsfräken tonight. He's on his back with his arms spread, taking full advantage of the space. I watch him. The top of his bare sculpted chest is coming out of the duvet, and I can just about see it rise and fall in the dark. The details of his face are lost, meaning it could be any strange man lying in my bed right now – an unknown stranger who could do anything to me. Why wouldn't someone want to have sex with me right now? I'm a 29-year-old woman in a sensual red dress, no man would turn me down. A tingle goes down my body. I stretch my arms behind, tug down the zip of my dress and let the red material fall onto the floor. I walk slowly to my side of the bed, carefully get in and mirror Josh's position by lying on my back. I close my eyes, put my fingers between my legs and imagine Josh is a faceless man who will throw me down on the bed and kiss my neck, my nipples, my belly until I feel his breath between my thighs, and . . .

'Amy . . .?' Josh suddenly croaks.

I yank my hand away, my heart thumping.

'Josh?' Has he been awake this whole time? 'Did you win the quiz?' I squeak.

'No. We needed you,' he says in a haze.

'Who won?' I ask.

His breathing fades back into a whistling snore. I get my breath back. How did it get this pathetic? Me, secretly masturbating *next to* Josh? Nina told me that the Ancient Greeks used to leave sex toys for their wives when they went to war to stop their wives from getting hysterical without sperm. I remember laughing at the time, but now I think I may have gone mad in my sperm-less state. I take my phone from the bedside table. I would usually listen to the *Science Vs* podcast when I can't sleep, but a song from *Tosca* won't stop playing in my head. It's the one that Cavaradossi sings while he's waiting to be executed, believing he will never see the love of his life again. It's sung in Italian, but I read the subtitles above the stage. The first line he sung about how the stars were shining, and the earth was smelling. I find the song and turn it up. From nowhere, a tear.

Foetal Position

203 Nights

Crying to opera at 1 a.m. now makes sense because I've started my period. I can't remember the last time I had a real one; I get PMS and a bit of spotting, but not the whole show. I have been meaning to go to the doctor for a new batch of pills, but Christmas and then the wedding distracted me. And besides, when the probability of getting pregnant is zilch, it feels rather pointless to make the effort. So now I'm twisting and turning in bed, as my stomach and back play tug of war with my womb. To make matters worse, I have no tampons in the house, so I have stuffed my pants with basic range tissue. The Apple Radar sound goes off, and Josh wakes up to find me in the foetal position.

'Period,' I groan, and twist the other way in the hope that it will relieve the pain. It doesn't. He looks baffled as he puts on his boxers.

'They still happen?' he asks.

'Yes, Josh, they still happen,' I snap. I am not going to explain the whole Pill scenario because that will invite the elephant into the room. The day ahead seems like a torturous to-do list: I have 30 tests on magnets to mark; I need to see if Nina is still angry about the promotion situation; and then I need to force Year 10 to do work on plastic in the ocean, knowing that my boss hates the idea, so it's all a big waste of time. I whimper and Josh comes round to my side of the bed and rubs my head.

'Can I do anything, Lab Rat?'

'I need tampons,' I whine. Josh looks uncomfortable.

'Ah . . . oh . . . um . . . well . . .' he stutters.

I sigh.

'I can get them.'

'Sorry, it's just that Tony is waiting for me. We've planned to do a circuit and—'

'I can get them,' I repeat in the same monotone voice. 'I'll meet you at school.'

Josh hovers over me as his brain battles with what he should do (help his bleeding, pained fiancée) and what he wants to do (bicep curls).

'Are you sure?' he says, as if he cares.

'Yes.'

He kisses me on the head, rubs my hair and leaves. Fuck men.

I stagger out of bed and get ready for work whilst in a right-angle position. The thought of buckling up work trousers around my melon tummy right now is making me feel ill, so I pull on my very loose wool dress and put on my ugliest, but most comfortable, flat black pumps. I then wobble to Tesco.

If I were prime minister, I would make it the law to have a period section by the till that would include tampons, chocolate and paracetamol. It would mean that in situations like these, I can just grab it all and go. But no, everything is spread out across the store, so here I am, hobbling from aisle to aisle, collecting all the things I need to survive this womb war, all while hoping that I am not leaking through my DIY pad. I get to the menstrual section and find on the packaging of the tampons, logos of turtles with skulls on them, reminding us that we are using single-use plastic. It's like they think we want to buy this stuff. I pick up two boxes of super and regular tampons from my trusty brand, despite the threat to turtles. I like to think I do my part; I don't drink through plastic straws, I recycle and I avoid buying fruit in wrapping, but when you're bent over in cramps and your fiancé can't even spare the gym for one morning to help you, then the last thing on your mind are the turtles. I never thought I'd say this but, Year 10, as horrible as they, may be on to something.

What's the point of sticking to the rules? Good behaviour doesn't get you the promotion. It doesn't get you laid. It doesn't even get you the cake flavour you want at YOUR OWN WEDDING.

I begin to fill my basket with menstrual products. Sorry turtles, but womanhood is a bitch.

The Box

The door opens, and Year 10 loiter in the lab, clearly still pissed off that I have taken their Wednesday lunch breaks away for science. My pulse is pumping through the roof. I smile at them as they shuffle past me and onto their stools. They scowl at the cardboard box on my desk that reads, **TOP SECRET: SCIENCE CONTEST**. Apart from agreeing to get married in seven weeks, this is by far the craziest thing I've ever done. The last to arrive is Arabella. She comes in holding a flask as big as her head. She looks at the box, then at me, and I smile back at her.

'Stop smiling like that,' she says, clearly unnerved.

I keep smiling, enjoying her discomfort.

She sits down. 'Cheugy has lost it.' I hear her mumble, which sets off a ripple of giggles amongst the class.

'What's in the box, Miss Elman?' Beatrice asks sweetly as always.

'That is a very good question, Beatrice,' I say. I take out my desk scissors, and there is a big gasp. I suppose the smile and scissors combo is a little creepy. I slice open the cardboard box, take hold of the first thing my fingertips find and lob it across the lab. A pink object flies over the girls' heads and hits the papier-mâché Mars at the back of the lab.

'What *is* that?' Arabella yells. Ophelia runs over and waves it in the air.

'It's a menstrual cup,' she says, and the class look at me like I need to be locked up in a padded room. Maybe I do.

HAHAHA. I take a handful of tampons, and they fly like cotton bullets across their heads. Ping. Ping. Ping.

'What the hell, Miss Elman?' Arabella says as she ducks away from one of them. The sight of this makes me laugh, and the class start to laugh too. I throw out pads like frisbees (they don't fly so well), then more tampons and menstrual cups.

'Oh my God, stop!' Ashwini yells.

More tampons.

'Are you okay?' Beatrice cries as she covers her head.

More pads.

'Miss Elman, stop!' Arabella says. I can't stop, though. Every time I lob a period product, it feels like I'm throwing a punch at life. Dr Therone. Ping. Promotion. Ping. Linda. Ping. Joe Rogan. Ping. Carrot cake. Ping.

Soon, my Year 10 class are surrounded by menstruation products – my lab is covered. They're laughing, and I'm laughing with them.

'You're right, Ophelia. We need to do something more relevant and personal to us girls.' The girls turn to each other. They can guess where this is going, but can't quite believe it. I lift out a menstrual cup, inspect it and throw it. 'I mean, plastic in the ocean is a problem, and I feel sorry for the poor turtles, but we women have issues too.' I lob another tampon. 'And birth control is an issue.' I lob my empty packet of contraceptive pills across the lab and then some condoms. Arabella picks one up and puts it in her skirt pocket.

'Miss Elman? Are you saying we can do . . .' Before Ophelia can finish her sentence, I whack the keyboard and huge capitals fill the screen.

WHAT'S WRONG WITH THE WORLD?
THE PILL AND HOW IT AFFECTS US.

The class begins to cheer, and I do a little bow. Is this what losing your mind looks like?

★

I keep my smile for the rest of the afternoon. The class have volunteered to do extra work to catch up on the time we've lost and even agreed to an additional session on Mondays so they can practise their presentation. I know it's immature, and the ultimate goal for a teacher is not about being liked, but to have the class laughing with me instead of at me feels pretty damn good.

I go to the staffroom for the last hour of the day to do my marking. Nina is at her table, surrounded by mugs and typing away on her laptop. We always share this hour on Wednesday together, and I usually look forward to it, but today I'm not sure what to expect. I tap her shoulder gently. She glances at me and then takes off her headphones.

'I've done the craziest thing today,' I say.

She doesn't lift her eyes from the screen. 'Go on.'

I slide a chair next to her and can sense this is the wrong move from how her body stiffens up, but I carry on anyway. I tell her about my science contest rebellion, the way I threw tampons at my class, and how they cheered me. I hoped this would impress her, but she just carried on typing. I take a deep breath.

'Nina, I'm sorry about Josh getting the promotion. We all know you deserved it, and that's coming from me.'

She slams her laptop down. For a second, I am worried that she's going to storm off.

'Amy . . .' She takes off her thick-framed glasses and rubs her eyes. 'There are thousands of women being sex trafficked right now.'

'I know. It's horrific,' I reply, wondering what to do with that fact.

'I'm just saying, I can't be angry about this stupid promotion.' She looks down at her lap. This is classic Nina mentality.

'Yes, you can. It's devastating and disgusting what's happening to women in the world, but . . . you are allowed to be angry at your situation too. We all know it's bullshit. The pupils love you. You are the hardest worker, the most qualified . . .' She rubs her eyes again and seems frustrated at me. 'Sorry, I didn't mean to patronise you.'

'No, I'm sorry.' She sighs. 'I shouldn't say anything, but I find the whole Dr Therone and Josh relationship . . .' She contemplates her words. 'Hard. Sorry. I know he's your fiancé.'

'You find it hard? Nina, they have such a good relationship that Josh has invited her to my wedding.' Nina's face drops. 'Exactly.'

'I may have to pull out of being your bridesmaid,' she says.

'*I* may have to pull out,' I say, and this makes her smile for a second. 'Look.' I lower my voice even though we're the only ones in the staffroom. 'Between you and me, Josh didn't deserve that promotion, nor did Mr Rawlinson. Dr Therone is a misogynistic beast, and that's the only reason why this has happened.'

'Good. I'm glad you see it too,' Nina says.

I tell her that I'm thinking of applying for another job. She doesn't look surprised.

'It's a shame, but I understand. I don't know how you don't go crazy, working under the same roof.'

'It's not all that bad,' I say, brushing it off, conscious not to go down the road of bad-mouthing my fiancé, but Nina doesn't look convinced. 'What about you? You can't stay, surely?' I ask. She looks at me like I've just suggested something ridiculous.

'I'll never leave. I love the girls, the school and my classroom. It's my home.' She then looks me dead in the eyes. 'If anyone is going to go, it's going to be her.'

'What do you mean?'

She gives me a smirk and reopens her laptop and begins typing. This is my cue to leave. I go to my favourite spot – it's a desk with a view of the hockey field. I like to watch the PE lesson, especially when it's raining, like now, because it makes my subject more appealing. I open the first book, and Nina calls out.

'By the way, your science contest rebellion is the greatest thing I've ever heard you do. I'm so proud.'

Josh and Amy's Wedding 2025

To Do:

Ask Mum if Uncle Clarke and Aunt Margaret are still alive.
Add Dr Therone to the seating plan.
Request 11 vegan, 16 vegetarian and 5 gluten-free meals.
Go to Lace's final fitting of the wedding dress.
Rebecca's bridesmaid dress party.
Buy flowers from Petunia.
Tell Josh the band needs to be booked by next week, or else you will do it.
Talk to Mum about being civil to Dad and Jean-Ivy.
Try on <u>sexy</u> lingerie.
Buy Josh ski goggles for his birthday.
Bleach hair.

Birthday Boy

205 Nights

Today, Josh turns 30. I was going to throw him a party, but as our wedding is just over a month away, we decided to keep it low-key. There were thoughts about branching out of Southwest London to Camden or Soho, but in the end, we couldn't be bothered, so we are in the usual Cock and Bull. Josh's oldest friend Ben is lingering next to Josh and has yet to take off his coat. I used to take it personally how little he speaks to me, but Josh has reassured me that Ben is just terrified of women.

Pete is also here, loud and theatrical as always. He has cut his hair into a Paul Mescal mullet, which strangely suits him. He's telling us (and the rest of the pub) about how he tricked his client into taking a job in Liverpool. The story is far-fetched, but at least we're all entertained. Well, I say *all* – the woman Pete has brought along tonight seems very disappointed. She looks far too sophisticated for The Cock and Bull, with her cream trouser suit and electric pink manicure. She introduced herself with her first and last name, Cara Helm. She is older than all of us – around mid-thirties, but way out of Pete's league. I have no idea how on earth he manages to pull these women.

Pete raises his voice. 'And do you know what I did? I sent him the YouTube video of "Yellow Submarine" in his congratulations email.' He erupts into his big, horsey laugh. Ben smiles a little, and Cara Helm rolls her eyes.

'No, you didn't,' Josh says, laughing too. I take hold of the top of Josh's arm and squeeze it. Today was meant to be my slot to kick-start the sex again. Unfortunately, my period is restricting me. So, the plan is to do a noble birthday blow job when we get home tonight. I'm braving the Thrills & Frills lingerie for the comeback. It's mighty tight and scratchy. In hindsight, I should have put it on after work, rather than endure the discomfort for the whole damn day. It will all be worth it though if it saves our sex life.

Feeling the squeeze on his arm, Josh mouths, 'Everything okay?' I nod, and he goes back to listening to Pete. I let go of his arm.

Ben finishes his pint and mutters that he must go. Josh makes a small protest, but Ben insists he needs an early night. He wishes Josh another Happy Birthday and makes his way out of the pub. And now we're on a double date with Pete and a dissatisfied Cara Helm. Nina was supposed to be here, but she said she was too busy working on Operation: Dethrone. I am convinced that this is just an excuse because she doesn't want to be around Josh, but I'm going to stay out of that.

'Pete.' Cara Helm waves her empty wine glass in Pete's face. I prepare myself for one of his typical, sarcastic comments ('What did your last slave die of?') but he apologises for making her wait and asks if there is anything else she wants. 'Just a Chardonnay,' she demands. Pete takes the glass and goes to the bar.

Fascinating. I look at Josh to see if he is thinking the same as me, but he is distracted by something over my shoulder.

'Hello,' says a familiar childlike voice. I turn around; standing behind me in a black dress and knee-high leather boots, is Lace.

'Lace!' I throw my arms around her like I haven't seen her in years. 'What are you doing here?'

'You invited me,' she says. She reads the confusion on my face and elaborates. 'You were getting into the taxi last weekend when you said, come to Josh's birthday at The Cock and Bull next Friday night. So here I am.' The fuzzy memory replays as she says it. I really should drink less.

'Who's your friend, Amy?' Pete says, coming back with Cara Helm's Chardonnay. Cara Helm, meanwhile, is eyeballing Lace like she's a threat to her safety.

'This is Lace. She's making my wedding dress.'

Pete's face lights up, and Cara Helm pushes forward and introduces herself in the same professional way she had with the rest of us – a handshake, her full name and job title.

'Lace what?' Cara Helm asks.

'Just Lace for now,' Lace says, then turns to Josh.

'You must be the birthday boy.'

'And you must be the one who's been kidnapping Amy.' Suddenly, Pete barges in, kissing Lace on both cheeks like he's a French gentleman.

'Pete Randy. Are you good at pub quizzes?'

'Not particularly,' Lace says with a polite giggle.

'I'm good at pub quizzes,' Cara Helm states, but everyone ignores her.

'Would you like a drink, Lace?' Josh asks.

'A Merlot would be lovely.' Lace touches Josh's arm for a second.

'Merlot, great. Large or small?'

'Large,' I answer for her. 'And can I have another gin, please?'

When he's gone, Lace leans into my ear.

'Josh is very nice-looking,' she whispers. A pang goes off inside of me. Jealousy? Worry?

'Are you surprised?' I ask.

She frowns. 'What did I say about liking yourself?'

'Lace, what's your story?' Pete asks. Cara Helm is still glaring at Lace and is now wrapped around Pete's arm like a python.

'I'm a dressmaker who lives in East London. I like a dry Merlot and listening to saxophone solos. I don't like liquorice or the colour grey in clothes, and I have a birthmark in a place that only a few people have seen.'

Pete's mouth drops. Cara Helm rolls her eyes. Josh comes back with Lace's wine, my gin and his pint of sparkling water.

'I hope that's vodka,' Lace says.

'Josh isn't drinking until the wedding,' I say.

'Gosh, whatever for?' Lace says, touching her heart.

'I want to be in the best shape for it,' Josh says. And then repeats his favourite quote. 'Sacrifice today for . . .'

'A better tomorrow,' Pete finishes off his sentence. 'God, you really are a broken record, mate.'

I don't want to agree with Pete, but Josh's new gym-bro lifestyle has made him a bit dull, which is strange, because he was always better at the social stuff than me.

Josh ignores him.

'Best shape for the wedding *night*?' Lace asks, raising one eyebrow suggestively.

'Lad!' Pete says and clinks his glass on Lace's. Cara Helm tuts.

'Well, the wedding photos will be around forever,' Josh says. Nobody says anything to this.

'Josh goes to the gym every day. He's so disciplined,' I say, helping him out.

'Every day? Wow,' Lace says sincerely.

Josh straightens up. 'You know what they say, discipline is the bridge between goals and accomplishments.'

'They say that, do they?' Lace says. 'And what do you do at the gym?' She's going to regret asking that. I put my fingers in the corner of my eyes, ready for the monologue.

'Here we go,' Pete says.

Josh begins. 'Well, first I stretch, and how I stretch is . . .'

He goes into every detail about his stretching, lifting, HIIT, the high-protein-low-carb diet, and even shows her a video of him doing some bicep curls. I've got to hand it to Lace, she is a brilliant actress; she seems impressed by everything and asks questions I've never even thought of. I suppose she asked me a lot of questions when we first met too.

'What do you press?'

'Eighty.'

'Squat?'

'One-one-five.'

'Deadlift?'

'One-forty.'

At this point, bored, I excuse myself and go to the restroom. I check myself in the mirror and groan. It could be bad lighting that is making me appear haggard, or the mirror is telling the truth. I flip my hair over my head to make it big like Lace's, but it's thin and shapeless, so it just flattens back into one straight block around my face. I wipe the mascara smudges from under my eyes and pinch my cheeks to make them blush. I remain very unsexy.

The door swings open, and Cara Helm enters.

'Who doesn't have a surname?' she shouts. 'That woman is . . .' She goes to the mirror and presses a thick layer of candyfloss-coloured lipstick onto her lips. '*He* asked *me* out! And I'm here in this pub celebrating some gym freak's birthday, no offence, whilst listening to some *slag* pretending to be interested in Pete's dumb recruitment job.' She drops her lipstick in the sink, and it echoes. I don't know Cara Helm, but she has zero chill.

'Ummm . . . can you call a woman a slag in 2025?' I say.

'Well, whatever she is, an alpha female.'

'An alpha female?'

'Yes, alpha female. She is using her femininity to get what she wants. I tell you this now, she doesn't give a shit about other women, she just needs to know that every man in the room wants to fuck her.' She begins flicking up her eyelashes with jet-black mascara. We catch each other's eyes in the mirror, and she says, 'You think I'm crazy, but I see her type in PR all the time. You'll see.' She brushes her hair violently, then stares at herself for one long minute. 'Right, let's get back out there before she fucks them both.'

The first thing I see when coming out of the toilet is Josh holding Lace up in the air. His arms are clenched around her body, and she's squealing at the ceiling. He puts her down, but his arms linger around her waist as they laugh like naughty school kids. The pang goes off again, harder this time. I'm back in the student union watching Josh dancing with Natalie.

'Told you so,' Cara Helm hisses in my ear.

I think of Nina then; she hates when women go against women over men. She says it is the poison that paralyses us from moving forward. I can see what she means. Cara Helm's jealousy is making her horribly judgmental about Lace, and she doesn't even know her. Lace is not an alpha female who wants to gobble up all our boyfriends. She's one of the most thoughtful women that I have ever met. Who would tailor a red dress for another woman to make her feel better about herself? Lace would.

Lace squeals as soon as she sees me. 'Amy, let Josh pick you up.'

I catch Josh's eye. He doesn't want to, that's clear.

'Go on.' Lace takes my hand and pulls me towards Josh. I laugh to brush away the awkwardness.

'Josh won't want to pick me up.'

Lace shakes her head and pulls me closer. 'Come on, Josh, pick up your fiancée.'

'Go on, guys, give us a show,' Pete yells.

Josh and I shuffle towards one another. He puts his arms around my waist. I hear his intake of breath as he squeezes me up in the air. A second later, I'm back on the floor.

'How hot,' Cara Helm says.

★

Pete and Cara Helm stayed for another 30 minutes, but then Pete asked Lace what her secret talent was, and Lace did the splits. Pete predictably made an inappropriate comment, and that was the final straw for Cara Helm. She was on her feet and out the door in a second, and Pete ran off after her.

Now it's just the three of us sitting at the bar with Lace in the middle. Lace and I decided to split a bottle of Merlot, which Josh was reluctant to order.

'You don't like red wine,' he said.

'I do, *babe*, I just don't like that cheap stuff we used to drink at university,' I said. He frowned when I called him babe, and to be fair, it felt strange the moment it left my mouth. Still, Josh got the red wine in, and now I'm feeling it. I told Lace the story of our engagement, and she seemed very confused about why Josh did it in a cable car. Josh told her because he 'thought it would be cool to do it whilst floating up in the air'. This confused Lace further.

'So do you have a partner?' Josh asks Lace.

Lace doesn't hear the question. 'Hey, let's play. What do you find sexy about each other?'

'Lace . . .' I say. I know what she's trying to do, but I wish she wouldn't.

'What? I'm curious to know. Come on, Josh.'

Josh looks at her dumbfounded. 'What, like . . .'

'It's not hard. What do you find sexy about Amy?'

'I . . .' He stares at his pint of sparkling water as if counting the bubbles. 'Well, she's clever. She's a great teacher. She is good at pub quizzes, and . . .'

Lace interrupts. 'That's not sexy stuff. I mean, do you like her fruity lips, her curves . . . her bum . . . her soft skin.'

Josh takes a gulp and fidgets in his chair.

'Yeah, all those things,' he says, then grins at me like a boy at school. 'And she's a Lab Rat.'

'Lab Rat?' Lace says. 'What do you mean she's a Lab Rat?'

'It's a silly nickname he has for me,' I say.

Lace looks disgusted.

'Lab Rat?' she repeats. Josh shrugs again. She leans into my ear and whispers, 'No wonder you're not having sex.'

I burst out laughing.

'What did she say?' Josh asks, sensing he is the butt of the joke.

'She said nothing. It was nothing,' I say. I still can't help smiling. He frowns.

'Why are you laughing at me?'

'I'm not. Sorry.' I drop the smile. I could feel I was in hot water with Josh, which is a very rare place to be.

'What did she say?' he asks again. I wish he would drop it. I want to show Lace what a great couple we are, so she can understand why we're getting married.

'Nothing!' I say and give his thigh a good rub. 'I promise.' We share a half-second smile, and then he downs his water.

'I'm going to go. Big workout tomorrow.' He gets up.

'Come on!' I say, holding on to his arm. 'It's only 9:45, the night is still young.'

He frowns at my hand gripping on to his bicep and shakes me off.

'When have you ever cared about the night being young?'

'It's your birthday . . .'

'I know it's my birthday, and I want to go home. Why don't you come too?' I can see he wants me to, but it feels so lame (even for us) to end the night before 10. It used to be Josh who would drag me out to bars and make me stay longer than I wanted to. I would protest, but he kept me out. He was always good for me like that.

'Why don't you give the gym a miss tomorrow?'

'No, Amy. I'm on my Body Blitz before *our wedding*.' He emphasises *our wedding*, as if he's doing me a favour by tearing his muscle groups so he can look chiselled for our wedding photos.

'That's right,' I mumble.

'So, are you coming?'

'Um . . .' I glance at Lace, swirling her wine, like she's not listening to every word. I look back at Josh, who is impatiently standing with his hands on his waist, his shirt stretching over his chest. I am meant to be seducing him tonight, but I can't see it happening when he's in this mood, and honestly, I'd rather have a good time with Lace than lie in bed feeling rejected again. 'I may stay, if that's okay?'

'Yeah, fine,' Josh says, raising his eyebrows. It's clearly not fine.

'You sure?'

'Of course, Lab . . .' He stops himself and then turns to Lace. 'Nice to finally meet you, Lace.'

'I'll look after her, don't worry,' Lace says.

He gives me a loose hug and leaves.

*

The bell for last orders went a while ago and Lace and I are on the same bar stools finishing the red wine. I am offloading everything. I tell her about my dilemma of being happy for Josh getting the promotion, yet resentful because I believe he doesn't deserve it. I feel bad for saying it out loud, but Lace doesn't seem to be judging me. It's like having a therapist. I also tell her about Year 10 doing the contraception pill for the science contest. She is very excited about this.

'One tampon *literally* hit one of my pupils in the head,' I brag.

'How hilarious. You sound like a fabulous teacher,' Lace says.

'I may get fired, though.' I smile as if this gives me a high, but I'm being kept awake at night by the fear that it's all going to backfire. This fear wasn't helped by Josh, who asked if I had 'lost my mind' when I told him what I had done. I didn't think he would understand, considering he never makes his job difficult for himself, but a little support would have been nice. Lace slams her little hand on the bar.

'I say tell that Dr Therone to go swim with the jellyfish. You need to teach somewhere else, far away from your fiancé. This world is too small as it is. You guys need to have space away from each other. You need mystery, different stories – different people in your lives.'

'Well, there is this head of science job in Ealing . . .'
'Do it!'
'It's not that easy.'

She slaps her hand on my thigh. 'Amy Elman, you are a free young bird. One day, you will have a family and lose your freedom.' She clicks in my face. 'Just like that.' She drifts off, staring into mid-air with the saddest look on her face. When I ask if she's okay, she gets up. 'I'm going to the little women's room. When I'm back, you better have sent that job application off.'

'Are you sure you're okay?'
'Send it off.' She disappears.

And just like that, I go on my phone, to my emails and reopen the drafts folder. I look over the application form for any typos, and before I can think my way out of it, I press send. Oh God. Oh God. Oh God. When Lace appears again, I wave my phone in the air pretending that I'm not freaking out by what I've just done. She throws her arms around my neck.

'I'm so proud of you, Amy Elman,' she says, pecking my cheek with her soft lips. 'MWAH!' She sits on the stool and pulls her short black dress down an inch. She's wearing sheer tights like those women in black-and-white detective films. I wish I could pull off that look, but my legs resemble mince stuffed into sausage casing whenever I wear tights like those.

'I can't believe he calls you Lab Rat. That makes me so sad,' Lace says.

'It's meant to be sweet. Your boyfriends must have given you nicknames.' Her eyes flicker down at the floor, and I see her disappear into her head for a second. 'Why did you look so sad when I said that?'

'I didn't look sad,' she insists.

'Yes, you did. Come on, tell me. I've been talking about myself all night.'

'Amy Elman, I like talking about you.'

'But what about you?' I poke my finger just below her shoulder, a bit above her heart. She tips her head back in a laugh.

'Your life is far more interesting,' she says with a slight slur in her voice.

'Ha!'

'Don't laugh.'

'I'm just a Lab Rat,' I say.

She stops smiling and leans into me so there is only a slither of space between our faces. She seems very serious all of a sudden.

'Don't call yourself that,' she says.

'Ha!'

'Stop laughing.'

'Sorry.'

We're sharing the same air now, and I watch her eyes flicker as she searches my face for something. Her rose scent drowns me. Hypnotised, I don't realise my body is falling forward and closing the gap between us. I feel the texture of her soft, full lips. My whole body comes alive for a moment, and then I realise what I'm doing. I pull away and cover my mouth.

'Shit, sorry,' I say. 'Sorry,' I say again. Lace is giggling.

'Amy Elman, you need sex,' she says. She doesn't seem bothered in the slightest. I shouldn't be surprised. People must accidentally kiss her all the time.

Batman
206 Nights

I wake up late Saturday morning to the sound of someone banging around in the kitchen. Fifi never bangs around, so I know it's Josh. There's a tight, itchy band around my hips, and I realise I'm still wearing – only wearing – my Thrills & Frills lingerie. I thought Josh would wake up and get turned on when he saw me, but alas, that didn't happen. In reality, I can imagine he woke up, saw me lying with my tummy flopping over the edges, and didn't have the desire to go near me. I take it all off and add another tally mark.

The pub closed not long after I accidentally pecked Lace on the lips. I said sorry again and again until she told me that if I apologised one more time, she would refuse to make my wedding dress, so I dropped it.

We walked to the Tube station and said our goodbyes. Lace was sad that the next time we'd see each other would be at the wedding dress-fitting party she was planning. What she doesn't know is that I'm going to surprise her tomorrow. She told me I should get highlights in my hair, so that's what I'm going to do. I've booked a hair appointment in Shoreditch, near Lace's studio. I figured a salon in East London would automatically make me cool. And I'm hoping being blonde will make Josh think I'm another woman. I've read that this is a thing. Some wives even go as far as to have a wig collection so that they can pose as different characters to keep it interesting for their husbands. That feels too much right now.

I wouldn't know what wig to start with or what voice to put with the wig. I'll see if a few highlights will do the trick first. Baby steps and all.

*

I finally roll out of bed and go see what all the noise is in the kitchen. Josh is cleaning. There are bubbles covering the bench, and Josh is rubbing them off with the oven glove. He has his earbuds in with angry rap blaring into his ears. I tap his shoulder, and he whips one of them out.

'You'll damage your eardrums,' I say.

He vigorously rubs the bench. 'Morning.'

'Good gym session?'

'Yup.'

'How was Tony?'

'Fine.'

'Is everything . . . okay?'

'Yup, just cleaning the kitchen,' he says. He rubs off the last of the bubbles and then plonks the oven glove in the dirty sink for someone else (me) to deal with.

'Sorry, I stayed out,' I say.

He pulls down the dishwasher door and begins unpacking the plates very loudly.

'You're allowed to stay out,' he says, frowning like I'm accusing him of something. The doorbell goes. 'That will be them.'

'Who?'

'Birthday cake?' he says, as if I couldn't have forgotten.

I shut my eyes in despair. Birthday cake. How did I forget about birthday cake?

Linda, Jason, Laura and Ray all come into the flat and make themselves at home in our living room. Ray goes straight to the kitchen area and puts the kettle on whilst

Jason and Laura plop themselves on the sofa. Jason makes a comment about how handy it is to have the kitchen in the living room.

'It means you can get a beer without missing the game,' he says and sniggers to himself. Meanwhile, Linda is flapping about with her M&S bag for life.

'Josh, you need to vacate the area. We will call you back when we're ready,' Linda orders. Josh does as he's told and goes and has his shower, leaving me with his family. 'Amy, come see this. What do you think?'

Linda pulls the birthday cake out from the bag. This year, it's Batman's face. I suppose it's better than last year's Action Man cake, and leaps ahead of the Shrek one he had at 25. Linda is chuckling to herself.

'So funny,' I say as brightly as I can. Linda then unpacks two white candles, a three and a zero, and pushes them into Batman's cheeks.

'Oh no, I am such a silly clog,' she says, furiously rummaging through the bag.

'What's wrong, pumpkin?' Jason calls out from the sofa.

'I forgot the matches. Ray, do you have a lighter?' Linda says. Ray shakes his head cluelessly. 'Laura?'

'Why would I have a lighter? I haven't smoked for 10 years,' Laura says.

I take Fifi's lighter from the drawer, and Linda sighs with relief.

'Oh, you're a lifesaver,' she says. The crisis of a 30-year-old man having unlit candles on his birthday cake is avoided. She yells out for Josh. 'Josh! Josh! We're ready!'

A few minutes later, a freshly washed Josh comes back into the kitchen to the sound of his family singing Happy Birthday. He stands with a childlike grin on his face. I'm never sure if he truly enjoys this tradition or is too scared to tell his mother to stop it. If I were him, I would have put an end to it 15 years ago.

'Make a wish,' Linda orders. Josh pauses momentarily to indulge his family, then blows out the candles.

'What part would you like, Joshy? Come on, no diet today,' his dad says as he starts slicing the cake. Josh goes for the bat ear and part of the head. I'm given Batman's line mouth and flicked-out, cocaine-damaged nose tip. I have no appetite, so I slice layers off with my fork until it disintegrates into tiny sponge balls. Meanwhile, Josh is announcing the news of his promotion and the news of my non-promotion to his family. Linda squeals with excitement.

'My son, the Head of Humanities at Clapham High for Girls,' she says. She then pulls a face at me like I'm dying. 'Sorry, Amy, you did deserve it too.' Her hand is on my knee. I take my frustration out on the sponge balls on my plate, pressing on them with my index finger.

'Yeah, good effort,' Jason adds.

'Well, our boss favours men, so it's no wonder,' I say, still pressing the sponge balls. The only noise is of plates being scraped by forks and cake moving around mouths. I peer up and see the crushed look on Josh's face. *Crap.* 'But Josh deserves it. He's a great teacher,' I add.

'He's a great, *great* teacher,' Linda says whilst she rubs her son's arm. 'The best there is.'

Taylor Swift

The Butters Family left eventually, but I'm now 30 minutes late for my bridesmaid dress party.

Rebecca's home isn't a stylised abode; it's more of a temple of good bargains. Every piece of furniture comes with a story of where her husband, Tight Tim, found it and how cheap it was. I'm sitting on the third-hand brown leather sofa, which Tim is proud to have obtained from his grandma, and on the coffee table (found on Facebook Marketplace) is an unopened bottle of Tesco Value Prosecco.

Rebecca, Nina and Abi are standing in a line-up, modelling the same dress in different ways. It's a brick-coloured strapless chiffon maxi to go with my rustic theme. Nina keeps pulling the dress up around her cleavage, conscious that she's showing skin that hasn't seen the light of day since she was a student. Abi, who I met in the lab at Leeds University, is barely 5ft and the dress pools around her ankles. Rebecca's is stretched around her post-pregnancy shape. She looks fantastic, apart from her exhausted face, which is glaring at me, waiting for my answer.

'You all look beautiful, but you don't have to wear the same dress. It's not a cult,' I say.

'We *do* have to wear the same dress. It's tradition,' Rebecca says with exasperation. I'm getting the feeling she's running out of patience for this wedding.

'It's also tradition to be a virgin when you get married,' Nina cuts in.

'And to not get divorced, but most do,' Abi says.

'Reassuring, thanks,' I say. (Abi has spent most of her adult life in a lab experimenting on mice, so I forgive her for her lack of human skills.)

'So, is it a yes?' Rebecca asks.

'Yes. Perfect. Thanks,' I say.

'Great. Done. Let's open the bottle. I have four hours without a baby, and I plan to take full advantage of it,' Rebecca declares, already unzipping herself.

A minute later, they are all back in their regular clothes and opening the bottle of Prosecco.

Three bottles later, Abi is dancing and singing aggressively to 'I Can Do It With a Broken Heart'. She can't sing, but what she lacks in pitch, she makes up for in passion. She closes her eyes and throws one arm in the air as she shouts the chorus. If there is anything she likes more than her mice, it's Taylor Swift. I'm watching her from a battered green leather footstool from Oxfam. Nina, meanwhile, is ranting at Rebecca about everything that is wrong with the world, from the manspreader on the Northern line to the way social media has knocked the confidence of young girls, and now she's digging into Dr Therone.

'She obviously wants to have sex with Josh,' Nina says quietly. 'That's why he got the promotion . . .' She drifts off, and I can sense it's because she's worried I am listening, which I am.

'Everyone loves Josh,' Rebecca says, not in a friendly way. I pretend I'm too distracted by Abi's dance to 'Love Story' to hear them. Rebecca said something to me once that made me think she wasn't *entirely* on Team Josh. I was training to be a teacher, and Josh was chilling at his parents' house. After months of him whining about the prospect of a job, I persuaded him to become a teacher. I filled out the forms and got him onto the course, and when I told Rebecca this, she said, 'Oh, Amy, you'll forever be making that man's life happen for him'. It stuck with me for some reason.

'I don't,' Abi says over the music.

'You don't what?' I ask.

'Love Josh,' she says and does a twirl. She's being her usual overly accurate self.

'Not love him, but you like him,' I say.

'Nope.' She does another twirl. I count the empty bottles of Prosecco in front of me; now there are four. She sways and says dreamily, 'That night at Leeds, when he was dancing with Natalie, I realised then he was a knob.' She does another twirl and mimes the chorus. I didn't think anyone remembered the Natalie night, let alone had an opinion on it. I jump to his defence.

'Oh, that was so long ago, Abi! And also, it was me who overreacted!'

She's still dancing when she says, 'I don't think calling him pug penis was an overreaction. He deserved it.'

Nina and Rebecca choke on their Prosecco. Abi keeps dancing.

Josh and Amy's Wedding 2025

To Do:

Wash the purple dress before the hen party.
Show Josh the seating plan.
Buy flowers from Petunia.
Email Velvet Cats to ask if they do song requests.
Talk to Mum about being civil to Dad and Jean-Ivy.
Do Josh's Seven-Week Wedding Body Blitz Diet.
Bleach hair.

Woolly Hat Man
207 Nights

I've made a catastrophic mistake. I had planned to go blonde like Lace told me to, but I picked up *Vogue* whilst I was waiting in the salon's reception and saw a photo of Selena Gomez. She and Lace have the same luscious, big mane of chocolate hair. I felt inspired, so in a moment of madness, I decided that instead of blonde, I'd go brunette.

I try not to cry as I'm faced with my reflection.

'Maybe invest in some bronzer,' advised the hairdresser. I whimper at the mirror – at my pale, knackered face, and my emo-coloured hair. What the hell have I done? I leave the salon, poorer and whiter than ever. I need Lace's help. Now.

My new hair keeps jumping out at me in the reflections of every shop window. What was I thinking, dying it four weeks before my wedding? I wonder if it's possible to impose a camera ban on the day so there's no evidence of me looking like this. And I can't even begin to think about my sex life with Josh. One thing is for certain: he won't want to get under the covers with *The Walking Dead*.

I get to Lace's studio and ring the buzzer five times, but there's no answer. I try her phone and it goes straight to voicemail. This is not the day I had in mind. I retreat to Beanie to get a coffee, hoping she has just nipped out and will be back shortly. I often think of her when I'm doing something mundane like feeding my fish or marking tests. In my mind, she's always up to something fabulous, like drinking red wine on a rooftop or eating sushi with Frankie. Beautiful people love sushi.

The same hairy-bearded barista takes my regular latte order. I sit on a spare crate close to the window and watch the tourists and hipsters go by. Opposite is a sustainable homeware shop selling bamboo brooms for £50 and jars for seeds and pulses. I can't wait to have my own home. I'll put dried food in jars and have a linen tablecloth and lots of (alive) houseplants. There will be no limescale in the shower, mouldy corners or unexplained stains on the carpet. Our kitchen cupboard doors won't be hanging off their hinges. And, best of all, we won't have flatmates filming erotic onion-eating videos in the kitchen. Our home will be spotless – a refuge from the rest of the world. I'll learn how to make my own gooey flapjacks, like the ones from Clapcake. Maybe I'll even bake a batch for my friendly countryside neighbours. Maybe.

I see Lace. She's walking away in a brown leather coat and knee-high boots. I leave my coffee and run outside, shouting her name. She walks around the corner onto Club Row. She is with a man, not Frankie or that cat bloke. This one I don't recognise; he's not that tall and has dark hair coming out from under his brown woolly beanie hat. He's wearing a baggy blue jumper and looks a complete mess compared to Lace. They are walking side by side, rigidly. Neither one speaks. I go to shout her name again but stop myself. Maybe this would be a good opportunity to find out more about her.

I know it's creepy to stalk someone, but considering she knows so much about me, and I know zilch about her, I feel intrigued to have some insight into her world. Besides, London is a free land, and I just so happen to be here today – walking in the same direction as her. I keep my distance as I follow them to Spitalfields Market. It's heaving, as it would be on a Sunday. People are getting in the way as they wander from art stands to t-shirt stands. I almost lose them, but I spot the woolly hat bouncing between heads. From what I can tell, they still haven't said a word to each other, so I can only assume they're in an argument. The Woolly Hat Man points to 'Flags', a bar with football on the TV, and shuffleboards and ping pong tables. Lace would hate that kind of place, but to my surprise, she nods and follows him inside. I hide behind a tuk-tuk van selling those flimsy coloured rope surfer bracelets.

They sit in a window, which gives me a perfect view. I can finally get a good glimpse of what the Woolly Hat Man looks like; he seems to be around our age with a bulky nose and sad, slanted eyes. Unlike Frankie and the other people in Lace's world, there is something real about him – he looks like the type who could put up a shelf.

They each read a menu, and then the Woolly Hat Man goes off to the bar and leaves Lace sitting alone. She doesn't take out her phone like ordinary people do. Instead, she stares at the market like a doll in a toy shop. I see heads turn to check her out as they walk by, but she stays looking out vacantly as if she can't see a thing. The Woolly Hat Man comes back with two glasses of what seems to be orange juice. I wasn't expecting that.

My phone begins to ring, it's Josh.

'Where are you?' he asks.

'Er . . . shopping. Wedding stuff.'

'Still? What have you got?'

'Um . . . like stuff I need. Make-up.'

'Could you get me a bottle of Radox?'

'Sure.'

'When will you be home?'

I exhale. 'In an hour or so. I have to go. See you then.'

'Great. I'll make you your first salad dinner. Bye.'

The thought of eating salad tonight is very depressing but after seeing how my hip fat engulfed my red thong,

I realised I needed to do something. Before leaving the house today, I stupidly told Josh I'd do his Wedding Body Blitz Diet. He was overly excited about this and has already made me download a calorie-counting app. It will be hell, but hey, like Lace said – a shy woman is a dry woman.

When I turn back to Lace, things have become more animated. The Woolly Hat Man is waving his hand around and not in a happy way. Lace is staring at her orange juice; now and again, I see her lips move as she says a word or two. Whatever she is saying, it's aggravating the man even more. He pulls off his hat and throws it on the table, rubbing his hands through his messy, floppy hair. Lace reaches out gently, but he shoves her off. He gets up and leaves the table, and a moment later, he's storming out of the bar. He passes me with his teeth clenched and his eyes tearing up. My first instinct is to get up and run to Lace, but I stop myself. She remains in the seat, staring coldly into nothing. Suddenly, she ruffles her hair and straightens up as if resetting herself. She takes another sip of her juice. She inspects her fingernails, appearing not to be bothered by the conflict. Suddenly, she looks out of the window, right in my direction, and for a second, we lock eyes. I duck out of view.

'Er . . . excuse me.' The man selling the bracelets is standing over me. 'If you're not going to buy anything, could you please step out of the way? Otherwise, I'll have to start charging you rent.'

'Oh, sorry,' I say. 'Two minutes.'

'No, you've been here long enough.'

I take the closest bracelet, a pitiful pink rope with a plastic smiley face on it.

'I'll take this. How much?'

'Five pounds.'

'Five pounds?' I yell. 'This city is a joke.'

He brings the card reader down to my level, and I reluctantly tap my card.

'Receipt?' he asks smugly.

'No, I don't want to be reminded of this.'

I stuff the bracelet into my pocket and look up again, but Lace has disappeared. My heart starts thumping. Where could she have gone? It's like having a spider let loose in a room. I stand and do a 360, but there is so much going on and so many people that she could be anywhere. I do another turn. The surfer bracelet man is watching me like I'm crazy. I sarcastically thank him for his hospitality, and then I make a run for it out of Spitalfields, through Shoreditch and into the Underground. A Tube arrives as soon as I get onto the platform. I grab a seat in the middle of the carriage and catch my distorted reflection; my forehead is stretched, my eyes are holes and my dyed brunette hair is lost in the black tunnels.

For the rest of the journey home, I can't stop thinking about Lace and the Woolly Hat Man. I wish I could ask her what it was all about, but I know that wouldn't go down well. *'Oh! Hi, Lace, I was following you earlier. Please could you tell me who that man was and why you were arguing with him?'* Gosh, I am a creep. A brunette creep.

When I get home, all I can smell is the familiar scent of boiled chicken. Gag. Josh is vigilantly cutting up a skinless chicken breast and placing it on a bowl of leaves. He glances up and jerks his head.

'Amy? Your hair,' he says, not smiling.

'Yeah,' I say. I do that thing that Lace does and twirl a strand of it. His mouth remains open, and I'm unsure if this is a good or bad thing. 'Do you like it?'

'It's cool,' he says with a high-pitched voice. 'It's dark.'

'Yeah, that's what I was going for. You sure you like it?'

'Yeah.' Still high-pitched. 'It's cool,' he repeats. Then picks up the bowl of dry salad, stares at it for a long time, and says, 'Dinner is ready.'

Nina's Assembly
208 Nights

Nina has always taken her assembly slots as a chance to fight for feminism. They have become iconic at Clapham High. The last one was on 'Me Too', where we listened to 14-year-olds tell the story (perhaps in rather graphic detail) of Harvey Weinstein. The one before that was about the women accused of being witches and being burnt at the stake. She has done these assemblies for years, even before I started here. Dr Therone, unsurprisingly, hates them. After the 'Me Too' one, there was an infamous debate in the staff meeting, where Dr Therone told Nina that they were grossly inappropriate. Nina argued back that appropriateness is irrelevant when it comes to history and that if we are not telling the future women of this world what happened to the women of the past, then we are not doing our job. At that point, Dr Therone slammed her fist on the table and threatened if she did it again, she would get an official warning.

The assembly began with the girls marching into the hall carrying signs. 'Get the Vote', 'Yes to Women'. Dr Therone put her head in her hands. The girls then proceeded to act out famous events, like Rachelle being held down and screaming whilst two girls in lab coats pretended to force-feed her. Now, a sign is being held up saying, Epsom Derby 1913. We all know what we're in for. Half the class gather on the stage, cheering as if they are at the races. Sasha runs out in an Edwardian dress, and they shout, 'Emily! Emily! Emily!'

Two girls in the shaggy pantomime horse costume come galloping on and collide with Sasha. They drop on the floor, the class screams, and the lights go out. For a moment, all is silent, and then 'Sisters Are Doin' It for Themselves' by Eurythmics fades in and starts blasting out in the hall. A very proud Nina and her class emerge from the curtains and take a bow.

'Turn that off,' Dr Therone orders. The music stops. She glares at Nina for a moment, then turns back to the school. 'Announcements? Yes, whoever's hand that is.'

The head girl, Henrietta, stands, simultaneously yelling at her friends to shut the hell up. Out of everyone in this hall, Henrietta hates her job the most. When she first began the year as head girl, she came in bright, clean and enthusiastic, but the weekly meetings with Dr Therone have taken their toll. She mumbles something, and Dr Therone asks her to speak up, so she begins to shout. 'School committee is this lunchtime. The Year 11 cake sale is on Thursday. And once again, stop leaving your bags outside the door of the lunch hall. It's a fire hazard, which means if the cooks fuc— . . . . mess up, we'll be trapped and will burn to a crisp. Don't say I didn't warn you.'

'Yes, okay, Henrietta. Any more?' Dr Therone looks around the hall. 'No? Miss Pascoe, please see me in my office at 1 p.m.' Nina smiles and nods. She really does have balls on her.

At lunch, Josh and I are having Berry Burst protein shakes. It's so depressing when today is pizza, and the hall is smelling of bubbly cheese and crispy ham. Berry Burst sounds and looks like it should taste like a TGI milkshake, but it's like drinking a cleaning product. I take another gulp and grimace. It will be worth it.

A shy woman is a dry woman.

'Ben told me that his sister and her boyfriend are moving out of their flat in Clapham. Rent's a little more, but now with the head of department role . . .' Josh says.

I frown. 'What's the point in moving flats in London? We may as well stick it out until we can put the deposit down. No?'

He takes a long gulp of his shake.

'It's a long way to commute for work, isn't it? From the countryside,' he says. It's the first time he has mentioned anything about the commute.

'Most people commute into London,' I remind him.

Josh shrugs and takes another gulp. Nina comes into the lunch hall. We watch to see if she's displaying any signs of distress from her meeting with Dr Therone. She fills her plate from the salad bar happily enough and comes and sits down without a word.

'Did everything go okay with Dr Therone?' I ask.

'It went exactly to plan. I got what I wanted, thank you for asking.'

Josh leans across. 'What did you want?'

'Evidence, Joshua,' she says, and stabs a potato with her fork and puts it full into her mouth. She then turns to me. 'What did you do to your hair?'

**You are invited to Amy's Wedding Dress Fitting.
10th February at 1 p.m.
Redchurch Street. Black door by Beanie cafe.
Red wine and cheese will be served.
(PRESS BUZZER 5 TIMES)
Lace xxx**

OnlyFans
209 Nights

Pete is missing the pub quiz because he is taking Cara Helm out. He never misses a quiz, so it's:

A. A surprise that he's ditching it for a girl.
B. That the girl is Cara Helm.

Nina is taking her sixth formers to *Hamilton*, so this means Josh and I are doing the pub quiz alone. We always have other people with us, so I thought this would be a cute thing for us to do, but as the questions go by, it's becoming excruciating. We are bickering over whether there are five or six human players on a polo team. I think six. Josh insists it's five.

'Fine, go with five,' I say. 'But I really think it's six.'

He scribbles down five and drops the pen, and we sit in another silence. GEEZ, this is painful.

'Shall we just go?' I say, trying to give him an out.

'Why would we go? We still have 10 questions left,' he says, pretending to be unaware of the hostility.

'Because we're obviously not in the mood tonight.'

'*I'm* in the mood,' he says, hinting that all the hostility is coming from me. He laughs, in a slightly unhinged way. So, we carry on.

The science ones are in the bag, of course. And Josh is confident with the geography and football questions, but any other question continues to be a frustrating battle. How many keys are in the octave chromatic scale? 10 or 12.

It was *Oliver Twist* that started with the line, 'It was the best of times, it was the worst of times.' No, it was *Great Expectations*. Wasn't it? We both knew the Banksy question; everyone knows he's from Bristol. Now it's question 30, and neither of us has the energy to fight over the name of the film about the Watergate scandal starring Robert Redford.

'Something about the president's men. Shall I put that down?' Josh mumbles.

'May as well,' I mumble back. He scribbles it down and passes the paper to the North London Invàsion team to mark.

15 out of 30?! That can't be right. We huddle over the paper, scanning each answer, trying to find where North London Invasion had made a mistake in their markings.

'See, I told you it was 12 keys,' Josh says as if he hadn't got anything wrong.

'And I told you it was 1975,' I argue back.

We both were wrong on the Dickens question and the number of human players on a polo team. There are four. We also didn't get a mark on question 30 because we didn't put 'All the' in *All the President's Men*. I thought this was particularly harsh of Daz.

'Not even third place?' Daz says when we don't raise our hands. 'Wow. How the mighty have fallen.' He raises his eyebrows sarcastically and, with a smile, mutters something away from the mic.

'I don't want to come here anymore,' I tell Josh.

'No, nor do I.'

It's the only thing we have agreed on all evening.

We get home, and Josh goes to have a shower. I lie in bed and watch @DrLabby's latest video, where she is recommending the best shoes for teaching. A sponsored post by Skechers. I get bored and put it down. Not her best video. Judging from our friction at the pub quiz, I assume that we will not break the drought tonight. I listen out to check if the shower is still going, then I put my earbuds in and hide under the covers.

Dennis's voice trickles into my ear. '515,000 mph is the speed at which our solar system orbits the centre of the galaxy. 230 million years is how long it will take to complete one single orbit around the galactic centre.' The door opens. I bolt up and out of the covers to see Josh in our bedroom. He's staring at his phone, so he didn't catch me in the act.

'Look what I found,' Josh jumps onto the bed. My heart is still thumping, and so is everything below. 'Are you okay?' he asks, noticing my flushed state.

'Yeah. Course. Why?' I say defensively. He shrugs and shows me his phone. I am expecting to see another gym video of some turtle man lifting something heavy, but it's not that at all. It's the video of Fifi in her pink lingerie chopping onions. I almost fly off the bed.

'Why are you watching that?' I ask, horrified. Josh is still staring at the screen as if he's watching a typical cooking programme.

'It's only Fifi,' he says.

'I didn't realise you watched OnlyFans.'

'I don't,' he says quickly. Too quickly? 'I wanted to find the video of Fifi. Thought it would be funny.' I peer at the screen again. Fifi is cutting up the onion slowly into slices; now and again she looks up at the camera with a sultry expression. Her nipples are more prominent on screen than they were in real life. She holds the edge of the table and sways her hips seductively whilst pretending to consider her next move. There is a very obvious cut, and that must have been when Josh and I came in. She then takes a slice and puts it slowly into her mouth. I gag and put my hands over my face. I watch the rest through my fingers. She eats another slice and then another, and slowly but surely, we watch her eat the whole raw onion. Josh goes on her profile, where there is a collection of her eating strange food in our kitchen in her underwear.

'Is she struggling for money?' I say, genuinely concerned. 'Like, perhaps, we need to see if she's okay.'

'Lab Rat, she's fine. She's making more money than we ever will. Look how happy she looks.' He points to a thumbnail of her smiling seductively whilst holding up a chilli. The title is 'Watch Me Eat a Whole Chilli'. 'See. She's having fun.'

'Do you think it's hot?' I ask.

'The chilli, yeah, I imagine so.'

'No, Fifi eating food in underwear?'

He pauses. 'No, of course not. It's weird as fuck. Night, Lab Rat.' He turns over.

That's a yes then.

Lobster

212 Nights

I thought I was going to be the late one, but Mum is still not here. Classic. I was held back at school because Beatrice needed to go through her lines from the science contest presentation. She can't practise at home – her mum will freak out if she hears her rehearsing a presentation on the Pill. I understand. Her mum is the worst helicopter parent there is. If Beatrice doesn't score at least 90 per cent on a test, then I can be sure to receive a frenzied email from Mrs Berryman.

So, I stood at the back of the lab, and Beatrice stood at the front, and she went over her lines until she nailed it. We only have Monday and Tuesday left, and then it's the presentation. On the one hand, I'm bricking it because of the topic, but on the other, the girls have worked their arses off, and it's a bloody good presentation. The best I've ever done, in fact. The judges may look past the controversy, and we may even win it. And if we win it, Dr Therone will have to reconsider me for the head of the department role.

Mum finally appears. She unwraps herself from her wool coat and scarf and hands them to the man at the front desk. When she was Robert Elman's wife, she dressed in a conservative white shirt and straight beige trousers, with a silk neck scarf that changed depending on her daily activities. When she was working, it was navy blue. When she was lunching with the girls, it was orange. She saved the brighter ones for holidays. I'm not sure where the inspiration came from to dress like a Republican from Virginia, but that fashion phase ended abruptly with the marriage. Now, Charlotte Dennis is a woman who dresses in vibrant, flowy dresses that she buys from cruise ship shops. Today, it's bright pink with sequins sewn on it.

'Gosh, I forget how cold this silly country can get,' she says. We give each other our signature loose hug. Mum picked her favourite restaurant, Shell off Marylebone High Street, for our reunion. It has thick, dusty velvet curtains and a tank of gloomy lobsters, who slowly wave their claws at customers as if waving for help. We sit in comfortable silence as we scan the menu.

When the waiter comes, I order the prawn pasta; I need to eat all the carbs while Josh isn't around. Mum orders lobster. She selects the most aggressive one in the tank – the one walking over the others. 'That will teach him for being a bully,' she says. She orders a bottle of Whispering Angel to go with her bullying lobster. As soon as the waiter is gone, she launches in.

'So, three weeks . . .' she says, laying the napkin on her lap.

'Three weeks . . .' I prepare my napkin in the same way.

'And how are you feeling?'

I go through my list. 'Venue is signed off. The cake is a carrot cake, but I'll survive. Bridesmaids are happy with their dresses. The hen party is tomorrow in Reading, but again, I'll survive. So, yeah, good.'

Mum doesn't look impressed, but before she can comment, the Whispering Angel arrives. She takes her time tasting it properly, swirling the wine in the glass, sniffing it, swirling it some more, and finally tasting it. A few years ago, she went on a two-day wine course and now fancies herself as a wine connoisseur. She gives the waiter a nod.

'Cheers,' she says, raising the glass of rosé. 'To your last three weeks of being free.'

'I suppose that's one way to put it,' I say and clink her glass.

'Are you still going to change your name?'

'Why wouldn't I?'

'Amy Butters?' she says with a scrunched nose. I know it's not the sexiest name in the world, but it's not like I'm a model or an influencer. I'm a teacher who's going to live in the countryside and spend evenings looking at the stars through my telescope. Besides, it will make it easier when we have children. Amy Butters will do.

I shrug. 'It's tradition.'

'A lot of paperwork if you ever have to switch back . . .' Mum says this like a warning. It's bizarre; most mothers would be over the moon that their daughter is getting married, but I feel like I'm being discouraged from signing up for the military.

'Hopefully, it won't come to that,' I say with a smile, and then distract her away from the anti-marriage talk. 'Have I told you about my science contest?' I launch into the story from beginning to end before she can stop me. Usually, I don't brag about my job to Mum or Dad, but I'm feeling oddly proud about what I'm doing at work.

'And you're not going to get into trouble?' Mum says once I'm done. Before I can answer, our food arrives. I waste no time digging into my pasta. I swirl the doughy carb strands around my fork and stuff them into my mouth. Mmmm . . . God, I've missed food. Mum is scraping the flesh out of the belly of her lobster. She takes the first bite.

'Good?' I ask.

'Delicious. You?'

'The best.'

She wipes her mouth with her napkin. 'A week before marrying your father, I discovered he had seen this other woman throughout our engagement.'

'Barbra Speck. I know,' I say. Mum mentioned Barbra Speck a few times when Dad left. She was so mad at herself for not leaving him then, and I had this thought that if she *had* left him, then I wouldn't be alive, and it made me realise how flimsy our existence is. One dick move can change the course of a family tree.

'I confronted your dad,' Mum carries on as if I hadn't heard the story. 'He said he would never do it again, putting it down to cold feet. I was the idiot who believed him, and 20 years later, I find an erotic text conversation with a moulding punk singer on his phone.' She drifts off. I also heard about the erotic texts that Dad sent Jean-Ivy, and they have scarred me for life. It's not as bad as Charles wanting to be Camilla's tampon, but it was close enough.

'Josh and Dad are very different men,' I say.

'Still men.' She snaps a claw off.

'Yes. Men. Humans – not snails or monsters.'

'All I'm saying is that ring is not magic, it's a piece of jewellery. It's not going to solve your problems.' She glances at my ring and scrunches her nose again. Like everyone else, she hates it.

'Josh and I are happy,' I say.

'Well, if you're happy, then I'm happy.' She takes a mouthful of claw flesh. I'm surprised she can fit anything into her mouth after that loaded comment.

'I mean, every couple has their problems, but . . .' I stop. It's too risky even to hint that things aren't perfect. If she knew about the dry spell, I imagine she would tell me to pack my bags tonight. 'I'm happy. I'm really happy.'

Mum snaps off the next claw. 'Good,' she says. We carry on eating, and I know in my bones she still has more to say. 'Be prepared . . .'

Here we go. I exhale as I put down my cutlery.

'Be prepared to hate him when you're 60.' She glances up from her plate. 'Don't look at me like that, Amy. Find me a postmenopausal woman who doesn't roll her eyes when she says her husband's name.' She gestures to an elderly couple in the corner who are dressed to the nines but haven't said a word to each other all evening. The woman does look particularly miserable.

'You really don't want me to get married, do you?' I say.

'You can do what you want, darling. But you were born after 1970, which means you may not be able to afford a house, but at least society isn't pressuring you to have a husband.'

'But I don't want to be old and die alone.' That came out wrong. 'Sorry. I mean I want to give the family thing a go.'

Mum takes her glass and swirls the wine around again before taking another sip. I need to change the subject. She's nearly at the end of her second glass, which means she's tipsy enough for me to talk to her about Jean-Ivy. I do a big inhale as I think of how to approach it. 'So, speaking of moulding punk singer.' Her eyes shoot up. Even the hint of Jean-Ivy kicks Mum into killer mode. She's like a shark with blood, ready to dig her teeth into the woman who ruined her life.

'Oh, Jesus, she's not performing at your wedding.'

'No,' I say. I then remember what Dad said about getting the band back together for my wedding. 'Well, I hope not.' (Note to self: tell Dad, no surprise performances.)

'You'll be doing your first dance to "Choke! Choke! Choke!"' Mum laughs into her lobster. I smile even though I don't find it funny.

'Mum,' I say. I pause to think of the best way to word this without seeming like I'm attacking her. I focus on the lobster carcass, knowing that if I look her in the eye, I may be unable to say what I want. 'I understand it's not easy for you, but for this one day, could you just . . . hold it in? You don't have to drink champagne with them, or do the Macarena, or be friends, but could you please not make any snide comments? It really winds them up.'

I finally look up. She's not mad, she's smirking.

'Snide comments? Me?' It's as if she is proud of her mean streak.

'Please?' I plead.

She rolls her eyes. 'Just don't put me anywhere near them. Where am I sitting?'

'On the top table next to Dad.'

'She better not be sitting with us,' she says and goes pink at the thought of it.

'No.'

'But your dad and I have to sit next to each other?'

'Yes, it's tradition,' I repeat. She slouches in her chair like a teenager being told to be on her best behaviour for her relatives.

'Heaven's sake,' she mumbles. I choose to ignore it.

'Linda will want to talk to you. She's really excited about seeing you again.' If Mum rolls her eyes one more time, they may just roll out of her skull. I didn't have half this attitude when I was a teenager. 'Mum, it's one day, and it's my day, so can you please—'

'Oh, Amy, what kind of mother do you think I am? Don't answer that. Let's get more wine and talk about this new hair colour of yours.' She searches the restaurant. 'Waiter?'

Bessy's

213 Nights

Josh's stag is going to be watching football and going on a bar crawl. I'm not sure about the kind of bars, but Pete is organising it, so I imagine the worst kind. It's also a big day for Josh because he's going to be having his first alcoholic drink of the year. He has given himself the rule of only vodka and soda water like he's a working woman in the eighties.

Rebecca has instructed us all to meet at Paddington at 12:45 so we can get the 13:00 train to Reading. I'm still a little gutted that my hen party is in Reading, but I keep reminding myself that it's not about where you are, but who you are with.

I go to the bathroom to take a shower. I open the door, and it takes me a second to gather what's happening. JOSH. WANKING. PORN. Josh slams the laptop down, and it falls onto the tiled floor. SMACK. I close the door. I go back into the bedroom, sit on the bed and stare at nothing as I process what just happened.

I know he has to masturbate like I have to masturbate, but seeing him do it in the bathroom like that makes me cold all over. Here I am, waiting for him to leave to go to the gym so I can orgasm to a Texan who talks about galaxies. And there he is, locking himself in the bathroom, watching strangers have sex so he can orgasm. How did we get here? I used to know every new pimple on his body. He knew when I had a new lotion on. Those days when we were living apart, we would be so desperate to see each other because we knew we made each other feel better than anyone else in the world. Now, though, we're hiding from each other so we can feel pleasure. I don't know how I let this happen to us, but I know we need to change, otherwise we're going to be together, but lonely, for the rest of our lives.

We meet again in the kitchen. It's been an hour since the 'walk-in'. I've got more make-up on than usual, and I've even tried to blow-dry my hair for the occasion. Josh glances at me.

'Ready for the big hen then, Lab Rat?' he says.

'Ready for scones,' I say, pinching the elastic waist of the purple dress to show how elasticated it is. He nods slightly disapprovingly. This would be something he would have found funny when we first met, but his new muscles seem to have squeezed out his sense of humour. I get a coffee mug as he rinses out his flask. Silence. The elephant has arrived in the kitchen. Hello, elephant. I'm not going to bring up what happened in the bathroom, but I am curious to see if he'll try to explain it . . .

'So,' he says. I grip the mug handle in anticipation. 'I was thinking I will allow myself three pints as well as the vodka. What do you think?' he says, frowning at me like it's a serious question. There's my answer: the bathroom incident will be swept under the rug, along with everything else.

'You don't need my permission. I'm not your mum,' I say.

*

I meet Nina and Abi next to the Burger King in Paddington station. Rebecca comes walking through the crowd on her phone. She clearly didn't have time to dress for her own purple theme. She's in all black, apart from a thin purple scarf that still has the tag attached to it. As soon as she gets to us, I snap it off.

'He's just tired, Tim. Maybe take him for a walk around the park and then try again. No, you can't feed him now. It will mess up his meal times. The girls are waiting, so I have to go. Any problems, give me a call.' She hangs up and exhales. 'Sorry about that, Tim is looking after Benson for the first time.'

Tim calls again when we're boarding the train. We find a table of four. I sit next to Abi, and Nina and Rebecca sit opposite us. 'Yes, he will need his pram blanket if you're going out . . .' Nina widens her eyes as Rebecca continues instructing Tim. It's like Tim has never seen a human baby before. As Rebecca talks, she lifts four small bottles of Prosecco from her bag, and then Abi goes into her bag and takes out four willy straws.

'It's a hen party, isn't it?' she says and takes a long suck of her drink.

Rebecca glares at the straw as she finishes her phone call. 'Okay, Tim, I've got to go. Yep. You'll be fine. Play Elton John, he loves Elton John.'

'Elton John?' Abi mouths to Nina and me. We're as confused as she is.

'Okay, bye. Bye. Love you too.' Rebecca turns off the phone and looks away, pensive. Nina opens her mouth. I can tell she's about to say something feminist.

'Nina,' I say and shake my head. She closes her mouth.

'Everything okay?' I ask Rebecca.

It takes her a second, and then she raises her Prosecco. 'Yes! Let's go, girls! Amy's hen! Woooo!'

*

We get to Reading. Rebecca leads the way from the station, past the closed clubs and bars. We go through The Oracle shopping centre. Rebecca and I used to walk around here aimlessly when we were teenagers. Girls from our class and local boys would hang by the McDonald's. Rebecca and I would sit on the steps with hot chocolates and watch how our classmates changed around the boys. They played with their hair and squealed at everything. Rebecca and I convinced each other that we weren't over there, because we were more mature. In reality, we were terrified. We wouldn't have had the slightest idea of how to act if one of the boys ever spoke to us. That's why we made sure we stayed together, and far away on the steps.

Rebecca stops us outside a cafe called Bessy's. 'Here we are,' she announces and goes inside.

My stomach drops with disappointment. Bessy's is a small, yellow-painted cafe with pink bunting and a laminated menu stuck on the window. Nina, Abi and I share the same confused look before we follow Rebecca inside.

Apart from a few elderly people clinking their tea mugs, the place is dead silent. The tables are covered with flower-patterned cloths, the chairs are painted yellow, and each table has a plastic carnation in a plastic vase. We're greeted by Bessy herself, a widow. We know she's a widow because there is a candlelit shrine of her dead husband, Larry, next to the window.

'Say hello to my Larry, girls,' she says. We all laugh at the joke, but she stands there expectantly.

'Hello, Larry,' Abi says first, far too enthusiastically.

'Hey, Larry.'

'Hi.'

'Hey . . . Larry,' Nina says slowly.

Once that is done, Bessy leads us to the back, where a group of elderly women are buttering their scones with shaky hands. As we sit down, Tim rings again.

'The wipes are on the top shelf in the bathroom. Yes. Just lift the legs from the ankles . . .' Nina listens and shakes her head while Abi scans the coffee-ring-stained paper menu. Rebecca gets off her phone with a gigantic sigh.

'Right, ladies, what are we having?'

'Tim knows Benson is a human baby, right? Like, not a baby giraffe?' Nina says.

'He's nervous,' Rebecca says, defending him as always.

'I don't think they serve alcohol,' Abi says, scanning the menu.

'Well, we can't drink tea,' Nina says. Rebecca suddenly goes a little pale. She's clearly booked an afternoon tea place without checking if it serves alcohol. She calls Bessy over.

'Oh, no, dear, this is a cafe,' Bessy says. 'But the sandwiches are on their way.' She shuffles away and disappears into the kitchen. We look at Rebecca.

'Fuck's sake,' she says and puts her head in her hands as if she is about to explode.

I comfort her. 'Don't worry, we'll have a nice, civilised tea, and then we can drink after. Right, girls?'

Nina and Abi are clearly not happy, but they put on their best performance.

'I love tea,' says Abi.

'It's always useful to have a clear head,' Nina says, grasping at something. A horrific squeaking sound comes from behind. We all cover our ears and turn to see Bessy wheeling a trolley with a tower of sandwiches, a teapot, milk and sugar on it. She parks it next to us, and we wait patiently as she lays it all out on our table and then wheels her squeaky trolley off again. Rebecca suddenly leans into the table like she's about to reveal a secret.

'So, I've done something a little cheeky and organised a Mr and Mrs with Josh. I've asked him some questions, and I will ask Amy them now to see if their answers match.'

'And if they don't match?' Abi asks, with a mouthful of cucumber sandwich.

'Then they're not compatible,' Nina answers.

Abi scrunches her nose. 'Bit late now, isn't it? We're at her hen party.'

I agree. What good is it now if we're on different pages about who would most likely go to prison? Or who is the least likely to do the ironing? Still, I'm curious about what questions Rebecca has asked Josh.

'Go for it, Rebecca,' I say.

She sits up and begins to read from her phone.

'Okay, so, how many kids will you have?'

This one is easy, we used to talk about having two kids. Everyone wants two kids, a boy and a girl, who will fit neatly into family holiday packages and taxis.

'Two.'

'Correct. Josh said, two.'

'What is Josh's happy place?'

'Easy, the French Alps.'

'Nope, the gym.'

We all groan in sync. The gym? I know he has a gym obsession, but surely his favourite place in the whole wide world is not some dark room in Vauxhall.

'Who do you think is the hotter one out of you two?'

'Josh,' I say without a beat.

Rebecca doesn't look at me when she mutters, 'Yeah, Josh said Josh. Strange.' She raises her voice. 'Okay, next question.'

'Wait . . .' Abi puts up her hand. 'He actually said he was the hotter one? What a fucking knobhead.' She shouts so loud that the elderly woman on the table next to us covers her ears.

'Abi . . .' Rebecca whispers.

'What? It's a knobhead thing to say,' Abi says.

'I agree,' Nina mumbles.

I feel them all waiting for my reaction, but what is there to say when your fiancé tells your best friend he thinks he's hotter than you? I had always known it to be true, but somewhere in me, I've carried a hope that he sees me differently than I see myself. Even so, it seems unnecessarily cruel, very un-Josh-like, to confess this to my best friend.

Nina puts her hand on my arm as a bit of comfort. I feel too embarrassed to talk. I want to forget this moment, even though I am sure it will haunt me forever. I give Nina a reassuring smile and move things along.

'What's the next question?' I ask.

'Who is smarter?' Rebecca says.

'Me.'

'Yes, you.'

'Which is why the promotion makes zero sense, but oh well. Karma is coming,' Nina says.

'What do you mean by karma is coming?' I ask.

Nina raises her eyebrows and smiles to herself. She's definitely up to something.

'Hey! No work talk,' Rebecca demands. 'Okay, what is the best sex position?'

'Missionary?' I guess.

Rebecca sucks some air in. 'Nope. Doggy.'

Doggy? I can't remember the last time he came from behind.

'Surely you guys must be in sync about that stuff now?'

Again, another silence.

'Maybe he likes doggy because he doesn't like looking at my face?' I joke. Nobody laughs. 'Or maybe I—'

I stop talking and almost drop my mug of tea. Linda Butters is in the cafe, coming towards us. What. The. Actual. Fuck.

'Sorry we're late,' Linda says.

'Linda,' I say as I get up and hug her. 'You're here.' I stare at Rebecca behind Linda's back. Rebecca looks at me as if she thought I knew Linda was coming. There was an extra chair at our table, but I didn't think anything of it. In fact, there are *two* spare chairs. Did she say, sorry *we're* late?

'Laura is just parking the car,' Linda says as if reading my mind. Oh, Josh's sister is coming to my hen party too. Isn't that brilliant?

Linda doesn't take long to dominate the conversation with her favourite topic – Josh. She tells us about when he shoved a button up his nose as a toddler. And how he used to eat all his advent calendar chocolates on the first of December. Rebecca keeps adding fuel by asking questions. Nina looks bored as sin, whilst Abi is entertaining herself by cutting a slice of cucumber into tiny pieces. Laura is on her phone as usual. She doesn't want to be here as much as I don't want her to be here. The squeak of Bessy's trolley gives us all a moment of peace from Linda. Bessy takes the empty sandwich plates away and then replaces them with a cake tower. Rebecca is on her phone again.

'If the temperature is not too hot or cold, then put Benson in. Yes, he does cry a lot.'

Abi and Nina are slouched in the yellow chairs, slowly being put to death by Linda as she goes on about Josh's teen era.

'Is that a policeman?' Laura says, interrupting Linda mid-flow.

We all look up and see a policeman in sunglasses, his head inches from the ceiling. His light blue shirt is too small for his muscles, but I'm guessing that's the point. He speaks to Bessy, and she nervously points to our table. Oh no.

'Officer Harry Hung here. I am looking for an Amy Elman,' he says, in a Liverpudlian accent that reminds me of Sporty Spice. He bends his hips forward. 'One of you must be her.'

I hover my hand in the same way my pupils do when they don't want to be noticed.

'Oh, Amy, you've been a bad, bad girl,' he says. 'I'm going to punish you with my baton.' He gets his Bluetooth speaker out from his bag. 'Just give me a second.' He puts it on the table and then tries to connect his phone to it. 'Fuck's sake,' he mutters.

'We really don't have to do this,' I say.

The music begins to play 'SexyBack'. Officer Harry Hung yanks my chair and spins me to face him. Linda makes a little 'Oh' sound. He throws off his sunglasses. He must be about 35. He begins wriggling about, doing that funny roll with his belly. I sit on my hands and try to look at anything else but the thrusting man in my face. All I can focus on are the pictures of dead Larry staring at me. Officer Harry Hung unbuttons his tight light blue shirt, revealing his waxed, tanned, slightly wrinkled four-pack. He takes the shirt off, and I see a snail trail of thick dark hair from his belly button to his belt. Suddenly one leg is up on the chair, and all I see is his bulge. The music stops.

'Oi! You're messing up my act,' the stripper snaps, with his crotch by my mouth. Bessy has the speaker in her hand.

'What is wrong with your generation? So sexual, all the time,' Bessy shouts. We don't reply. 'This is not a whore house. This is *my* cafe. Please take your ... your ... policeman and leave right now.' The elderly customers look horrified; the one who was covering her ears earlier is now covering her eyes.

'Eee ... I thought this was odd,' Officer Harry Hung is frowning at me as if it was my idea for him to strip in an old ladies' cafe, in the middle of the afternoon.

'*You* thought it was odd?' I say.

'The bird who booked me said it would be sound.'

'What bird?' I ask.

'Women are not birds,' Nina shouts across the table.

'I don't know. Lucy? I speak to a zillion women a week.'

'Lace?' I say.

'That's the one.'

I had an idea that this was Lace's doing. I would typically be furious, but Officer Harry Hung has been a blessing in disguise. I don't know how much more Battenberg cake I can stomach, and the tea is not cutting it now that Linda is here. If she insists on talking about the wonders that is Joshua Craig Butters at my hen party, then I will need something a little stronger. Or even better, to go home.

Bessy comes back over with her hands on her hips to hurry us up.

'YES, we're leaving,' Rebecca snaps. We get up, and Tim rings again. As we leave, Bessy makes us apologise to Larry and tells us never to come back to her cafe. That won't be difficult.

We're waiting by the river for Rebecca to finish her phone call. I am now £10 short because Officer Harry Hung guilt-tripped me into tipping him for doing a one-quarter striptease. I told him I had no cash, so he whipped out his card reader. Somehow, I've ended up spending £10 to see a man's belly fluff.

Abi walks in circles to keep warm while Nina and I stand close together. Linda and Laura have an in-depth conversation about Tupperware.

'I may get a circular set of Tupperware,' Laura says.

'It's harder to store than the rectangular set. And if you want to use it for your lunch box, a circular Tupperware is not ideal for sandwiches.' Linda replies. She sounds like she could be talking about something as serious as a cancerous mole.

I zone out as I try to think of ways to escape my own hen party. After the bathroom incident this morning and having Josh admit that he thinks he's more attractive than me, I'm not feeling very bride-to-be-y. I think of that woman on her hen party, Beth, I think her name was, who was pole dancing on the Victoria line. She was on top of the world, glowing with confidence, the way she is supposed to be. She was, after all, about to marry the love of her life. I deserve to feel like that on my hen party – so why don't I? I do the last button up on my coat and hold in my tears.

Rebecca is off the phone and is walking towards us. Something isn't right.

'Benson won't stop wailing. I've never heard Tim sound so stressed. I need to go back.' She looks like she is about to cry herself. 'But guys, please carry on. I have a table booked at Be At One.'

I want to hug Tim for being so useless. 'Please don't worry. I think I'm done anyway,' I say.

'Amy, it's your hen party,' Rebecca says.

'Honestly, I don't feel great.' I rub my stomach. 'Don't think that Battenberg agreed with me.'

Nina and Abi put on a good show of trying to persuade me to stay out, but I can tell they are relieved. Laura, too, seems pleased.

'Ah, shame,' she says and makes a sad face for a second. The only person who is genuinely upset is Linda.

'But we've just got here,' she says, and her Clarks heel does a little stomp. I rub my stomach again to double down on the Battenberg excuse.

LB29

The night of my hen party, I have the house to myself. A chicken pizza with extra cheese is currently being made for me in a place called Red & Yellow Dough in Lavender Hill. Soon, it will be on the back of a stranger's bike and hurtling towards me. I plan to watch *Game of Thrones* and pretend to be disappointed that I'm not at Be At One with Linda.

I take off my purple dress. Josh's laptop is on the bedside table next to our engagement photo. It's screaming at me to open it. I get a flash of what happened this morning. Opening the bathroom door, the laptop crashing on the floor and the look of horror on his face.

No. It would be very, *very* wrong to snoop. I am not that woman. I put on my purple hoodie and star pyjama bottoms. I go to leave the bedroom. I stop at the door. I turn. I grab the laptop. I am that woman.

Logging on is simple: LB29, Linda's initials, and their family house number. The Butters use it for everything in case of an emergency. I don't even know where the spare key to Dad's house is, let alone his passwords.

He has left the internet browser open on Pornhub. The video is paused on a full screen of blurry skin. I press the space bar. A man starts screaming. I hit mute. It goes to a wide angle. A man is naked, leaning across a desk. A tall woman with tattoos all up her arm is behind him, violently thrusting. She's like a gladiator: muscular with jet-black hair, purple lips and over-arched eyebrows. I press unmute. The man is screaming blue murder.

'You're a fucking waste of space, aren't you? Aren't you?' the woman shouts.

'Yes,' the man cries.

I pause it. The title is 'Employee Gets Pegged by Boss'. I slam the laptop closed and push it away. I feel sick.

It was Pete who told us what pegging was. Nina had heard the word and made the mistake of asking him. In graphic detail, he explained it was when a woman uses a dildo on a man. The face he was pulling when he told us about it made it clear this wasn't something he had ever done or wanted to do. I don't remember Josh's reaction, and I don't remember him even being there, probably because we avoid each other's eye contact whenever sex is being spoken about. 'It's a power thing. A humiliating thing.' Pete explained the concept to Nina, who was bewildered by it.

So, that's it. Josh wants to be dominated in the bedroom. He doesn't want a star-patterned-pyjama-wearing teacher who does missionary and thinks doing it in a chair is wild. He wants someone who is more attractive than him. He wants a seductress. Someone who is not me. That's why he hasn't touched me for 213 nights.

I reopen the laptop. His search history shows it's not a one-off. Most days, multiple videos are being viewed, all titled things like, 'Pegging', 'Man Humiliation', and 'Female dominatrix'. How does the boy get time? I click on a video viewed on the day I went cake tasting with his mum. It's in some abandoned car park, and the woman, again, is muscly and dark-haired. The man is naked and on all fours with terror written all over his face like he's about to be killed.

'Tell me your full name and job,' the woman orders. The man says something, but you can't hear it, so she gives him a whack and demands that he says it louder. He screams out in pain. I slam the laptop closed again.

Josh and I once watched porn together; we were drunk at the time, and I told him to show me an example of what he liked. We watched a man and a woman going at it, but it was friendly enough, and everyone seemed to be having a good time. I assumed, going forward, that's the kind of thing he'd be watching, and I didn't mind that. I read a statistic that 80 per cent of men view porn every single week, so I would be naive to think that Josh didn't dabble. BUT THIS? The violence, the frequency, is something I can't get my head around. I don't understand how he hasn't got PTSD from watching it, let alone getting pleasure from it.

I put the laptop back and sit at the end of the bed, staring at it, not sure what to do next. I call Lace. She picks up after three rings.

'Lace, I need your help,' I say.

'Oh, hey.' The low tone of her voice catches me off guard. I'm guessing it's something to do with the Woolly Hat Man.

'Everything okay?'

'Oh, yes, yes. Everything is bright and beautiful.' It sounds forced. I wish she would be more open with me, especially as I weirdly feel I can tell her anything, even if we have only known each other for less than a month.

'No . . . man troubles?' I push. I wish I could directly ask about the Woolly Hat Man, but I can't without revealing that I followed her like a little creep.

'Man?' she says, as if she's never heard of the word.

'Yeah . . . you know, the other type of human.'

'Aren't you supposed to be on your hen party?'

'Well, Officer Harry Hung saved me from a night in Reading with my mother-in-law. Thanks for that, by the way . . .'

'You can always rely on Officer Harry Hung.'

'You can indeed. Look. I called you because . . .' I stop and contemplate how I'm going to say this. I suddenly feel shy and stupid and wonder what came over me to ring her about something so personal.

'Are you still happy that you're getting married to Josh Butters? Because if not, let me know. I'm stitching your wedding dress together right now.'

'I'm happy. I am happy, but . . .' I look at the laptop. 'Here's the thing,' I say, trying to sound light-hearted. 'I've found Josh's porn, and, well, it seems like he has taken to . . . pegging.'

'Pegging?'

'It's when you put the dildo into the man's . . .'

'Bottom. I'm aware.'

'Should I be worried?' I ask.

She exhales. 'Do you want to peg him?' She suddenly sounds very tired.

'Erm, I don't know. Do you think I should?'

'You need to do what you feel comfortable doing.'

'That's very politically correct of you,' I say.

'All I'll say is sex is meant to be a fun and loving way in which humans connect.'

'Let me tell you, the men in the films don't look like they're having fun. You should hear the noises they make. They were like, AHHHHH!'

'Amy. You need to talk to your fiancé about this,' she says firmly.

'Trust me, I would, but I don't know how to talk to Josh about basic sex, let alone . . .'

'Have you got those types of toys?' Lace asks.

'Do you think I should get some toys?'

'If you want toys.'

I groan. Sex is like the arts; there are no wrong or right answers. Nothing is black and white, just a mash-up of emotionally led actions. That's why science is so easy; you do tests, and something is wrong or right.

'I'm sorry to do this, doll, but I need to get on with this dress before the red wine kicks in.' She says, obviously losing all her patience with me. I don't blame her, I'm sick of me too. Here I am, ONCE AGAIN, moaning about my love life when she is going through her own man issues.

'Lace, I'm here if you need to talk about anything.'

'I know. Good night, doll.'

She hangs up.

Petunia

214 Nights

Josh managed to go to the gym today despite his hangover. He came in around 2 a.m., a little drunk but not in the state you would expect a man to be after his stag. While he collapsed into bed and fell into a deep, peaceful sleep, I lay next to him, scared for us. Not only do I now know for certain that my fiancé thinks he's hotter than me, but also, he's been harbouring a pegging fetish. I thought I knew everything about the man I'm about to marry, but apparently, there is still stuff to discover. It's been like finding a room in my own home that I didn't know existed.

'Mum said you went home early from your hen party. Are you okay?' Josh says, bringing me back into the room. We're in the kitchen and he's stirring his protein shake.

His chest is all sweaty, and his tank top is stuck down to show the outline of his new pecs. It was Arm Day today. I can tell because his biceps are more inflated. He can get as toned and muscly as he likes, but the problem still lies under those thin nylon Nike shorts. He downs his shake and leaves it dirty in the sink. 'Why are you staring at me like that?' he asks.

What I want to say is, 'Well, honey. I discovered your pegging fetish last night, and I'm not quite sure what to do about it right now. Do you want me to peg you? Do you want another woman to peg you? Is this deep-rooted issue stemming from your dominant mother that perhaps you need help with?'

I don't say this. 'Sorry. Yes, yes, I'm fine. Just a dodgy Battenberg.'

'Pure sugar.'

'Mmm. Well, we have to go to the florist today,' I say.

'Kick-off is at 3 p.m.'

'Well, we should get going then.'

'I'll get ready. Are you sure you're okay? You look a little . . . vacant?'

'No, no, no. Not vacant.'

'You're overthinking things, I can tell,' he says, laughing.

★

On the Tube, I find out that Linda has told Josh everything about my hen party, including the failed stripper, and how disappointed she was that her evening was cut short.

'She was so disappointed,' Josh says.

'Poor Linda,' I mutter.

We move on to his stag do, which Josh describes as 'a mess'. I am shown a video of Pete singing 'Stacy's Mom' in a neon-lit karaoke bar and then a photo of him taken a few hours later, trying to climb one of the lions in Trafalgar Square. Josh said it was one of the funniest evenings he has had in a long time, and I tried not to be offended by this.

Petunia is Rebecca's recommendation, and it's clear why. It's not one of those Instagram flower shops with flower arches and giant bouquets. Petunia is basic and small, with wooden shelves and buckets of slightly droopy flowers.

'What about lavender?' Josh says as he points to the bucket full of lavender with his foot. 'Grandma's favourite flower. Gramps would be made up.'

'That's nice, but no,' I say and move on. I can't have another element of my wedding dictated by Gramps. The flowers will be my thing (even though I have no idea about flowers).

Some women are obsessed with flowers and know precisely what they like. Mum for instance loved peonies. Dad would get her a bouquet of them for her birthday or whenever he did something wrong – which was often. Even when Dad left Mum for Jean-Ivy, he sent her a bouquet, but that was a big mistake. The flowers ended up torn to shreds and sprinkled over the seats of his Bentley. Dad hated Mum after that, and Mum hated peonies.

Josh doesn't get me flowers. Instead, on Valentine's Day, he gets me a Lindt Christmas reindeer, which he puts a heart sticker on and calls a love horse. It's those things that made me believe he was more innocent than my dad, and therefore safer. But maybe Mum is right when she says that all men are the same.

'These?' I point my foot at a bouquet of a mix of orange roses, white carnations and yellow asters. Below is a sign saying, *'Recommended for the wedding day.'* Josh glances at them for a split second.

'Yeah, alright. So, these will go everywhere?' he asks.

'Yes. They're for decorating the venue and for me to hold when I'm coming up the aisle,' I say tightly.

'Okay. Yeah. Sure,' he says and wanders off. I feel like I could be pointing to a row of cacti, and he would react the same. I crouch down to get a closer look at them, then suddenly I feel a tap on my shoulder, and I turn to see Josh standing over me with a rose in his mouth.

'What are you doing? Where did you get that?' He ignores me, drags me up by my hands, and then adjusts us into a ballroom dance position. 'Josh, what are you doing? Josh? Josh?' He starts pulling me round the shop like we're dancing. The music is not appropriate, but Josh moves as if it's a slow romantic tune. I start to laugh, and his dimples emerge.

'Excuse me,' the shop lady shouts from over her book. Josh stops mid-dance but keeps the rose in his mouth. 'You better be paying for that rose.'

Josh nods, spins me around, and then waltzes me to the counter. He takes the rose out of his mouth and points to the orange flowers.

'I'm terribly sorry,' he says in a fake posh voice. 'I would like this rose and a ghastly amount of your wedding flowers, please.'

I laugh. I love him like this. Silly. Safe.

We leave the flower shop, giggling, with an order for our wedding flowers. On the Tube home we play a game of guess-the-name-of-the-passengers-and-their-coffee-order. Her name is Eloise, and she would order an oat milk flat white. His name is Noah, and he will only drink Americanos. Stupid but riveting fun. We used to do this a lot, making games out of nothing.

We are still joking around as we go through the front door. As we take off our shoes, we lock eyes, and I sense something strange but familiar – that spark. It's right there between us.

This is it. We're going to break our dry spell.

Josh throws his hand in the air and turns away. 'Come on, Man-U!' he shouts and goes into the living room. The football is turned on. I sigh in the empty hallway, then line our trainers up before joining him on the sofa.

It's Manchester United vs Tottenham, and Josh is yelling at the TV as if the referee can hear him. The man in the flower shop is long gone and is now possessed by the FA. He's glaring so intensely at the screen that you would think he was hypnotised by it. I am on the other side of the sofa on my phone. I'm not watching @DrLabby for tips, I am on *Cosmopolitan*'s online sex manual, Sexopedia, researching pegging.

'What's that face for?' Josh asks, I turn and see that he's looking at me from the other side of the couch.

'Nothing. I was just thinking,' I say.

Amy Elman Doesn't Feel Sexy

'Are you looking at new houses again?' he says with an eye roll. Before I can reply, he is back watching the football. 'Fernandes, what the fuck?' he yells at the screen.

I learnt early on in our relationship that trying to have a conversation with Josh during a football match is a complete waste of time. It's like he's going in and out of a parallel universe, and it's completely out of his control. Even when a match is finished, it will take him a minute to be fully present on this planet.

I leave the Sexopedia page and type 'sex therapist in Southwest London'. I'm surprised that there are ten in a five-mile radius alone. The therapists are smiling too hard at the camera, like they enjoy their job a little *too* much. The reality of Josh and me sitting opposite any of them and stumbling through the details of our desires makes me want to cringe into oblivion.

Josh makes an animal noise, and I jump out of my skin. 'What are you doing with your life, Maguire?' His mouth is wide open, and his hands are gripping his hair. Man United are going to lose.

I bookmark a therapist, just in case. Dr Greenwood is an 18-minute walk away and is the only one who's not smiling in her photo, which makes me trust her the most. The whistle blows, Josh throws the cushion across the floor. Manchester has lost 2-1.

Josh and Amy's Wedding 2025

To Do:

Ask Josh if he has any changes to the seating plan.
Go to Lace's for the final fitting of the wedding dress.
Book Velvet Cats.
Lose half a stone so you can pull off your wedding lingerie.
Go to the gym with Josh.
Dye hair back to mousey brown.
Research sex toys.

Tosh

215 Nights

The Wedding Body Blitz Diet hasn't budged a pound off me. Josh is surprised, but that's because he doesn't know how many Maltesers I've been nibbling in my lab. As good as they tasted (like heaven), I realise if I want my partner to want to have sex with me, then I'm going to have to put a bit more effort in. The wedding is two and a half weeks away, so I'm not expecting miracles, but hopefully I can at least look better than I do in my lingerie.

I'm already out of bed, squeezing into an old sports bra when the Apple Radar alarm goes off. Josh is ecstatic when he realises what's happening.

'This is the first day of the rest of your life,' he says, gripping my shoulders.

I gulp. 'It is?'.

Vaux-Box Gym is in the arch of the railway bridge at Vauxhall. The place smells of armpit and is full of people I would dodge in an alley. Josh proudly gives me a tour of the place as if it's his home. It's like every gym; machines, mats and sweat puddles. Across the walls are motivational quotes that I've heard Josh say numerous times. *'A one-hour workout is four per cent of your day'*, *'Only losers quit'*, *'Be stronger than your excuse.'* My favourite is printed above the treadmills, *'If you can dream it, you can do it.'*

'Now for the best part,' Josh says. We're at the back where all the weights and humongous humans are. There is a wall-length mirror with a line of men watching themselves bicep curl. Josh looks tiny compared to them, which explains his obsession with building muscle. It reminds me of the size zero trend, when the older girls at school were supposedly eating less than 500 calories a day. It's sad the pressure we put our bodies under to fit in.

'And this is Tony, my gym partner,' Josh says. It takes me a second to realise who he is talking about, and then it hits me.

'Tony is a woman?' I say slowly.

'Course she's a woman,' Josh laughs as we approach Tony – his female gym partner.

He has mentioned Tony quite a few times over the last year, but either I wasn't paying attention, or he has purposefully not elaborated on who Tony is. 'Tony, Amy. Amy, Tony.'

Tony looks like she could save the world from an apocalypse. She has gelled-back dyed mahogany hair in a high ponytail and high 'don't mess with me' eyebrows. Her tank top reads, WATCH THE SQUAT! On her left shoulder is a coloured peacock tattoo with its feathers spread out across her bicep. Her cycling shorts are stretched over her solid thighs and peachy bottom. Now I understand how she beat Josh at the squat challenge.

She scans me up and down without smiling, and then gives Josh a friendly punch in the arm. 'You soft thing, bringing your fiancée.' Josh flinches from the impact. She then points in my face. 'Are you ready for destruction, Amy?'

'Pardon?'

'It's Amy's first day so she will take it slow,' Josh says, coming to my aid.

Tony shakes her head. 'You know what we say about excuses! Find the heaviest weights you can lift, Amy. LET'S GO, GO, GO!'

I hover by the weight rack. I try a set of 7kg. Nope. Maybe 5kg. Nope. I pick up the 3kg; they're still painfully heavy, but

I guess if I want to change my body in under three weeks, I'm going to have to endure it. Josh and Tony have already started when I get back. They are standing side by side, curling in sync. I stand next to Josh and join in with their rhythm. I look over to Tony lifting her 10kg weights as if they are toilet rolls.

'Are you okay with those?' Josh asks, inspecting me in the reflection.

'Of course,' I say through breaths. I try to make it look effortless, even though my arms are being torn at the seams.

'TWENTY!' Tony suddenly shouts. And they both drop to the floor and start doing press-ups. I get into a 'woman' press-up position and slowly press down, like an elderly chicken pecking at crumbs. Tony counts faster as they press up and down at lightning speed. '18 . . . 19 . . . 20. Done.' They're back on their feet.

I wobble up. The exercise has now changed. They're now opening and closing their arms with the weights in each hand. I try and copy them, but it's impossible.

'I'm so weak,' I laugh, hoping to get an ounce of support from Josh, but he's too focused on his reflection to notice me.

'Go down a weight,' Tony demands, her arms flying in and out. I go to pick up the 2kg weights. By the time I return, they've changed the exercise to tricep dipping without weights. 'Sorry, Amy, the Tosh train is a fast one to board,' Tony says with a straight face as she dips up and down.

Did she say Tosh train? What's a Tosh train? Oh, Tony and Josh. It's their names merged, like Brangelina. Is this typical for gym partners?

I go close to Josh on the bench and start dipping up and down with him.

'My arms are going to fall off,' I say jokingly in his ear. Again, he doesn't say anything. It's as bad as when I'm trying to talk to him while football is on. I try again. 'No wonder your muscles are so—'

'Thirty!' Tony yells, and they're back on the floor doing press-ups. I don't even try to do 30; I barely do 5, and that's on my knees. Tony counts to 30, and they're back on their feet.

'Round two!' Tony screams.

'Round two!' Josh repeats.

I pick up the weights and feebly join the Tosh train for round two. They're no longer concerned that I'm not keeping up. It reminds me of those dark days of the beep test in PE. Rebecca and I were always the first out.

Finally, after three rounds, it comes to an end. I collapse onto the mat, trying to catch my breath. Josh nods at me to see if I'm okay. I manage to give him a thumbs up for a microsecond. He turns to Tony, who is inspecting her arm, twisting it around.

'Did you hurt it?' Josh asks as he puts his sweaty hand on her sweaty peacock tattoo.

'No. I'm still sore from yesterday,' she says. 'Just need to add extra—'

'Protein,' Josh says, finishing her sentence.

'Exactly.'

They share a smile.

'Workout rundown time?' Josh says.

'Workout rundown time,' Tony repeats. And they begin reviewing the last hour in painful detail, of how they could improve and how they have progressed. They are both so eager that they keep talking over one another. Meanwhile, I'm lying flat on the mat nearby, feeling like a third wheel to my fiancé. I'm waiting for the jealousy to hit me, but I'm far too distracted by how passionate Josh is right now. His hands are animated, and his voice has this authoritative tone as he instructs Tony about her curling technique. You could be fooled into thinking he's talking about something that actually matters. I will never understand his love for this place, like he will never understand my love for astronomy. I guess we're just very different like that.

I finally peel myself off the mat and hobble over to them. Tony seems marginally disappointed to have me back alive, but she welcomes me anyway with a playful smack on the back.

'Good effort, Ames!' I jolt forward from the power.

'Thanks,' I say. I try to slap her arm, but my body has turned to jelly, so I end up stroking the peacock instead. 'Um, we've got to go, Josh, we'll be late for work.'

'Eurgh, work,' he grunts.

'Are you going to come back tomorrow?' Tony asks me, more concerned than encouraging. She needn't be worried, there is no way I'll be returning. I know I need to change my body, but I'll just eat less Maltesers and squat . . . occasionally. Nothing is worth this torture.

'Ha. I think I've reached my final destination – I won't be reboarding the Tosh train.'

Josh doesn't laugh, nor does Tony. Geez, they really need to chill out. Tony grabs my shoulders and looks me in the eye.

'Change starts at the end of your comfort zone, Amy,' she says. And that is all the motivation I need to know that I am never coming back here again.

Bunsen Burner

The whole school has been evacuated. We are all standing on The Common as they try and stop the fire alarm. Turns out, Mr Rawlinson was reading a book over a Bunsen burner. If it hadn't been for the lab technician saving the day, Josh's prediction about Mr Rawlinson burning the school down would have come true. The lab technician ran in with a bucket of water, but by that point, the alarms were triggered, and now we're waiting in zero degrees, without coats, whilst the maintenance team try and turn it off. Josh keeps the pupils warm by making them do jumping jacks.

'One, two, three, four . . .' he chants as they all jump in sync. I don't join in, because I physically can't move my body after this morning's torture, but I am getting my class to shout out the periodic table at me as they jump about. I feel a tap on my shoulder and turn to see Dr Therone.

'My office. 1 p.m.' She struts away. This is it – my chance. She has finally realised that Mr Rawlinson is not fit enough for the head of the department. The fire alarm suddenly stops, and the whole school cheers.

At exactly 1 p.m., Dr Therone calls out from the other side of the door. I come in with the confident stride I learnt from @DrLabby and sit on the familiar low chair on the other side of the desk.

'We've received a complaint from a parent. Can you guess why?'

I frown and shake my head in bewilderment.

'Beatrice's parents. Something about you doing some birth control project for the science contest. I said to them, no, not Miss Elman, she's doing plastic in the ocean. She wouldn't dream of doing something so inappropriate.' She raises her eyebrows at me. Oh God. I feel my pulse in my throat. She sits back in her giant chair.

'Um, the girls wanted to explore it. They were passionate about—'

She slaps a hand on the desk, making me jump.

'Of course the girls wanted to explore it. They're 15 – they thrive on being controversial. That's why you're here, as an adult, as their teacher, so that you can tell them no.'

I feel shaky and teary. I've never been good at being told off.

'But you said plastic in the ocean was boring,' I remind her. She scrunches her hands into tight fists. I think she may punch me.

'Miss Elman, I will pick boredom over embarrassment any day,' she snaps and takes a deep breath. 'Now you are going to do this science contest on plastic in the ocean like a normal teacher.'

My stomach drops. Not just because I think the presentation we have is so good that it could win, but also because, for the first time ever, the girls have worked their arses off. They're going to be gutted.

'Dr Therone, the girls have worked so hard—'

'I don't care.'

'There is no way we can prep another presentation in two days.'

'You should have thought about that before you let a bunch of teenagers influence you into doing a presentation about birth control, in front of all the schools in London. Now go and fix this mess.'

Tampons
217 Nights

I peek from the wings of the Royal Festival Hall, and my heart thumps. Sitting directly at the front is a line of five stern judges from Imperial College, viciously writing notes. Behind them are rows and rows of restless teenagers in different coloured uniforms. This is the eighth presentation of the day – it's on chemicals in denim and is being presented by a stuttering group of boys and girls from Richmond College. So far, every presentation has been about the environment in some form or another, probably because it's relevant . . . and appropriate.

'Miss Elman, are we next?' I hear a whisper and turn. Ophelia, the student whose idea this was, is behind me with an eager smile. She is dressed as a human-sized tampon. Her head, arms and legs are sticking out from a white cotton tube that even has a string attached to it. I had heard that Daisy was good at textiles, but even so, our costumes are extremely impressive for a 15-year-old girl. Behind Ophelia are Beatrice and Arabella in identical tampon costumes. Beatrice spirals in circles, repeating her lines, while Arabella films herself talking to her followers.

'We are,' I say tensely. The reality of what I'm doing is suddenly hitting me, and I'm beginning to regret it.

I tried to revive the plastic in the ocean presentation after the meeting with Dr Therone. I was in my lab making a new slide show and writing a half-arsed script when Nina came in.

Amy Elman Doesn't Feel Sexy

She saw me frazzled, surrounded by textbooks and printouts. She thought I was losing the plot. I told her what happened, and her response was, 'Dr Therone should go fuck herself', before convincing me that this wasn't just a science contest but a platform for freedom of speech, and if I was to silence a group of young women for talking about something so natural, then what kind of teacher would that make me? I'd never seen her so passionate for my subject before. I had to listen.

'Please welcome to the stage, Clapham High for Girls,' the host announces. That's us. Oh crap. Oh crap. Oh crap. My three menstrual-clad pupils wobble past me and onto the stage before I can say anything else. The tired audience's applause turns to laughter and gasping. At least they're not being booed. I try to take a breath to calm myself down, but there seems to be no oxygen around me. The girls stand in line under the stage lights and wait for the audience to settle down, and then, oh-so-coolly, Arabella begins.

'The menstrual cycle can be funny, it can be embarrassing and disgusting, but above all, it is nature, and around 50 per cent of this room experiences it first-hand.' Her voice commands the audience, and they are silent. She's got them. The first slide appears on the big screen behind them. 'THE PILL AND HOW IT AFFECTS US'.

Beatrice goes next to explain the nitty-gritty facts about the menstrual cycle. On the screen is a video showing the egg leaving an ovary and floating down the fallopian tube, like a ball in a pinball machine. 'And this brings us to . . .' Beatrice says, and then as rehearsed, Ashwini comes onto the stage, dressed in a round pink fluffy costume, with 'The Pill' written on her front and back. Again, I'm very impressed by Daisy's work. Ashwini waits for the audience to stop laughing and then introduces herself.

'Hi, I'm The Contraceptive Pill, and I have been around since the 1960s. I gave women sexual freedom; it meant they could finish their degrees without risking an unwanted pregnancy and have careers. Because of me, they could take control of their lives and not be at the mercy of biology. I am the greatest thing that has ever happened to women.'

'Hold on there, Pill,' Ophelia says. 'You haven't been *that* great to women, have you?' She then changes the slide to a photo of a brain. 'New research says that women on the Pill can have a blunted cortisol response to stress. What does this mean? Well, cortisol is the hormone that helps us deal with stress. If your teacher gives you a test at the last minute, or you fall out with your best friend, you probably will get a little stressed out and the cortisol helps you cope with it. So, for us to mess with this natural chemistry could negatively affect women.'

I spot the woman judge raising her eyebrows and then scribbling something down. I can't tell whether she's impressed or disgusted. Arabella then takes over.

'There have been studies to show that when a woman is ovulating, they are subconsciously attracted to men with thicker jawlines and deeper voices.' Timothée Chalamet comes onto screen. A few girly 'woos' come from the audience. 'So, you could think you're attracted to this guy whilst on the Pill, when in fact . . .' The slide changes to a picture of Paul Mescal. 'Off the Pill, you could like this guy.' The audience woos louder. I peer around to recheck the judge's faces. Nothing. I bite my nails. Beatrice is next with the physical risks, and I find myself mouthing along to her script about blood clots. She was nervous about this part but is doing it flawlessly, not one word out. She subtly turns to me as soon as she finishes, and I give her a thumbs up.

Arabella takes the mic back for the finish. 'We're 15-year-olds, and it's not uncommon for our GP to put us on the Pill for medical reasons or to prevent unwanted pregnancies, but it's scary to think that there's still not enough research into the actual long-term effects on our brains. This is why we propose that the funds go towards more awareness in this area. Most of us will be offered the Pill at some point in our lives or have a loved one who will be. What a privilege to have this freedom, but to *truly* have freedom, we should know exactly what we're putting into our bodies.'

I didn't realise how tight I was clenching my arms until the applause erupts. It's a huge applause. The biggest of the day by far. I unravel myself and clap. It's over. It's done. The girls are bowing. I breathe. The rest of the class is on their feet, cheering in the audience. A group of girls behind them stand up too, and then a group to the right, and then a few random people also rise to applaud. Arabella, Beatrice, Ashwini and Ophelia bow one more time and then come bouncing off the stage. I find myself breaking all professional barriers and squeezing each one of them.

There is one more presentation on BPA in cans by Ealing Boys School. I haven't heard a word from them after I sent my job application, so I can only assume they've rejected me. Perhaps it's for the best. If we win this competition, I won't need a new job because Dr Therone will be eating out of my palm.

The Ealing Boys teacher is a lanky man, around mid-thirties, wearing glasses and a beige wool suit. He is hovering next to me, biting his nails very loudly. He should be nervous – their presentation is boring as hell compared to ours. I hope he regrets rejecting me.

The boring BPA presentation finishes and is met with tired applause. We are sent out for a 20-minute tea and biscuit break as the judges deliberate the winner.

The class are on a high and want a photo, so we go outside by the river. They insist I should also be in it too, so I hand my phone to a stranger and stand in the middle of them all. I've never had a candid photo with the pupils before. I send Josh the one of us jumping, with a message saying:

> **Waiting for results but the girls were AMAZING. I ♥ my job!**

He thought I had lost my mind to go against Dr Therone, that I was making life difficult for myself. He doesn't understand, though, that my job is already difficult. I don't have the luxury of walking into work, doing the bare minimum and then being rewarded. I used to resent it, but if I had it as easy as Josh, I wouldn't have pushed myself out of my comfort zone. And because of that, I now have a class of 15-year-old girls jumping with excitement over a subject they once detested. I always thought teaching was about getting the highest grades from my pupils, but that doesn't even come close to seeing Arabella today – she'll never admit it, but it is clear how much effort she has put in. She made that presentation what it was. I may have lost my mind, but if that makes me a better teacher, so be it.

We are called back into the main hall for the results. The host appears on stage – a shiny man in a lab coat. He sees himself as a showman, even though he's just presenting a schools science contest. Fair enough. Go big or go home.

'Ladies and gentlemen, today has been a whirlwind of knowledge and inspiration brought to us by the youth of this city. The panel of judges from Imperial College want to thank you for your time and energy; they have thoroughly enjoyed each one of your presentations, even the more . . . controversial ones.' The audience chuckles a little. I hope he doesn't mean us. 'I know it's been a long day so I'm going to read out the results. If you hear your school's name, please come up to the stage. So, here we go. The results for the London Science Awareness Contest 2025 . . .' I grab the two hands closest to me, Arabella's and Beatrice's. 'In third place is salmon farms by Brixton Boys.' There is a rumble of applause as Brixton Boys come up to the stage.

'Second place is Joseph's House, with their fabulous presentation on wind energy. And first place . . .' Arabella squeezes my hand so tight that it hurts. 'Ealing Boys on their spectacular pitch on BPA in cans.'

What? No. How? Their presentation put the hall to sleep! The girls look as surprised and deflated as I am. I tell them to keep applauding, though. We are not bad losers – even if the winners were crap.

As we leave the Royal Festival Hall, I decide I must be diplomatic.

'Right, girls, meeting by the books under the bridge,' I say. When they're all in front of me, I notice the teacher in glasses from Ealing Boys watching me from afar; I turn away, so he's not in my eyeline, and begin.

'Girls, science is not about winning money. It's about looking at the world around you and putting it to the test. You did that today. You bravely questioned how science is affecting you personally, and for that, you are winners. I, for one, have never been so proud, and I . . .' I'm going to cry. I take a breath, and the girls let out an 'Aww'. 'I want to thank you for teaching me how to be a teacher. Ophelia, without you putting your hand up in the first place, we wouldn't be here. Beatrice, you might have the best work ethic I have ever seen, and I hope you can use that to do exactly what *you* want in life.' Beatrice smiles. She knows what I'm saying. 'Daisy, one day you'll win an Oscar for your costume designs. And Arabella . . .' I notice she's filming, but I don't care. 'Arabella, you're a challenging woman, but it's challenging women who have made some of the best scientific discoveries, so keep being challenging. And that goes for all of you, whether in science or in life, keep questioning the world. The world needs your questions.'

The girls start applauding. Who cares about weddings and countryside cottages? This moment, right now, is what life is about. 'Hot chocolate?' I shout over the applause, and the girls start cheering. Above their heads, I see the Ealing Boys teacher walking away with a smirk on his face.

I should have known they wouldn't stick with hot chocolate; we have caused chaos in Starbucks with Frappuccinos, coffees, teas, oat milk, almond milk, caramel syrup . . . The girls take more selfies, videos and group photos as we wait.

'Miss Elman,' Daisy says, suddenly at my side, looking sheepish. 'I didn't make the costumes.'

'I thought they looked very professional. Who made them then? Your mum?' It was then, and only then, that I recognise the red garment covers over the costumes.

'Your friend, Lace.'

'How on earth . . .' I say, not angry, just very confused.

Daisy begins to talk very quickly. 'I was talking outside the gates with Ophelia, and she was in her sunglasses reading *Vogue*, like, the actual magazine, so I knew she must have been around your age. She overheard me talking about the science contest and how worried I was about the costumes and said she'd help me. And before I knew it, she dropped all these costumes off at school.' She cowers as if I'm about to lose my head. 'Are you mad?'

I laugh. 'No. I'm not mad.'

'Daisy! Miss Elman! Come here, you need to be in this,' Arabella yells out. The class are posing again for another photo. We go over and join them. 'Ready,' Arabella shouts.

I think of Lace sitting in her studio, stitching giant tampon costumes. I laugh out loud as the camera snaps.

Sofa

218 Nights

I'm walking to my lab with a new box of magnets that I'm excited to try with my Year 8 class.

The week is off to a good start. Our to-do list for the wedding is almost all ticked off. We just need to confirm the guests and book the band. Saturday is the wedding dress fitting and I'm looking forward to it much more than I did my hen party. At least there is no threat of Linda or Officer Harry Hung being there.

The doors at the end of the corridor fly open, and Dr Therone comes strutting towards me. She looks fired up like she is heading into battle. She points her finger at me.

'My office, now.'

This can't be good.

I sit on the chair at her desk, twisting my hands together in anticipation of Dr Therone's arrival. The door slams.

'Have you lost your mind?' Dr Therone yells. I take a wild guess that this is about the science contest, but just in case, I play dumb.

'What do you mean?'

'The Pill, at a science contest for 15-year-old girls! Miss Elman, I specifically told you not to do it. I have never been so disrespected in my whole career. You have embarrassed the school, me, and most of all, you have humiliated yourself. Are you trying to sabotage your career? Is that what this is about? Because you didn't get your promotion, so now you're throwing your toys around like a pathetic child?'

I swear it isn't legal for a boss to talk to an employee like this.

'No, I wasn't doing anything purposefully controversial. The Pill is just science, and the girls were so passionate about it. Dr Therone, if you could have seen how well they did . . .'

'Science? Wasn't there a photo of the kid from *Dune* in the presentation?'

'It's not like that . . .'

'And if they did *so well*, why didn't they win the money?'

'It shouldn't be about winning . . .'

Dr Therone growls in the air, making me jump out of my skin. She catches her breath, leans over her desk and says, 'Miss Elman, you are suspended with immediate effect.'

I shoot up.

'You can't be serious?'

'When have I ever joked?' she says, then points to the door. 'You need to leave the premises now. George will show you out.' I turn around and jerk at the sight of George, the 100-year-old school gardener, hunched by the door, ready to escort me.

'This is a bit over the top, don't you think?' I say.

'George can you . . .' Dr Therone waves her hand at me like I'm a bag of rubbish that needs to be disposed of. George tries to usher me out, but I tell him I'll do it myself, and I walk out of the building.

I get on my bike, my heart thumping. *Suspended?* I never do anything wrong. I would be crying if I wasn't so angry about the injustice of it all. I look back at the school building, push down on the pedals and wonder how I will explain this to Josh.

*

'Suspended?' Josh says, standing over me. I've been a lump on the sofa since 10 a.m. 'I told you not to listen to Nina.' He still has his backpack on and looks more distressed than when I caught him masturbating in the bathroom. I frown at him.

'That's not helpful,' I say. 'Besides, Dr Therone is wrong. There is nothing taboo about—'

Josh butts in. 'Fifteen-year-olds talking about birth control in a public competition? Amy . . .' He says my name like I'm crazy. I pretend to watch *Friends* even though it's been muted. Rachel, Monica and Phoebe are sitting in wedding dresses, eating popcorn.

'What are you going to do?'

'Well. It's not all that bad. At least I have time now to do the last bits for our wedding. This afternoon I booked Velvet Cats.' It was Josh's one and only job to book the wedding band and he knows it too. He looks away from me, feeling that back foot.

'Oh, right. Yeah. Well. Thanks for doing that. I completely forgot,' he mumbles.

'They're happy to play a general wedding playlist for us and do requests. I have also emailed The Chipping Barn and given them the final number, 55. Uncle Clarke and Aunt Margaret can't come. Oh, and I'm uninviting Dr Therone, obviously.'

'Okay, fine,' Josh says. 'But, wedding aside. What happens if you get fired?'

I bite my lip, contemplating if I should say it now or save it for when things are less heated. Josh reads my face like a book.

'What is it?' he says.

'So, I may have another job . . .' I thought if I said it quietly, it would make my revelation a little less shocking, but Josh's eyes have bulged out of his face, so I don't think my theory has worked.

'Huh? How?' He's almost yelling.

'Ealing Boys School want to interview me. They were at the science contest and thought I would be a good fit.' It was a half truth – there's no reason why he should know that I sent my application off beforehand.

The phone call came this afternoon. The man introduced himself as the one who was 'spying on me at the science contest'. His name is Alex, he's the biology teacher at Ealing Boys, and he bumbled through how he saw my application before the competition and was observing me from afar. Not that far, I thought to myself. He told me he was 'blown away by my passion for the subject and the rapport I had with my pupils'. They want to interview me in two weeks' time.

Josh dumps himself onto the sofa next to me in a daze.

'You can't go . . .' he says, suddenly sounding like a boy whose mother is leaving him.

'I may not have a choice.'

'How would that even work? You'll have to commute to the other side of London. We'll never see each other.'

'We'll have to commute from the countryside soon anyway, either that or find a local school to work at.' Josh sulkily rolls his head. 'What?' I ask.

'You're obsessed with the countryside,' he says, staring at the ceiling.

'I thought we were both obsessed with the countryside. Isn't that the whole point of everything?'

'Yeah . . .'

'Josh, if you don't want to move out of London, say now . . .'

'I do. I do,' he mutters. He plays with the tatty pillow, pulling the zip back and forth.

'It's been the plan for years . . .'

'Yeah, I know. It will be great. Don't worry.'

There is a long silence as I watch him play with the zip. 'Well, I may not get the job at Ealing,' I say. I look back at

Friends. Rachel has just opened the door to Joshua in her wedding dress. He looks terrified as he runs away.

'I hope not. Who would I sit next to at lunch? And what about the fish? They will die without you,' Josh says in a childlike tone. I laugh. 'I don't want you to go.'

'Well, hopefully, it won't come to that.'

I'm lying. That phone call from Alex made me realise just how desperate I am to move away from Clapham High, Dr Therone and even Josh to some extent. Even if I don't get the job at Ealing, I know now I can't go back.

Debbie Harry

219 Nights

I'm spending my first full morning of suspension researching Ealing – just out of curiosity. Ealing is the greenest borough of the city, apparently. Abi lives there too, so it will be nice to have a glass of wine with her after work – that is, if I get the job. What I learnt in the last month is to not get your hopes up before an interview.

Fifi comes into the living room wearing a tiny pink dressing gown. It's 1 p.m. She takes out a Heinz Cream of Tomato soup.

'I didn't realise you were at home,' I say, trying to fill the silence.

'You know what baffles me?' she snaps. Crap – she must know about the two slices of bread that I took from her Hovis loaf. 'You still haven't invited me to your wedding.'

For a moment, I'm taken aback. I never thought to invite Fifi because, well, I don't really know her. This is odd considering we have lived together for over a year, but it's the truth. All I can say about her is that she's an introvert who likes canned soup and gets paid to eat in her pants. That's it.

'I didn't think you would want to come.'

'Everyone wants to go to a wedding. It's the only opportunity to meet people when you're in your thirties.'

'You're in your thirties?'

'I'm 35.'

'You look great,' I say, surprised. I always thought she was younger than me. This Heinz diet is a miracle.

'I'm 35, not 45.' She throws the soup lid into the recycling bin.

'You can come to our wedding,' I say, even though I have no clue what I would do with Fifi there. Where would I even sit her? She makes a little 'Hmm' sound as if not completely satisfied with my invitation. She puts the soup into the microwave without another word. Assuming the conversation is done, I turn back to my phone.

'And you know another thing that bothers me,' Fifi shouts, holding up her knife with a chunk of butter on it.

'No,' I say, not caring.

'Why don't you guys fuck?'

My jaw drops.

'Excuse me?' Maybe I haven't heard her right.

'You haven't fucked in an excruciatingly long time.' She licks butter off her finger.

'We fuck,' I say defensively. The microwave beeps.

'No, you don't, and you need to do something about it. I'm getting sick of him hogging the bathroom to wank. Oh, and stop stealing my bread,' she says, then flees the kitchen with her soup and toast, leaving me flabbergasted.

*

In the afternoon, I receive an ominous text from Dad.

> **Hi Amy. Are you around after work?**
> **Jean-Ivy and I have a gift for you.**

> **Yes. After 5pm.**

> **Good. Meet Pink Bar Maddox Street 6pm?**

> **Ok.**

I would usually think of any old excuse not to see Dad and Jean-Ivy, but after the bizarre exchange with Fifi, I'm keen to get out of the house. I put my work clothes on and take my empty work bag with me. If Dad found out his daughter was not just a teacher but a suspended teacher, it could trigger a heart attack. We have our differences, but I'd like to keep him around.

Everything in the Pink Bar is pink: the chairs, the walls, the glasses, the feathered chandeliers, the carpet, the candles, and even the servers are dressed head to toe in bubblegum pink. Dad and Jean-Ivy are sitting at the bar. Dad looks like a rain cloud in Barbie World. Jean-Ivy, draped in a red cloth, has one hand on my dad's thigh, the other holding a champagne glass. Classic.

'Your hair. It's so . . . dark,' Jean-Ivy says, in a non-complimentary way. She wraps her wiry arms around me, and her rings and bracelets press into my back like tiny daggers. She lets go eventually, and I get my oxygen back. 'Sit here, little Amy,' she says, pointing to the pink, fluffy bar stool beside her. 'Champagne? Yes, champagne.' She clicks the bartender for service. 'Isn't this place adorable?'

'Yes. Adorable,' I say, staring at the portrait paintings of pigs in suits on the wall.

'How's work?' Dad asks.

'Great. Very productive.'

'Did you get that promotion?' he says, forgetting that he had disparaged this promotion only a few weeks ago.

'No.'

'Oh, I thought it was a done deal?'

'A man who has been at the school for longer got it in the end. A bit of a stitch-up, really.' I have figured out the best approach when dealing with Dad's expectations and inevitable disappointment is to blame the system.

'Stay there for another 20 years and then hopefully they will give you the next one,' Dad responds in his favourite condescending tone that scratches on me. I want to go home now.

'So, you mentioned something about a gift...'

'Yes.' Jean-Ivy claps. 'But first, let me show you our photos of Barbados.'

A champagne glass is put in front of me, and I drink half of it as Jean-Ivy gets out her phone. She shows me a photo of her first-class seat, the piña coladas that were served in pineapples, a grinning waiter whose name they have forgotten now, a blurry sunset and my half-naked dad stooped in a pool, his grey furry belly sticking out of the water.

'Looks delightful,' I say.

'Jeany, we've got a reservation. Let's just get on with the surprise,' Dad says.

'Is it a trip to Barbados?' I joke.

They don't laugh. Jean-Ivy theatrically gets up, goes to the side of the bar and lifts a black guitar-shaped case. Oh God, no. That better not be...

'As an early wedding present, I want you to have my signed Debbie Harry guitar.' Her eyes well up as she hands the guitar over.

I narrow my eyes. You've got to be kidding me. The 'signed' guitar that Dad's been trying to get rid of from his lounge for the last eight years. It's not even signed by Debbie Harry – we've repeatedly cross-referenced the autograph with ones from Google Images – but Jean-Ivy is dying on that hill, insisting it was Blondie in that club toilet in 1978. How do I leave this place without taking it home?

'I couldn't take that from you, Jean-Ivy. I can't even tap my fingers in a rhythm. You should give it to Woody; he's in a band, and he's your family,' I say in my pathetic voice. I know Woody won't take it because he also knows that it wasn't Debbie Harry.

'We may not be family in blood. But in here . . .' She taps her heart. 'Here, you are my family.' Dad puts his arm around his second wife.

'You're very much our family, Jeany,' he says.

'The thing is,' I try again. 'I have nowhere to put something *so* valuable. I would hate for it to be damaged.'

Dad jumps in. 'I'm sure you'll find space, Amy.' And he pulls that non-negotiable face of his. The one that I'm still marginally scared of, despite being a fully grown woman who pays her rent and has endured two smear tests.

Still, I try. 'I really can't take . . .'

'Amy,' Dad snaps. He crosses his arms and frowns at me like I'm a kid who has forgotten their manners. I want to fight my corner, but it will be easier to take the guitar now and find a way to get rid of it than to keep arguing with Dad when he's in this mood. Heck, perhaps I could sell it on Vinted and use the money for a telescope.

'Thank you. That's very generous of you,' I mumble. Dad excuses himself to the toilet. I catch him smirking to himself as he walks away. Bloody swindler.

Jean-Ivy turns towards me. 'So, Amy. I need to ask about the seating plan at your wedding. I presume I'm sitting next to your father?'

I take another gulp of my champagne and pray that Dad will be quick. She wouldn't ask me this if he were here.

'You'll be really near him,' I say.

'On the same table?'

'In the same room.'

She pinches her mouth.

'So, I'm not on the top table?'

'You're on the front table, the closest to the top table.' I wish Dad would hurry up.

'And so, Robert will be on the top table with your mum?' she says fiercely. I want to tell her that, if it was up to me, I would have all the bridesmaids on the top table and all the parents together on a table inside a soundproof transparent box.

'Josh is keen to keep it traditional,' I say.

'Traditional. Right. Well, I'm sure Charlotte will enjoy herself,' she says with gritted teeth. She takes her glass in a very stiff hand and sips the champagne. I'm surprised that the flute doesn't crack in two.

'Jean-Ivy, I'm hoping we can all put the drama aside for my wedding,' I say.

'It's not me,' she squeals, but then Dad appears, and she instantly switches back to being delightful. Sometimes, I wonder if she is doing what Mum did – playing a role. Maybe it's something all wives do.

'Jeany, we've got to get to the restaurant now,' Dad says, tapping his watch. 'Look after that guitar, Amy.' He pats me on the back. 'Come on, Jeany.' Jean-Ivy stands and adjusts her dress.

'I'll see you tomorrow,' she says.

'Tomorrow?'

'Your wedding dress fitting, darling.' She's mirroring my confused expression.

My stomach drops. NO. NO. NO. Lace, what have you done?

'You're coming to that too?' I blurt out.

'Poor lamb, you must be exhausted,' she says as her cold hand slips down the side of my head. 'Yes, I'm coming. I paid for the dress, didn't I?' Dad pulls her arm. 'Yes, Bobby, okay. The table hasn't got a time bomb on it.' They leave arm in arm through the pink bar.

This is terrible. I call Lace, but she doesn't answer. What was she thinking? I knew Mum was coming, but not Jean-Ivy. They cannot be in her tiny studio together. It's risky enough to have them in the same barn on my wedding day. I'm still not convinced there won't be blood on the dance floor by the end of the night. I down my champagne, haul the guitar onto my back and leave the bar.

The Big Purple Pleasure

I carry on trying to ring Lace as I make my way up Oxford Street. Josh is doing an evening HIIT class with Tony tonight, and I'm not in a rush to go home to Fifi after her earlier comments. What does she know, anyway? She hasn't had any relationships since I've known her; the odd person stays the night, but we never see them. It's easy-peasy to keep the passion alive for a day, a month, even a year, but after 10 years, it can feel like trying to keep a flower alive in the desert. As I think this, I stop at the window of Thrills & Frills. There are two mannequins dressed as sexy nurses. The sign reads, 'Cure his winter cold tonight, ladies!' I walk in.

I'm barely in the shop when I hear Gemma, the assistant. 'Oh, it's you! I'm dying to know, did the red work its magic?'

'It did,' I lie. She claps and looks genuinely happy for me. If only she knew.

'So, what's it today? A nurse outfit? Perhaps something for the honeymoon?' she asks. I look around and find I'm surrounded by people checking out the lingerie. Friday night – I suppose they're all getting set for a weekend of excellent sex. I lean into Gemma with my hand half covering my mouth. 'Do you have any strap-ons?'

'STRAP-ONS, YOU SAY? Oh, you're in for A TREAT!'

I follow Gemma sheepishly through the shop. The guitar on my back is bashing the racks of bras and pants. Gemma stops at the toy section. It turns out dildos come in many shapes, colours and sizes. She holds a huge bright purple one in the air called 'The Big Purple Pleasure'.

'This one is your best friend,' she says. 'It has a wireless remote, seven vibration modes, and veins.' She runs her fingers across it, as if exhibiting a prize on a game show.

'Do they like . . . veins?'

'Oh God, yeah! My boyfriend loves veins,' she says with big, wild eyes. I have an unwelcome vision of Gemma.

'Do a lot of women . . . you know?' I do a subtle thrust.

She laughs loudly. So loudly. 'Oh, honey, we're all at it.'

And with that, another £60 investment is made to get my sex life back.

*

I lie it on the bed. It looks ridiculous; a bright purple rubber penis attached to a black bungee harness. I turn it over: *Made in China*. Homo sapiens have come a long way from humping each other in their caves to making plastic genitals in factories and shipping them overseas for other Homo sapiens' pleasure.

'It's just a toy, Amy,' I reassure myself, and put one leg in the strap, then the other, tightening it around my hips. My wool dress rises and sticks out in weird places. The weight feels so alien. I bounce and it wobbles. Is this what men feel like all the time? I walk over to the mirror and confirm what I thought would be true – I don't look sexy, I look bizarre. The wool dress is not helping, but I can't see how being nude will improve the situation. I stand to the side to get a profile view of a thrust. Slow at first, and then gradually faster, and the dildo bounces and shakes as I move. I press a button on the remote, and The Big Purple Pleasure comes alive. A loud vibrating buzz tingles up my body. It feels strangely and shamefully nice. I press another button; the vibration gets harder. Harder again. Then, like Christmas lights, the vibrations form different patterns – long and slow to intense, rapid pulses. I press through them all until it goes off. I need some help. I get out my phone and search for a video on Josh's favourite porn site. I remember one was called 'Wife Finds Out Husband Is Cheating and Punishes Him'. I liked that this couple were at least married, unlike the other videos, which seem to have a lot of inappropriate dynamics.

I find it and press play. Here we go. The wife appears in a strap-on, yelling at her husband to 'Shut the fuck up'. I rewind it and examine her movements, mimicking her as if Josh is bent over the bed. I watch the rhythm of her thrusts – very hard and fast. Her husband is wailing with distress, so I think I'll go for a gentler approach to begin with. I assume yelling degrading words is part of the pegging experience.

'FUCK YOU, USELESS PUSSY. WHAT ARE YOU? SAY IT. SAY IT,' she shouts. I mouth the words along with her, then I whisper them, and now I'm yelling them. It's strangely therapeutic to yell out 'Useless pussy'. I reckon it could solve the big divorce issue.

'PUSSY MAN! PUSSY MAN! PUSSY MAN,' I yell.

'Amy? Amy? Can I use your knife again?' It's Fifi in the hallway. I trip on the bed.

'Yes, Fifi. Yes,' I call back. I throw off The Big Purple Pleasure and hide it amongst my knitwear.

Josh and Amy's Wedding 2025

To Do:

Chase Josh about the seating plan.
Go to Lace's for the final fitting of the wedding dress.
Dye hair back.
Peg Josh (???).

Wonderwall

220 Nights

Josh is on the bed poorly strumming 'Wonderwall'; like the rest of the white male population, he stopped learning the guitar after this one song. I, meanwhile, am rummaging through my drawer, trying to find a single pair of matching socks. Lace never called me back, so now I'm about to face the reunion between Jean-Ivy and Mum, which will be like one of those reality show reunions where women scream at each other on a sofa.

'I don't want to go. Please don't make me go,' I beg the universe.

'It will be fine,' Josh mumbles at the guitar strings. He, out of everyone, should know how distressing this is for me, to have my mum and stepmum in the same room with all the history.

'You could be a bit more supportive, Josh,' I murmur back.

He stops playing. 'Sorry. What do you want me to say?'

'I don't know. Just. Just. Just. I don't know.'

'Well, at least Mum will make sure they don't fight.' He strums a chord. I twist to face him.

'Your mum?'

'My mum. Short, blonde hair, named Linda, wears a coat all year round.'

'I'm aware,' I say tightly. 'You made it sound like she was coming today.'

Josh nods.

'Lace invited her. I told you, didn't I?'

'No, you did not.'

'I didn't? Oh. Oops. Well, she's on her way to East London now.'

'For fuck's sake,' I shout. Linda Butters? Really? What is Lace thinking?

'Hey,' Josh snaps. 'Mum is looking forward to seeing you.' He's scowling at me.

'I didn't mean it like that,' I growled, even though that's exactly what I meant it like. 'Sorry.'

I find two socks that match, white with pink spots. Hooray. I plonk myself next to Josh on the bed. 'I just don't want a big crowd today,' I say to cover my back. What I *really* don't want is fusspot Linda Butters crying on the sidelines of the fight between Mum and Jean-Ivy. I put one sock on, and my big toe pokes out of a hole. 'EURGH! Why is this happening to me?' I shout.

'Because you don't throw away old socks,' Josh jokes. He doesn't see my daggers because he's too occupied pretending to be able to tune the strings.

'I may learn guitar again,' he says.

'Oh, please don't.'

Five

I close my eyes and press the buzzer five times. The door opens, and I step back. Rebecca is standing with red lips and flicked-out eyelashes that are highlighting her slightly pissed eyes.

'The bride is heeere,' she calls up the stairs.

'Your face,' is all I can say.

'Lace did it, isn't she fabulous?'

'Fabulous?' I repeat back. I don't think Rebecca has ever said that word in her life.

I follow Rebecca up the stairs, and we go into Lace's studio. There's a big cheer for my arrival. Nina and Abi both have a mouthful of cheese. Jean-Ivy pounces on me, saying something in my ear, but I don't hear what it is because I'm too distracted by Linda Butters.

'Amy, you'll have to come here for a hug because I'm not getting up,' Linda says with a chuckle. She is sitting on the French daybed with a plate full of cheese and biscuits. In a daze, I do as I'm told. 'I almost didn't recognise you with your hair,' she says. 'It's very dark.'

Nina slips a glass of red into my hand.

'You may need this,' she says.

I do, very much so. I take a gulp. I see Mum hasn't arrived yet. Classic. We're talking about the woman who left so late for the hospital that she almost gave birth to me in the car.

'Doll, there you are,' Lace says as she comes into the room, cuddling two extra bottles of red wine, wearing a black shift dress. She inspects my hair for a long second, then takes my hand and announces, 'Everyone, please make yourself comfortable. We won't be long.' We go down to the next floor and open the door to an empty room. There is peeling wallpaper and exposed floorboards with paint splashes. The only piece of furniture is a floor-length mirror balancing against the wall. On the back of the door, the dress hangs in its cover.

'Why do you look so nervous?' Lace says, unzipping the garment.

'Jean-Ivy and Mum. It's going to be a disaster.'

'It's tradition to have your closest women present when trying on your wedding dress.' She steps away, revealing the dress. 'What do you think?'

I step back. There are no patterns, no frills, no diamonds – a simple white dress. It's stunning.

'Lace, you made this?' I go to touch it, but Lace grabs my hand.

'No, I bought it from Primark. Of course I made it. Do you like it?'

'Like it? It's exactly what I wanted.'

'No, you wanted your mum's dress.'

'What was I thinking?'

'I mean, I wanted to make you something more va-va-voom, but, actually, I think this will be perfect.'

It takes time to put it on because Lace makes me go super carefully, as if the dress is made from cobwebs, but we get there in the end. I stand in front of the mirror, stunned at seeing myself in a real wedding dress. In *the* wedding dress that I'm going to get married in.

'I want to ask you something,' I say.

'What to do with your hair on the wedding day?' Lace says, eyeballing the dark nest on my head.

'That. And I want you to be my bridesmaid.' I smile in the mirror and see her pinching her lips together. 'I know we've just met, but I feel like you've been such a big part of this wedding frenzy that it would be strange not to have you there for the big day.' She fiddles with the back button of my dress and shakes her head. 'Come on, it will be fun. Lots of red wine.'

'I'm not going to be able to make it,' she says, a hint of disappointment in her voice. 'I'm sorry, but I can't.' She looks down, avoiding my eyes. Jean-Ivy shouts from the top of the stairs.

'Hurry up, girls! I'm BURSTING with excitement.'

There is silence. The disappointment that Lace won't be there on my wedding day hits me harder than I thought. I had assumed she would say yes. I want to ask why not, but I know her well enough now to know she won't tell me.

'Right,' she says, flicking my hair out. 'Before we show them the masterpiece, let me make some tweaks.' She puts pink lipstick on me, lines my eyes with thick eyeliner and clips my hair up. It has somehow made me look . . . pretty.

I come into the studio, hand in hand with Lace. Rebecca starts squealing and waving her arms whilst Nina and Abi repeat, 'Oh my God, Amy.' Jean-Ivy has her hands over her mouth very dramatically. And Linda . . . Linda is sobbing, of course.

I don't know how to stand. My arms feel awkwardly attached to my body, so I cross them, but that feels strange too, so I clasp them behind my back. Lace pulls them apart and then lifts my chin with a single finger. The buzzer goes. My heart thumps. Mum is here.

'I'll go,' Rebecca says. She runs out of the door and down the stairs. Lace takes my hand and squeezes it. Jean-Ivy fills her wine glass up to the brim.

'What is it with your generation and fussy coffee?' Mum says, waltzing into the room with a Beanie coffee in hand. 'Well, let's have a look then.' She stands in the way of Abi and Nina and inspects me up and down. I wait for some remark about the dress not resembling hers, but instead, her face softens. 'Amy, you look—' Mum suddenly stops. She breaks eye contact with me and glares at Jean-Ivy. 'Pity I have to share this moment with her.'

Pop. The moment is over.

'Mum, we spoke about this.'

'Oh, look, Rose has returned from the ocean,' Jean-Ivy mutters into her wine.

'Ladies, let's keep it civil,' Linda says from the French daybed.

'I think you have a little something on your face,' Mum says to Linda, not kindly. Sure enough, a piece of cracker is sticking to Linda's cheek. Linda wipes it away, and the crumb falls on the floor. 'Good woman,' Mum says, in that patronising way that rubs everyone up the wrong way. If the room felt small before, it feels teeny now. Lace takes Mum's arm.

'Rebecca, will you get Charlotte a glass of red? Charlotte, please make yourself at home. You get the red velvet chair as the Mother of the Bride.' Mum glares at Jean-Ivy as she makes her way to the chair, and Jean-Ivy raises her glass to her mockingly.

'Jean,' I snap. Jean lowers her glass.

'So, it's a yes to the dress?' Lace asks.

Linda cheers with two arms. 'YES.'

'Absolutely,' Jean-Ivy says.

'I love it,' Abi says.

'Pardon?' Jean-Ivy says. She's staring at Mum with one hand to her ear. 'What was that, Charlotte?'

'I said it doesn't matter what you think,' Mum says.

I sink. Here we go.

'I bought the dress actually, so it very much matters what I think,' Jean-Ivy retorts.

'Purr-lease. My ex-husband bought the dress like he bought your implants,' Mum snaps back.

'Both of you, stop being so blooming selfish,' Linda cuts in. I'm surprised she's even trying; she'll get eaten for dinner by these two.

'Selfish?' They both say at the same time.

'The whole reason my daughter is having to rush this wedding in the first place is because of you,' Mum snaps. Linda glances at me, hurt. I want to bury myself.

'Mum!'

'My dad has dementia, Charlotte,' she cries. 'I'm sorry there is a small sacrifice on Amy's part, but that's what families do. They SACRIFICE for each other.'

'Well, old leather pants here certainly sacrificed my family, didn't she?' Mum points to Jean-Ivy, who is swirling the wine in her glass, sniggering to herself.

'You didn't put out for five years, Charlotte. What do you expect the man to do?' she says. The room goes silent.

My dress tightens around my lungs. Five years? That's like 1,800 tally marks. I feel a wave of heat come over me, and the dress gets even tighter. That could be me and Josh. We're already over the six-month mark. What if we get married, and then it gets to a year, then two, then a decade. I'll be an old lady with a wrinkly, paper-thin hand, still marking tally marks in my notebook. I pull on the dress to try and get air, but it's tailored so wonderfully that it's stuck to my body.

'I need to get out of this,' I say and begin reaching behind for the zip. I call for Lace. Where has she gone?

'Ladies, we've got to stick together in this man's world,' Nina says in her teacher's voice.

'Five years . . . really?' Linda says with surprise.

'Oh, please Linda, as if you're getting it all the time,' Mum bites back.

'I have a very healthy sex life, Charlotte,' Linda brags. I want to be sick.

'Do you even remember what an erect penis looks like?' Jean-Ivy laughs.

'Well, sorry I can't get wet over tucked-in checked shirts and cord trousers,' Mum argues back.

I keep reaching for the zip. Why is this dress so tight? My hairline is damp, and the clip Lace put in has slipped out. They're yelling in each other's faces, and I can't make sense of what they're saying anymore. I need to get out of this dress.

CRASH! Everybody freezes. A mannequin is on the floor. Suddenly, everything loosens. I can breathe again; my zip is undone. Lace is standing next to me.

'If you're not a bridesmaid, please vacate my studio instantly,' Lace announces. She has her hands on her hips and is staring at Mum and Jean-Ivy. I've never heard her sound so cold before. There is a pause, and then they all start on Lace.

'You can't kick me out, I'm her mum.'

'I paid for the dress.'

'I've done nothing wrong,' Linda says and starts to cry again.

Lace points to the door. 'This is my studio, and I want you to leave,' she says.

Mum, Jean-Ivy and Linda all turn to me.

'Amy?'

'Amy?'

'Amy?'

I am staring down, still trying to get the oxygen back in me.

'I think it's best if you go,' I say, breathless.

'Amy?' Mum says, shocked, as if it's *me* who's let her down today.

'Excuse me, I bought the dress, Amy,' Jean-Ivy says, waving her hands frantically.

'Amy, you wouldn't kick me out?' Linda snuffles.

'It's my wedding. It's my wedding day. I'm getting married,' I say. This is the one time in my life it should be about me, but none of it is. 'Please, can you just go.' I point to the door. Jean-Ivy huffs and storms out. Mum is next.

'I can't believe you're kicking me out with *her*,' she mutters aggressively, then storms down the stairs. I'm too angry to feel bad. All I asked was for her to keep the peace for my wedding, but she couldn't even hold it in for 15 minutes. The last to go is Linda, who doesn't say a word to me but sniffs into a tissue as she leaves. I can't keep her happy for the rest of my life, no matter how much Josh wants me to.

They don't even reach the front door before they start arguing again. They shout over each other as they go down Redchurch Street until their voices fade.

A movement from inside a drawer gets everyone's attention. Peppy stumbles out and waddles to the French daybed. It takes him two attempts to lift his weight up and onto it.

I'm the first to speak. 'Lace, what the hell are you feeding that cat?'

The Peg

We're in a club. Lace and I are waiting at a bar to order more sambuca. I can't remember the name of the club, but it was my idea to go.

After the mums left, Rebecca suggested that we should have a proper hen party. We've since crawled from tacky bar to tacky bar, drinking the most garish cocktails on the menu. We booed Rebecca when she had to go home. We told her that Benson is big enough to look after himself, but it didn't work. Nina, Lace, Abi and I remain.

Abi is on the dance floor with a man who matches her cheesy dancing style. Nina is sitting in a booth having a deep conversation with a woman she found in the toilets.

'My parents didn't have sex for five years,' I say into Lace's ear. 'Five years!' I hold up five fingers. Lace nods.

'I'm aware,' she shouts. It's not the first time I've said it tonight, but I can't let it go. What happens if it's a genetic thing? There are women like Jean-Ivy and Natalie, who men want to have sex with, and there are women like Mum and me, who men have relationships with, even love, but never truly desire.

'That's going to be me. Isn't it? I will be just like my mum,' I shout to Lace. She leans in and puts her mouth to my ear.

'Did you try my sex tips?' she shouts. I give her a defeated nod. 'And still nothing? Did you ever do the pegging thing?'

'I don't know if I can. I mean, how do you even begin?'

Lace puts her hand on my shoulder and looks at me with empathy. 'Sex is not your problem,' she says. Then points to my mouth. 'That's your problem.'

'Kissing?'

'No, you need to talk to him.' She makes a talking mouth with her hands.

'I don't know how.'

'Exactly, that's your problem, and it's huge.'

'No, the problem is he wants to be pegged,' I shout.

Lace is about to say something, but the barman gets her attention. She turns away from me and orders another round of shots.

That's the problem, he wants to be pegged. He needs something, and I'm too frigid to do it, like I was too frigid for Hugo. I'm still that same girl who laughs at ball sacks because they look like Jabba the Hutt. That's what divides the Amys from the Natalies – sexual confidence. I give Lace a hug from behind. 'Thank you, Lace.' She turns back. The barman is filling up a line of shot glasses with sambuca.

'Where are you going?' she asks.

'I'm going to peg him,' I yell.

'No! Amy, not tonight!' she says. She tries to grab my hand, but I pull it away.

'Yes, tonight! If I can't peg my own fiancé now, then when can I?'

'Amy,' Lace pleads. I kiss her on the forehead, grab a shot and down it. I push my way back through the crowd. I wave to Nina in her booth, but she's too engrossed in her conversation to notice. Abi and the man are still dancing. They're doing the night fever dance to Beyoncé. I get outside and order an Uber. There are five missed calls from Josh. How strange, he never calls like that. I try calling, but he doesn't pick up, so I text him.

Coming home! Stay Up!!!! I have a surprise!

Amy Elman Doesn't Feel Sexy

Dino, an old Italian man with 4.3 stars, picks me up. After two attempts, I manage to open the door of his car.

'Amy?' Dino asks. He has a gorgeous accent. Tanned with grey hair. I bet he was stunning when he was young. Or maybe I'm just beer-goggling the Uber driver.

'That's me.'

We drive off. There is a fresh bottle of water in the back which I help myself to. Dino is playing Classic FM and I suddenly become very excited because, for the first time ever, I recognise the music.

'OH MY GOD, *TOSCA*!' I clap.

'You know the song?' Dino says, surprised.

'Yes, it's Tosca's lover. He's singing about how the stars are shining.'

'And the earth is smelling,' Dino adds.

'Right!'

I'm impressed that I remember this, and Dino seems very impressed too. He turns it up, and we smile at each other in his rear-view mirror. He's going to get five stars.

★

I get home. Josh is in bed; he didn't stay up for me, so I'm going to have to wake him up. I know I can solve our issue tonight. I turn on our bedroom light and stumble over to the drawers.

'What are you doing, Amy?' Josh moans and puts Skogsfräken over his head.

'I've got a surprise. You'll love it,' I say. I am rummaging through my knitwear drawer. I throw the cardigans out, and then I see it in the corner. 'Don't look,' I say. Josh groans with exasperation. He's moody now, but I know he'll be so happy when he finds out what I am going to do to him. 'Don't look . . . Don't look . . .' I get naked and put on the strap-on. I turn around, remote control in my hand and press the on button. It begins to vibrate. The sound makes Josh jolt up. 'Get on all fours,' I demand as I walk towards him. I stumble on my dark matter book but recover. I stand over him. He looks at my face, then at The Big Purple Pleasure around my hips. His eyes are wide. He looks as terrified as the men on his porn videos, but that's all part of the role play.

'What the *hell* are you doing?' he shouts, eyeing up the dildo.

'Get on all fours, you . . . you . . . pathetic pussy.'

'Did you take something? Are you okay? Amy?' He holds on to Skogsfräken.

I grab the pillow and throw it away.

'What the fuck?' He jumps up and stands on the opposite side of the bed with hands out ready to defend himself. I notice his boxers, and how flat they are. This isn't the reaction I was expecting, considering it's been 220 nights and I'm performing his kink. 'Amy, I don't know what you're trying to do, but you're drunk, and you need to go to sleep.'

'I'm trying to peg you,' I tell him, in case it's not obvious already.

'*You're* trying to *peg* me?' he says back, like it's the craziest thing in the world that his fiancée is trying to do something sexual to him.

'I saw your porn history. I know you want to be pegged like the . . . bad boy you are.' As I say it, my jaw tightens with discomfort, but I have to carry on. 'You bad boy . . . allowing carrot cake at our wedding!'

'I thought you wanted carrot cake!' He seems distressed and not at all turned on. Still, I don't want to give up. I crawl onto the bed and kneel up.

'I want to stick these veins in you.'

'Veins?' He frowns. I point to the vein details on the dildo, and he looks like he may be sick. (Note – Gemma was wrong; not all men like veins.)

'Wait,' Josh says, pointing at me. 'Did you say you saw my porn history?'

'We're going a bit off course,' I mutter, still kneeling with the dildo on full blast vibration.

'Did you go through my laptop? Because that's bang out of order if you have.' He picks up my notebook. 'What if I looked in here? How would you feel?' He starts flicking through it.

'No, don't. Put that down,' I yell. Panicked, because I wouldn't know how to explain the pages of tally marks. He drops it. Thankfully. 'Sorry,' I say quickly whilst I regain my balance. The strap-on is quite heavy. 'Can we just do this pegging thing, and then we can go to sleep, and live happily ever after?' I say. I know I've drunk a lot tonight, but surely, he can see the sense in that too.

'No.'

'Why not?'

'I don't want to do that with you,' he snaps.

I get off the bed.

There it is. The rejection in black and white. *I don't want to do that with you.* Josh gets back into bed and pulls the cover over himself. 'Turn that thing off and go to sleep.'

'Josh . . .?' I plead.

'Go to sleep, Amy. You've done enough damage for one day,' he says coldly.

'What do you mean?'

'We'll talk in the morning when you're sober.'

I press the button on the remote, and it goes through the seven vibrations until it's completely off. I feel like the unsexiest woman alive. There are probably farm animals that feel sexier than I do right now. I chuck The Big Purple Pleasure across the room. It hits the wall, making a loud bang. Josh doesn't even flinch.

Haze

221 Nights

I peel one eye open. I'm in my bed. Thank God. For a second, I feel nothing, and then, everything. Pressure squeezes my head and I think my skull is going to implode. This has got to be the worst hangover in the history of hangovers. Josh is not next to me. I assume he's planking with Tony.

A quick flash of singing badly to *Tosca* in the back of an Uber springs to mind, and then I see The Big Purple Pleasure against the wall. I want to crumple into the mattress and die.

The front door slams. I hear Josh dropping his gym bag by the door, and then him coming towards the bedroom. The door opens, and Josh has a face of thunder on him.

'How was the gym?' I ask cautiously, half hiding under the duvet. He's exceptionally sweaty today. His black tank is stuck down to his chest. He takes it off and drops it on the ground.

'Do you even remember what happened?' he yells. The aggression catches me off guard. I've never heard him sound so angry before.

'I tried to peg you?' I say with a grimace.

'You kicked my mum out of your dress-fitting party. She's in bits. She thinks you hate her.' He's still shouting. Of course, this is about his mother, not us.

'I don't hate her,' I say with a sigh. I'm either very hungover, or I've just resigned myself to Linda being upset about something all the time. Josh is staring at me as if I've shrugged off a story about a bag of puppies being drowned. 'I'll call her,' I say, like it's a chore. It's clear he's unsatisfied with my response. 'What?'

'Mum and Dad booked us into a space-themed escape room in Soho. Mum wanted to give it to you yesterday as a surprise, but you kicked her out before she could. Our slot is at midday, so we need to go in 30 minutes . . .'

Josh storms out to have a shower. I go under the duvet, away from the very messy world I have successfully created for myself in the last 12 hours. Maybe we'll do what we do best. Josh will come out of the shower, and he won't mention anything about the pegging. That will suit me and my hangover today. I'll buy Linda some flowers and blame my actions on being a Bridezilla. Then I'll throw away the dildo, and we'll get married and move to the countryside. And the sex will come back . . . hopefully . . . before it gets to five years. I squeeze myself into the smallest ball possible and scream into the pillow.

HWSS Suzanna

The Room Master of the escape room is barely 20 and looks like he's had as heavy a night as I did. He takes us to the door of the escape room and taps his key card onto the scanner. He pushes the door, but it's still locked. He swears under his breath and tries again. This time it opens, and Josh and I go into a room that is designed like a budget sci-fi spaceship. It has a childlike control panel made up of coloured flashing lights and glow-in-the-dark buttons. There is a windscreen taking up the back wall with a drawn-on galaxy. The Earth, Moon and Sun are in the distance – they're inaccurately sized and spaced out, but I'm too tired to care.

'The spaceship manual will give you your first instructions,' the Room Master says. He points to the corner at a small security camera. 'We will be watching you at all times, and if you need a clue, use this.' He hands Josh a walkie-talkie. 'Okay?' he sounds like a zombie. We nod. 'Good. May the force be with you.' He closes the door. A big flash and a theatrical American voice starts to blare out of the speaker.

'Space Cadets. The signal is terrible. There is something wrong with the passenger section of HWSS Suzanna. Your only hope is to fix her yourself. We will have to abort the mission in 60 minutes, which means, cadets, we're going to have to leave you behind if you can't fix her on time. Good luck.' A noisy techno track starts to play.

I massage my temples, trying to relieve the ache. 'I'm no engineer, but that storyline doesn't make any sense,' I say, trying to make a joke.

Josh has hardly said two words since this morning. I hoped the escape room would shift his mood, but so far it hasn't done the trick. He is reading the laminated card from the 'spaceship manual'. I look over his shoulder, still massaging my temples. There are lines of blue, yellow and red dots in different patterns on the page.

'We have to match the patterns with the buttons over there,' I say, gesturing to the control panel. He goes over and puts in the patterns without a word. There is a white flash and a jingle. We've completed the task.

'Wow, look at us go,' I say, still committed to livening the mood, which is hard when I feel like death.

Josh, again, ignores me. It's as if we have actually broken down on Mars, and it's all my fault. A locker pings open, and a bucket full of black foam balls is inside.

'Maybe we need to put the balls in there.' I point to a tube with 'Gas' written on it. Again, he doesn't say anything. He just stuffs the balls into the tube. The flash and jingle play again. We go to the next task and the next without a word. This is a thousand times worse than the time we did the pub quiz together.

We're stuck now. Josh is standing at the front of the ship by the control panel. He is pulling a squeaky lever back and forth, and the noise is like shards of glass scratching my brain. I cover my ears.

'I don't think that's right,' I shout over the squeaking. He keeps pulling the lever. 'Josh, I think—'

'What do you think?' He lets go of it very dramatically. It's the most he has said since we entered the escape room 40 minutes ago.

'We need to ask for a clue.' I pick up the walkie-talkie.

'No. No clue.'

'I just want to get this done so that we can go home.'

'Amy!'

I press the button on the walkie-talkie.

'Would you like a clue?' The Room Master sounds like we've just woken him.

'Stop treating me like I'm an idiot!' Josh yells as he erratically pushes buttons.

I take my thumb off the walkie-talkie button.

'I'm not. I'm just asking for a clue . . .'

'You don't think I deserve the promotion.'

I laugh at the randomness. 'What are you talking about?'

The flash goes off, and the jingle plays out. The 'engine room' door swings open, and Josh storms inside. I call after him. Why is he talking about the promotion? I follow him into a tiny room. Just what we need – an even smaller space. There's a jigsaw on the wall. Josh picks up a piece and puts it in the wrong place, so I pick it up and put it in the right place. He slaps his hand on the fake wires. 'This is what I mean.'

'I'm just helping!' I say, feeling my patience slip away. 'And about the promotion. Yes, I thought Nina deserved to get it, but of course I'm glad you did, and I think you'll do a really good job.'

'So patronising,' he mutters.

That's it.

'Fine. Nina is more qualified, passionate and dedicated than you, so yes, I was very surprised that you got the job over her,' I shout and push the last two pieces of the puzzle together. Flashy lights, jingle. A locker opens.

He begins clapping sarcastically, as if he's been waiting for this moment. 'Finally, the truth. Admit it, you believe the only reason I got promoted was because you think Dr Therone wants to fuck me.'

'The whole school thinks that, Josh.'

Josh storms out of the engine room and into the main ship again. I find him staring out into the fake galaxy. I take a deep breath. 'Josh –'

'You've changed,' he says. I laugh because it sounds like something a teenager would say. 'Stop laughing at me,' he shouts. 'Fuck's sake. Old Amy wouldn't laugh at me. She wouldn't ditch me at the last minute to go to some opera. Or get suspended from work. Or throw my mum out. And she wouldn't get wasted and try to . . .' He stops.

'Try to what?' I push. I need him to say it out loud.

Josh goes back into the engine room. I follow him. He goes to a keypad and punches in a code. The light flashes, and the jingle plays, a door opens. I have no idea how he worked that out, but I'm too angry to ask.

There is a red floor and black walls with tiny lights for stars. We're on Mars. Josh empties a bag of sticks onto the floor. Each stick has a different star shape on the end, and on the wall are the slots to stick them in. He sits down close to the wall and slams a hexagram into a hole.

'Try to do what?' I repeat. He carries on, shoving the sticks into the holes. 'Josh?'

'I don't know why you had to throw out Mum,' he eventually says.

'Geez!' I want to bang my head on the fake crater. It's like we are speaking another language – we've been speaking another language for quite some time.

'You don't care that you upset my mum, do you?' he yells.

'No, I don't care about your mum. I care about us, Josh. For goodness' sake, why are we not having sex?' I shout back. I'm shaking, my heart is racing. Josh goes on inspecting the star shapes as if I hadn't said anything. 'We can't keep ignoring the elephant.'

'Elephant?' he says, frowning.

'Yes, the big fuck-off elephant in the room, Josh! We've barely touched each other in over six months. And I've tried everything. Everything! I tried not having phones in the room. I squeezed into lingerie. I dyed my hair. I did at least 20 press-ups with your gym-buddy wife . . .'

He's fiddling with one of the sticks. 'Well, maybe if you—'

'Pegged you? I TRIED!' The words bounce around Mars.

A crackling voice comes over the speaker. 'Space Cadets, you have one minute until launch, do you copy? You have one minute.'

Josh slams in the heptagram and then the decagram. The lights flash, and the jingle plays.

'Space Cadets, you've done it. You've done it. Quick, board HWSS Suzanna now. We are launching in 10 . . . 9 . . . 8 . . . 7 . . . 6 . . . 5 . . . 4 . . . 3 . . . 2 . . . 1.' All the lights come on, and Josh is still sitting on the red floor with his back to me. I'm leaning on the starry sky wall.

'I was going to say, maybe if you said something, we could have talked about it.'

'How can I, Josh?'

'I don't know. Just talk. Ask me questions,' he says, like it's been that easy all along. As if the whole reason why we're here, right now, is because I didn't do the obvious, but I'm not going to shoulder the blame for this.

'It's impossible, Josh. You shut down whenever sex is mentioned. Even last night, you said you didn't want to do *that* with *me*. It's ridiculous. We're getting married in under two weeks, and we don't even know each other's favourite sex position.'

'Are we?' Josh asks.

'What?'

'Getting married?'

The walkie-talkie crackles. 'Guys,' the Room Master says. 'Can you break up somewhere else? We have another group waiting.'

Hobnobs

The front door closes, and I know it's Josh by the sound of his breathing. He comes into the bedroom to find me on the edge of our bed. I stormed out of the escape room and ran to the Tube. I needed to be alone to gather my thoughts. Josh obviously had to do the same, because he's taken his time to come home. I've been waiting for an hour.

I launch in.

'You don't think I'm attractive, do you?'

He throws his hands in the air with frustration.

'When have I ever said that?'

'You said to Rebecca that you think you're hotter than me.' Tears pool in my eyes. Josh leans against the wall, next to the map we never hung, and stares down at his feet. 'I'm sorry that I'm not *obsessed* with how my body looks,' I say, intending to hurt him. It works. His head shoots up.

'I'm sorry that I think health is important,' he snaps back. I snort, and he hits the wall with frustration. 'You know, Amy, it wouldn't harm you to plank once in a while.'

My mouth drops open.

'When did you become such a knobhead?'

'Me?' He points to himself and laughs. 'What about you? On my birthday. Don't think I didn't hear what Lace said to you.' I frown, confused. 'She said, "No wonder you're not having sex", and you fucking laughed at me. That's why I went home. Did you know I ate dinner by myself that night? Happy fucking thirtieth birthday to me.'

'Lace was just trying to help me with the sex stuff,' I say defensively and then begin to cry, mostly because I feel ashamed of myself. I thought he hadn't heard that conversation, and now I feel like the bitchiest fiancée on earth. Josh hasn't been the most attentive partner, that's for sure, but I hate the thought of hurting him, because he's Josh.

'So, you were laughing about me, to her?'

'Not laughing. Talking.'

He's looking up at the ceiling, and I can see the tears in his eyes, and I have a sudden urge to hold him. It feels like we're on the edge of a cliff. I get up from the bed and walk to him. I put my hands on his arms and stare into his eyes, but he looks away.

'I shouldn't have laughed. I'm sorry. I don't know what's happened to us. I don't even recognise who we are anymore ...' I choke on my words as tears fall down his face. I wipe them away with my finger. 'But maybe it's nothing, just a bump in the road that we could work through. Perhaps once we're married and have moved to the countryside, we'll go back to how we were.' I can't help feeling as I say it, that I'm trying to convince myself. Josh sniffs and looks at the ground for a long time. It's making me nervous. 'Josh? What is it, Josh? Be honest.'

He exhales. 'The countryside thing. It's not ... really ... what I want.'

'What?' I step back as if his words have physically pushed me away. 'But that's the plan. It's what we've always wanted. Isn't that why we have a savings account? Why I've set alerts on property listings? Why we agreed to push our wedding to be in seven weeks, so we can speed it all up?' Josh does an infuriating shrug. 'So, what? You want to live in Southwest London forever?'

'Not forever, but maybe another 10 years.'

'Ten years?' I can't believe what I'm hearing. 'But what about having a family? You wanted two kids. That's what you told me. We were going to move to the country and have a garden with a BBQ and—'

'There's time for that,' he interjects.

'Time? I'm 30 this year, Josh. I don't have time to play with.' Josh doesn't know how to answer this, so I ask, 'Okay, what do you want to do for the next 10 years?'

'I dunno. I want to keep building up my body. Maybe compete in Ironman challenges. Pete was thinking of doing a lads' trip in a van around France next year. And, I dunno, we carry on with work, go to pub quizzes, go skiing, that kind of stuff,' he mutters. 'I don't see the need to overcomplicate it by moving away and settling down.'

We make eye contact for a split second before I look away. Why is he telling me all this now? I want to explode, but instead, I walk to the door.

'W-where are you going?' he stutters.

'To get a snack.'

I go to the kitchen in a daze and get the Hobnobs from my cupboard. On the bench is our wedding menu design, which was sent from The Chipping Barn yesterday. They want us to sign it off by tomorrow. Next to it, is the seating plan I did that Josh was supposed to look at two weeks ago. And then there's my wedding dress, in its red cover, hanging on the only hook in the flat. I think about how beautiful I looked yesterday standing in front of the mirror, and it brings fresh tears to my eyes. That woman deserves more than this.

No matter how perfect The Chipping Barn or the wedding dress is, I know in my bones that marrying Josh would be wrong. The only thing we have in common is history. We have given each other 10 years of our lives, but that doesn't mean we should give the next 60. We both deserve better, and that means not being together.

I take a deep breath and walk back to the bedroom.

Josh is where I left him, leaning against the wall. I sit on the bed and open the packet of biscuits. 'Want one?'

Josh waves his hand. 'No, thanks.' He watches me as I put one in my mouth. He comes over and takes one, then sits on the edge of the mattress.

We eat Hobnob after Hobnob in silence. I am trying to think of how to say what needs to be said. Josh looks like he's thinking too, but I can't be sure. It's becoming clear that he hasn't thought too deeply about us for a long time. If ever at all. He's nodded along and gone with the flow. And I've let this happen, because I was so desperate to have my own home, my own family. Tears fill my eyes. I sniff and look down at my shaking hands. I have a strange feeling in my chest, like a hole is expanding. I open my mouth.

'This isn't going to work, is it?'

*

It's 11 p.m. I'm lying near Josh's feet, staring at the ceiling; we are surrounded by Kleenex balls and biscuit crumbs. We've been going round in circles for hours. Maybe if we get a sex therapist? *If we get a sex therapist now, what hope would we have when we're 50?* Maybe if we pack up everything and go travelling for a year? *If we go travelling for a year, we will still have the same problems when we get home.* Even after we discuss every possible way to make this work, we always end up at the same outcome – to break up.

'I will move out tomorrow,' I say. 'We can tell our families over the next few days.'

I feel Josh's hand on my foot. I look up and see his red, raw face. 'You can't move out tomorrow. It's not right. It's stupid. We hardly argue. We don't cheat. We're happy, Lab Rat, we're so fucking happy. Everyone says so . . .' His voice breaks off.

I exhale, exhausted at the thought of going through it all again. I care, but not enough to fight for it, and that breaks me.

'We're not happy. Not really,' I say through tears.

'No,' he yells. He crawls over and lies next to me. There is a dot of blood on his cracked lips from where he has chewed on them. 'We are happy. We are. Let's get married and we can move to the countryside, like you want. Let's forget this whole thing ever happened. We're just scared because of the wedding. It's normal. Come on, let's forget it, yeah?' He rests his hand on the dip of my waist. It sits there, heavy and awkward. 'We love each other. Yeah?' he says, rocking me.

I can't remember the last time we said we loved each other. I blink and let the words fall out.

'Not in the way we should.'

*

I pretend to sleep as Josh gets changed for work. After I said what I said, he took Skogsfräken under his arm and slept on the sofa. I don't remember falling asleep, but Josh's shower woke me up, so I must have drifted off at some point. I don't think he made it to the gym this morning.

He leaves the house. The sound of the door shutting behind him makes me tear up. I want to run after him and hold him again, but I don't move. Instead, I keep my face pressed into the pillow and cry hard. It feels like bats are swooping around my stomach, down and up, down and up . . . I fall back to sleep.

At 11:13, I wake and run to the bathroom. Ten Hobnobs come out in a big mush. It makes me feel *a bit* better, but I still feel the bats swooping around.

As much as I want to, I don't get back into bed. If I do, I know I won't get up again, and I must leave this flat before Josh comes back from work.

I text Nina, asking if I can stay at her house tonight. She texts a second later. She must have seen Josh this morning and worked it out.

I'll make dinner X

I open the top drawer and stare at the creased clothes inside. It takes me a minute to mentally prepare myself to start packing. I pick up my purple hoodie first, and then my jeans, and then my black woolly dress. Soon, the drawer is empty. It is surprisingly therapeutic doing something practical. Next, I start on my books, stacking them into a cardboard box. I remember Mum furiously packing her things up when she left. It felt so cold back then, but now I understand; if you stop moving, you won't start again.

The bed sheets are covered in mascara splodges and crumbs, so I put fresh sheets on for Josh. Herbert, the dead plant, finally meets his fate and goes into the bin. I pick up my notebook from the bedside table. The wedding to-do list has everything ticked off. All that's left is to say *I do*. I flick to the back, where the tally marks are: 221 frustrated lines fill the pages. It's both terrifying and sad that we thought we were ready for marriage. I am about to throw it in the bin but decide to pack it instead. If I ever feel vulnerable about making this decision, it will be there to remind me why I did it.

The bedroom is done. I stare at the bare space and feel the bats swooping inside of me again. I move on to the kitchen before I crumble again. The four ceramic mugs Mum bought me for Christmas and my gin-making kit go into a box labelled **'AMY'S KITCHEN'**. Fifi wanders in, making me jump. She eyeballs the cardboard box and nods, then turns and leaves the room. I'm going to miss her, strangely.

I carry the box to the bedroom and add it to my cardboard tower. My life is in boxes, and I have no idea where they will end up. The girl who plans everything suddenly has no plan at all.

'It's for the best,' Fifi calls out from the hallway, as if she could sense my fear through the walls.

'Thank you,' I call back to be polite.

I leave a note on a torn-up piece of paper, telling Josh I'll come and collect the boxes on the weekend. Next to the note, I leave his grandma's ring. I stick a Post-it note on the Debbie Harry guitar and write 'For "Wonderwall"'. At least that solves that problem.

I will let my family and friends know the news as soon as I can stomach their questions. But right now, all I need is the reassurance that I'm doing the right thing. Lace can give me that; she is, after all, the only person who knew the truth about Josh and me. I send her a text.

> **Hi Lace. Are you free to talk?**
> **Something has happened.**

Everything is packed, but there is still time to kill before Nina finishes work. I don't want to sit around and think. Thinking means tears. So, with my backpack of clothes, I leave the house and cycle to Clapham Junction. I need to cancel the wedding cake.

Exhaustion hits me as soon as I walk into Clapcake, and it takes me a second to remember why I'm there.

'I need to cancel a wedding cake. Butters and Elman. February the 22nd. The carrot one.'

I recognise the lady – Gramps was mansplaining cake to her last time we were here. She tilts her head sympathetically. I suppose I should get used to that look. Sad Amy, the bride who cancelled her wedding.

'You did seem a bit tense that day, if you don't mind me saying,' she says. It surprises me. I assumed my frustration was well disguised, but obviously not. I wonder how many other times people could see through the charade. She smiles. 'I'll get it all cancelled for you, sweetheart.'

I feel strangely relieved. Not just because I don't have to have a carrot wedding cake, but a weight has been lifted off me, knowing that I no longer have to accommodate Josh's family for the rest of my life. They are not bad people, quite the opposite. They are genuine family people with big hearts. There will be another woman one day who will love the way The Butters Family are, or at least know how to manage them better than I did. Or, like most people, she'll learn to endure her in-laws because she is in love with Josh. That's the way it should be. As much as it feels impossible and gut-wrenching to think of Josh with someone else, I hope it happens for him one day. He deserves it, like I deserve it.

I leave Clapcake with a buttery flapjack. A hug from the inside. I cycle to Nina's house in Lavender Hill. Before I even open the gate, she opens her front door and runs towards me.

'Amy, you've got to see this,' she says.

Viral-ish

It turns out Arabella has more TikTok followers than I thought, and the video she made of the science contest is getting quite a bit of attention. I wouldn't say it's viral, but it's been viewed 50,000 times and has over 3,000 comments, which is more attention than I have ever received. The video is titled, 'My Science Class Takes on Birth Control'. #WeNeedYourQuestionsGirls'.

It begins with Arabella's happy face filling the screen. 'Hi guys, so our class are doing this London science contest this year, and we've chosen to discuss how the Pill affects us. The winner gets funding for research and awareness of their chosen topic. We wanted to do something that doesn't get talked about a lot and is important to women.' She does a peace sign. Dance music begins to play and it cuts to the class preparing the presentation in my lab. I appear next to the board, teaching them about the fallopian tube. (How did Arabella film that?) It cuts to the day of the contest, with Arabella pulling a nervous face backstage. The next clip is of Arabella, Ophelia and Beatrice presenting on stage in their tampon outfits. It ends with Arabella on the Southbank, watery-eyed and saying that we lost. Then, it's me doing my speech. '*Whether in science or in life, keep questioning the world. The world needs your questions.*' It cuts back to Arabella. 'You heard Miss Elman, the world needs your questions, girls!'

The video stops, and I immediately scroll to the comments expecting the worst, but to my surprise, they're mostly positive.

This is so inspiring!!!!! #WeNeedYourQuestionsGirls
Yes! There 10000% needs to be more information on the pill.
Elman for President!!
LOLOLOLOLOL LOVE THE TAMPON OUTFITS!
Fuck. How did you not win?!
What school is this??? Amazing.
Elman is a legend! #TEACHERGOALS

'This is only the start of it,' Nina says as she puts my dinner down, a full plate of chicken pesto pasta with a mountain of melted mozzarella. I don't remember, but I must have told her this was my favourite meal at some point. 'Dr Therone will want you back.' She settles down opposite me.

She has laid the table like we're in an Italian restaurant, with a gingham cloth and a dripping candle in an old wine bottle. I pierce one piece of pasta at a time. All I've had today is my Clapcake flapjack, but my stomach is stuffed with emotion that makes my appetite obsolete.

'I won't go back there. Josh has got his head of department role, and I . . .' I think of my lab, my fish. How they go crazy when Josh taps their tank. I choke. Nina's eyebrows dip as she reaches her hand towards me. I wave her away and dab my eyes with the matching gingham napkin. 'Sorry,' I say. 'I'm fine.'

'Could be cold feet, maybe?' Nina says gently.

I shake my head.

'No, this is it,' I say.

Nina gets up from the table with a smile. 'I have something that will cheer you up.' She leaves the room and comes back a moment later with her laptop. On the desktop is a folder called THE THERONE TAKEDOWN, and it's full of audio files.

'What on earth . . .' I ask.

'Just something I've been working on behind the scenes.'

She clicks on a file named *Assembly_StupidWoman_Feb25.mp3* and turns up the volume. Dr Therone's voice comes out of the speakers.

'You are a stupid, stupid woman, I told you not to do any more of these woke assemblies of yours. If you do it one more time, I swear I'll . . .' Nina hits the space bar and smiles.

'That's one clip of evidence where she is being a bully in the workplace, and I have 10 more like it,' she says, and then adds, 'If I can't be head of the department, she can't be head of the school.' She slams her laptop lid down. 'The beast is going down.'

Woman to Woman

My phone has been going off all morning with messages from strangers and journalists. They're asking me the same questions; why I did the science contest and my views on sex education at school. Ironic. There is no energy within me to come up with any insightful answers, so I've copied and pasted the same response to all of them. (I'll admit it's slightly inspired by Nina's speech.)

The girls were passionate about this subject, and what kind of teacher would I be if I didn't let them explore something relevant and vital for women of this generation? This had nothing to do with me, the girls did it all. I just trusted them to deliver it maturely and scientifically, and they did. I'm so proud of them.

When I come out of the shower, I have three voicemails. None of them are from Lace. Two are journalists asking the same old questions, and the third is a professor from Edinburgh University who wants me to do a speech to students about women in science. She says that I'm the 'kind of mentor women need.'

Me, a mentor? I have to laugh out loud. If only she knew me a month ago; I could barely get my pupils to listen to me.

I'm about to call the professor back, but then my phone rings again. This time, I recognise the number. Dr Therone needs to see me urgently.

*

I take my time cycling to school because I'd rather be anywhere else than in the same building as Josh or any place that reminds me of him. I can say goodbye to pub quizzes and escape rooms for a while, that's for sure.

The white sign of Clapham High for Girls comes into view, followed by the high iron gates. As I cycle in, I hear my name being called by a squeaky voice.

'Amy Elman. Amy? Amy?'

I break hard and look back. A tiny woman with a humongous camera dangling from her neck comes scuttling over. She tells me that her name is Mindy and she's from the *Metro*.

'Sorry, I've got a meeting,' I say and pedal off.

'I won't be long,' she pleads. I stop. She looks desperate. 'I just love your story, and I want to run it. I only have a couple of questions, promise.' She seems young and is swamped in a green coat, with red knitted gloves sticking out from the sleeves. Her naturally sweet persona reminds me of Abi.

'Three minutes,' I say. Mindy claps and makes a celebratory sound. She asks the same questions I've been asked all morning, so these are pretty easy to answer.

'And last question, what's next for Amy Elman?' Mindy says.

My mind blanks. I don't have an answer to that question anymore, but I do know one thing for certain that makes me happy now.

'To keep encouraging young women to ask questions.' Mindy smiles like I've said the right thing. 'Oh, and to keep learning about space. I love space.'

She stops her phone recorder. 'Would it be okay if I could get a quick photo?' She holds up her camera and senses my nerves. 'I'll be very, very quick. You don't have to do any strange poses or anything. You can just stand here and hold your bike.' I think about it for another second and then get off my bike. 'Oh, thank you so much,' Mindy says. I grip on to the handlebars, then pull a smile. Mindy looks down her lens for a long while, then tells me to relax.

'I don't know how to,' I say with an awkward laugh.

'Um ... drop your shoulders, and think about something funny, or someone that you like.'

My mind goes to Josh out of habit, then I feel a punch in my stomach as I remember.

'Oh, you don't like that person,' Mindy says, giggling.

I try hard to think about something or someone else. I think of that time that Peppy came stumbling out of the drawer and hobbling across Lace's studio.

'That's it. There,' Mindy says, taking multiple photos. She checks the images and gives me a nod. 'Got it. You're free. The story should run tomorrow,' she says and puts her hand out for me to shake, which I do.

'You are going to be nice, aren't you?' I ask. The last thing I need is for the whole of London to cancel me right now.

'Why wouldn't I be nice?' She seems genuine when she says this, but I guess journalists always do seem genuine at the time. 'If I had you as a teacher, I may have liked science,' she says, then runs off with her camera bouncing around her neck. I turn back to the tall iron gates of the school. My stomach plummets – time to face the beast.

*

'Amy, please, sit.' Dr Therone holds the door for me. 'Tea? Coffee?'

'Er, no, thank you,' I say. I want to get out of this place as quickly as possible. She sits on her chair opposite, with a thin-lipped smile. She is one of the few people on this earth who can't pull off happiness.

'This science contest has got everyone talking, hasn't it?' She is using her soft voice on me, the one she usually only uses on Josh.

'The same science contest that you suspended me over?' I remind her.

She waves her hand. 'Yes, well. I got the wrong end of the stick before, but I can now see the benefits it has had on Clapham High. Between you and me, this morning we've had over 100 calls from parents wanting to enrol their girls in this school.' She looks at me as if we're in business together.

'Well, that's good for the school, I guess,' I say.

Dr Therone, clearly unnerved by my attitude, leans forward.

'Miss Elman, you have proven yourself to be a contemporary, courageous teacher this term, and your hard work hasn't gone unnoticed.' I cross my arms and give her an unimpressed look so she knows I'm aware of the 180 she is pulling right now. She clears her throat. 'So, I have concluded that you would be a better fit as the head of department than Mr Rawlinson. Your promotion starts in the next academic year. I know that you've been eager for this role, and I'm very pleased to be offering it to you today.' She slides the contract across the desk towards me. I glance at it but keep my arms crossed. She taps the paper and laughs. 'Well, go on, sign it!'

I stand up.

'I'm resigning,' I say. I see the panic in Dr Therone's eyes and, God, it feels good.

'If this is about the rumours I've heard regarding your relationship with Mr Butters, then please, woman to woman, you're a more valuable staff member. We can work something out. Let's face it, he's not the best teacher in the world.'

I frown, and all I say is, 'Funny.' I begin to walk out.

'Miss Elman, I don't know what you're playing at, but you know you can't leave mid-school year.' I put my hand on the door handle and turn to her. She gives me an arrogant nod as if she knows she's got me trapped and then gestures to the seat again.

A smile spreads across my face. 'I've also heard a rumour. A rumour that there is audio evidence that you've created a toxic environment at this school,' I say. Her smirk disappears in a second. 'Woman to woman, I think you're fucked, Dr Therone,' I say.

'What are you talking about, Miss Elman? Miss Elman? Amy?'

I shut the door and walk to my lab to get my things.

Lab

I open the lab door and scream. Josh is feeding my fish. He gives me a cold look and sprinkles a handful of flakes in.

'Sorry, I need to collect some stuff.' My voice is cracking. Josh has gone from my comfort blanket to the person who makes me the most nervous in this whole world.

'I thought the fish may be hungry,' he says as he watches the fish wriggle up to the surface and suck in the flakes. I don't dare tell him that Nina has been feeding them. 'I hear you're going viral. That's exciting,' he says, sounding far from excited.

'Yeah, it's certainly strange,' I say, and then there is an awkward silence.

I go to my desk and start packing my bag. Josh looks over, perplexed.

'Isn't Dr Therone going to give you your job back?' he asks. I pack my lab coat into my bag and contemplate telling him.

'You should hear it from me first. I've resigned,' I say.

He freezes with his mouth wide open.

'Was this Lace's idea too? To quit your job?' he says fiercely.

I bite my lip as I put another book into my bag. I've never been so insulted, but I don't want us to fight.

'She wanted us to break up, and she got that.' I stop packing and look to see if it's Josh standing there or some crazed guy who sounds like him.

'Josh, she just made the wedding dress.' He scoffs, and the sound of it squeezes me. 'Why are you being like this? We mutually agreed that it was over.'

'Hardly mutual . . .'

'What's going on, Josh?'

'What's going on?' He lets out a sarcastic laugh. 'Ha. I don't know, Amy. We were fine before she came along. We were together and getting married, and you had a good job. And now all your stuff is in fucking boxes in our bedroom. Don't you see she sabotaged everything?' He sounds erratic as hell.

'Don't be so silly, this has nothing to do with Lace.'

'You were laughing at me on my birthday.'

'I know. You said, and I'm sorry,' I shout. 'You should have said something at the time.'

Josh runs his hands through his hair, and it sticks up at crazy angles.

'I didn't want to say anything before our wedding. In case—'

'We broke up?'

'I never thought we would break up.' I can see he's really trying not to cry, and it's killing me. I wish he would just leave before one of us says something we'll regret. I'm determined to not end up like Mum and Dad.

'Josh, look, I know you're scared—'

'I'm not scared!' he snaps. I take a breath and continue.

'. . . I'm scared too. But come on, let's be real, we didn't have sex for 221 days.' As soon as it's out of my mouth, I regret it. He narrows his eyes.

'You were counting?' he yells.

'Um.'

'Did you tell Lace it was 221 days? Did you laugh about it?'

'No, Josh, we didn't laugh about it.'

'Whatever. I don't know what's happened, but you're not the same person,' he says.

'No, I'm not, and nor are you, and that's why we're here.'

He throws up his hands and looks like he is about to say something, but stops himself, then turns and storms out.

The door slams behind him. The sound of the fish tank pump fills the room. I start shaking and gasping like there is suddenly no air. It feels like I've just run for miles. I shove one last book about the moon into my backpack. I murmur a sad goodbye to my fish and turn the lights off. It's not how I thought I would leave this place.

Outside it's drizzling, and the wind is biting my skin. I dream of my childhood bed and wish to be deep under the covers, away from this messy adult world I have made for myself.

Josh's bike is locked up at the end of the shed. I imagine him alone, locking it up, and it pulls my heart apart. No, I can't think like that, I shouldn't think like that. I crouch next to my bike and start twisting the numbers of the lock. My fingers are damp from the rain, so they slip as I twist. The number six at the end is the hardest to get into place, and I keep trying to push it and push it, and then I fall back onto the gravel with my head in my hands.

To Do:

Email all guests.
Cancel Velvet Cats.
Cancel flowers from Petunia.
Find out where Lace has gone.
Collect belongings from Josh's.
Start again.

We Can Do It!

I bury myself into the single bed at Nina's. My clothes are all over the floor and Rosie the Riveter stares at me from a frame, with her arm bent to show off her strength. She is telling us that we can do it.

'Are you sure about that?' I ask her. I reach for my phone on the floor below the bed and try calling Lace again. It goes straight to voicemail. I send her another text.

Are you ok? Worried.

Like the text this morning, only one tiny grey tick appears, meaning it's undelivered. I'm beginning to think she has blocked me, but why would she? The moment I put my phone down, it vibrates. Oh, thank goodness, I think, assuming it's Lace. It's not, it's Mum.

Call me. I know xxx

How does she know? I told Nina not to say anything. I am going to tell Rebecca and Abi soon, but I can't handle the phone conversations right now. The only person who could have let Mum know is Linda, and I'm guessing that exchange wasn't pleasant. I hover my finger over Mum's name. The last time we saw each other, I was kicking her out of my wedding dress fitting. Now look at me; my tail is so far between my legs I'm tripping on it. Here goes nothing. She picks up on the first ring.

'Amy . . .' she says gently.

'I'm sorry,' I say, tearing up.

'Don't be silly. Where are you now?' She sounds so worried; it's like I'm a child who has run off and got lost in the world. I guess I am to her. I explain that I'm at Nina's, and joke about how much food she has fed me and how relieved I am that I don't have to wear a wedding dress anytime soon. Mum laughs, if only sympathetically.

'Linda was . . .' She stops, and I know she was about to say something mean.

'She's upset, I understand', I say.

'Yes. She's a good family woman. I admire her values,' Mum says without a hint of sarcasm. I pull the phone away from my ear and frown at it. Did Mum just *compliment* Linda?

'You've changed your tune.'

She breathes out. 'We can talk properly when you're here, but so that you know, I've been feeling terrible about my performance at your wedding dress fitting and realised I needed to talk things over with someone. So, I've been *very* millennial and have found myself a shrink. I've only had one session, but . . .' She laughs nervously. I'm shocked to the core. This is the woman who, for the past decade, has gone on and on about how sea air cures everything.

'Well, I'm proud, Mum,' I say.

'Yeah, well, look, no pressure, but I've got your bed ready and a Waitrose order coming tomorrow, so if you want to come . . .'

'I'll be there Friday,' I say without a beat. Nina hasn't shown an ounce of annoyance that I'm here, but I know her well, and she needs her alone time.

Besides, I really want my mum.

★

Early evening, and I still haven't come out from under the covers, but I did manage to call the Edinburgh University professor back, and now I'm going to Edinburgh on Wednesday to meet her. So, next week I have an interview with Ealing Boys School and a trip to Edinburgh. All of that seems far-fetched right now, considering I don't even have the energy to wash my hair. The front door goes. Nina is home. The next thing I hear is Beyoncé's 'Run the World (Girls)' blasting from the kitchen. She's done something. I throw the covers off and see what's up.

As I walk into the kitchen, a loud pop goes off, and Nina is standing there with a champagne bottle, swaying her hips to the music.

'What's the occasion?' I ask as I sit down at the kitchen table.

'A historic event occurred today at Clapham High: "Nina Pascoe gets Dr Caroline Therone fired",' she says as she pours two glasses.

'How? I was just in a meeting with her,' I say.

She gives me a glass.

'While you were distracting her with your resignation, I was with the governors, showing them the audio files.' She raises her glass. 'To vengeance,' she says.

Autograph

'Ding-dong. Ding-dong. Ding-dong.' I open one eye and see Woody standing in the doorway. It takes me a second to remember where I am. I'm in Nina's guest bedroom. So why is Woody here?

'Morning, Sissy.' He is in head-to-toe denim and has a rolled-up newspaper under his arm. I open the other eye and slowly sit up. 'Your bag seems to have thrown up everywhere.' He steps over my scattered clothes with disgust.

'Woody, how are you here?' I ask.

He perches at the end of the bed.

'It was a whole thing. Dr Daddy told Mummy that you finally saw the light and are no longer with Joe Rogan 2.0. Mummy told me, so then I texted the ex and asked where you were, and he told me that you were at Nina's. And I was like, who the hell is Nina? He shared her number, and I was like, thanks, ya douche.' I gasp. 'Joking, I didn't call him a douche. So, I rang Nina. She said to come round anytime.' He looks at his phone. 'So, I've come at 9:39 a.m.'

'It's 9 a.m.?' I ask, horrified. 'Why didn't my alarm go off?'

'Relax, you've quit your job, remember?'

'Oh, yes,' I mutter. 'I have become single *and* unemployed in one week. What a year 2025 is cracking up to be.'

'I think it's great. Physics is the most pointless subject there is. You can't even see what you're teaching.'

'Erm. I'll still teach physics, just not at Clapham High.'

'Awkward,' he sings. He rubs his fingers together to get rid of any bacteria that may have come from my hoodie. I try not to feel offended by this.

'So, what are you . . .'

'Doing here? I need you to autograph my *Metro*. Page eight.' Woody passes me the rolled-up *Metro*. I let out a small cry. It's *actually* printed. I flick to the page and see the headline: 'Brave Teacher Takes on Birth Control in Science contest.' Under the headline is the photo of me. Mindy picked the one that I'm laughing in – I have two chins, and one eye is significantly more squinty than the other.

'Oh God.' A pen drops onto the paper. I look up at Woody.

'I want you to write . . . To Woodstock, you are the best. Love Sissy.'

'Woody, I'm not—'

'Sign it!' he demands. I quickly start scribbling the message. 'Dr Daddy is very proud,' Woody says, as I hand the paper back. 'He's telling everyone that his daughter is the rebellious teacher in the *Metro*.'

'He won't be proud. He hates this kind of stuff,' I reply.

'Don't be hard on poor Dr Daddy – he suffers from that illness where he can't show his emotions unless he disapproves of something. So sad, but extremely common in the old straight, British male.' He pushes his bottom lip out and I laugh. 'The second reason why I'm on your bed.' He pauses to give me a cheeky look. 'Is to invite you to my gig tonight. The Fox. Camden, 8 p.m.'

I'm about to give him an excuse, but he holds up his finger to stop me. 'No excuses. You're now young, free and single. And more importantly, you need to get out of this room. It looks like Zara on Black Friday.' He scans the room disapprovingly. 'So, are you coming?'

I visualise dancing in a sweaty dark room to Woody's band. It is not my scene whatsoever, but there is a small voice inside of me that whispers . . . *Hey, it may be fun.*

'Maybe.'

He claps. 'Yay, Sissy! And bring a friend or two or ten. We're massively undersold and the bloated manager is doing his nut.' He rolls his eyes. I wish I cared as much as Woodstock about what people think. As in, not care at all. 'Okay, I think that's it.' He jumps up onto his feet.

'Oh, Woody,' I say.

He sits back down. 'Tell me.'

'Have you heard from Lace? She's not texting me back. I'm worried something has happened.'

'Lace.' He thinks for a second. 'The dressmaker. Ah yeah, she's gone,' he says casually.

My stomach drops.

'Gone?'

'Flown away.'

'She's not a pigeon.'

'No, she is not.' He shakes his head as if sad about this. 'She left a note and fled. Word on the street is that Frankie looks as rough as a stray dog. Poor man, always falling for the flake.'

I throw the covers off me. Woody squints at my star-pattern pyjamas as if they are causing him pain.

'What if something has happened to her?' I say, panicked.

'Chill out, Miss Universe. She got bored and left. People do that all the time, like my Bio-loggy-Daddy. Poof. Gone.' He looks down and rubs something off his cowboy boot.

'You've never spoken about your Bio-log . . .'

'Bio-loggy-Daddy. There isn't anything to say.' He pauses, looking genuinely sad for a rare moment. 'Besides, you're my family. You, Mummy, Doctor Daddy. We're a dream team.'

He gets up again and begins cautiously stepping over my clothes towards the door.

I feel sorry for Woody's dad. He doesn't realise who he's missing out on. Woody is loud, exhausting, eccentric, yes, but he's like sunshine, lighting up every room. I've had him as a brother for a decade, but not fully appreciated how lucky I am until now.

'It's his loss . . . Bro-Bro,' I call out, and cringe immediately.

He turns with his mouth wide open.

'Did you just call me your Bro-Bro, Sissy?'

'No.'

'I think you did! Bro-Bro and Sissy against the world. Ha. See you tonight, Sissy!' He disappears.

I exhale and smile.

'Oh.' His head is around the door again. 'If you ever want to get laid, never, ever, *ever* wear that purple hoodie again.'

Buzz Buzz Buzz Buzz Buzz

I walk the usual route to Redchurch Street, passing the bearded hipsters with their beanies, rolled-up trousers and coffee obsessions. I can see from the top of the street that Lace's light is on, which means Woody was wrong. I run to the door and press the buzzer five times and wait and wait. I press it five times again and step back to check the window. She's ignoring me. Why is she ignoring me?

'Lace, it's Amy,' I shout, then go back to pressing the buzzer, not in five lots, but consistently. Buzz, buzz, buzz, buzz, buzz, buzz, buzz. I hear heavy footsteps slowly coming down the stairs.

'Stop pressing that buzzer! For the love of God.' The door opens. It's Frankie, kind of. He's not his usual clean self. He has bed hair and dark eyes and is wearing not much more than black boxers and a thin blue dressing gown. He looks awful, but I've got bigger worries.

'Where's Lace?' I ask.

'Good morning to you too,' he says with a waft of alcohol on his breath.

'I need to see her.'

'Good luck with that,' he says, and then he goes to close the door, but I stop it with my hand.

'Frankie, I know she's up there, and if you don't let me in, I'll um, scream.'

'You're not a screamer,' he says and sniggers at his own dirty joke. I open my mouth and let out a high-pitched squeak before he covers it with his clammy hand. 'FUCK! Okay! Come on in, but she's not here.'

The drawers are open and empty, and the French daybed would be bare if it weren't for a blanket and an uncovered pillow. I think this is where Frankie slept last night because there is also a half full bottle of whisky on the floor. I walk around, my footsteps echoing. It feels so much smaller without her and her stuff in here.

'See, gone,' Frankie says. 'Even that hippo cat has waddled off.'

'She can't have just gone. Where would she even go to?' I say irritably, because Frankie doesn't seem to be bothered that our friend has disappeared into thin air. He sits on the edge of the bed, inspects the whisky bottle and grimaces.

'Home, I guess.' He gets up with effort, wanders to the window and opens it, making the dust fly up like a fireball.

'This *is* her home,' I say like it's an obvious fact.

'This?' Frankie laughs. 'This is my storage space. What, you thought she lived here?'

'This is London. People live anywhere,' I say. He stares out of the window. 'Where is she then?' I ask. He shrugs with his back to me. 'Frankie, please, I need to talk to her.'

'She's packed up and left, what more can I say?' He looks at me, broken.

I drop down onto the French daybed. I can't believe how self-centred I've been. I've known something wasn't right since I spied on her and the Woolly Hat Man, but I have been too wrapped up in my own problems that I didn't make time for her. And now she's gone. How lonely she must have felt to pack up and leave without a word. I wipe the tears off my cheeks with my palms.

'Oh, where has granny's ring gone?' Frankie says, lighter. I sniff. He comes over, sits beside me with a sigh, and then rummages in his dressing gown pocket for two envelopes.

'Post arrived for her yesterday. I was going to send them to the original address, but the postal system can be dodgy. You can always hand-deliver them if you like?'

I inspect the white envelopes; they don't look like they are of much importance. The original address has been crossed out, and in wiggly handwriting, it says. *Please direct to No.8, Beanie Cafe, Redchurch Street, London.* The original address with the big cross-through is typed out and says *56 Primrose Street, Brighton.*

'Brighton?' I scrunch my nose at Frankie.

He scrunches his nose back. 'Unpleasant, I know.'

I then see the name *Olivia O'Shea.* 'Olivia?'

'You didn't think her real name would be Lace, did you?' he says. He bites his lip and takes another swig of whisky.

Nash

I exit Brighton station past a bunch of fat seagulls fighting over a couple of chips. I could get a taxi but decide to take a 30-minute walk to burn off the nerves. Impulsiveness does not suit me, and jumping on the first train out of London to Brighton was definitely not what I thought I would be doing today, but I had no choice. I need to know what is going on with Lace (or Olivia). She was a friend to me during one of the toughest times of my life; now it's my turn to be her friend. I just hope she's okay ... whoever she is.

Google Maps directs me through the city's backstreets, with graffitied walls and mystical shops where the smell shifts from salty air to incense to weed. The map directs me to a muddy park called The Level, which I follow until I cross the road onto Primrose Street. This can't be it.

Primrose Street is narrow with terraced houses in mismatched colours and two lines of cars packed tightly together. The pin in my phone suggests Lace lives in the middle house. There is no way she would live on a street as quiet as this.

Number 56 is cuter than its neighbours. It's painted pink and has two small palm trees in terracotta pots on either side of the white door. The curtains are open for the world to see inside the front room. There is a sofa facing a TV alongside a mantelpiece with candles and framed photos along it. I spot a headless mannequin in the corner and lean over the wall to see if there are any other clues of Lace. The front door opens. A man is standing there with a confused look on his face and a very familiar woolly hat on. Well, I never.

'Are you delivering an iPhone by any chance?' he asks.

'Erm . . . no,' I say. He looks disappointed. 'I'm Amy, I'm trying to find Lace.'

'Lace, did you say?' the man says, and lets out a big 'HA'. 'I haven't heard someone call her that since school.'

'Olivia, sorry.' I fake a laugh to cover my mistake.

He narrows his eyes. 'How do you know her?' I go to answer, but then he says, 'Actually, I'm dying for a cuppa. Come in and you can tell me.' He leaves the door open behind him.

He calls out, 'How do you like your tea, Amy?'

I am standing in a narrow hallway with a staircase and a line of shoes. There are women's white trainers, men's running trainers and black flat pumps that seem far too clunky for Lace. I peer at the envelope from my bag to double-check that I have the right number: 56. I do.

'Erm, milk and no sugar,' I call back. There is art everywhere. The walls are filled with framed abstract pieces; one of a ballet dancer spinning in motion and another of a blue blob. I step into a pastel pink kitchen. It's a cosy, homely space, with a round wooden table. There are succulents in the window and a row of Mason jars filled with seeds and beans on a shelf. On the wall, there are candid photos of people in frames, a farmhouse clock and a blackboard with 'Grab some sourdough' written on it. The man hands me a white mug that says *Home Sweet Home* in italic letters.

'I'm Nash,' he says.

I take the mug and inspect the tea; it's milkier than how I usually drink it, but I thank him anyway.

'So, how do you know Olivia?' He leans against the bench, coolly sipping from his mug. He seems a lot more relaxed than he did in Spitalfields Market.

'She recently made my wedding dress,' I say.

'Congratulations.'

'Oh, I didn't go through with it.' I wave my ringless hand in the air with a nervous laugh.

'Oh, sorry.' He sucks air with his teeth. His face shifts as if something has just clicked in his mind. 'Oh, wait! Were you the client who had to rush her wedding because the grandad had dementia or something?'

'Erm, sorry, who are you?' I ask. Whatever has clicked in his head, hasn't clicked in mine.

'Nash,' he repeats slowly, like I'm crazy.

'I mean, are you Olivia's . . . boyfriend? Brother?'

Nash puts up his hand, where there is a gold band on his wedding finger.

'I went through with it.' He smiles. My stomach drops. Lace has *a husband*. 'I'm guessing I wasn't the hot topic of conversation?' he says, sounding a little hurt.

I begin stuttering. 'Well, I was just a client, so—'

'It's okay,' he cuts in. 'It was a strange time for her. For us.'

'Strange time, how?' I ask. Suddenly the front door slams.

'Probably best if you talk to her yourself,' Nash says. We listen to the commotion in the hallway of keys being dropped and shoes being taken off.

'Got the sourdough,' a voice yells.

'We're in the kitchen,' Nash yells back.

'Who is we?' she says, and a moment later, Lace appears holding a bag with bread poking out of the top. She freezes in the doorway, like she's accidentally walked into the wrong room. She's not in a classic black outfit but in baggy jeans and an oversized beige jumper. Her hair is flat, her eyes are not lined with flicked eyeliner, and her lips are not painted Hollywood red. This is not Lace, this is Olivia.

'Amy. You're in my kitchen,' she says. Her childlike voice is now deeper and ordinary. The kind of voice that you don't really think about.

'I am,' I say.

She puts down the bread and offers me another cup of tea.

Comet

Olivia and I are sitting at the kitchen table with tea. Nash has gone upstairs to give us space.

'I gave Peppy back to his owner if that's what you're here to ask,' Olivia finally says. I know she's trying to make light of the situation, but I'm in no mood for jokes.

'Who are you? You have a house? A husband? You don't even have the same voice,' I say in a frantic whisper, cautious of Nash being in the house.

She flicks her eyes up at me.

'I'll explain,' she mutters. I lean back in my chair with my arms crossed, prepping myself for the story. She exhales and begins. 'Nash and I have been together since we were 12. We met on the first day of senior school in art class. We were asked to draw any animal and we both drew a platypus, and that was that. We went through school together, and both left at 16 and have been working ever since. When I was 22, we got married at the town hall, and then we bought this house. Recently, we started talking about starting a family . . .' She drifts off. I frown. It's not the traumatic story I was expecting. She's got the house and a man who clearly adores her, isn't that what people are striving for?

'Sounds like the perfect love story,' I say tightly. 'Unlike my one.' I show her my bare hand without the engagement ring on. She does a sharp intake of breath, like she has seen a nasty cut.

'Oh, Amy. I'm so sorry . . .' She winces and then says, 'But probably for the best, though. Right?'

'Probably,' I say as I stand up. 'But it still hurts.' I go to the kitchen window and look out at the garden, which is a concrete space with a rusting round table, bare flowerpots and a string of fairy lights dangling from one side to the other. In the corner, a BBQ is covered in shrivelled leaves.

'Sorry, I didn't mean that,' Lace says. 'I just meant—'

I cut her off.

'You knew more about my relationship with Josh than anyone else. I didn't tell my best friends the things I told you. And yet, I didn't even know your real name, let alone that you were happily married and lived in a lovely house with a . . . a . . . BBQ.'

'It's only a cheap thing from Homebase,' I hear her mutter.

'I'm just confused, Lace. Olivia. Whatever. I feel lied to.'

I look at her, and she dips her head.

'I know, I'm sorry.'

The photo hanging by the farmhouse clock catches my eye. I go over to take a closer look. Olivia and Nash are standing on wet concrete steps surrounded by confetti. She has lace from her neck to her wrists and a bright white skirt with a long train being held up by her bridesmaids. Nash looks like a true hipster in chequered trousers that hover above his ankles and a green bowtie that matches his green socks. They are a disgustingly cool couple.

'That was the first wedding dress I made,' she says.

'It's stunning. Naturally,' I say and sit back at the table.

'The thing about me and Nash is we're so close. It's like we've moulded into the same person. Where Nash is, I am. Where I am, Nash is. Our lives have been so intertwined that it's almost impossible to know who I am without him.'

'Sure. I get it. Relationships can be suffocating, but it's quite something to run away to London, change your identity, make friends with strangers, and let's not forget, *steal a cat . . .*' I pause. She avoids my eye contact. 'Surely a spa weekend would have done the trick? I just don't understand—'

'Mum left when I was eight,' she cuts in. 'She flew to America with some guy. She couldn't deal with *it* anymore. *It*, being motherhood. *It*, being me.' She laughs, even though we both know it's not funny.

Now I feel awful.

'Olivia. I'm so . . .'

'It's fine. Or it was until last year, when Nash and I started talking about having a family. The more I thought about it, the more I convinced myself that I couldn't do it. What if I get bored and ran away like Mum? That's another kid on this planet who's fucked up. I should have said something to Nash sooner, but I was terrified he would think I was broken. Society has never warmed to women who are not ga-ga about babies. So, I spiralled. I began making arguments out of nothing. The placement of the soap dish was a real lowlight. I knew I was being horrendous, and he didn't deserve it. So, I told him I needed some space. And that's when I came to London and became Lace.' She says this as if it were the most natural solution to the problem.

'Okay,' I say, pausing to absorb the story, which was upsetting, yes, but also very baffling. 'But why would you pretend to be someone else?'

'I didn't see it like I was pretending to be someone else. Lace is me, just a very exaggerated version. Does that make sense?' I nod as if it does, even though it doesn't. As far as I'm concerned, I am Amy Elman, there's nothing more to it, but each to their own. She continues. 'I always wondered what my life would be like if I hadn't met Nash, if I lived this alternative life in London. And so that's what I was doing.'

Nash appears in the doorway. 'Smuggins, do you know where my earbuds have gone?'

Did he say, *smuggins*? How could she laugh at Lab Rat, when she gets called bloody smuggins?

'By the sink,' she says, glancing at me, aware that I have noticed her nickname.

'Thanks,' he calls out as he walks away.

'He always leaves his earbuds by the sink,' she explains to me. 'He likes to listen to the *William Tell* Overture when he's brushing his teeth. He's done it ever since the iPod came out.' She shakes her head and smiles to herself.

'You really love him, don't you?'

'Yeah. I'm lucky.'

'Sounds like you won the love lottery.'

'I have. However, it's still hard work, which is why, God forbid, don't settle. Please don't settle, Amy. I see so many marvellous women settle for something that isn't real. Sure, Josh and you got on, he's a good guy. But I could tell immediately that he didn't set your world on fire. You didn't want to rip his clothes off. You weren't even excited about your wedding. You were ticking off a checklist of what life should be, rather than what it could be. Who you, Amy Elman, could be.'

I look down at my mug still full of tea and feel the weight of my current reality. 'I don't know what I want my life to be anymore. See, I thought I did, but . . .' I drift off.

'Not many people do, but you have the freedom of choice. That's more than most have in this world.' She reaches her hand across the table. I look at the ring on her wedding finger, a gold band with a sapphire. I slowly reach my hand out, and she squeezes it. 'I'm sorry I lied to you,' she says, looking me dead in the eye.

I want to be angry at her for making me feel like an idiot, but then, I can't ignore the fact that she saved me. She was a stranger who gave me confidence when I needed it the most. And without her, I probably would have made one of the most colossal mistakes of my life.

'The reason why I came here today was not to catch you out. I came here to see if you're happy. Are you?'

She nods and lets go of my hand. 'I am now.'

'Well, that's the main thing.' I spot the time on the farmhouse clock and groan. It's past three already. Time goes quickly when you're solving mysteries.

'I need to get back to London. I'm seeing Woody's band play tonight.'

'I didn't think you liked Woody's band?'

'I thought you only drank red wine, *smuggins?*'

'Touché.' She raises her eyebrows and smiles. 'I'll walk you to the station.'

I take my mug to the sink and have one last look at the garden. I suppose there is no dream life; everyone is paying a price somewhere.

Olivia links her arm in mine as we walk down her street. She tells me she and Nash are going to start trying for a family in the next few months. She also tells me she's going to stay away from London for a long time, if not forever. 'I'm not saying I didn't have fun,' she says, 'But they were dark days.'

'What was it that got you to come home?' I ask.

'Ah,' Lace said through a sigh. 'Nash rocked up one Sunday out of the blue, and gosh was I a bitch to him. He wanted me to come home, but I wasn't ready. When I went back to my studio that night, I had never felt so alone. I cried and cried. Poor Peppy sat on the French daybed, glaring at me like I had lost my mind. I suppose, in a way, I had.'

'You should have called me,' I say, feeling terrible because I knew where I was that evening, watching another episode of *Making a Murderer*, of course.

'No, it was my mess. I called Nash around 2 a.m. and finally said everything I was feeling about being a mum, and he understood me. Of course he did. He always has done. He said that we didn't have to be parents, but he thought it would be a shame, because he believes that I would be the kind of mum who makes costumes for plays and tries to solve every problem, even if it's just a silly playground drama. The kind of mum who would spend ages writing out tooth fairy letters in tiny handwriting to make it look more believable. And he was right, that would be me. It clicked after that. Life with Nash, motherhood, it was less scary because I wasn't focusing on how I could fail, but how I could be great. I know that sounds dangerously close to some Pinterest malarky . . . but it's true. I went home after the wedding dress fitting, and now we're patching ourselves back up again, slowly.'

'God, you didn't wait around for my dress fitting, did you?'

She tightens her arm around mine. 'I wanted to. I worked hard on that dress. It was one of the best I had ever made. Plus, I wanted to say goodbye to you properly that night. But you ran off to peg Josh before I could.'

I laugh, still embarrassed about that night. 'Ah yeah, that didn't go well.'

'Clearly. What are you going to do with the dress?'

I think of it lying on top of a cardboard box. It feels like such a waste that it's not going to be worn after all her hard work.

'Why don't you have it? Maybe another client will fit into it?'

'No. It's yours. I made it for you. Wear it for Halloween, or the next wedding, perhaps? I don't know. You'll find a purpose for it. Maybe sell it and buy a telescope.'

'Maybe.' I smile.

We cross the road at the traffic lights and begin the uphill climb towards the station, passing the rush hour traffic as we walk.

'Do you regret coming to London?' I ask her.

She takes a deep breath. 'I regret the lies, but selfishly, no. I needed to step out of my painting to view it from the outside, so I know just how beautiful it is. How lucky I am. If that makes sense?'

'You know I'm not good with poetic stuff.'

'You're better than you think.'

The smell of fish and chips makes my stomach rumble, and it reminds me to call Nina about dinner as soon as I'm on the train. She's not going to believe Olivia's story.

We go against the flow of commuters coming in from London as we go into Brighton station. There is a train to Blackfriars, which leaves in four minutes from platform seven.

We turn to say our goodbyes. I see every freckle on her face and how her eyelashes flick up naturally. She's still nauseatingly beautiful.

'Oh, these are for you,' I say, pulling out the envelopes from my bag.

'Ah, so that's how you found me.' She checks over the envelopes and whispers sadly, 'Oh, Frankie.' She looks like she's about to cry.

'Can I ask?' I say. 'Were you two *doing it*?'

'Amy,' she says in a disapproving way. 'Ask me the question like we're grown-ups.'

'Fine. Were you having sex with Frankie?'

'No, we weren't,' she says with a straight face. 'But, if I'm honest, I knew he wanted to have sex and more, and I used that to my advantage, which is worse, in a way.'

'Hmm, yeah. That's not great.'

'Could you tell him I'm sorry?'

'I'll try,' I say and grimace, because I can't imagine Frankie wants to hear a second-hand apology from me.

'Or, maybe I'll send him a letter,' Olivia says, reading my face.

'That might be kinder.' An announcement tells me my train is ready to depart. 'Well, this has been . . . surreal,' I say, laughing, awkwardly, unsure of how to navigate this farewell. But then, Olivia pulls me in, and we give each other the tightest hug. She lets go and begins walking backwards.

'Paint the most magnificent picture, Amy Elman,' she shouts across the people passing between us.

Again, I'm not sure what she means, but I shout back, 'I'll try.' She turns away and disappears into the crowd, like a comet disappearing into the night sky.

September

I think I just had my first 'hot girl summer'.

There were gigs in stuffy rooms, where Woodstock thrusted microphones in sparkling outfits. There were Hinge dates in overcrowded bars. One of these dates turned into Willy Three, an account manager who restored my confidence that I was not bad in bed. Nice guy, but I'm enjoying having my own space and time.

It was the middle of July when I found my new home. I had stayed in Mum's spare room until Abi and I, dizzy on Pimm's, had a lightbulb moment. *Duh. Why don't we flatshare?* Next thing, I was stuffing cardboard boxes into an Uber and unpacking them in a room that faced Ealing Common. I lined my science books on the shelf and put a plant on the windowsill. I hung up my (new) clothes, picked out by Woody. And for a few weeks, my wedding dress hung in the wardrobe too. I had planned to keep it for the next time I walked down the aisle, but changed my mind. It felt silly to put that pressure on myself. I may fall head over heels for someone tomorrow, or I may be wheeled up the aisle when I'm 80. I may not get married at all. The problem with love is you can't plan it. Nina told me about the bridal charity shop in Notting Hill. I handed the dress over to a very grateful lady. It was in the shop window for three days, and then it was gone.

As for Olivia, she ghosted me for three months after that day in Brighton. I was sure that I was never going to see or hear from her again. It was on my thirtieth birthday when she text me. She wished me happy birthday and invited me to dinner with her and Nash at their home. Since then, I've been down a handful of times. The most recent time, we were having tea in her kitchen and she told me through tears she was pregnant. She looked somewhere between ecstatic and terrified. She was, after all, Olivia from Brighton, the local dressmaker, the wife of Nash. But she was also, Lace, the mysterious cat thief who was hiding from motherhood above a Shoreditch coffee shop. We're complicated beings – us women.

Now, it's September.

I'm in the kitchen eating Marmite on toast. My academic diary, break-time banana, bike keys and helmet are on the table in a line. A Good Luck balloon – a sun with a toothy smile – is lightly spinning by the window. It came with a card signed by Mum, Matthew and Chums. Matthew being the first man Mum has let in since Dad. Chums being Matthew's dog. She had no men in her life, now she has two.

My phone vibrates; it's a video message from Rebecca. I take a bite of my toast and press play. Rebecca has Benson sitting on her lap. He's only one, but looks big enough to be allowed on most theme park rides.

'Benny and I want to say good luck. Benny, say good luck.' Benny starts to giggle at the camera. 'Aunt Amy is starting her new job-y-wob.' He giggles some more. 'Say we'll see you on the weekend, Aunt Amy.' She takes Benson's wrist and says in a profound voice. 'We'll see you over the weekend, Aunt Amy.' She cracks up, and the video ends.

I also have a DM notification on my TikTok. That's right, TikTok. It's from Arabella.

Good luck, from your favourite class ever!!!!!

Attached is a photo. It's me with the Year 10 class, taken that day on the Southbank after the science contest.

Don't cry. Don't cry. Don't cry.

Thanks, Arabella. Be nice to the teachers.
(Remember your physics textbook.)

It was because of Arabella that I'm on TikTok. After the press I received from the science contest, Arabella persuaded me to start creating science content. It began with a few bumbling physics fact videos, and then it snowballed. Now @AmyUniverse has a following of 100,000 science fans, including my favourite influencer, @DrLabby. A highlight of my year.

Abi comes bouncing into the kitchen holding a red-eyed white mouse. She brings them home to have a holiday. I'm slowly getting used to that part of our flatshare.

'Look who it is, Mouse 55. It's the new physics teacher,' Abi says and holds the wriggling mouse towards me.

'Morning, Abi,' I say, leaning away from it.

Abi puts Mouse 55 into the cage and goes to make her coffee. The mouse climbs up and starts aggressively gnawing at the bars with its long sharp teeth, making a desperate clanging sound.

'Right, time to go,' I say.

'Good luck,' Abi yells over the noise of the coffee machine.

I rush out the door and get on my bike. It's one of those blue-sky September days where every colour is popping in the park. It's not the countryside – yet – but I'll get there one day. I have my savings and rough idea of where I will end up, but for now, I am living each day as it comes and taking a break from to-do lists . . . and tally marks.

I leave the park and cycle a mile up the road. The Ealing Boys School sign comes into view. My insides start bubbling away. This is me, heading towards my new job.

There are groups of boys standing by the gate in green blazers and black ties. I ring my bike bell and they jump out the way and give me a curious look, trying to suss out who I am.

'Thank you,' I call back.

When I got the phone call to say I had been successful in the interview, I didn't accept the job straight away. After the break-up, I had an impulse to move far away from London. Start again. Refresh. Reboot. But I wandered around Ealing, and even though it's still London, it felt different from my world in Stockwell. But what pushed me to say yes was when they increased my wage a smidge, and that smidge would have been silly to say no to.

I park my bike in the teachers' bike shed and bend over to lock it up.

'Amy Elman?' a voice says behind me. I turn and see Alex, the biology teacher, standing with a backpack pulled up high on his shoulder and his distinctive thick-framed glasses that he wore that day at the science contest. I have a lot to thank him for, but I have to keep it professional for now.

'Hi,' I say, shaking his hand. My unclasped helmet falls off my head and drops onto the gravel.

'Oopsy,' he says and picks it up. I am blushing. I'm not sure if it's because I dropped my helmet, or because he said oopsy. 'Ready to see your new lab, Amy, or should I say @AmyUniverse?' He grins.

'Oh gosh, Amy, please,' I say.

'Very well, *Amy*. Follow me. You're going to love what they've done to the place.'

Alex opens the lab door for me. I walk in and step back. The lab is twice the size of the one I had in Clapham, and everything, from the floor to the benches to the whiteboard to the walls, is sparkling new.

'The science department finally got a makeover over the summer. It's all "state-of-the-art",' Alex says proudly.

'It's like something from a sci-fi movie . . .'

'You should see my lab,' Alex brags. 'Oh, and . . .' He runs to the corner where a blue sheet is covering a box. 'Duh. Duh. Duh. Duuuh.' He sings and takes the sheet off, revealing a fish tank.

'Are those my neon tetras?' I squeak.

'All 30 of them.'

'How?'

'The head teacher of Clapham High arranged it. Nina, is it?' he asks as if he doesn't know her name. After her takedown of Dr Therone, every teacher in London knew the name Nina Pascoe. The teaching world is not that dramatic, so when a scandal happens it spreads like wildfire. It was like our very own Wagatha Christie.

I put my face up to the tank. 'Hey guys,' I whisper. I hear a quiet snigger. Alex is laughing at me. I straighten myself up and clear my throat. 'Sorry.'

'No need. I talk to Joan all the time. She's a skeleton,' Alex says. 'My number one woman.'

'Is that because she doesn't talk back?'

'I wish she *did* talk back. No, it's her bone structure that got me.'

I laugh. A funny biology teacher, who would have thought it?

'Come and meet her when you get a chance.'

'Can't wait.'

We share a smile.

'Anyway, I better leave you to it. I'll see you at lunch, Amy.' He turns at the door. 'Oh, don't touch today's shepherd's pie at lunch. Go for the vegetarian choice. It looks like vomit, but tastes . . .' He kisses his fingers like a cartoon chef. I chuckle.

'I'll take your word for it.'

Alex leaves, and I can finally let out the excited squeal that I've been holding in. *My* lab. I send Nina a photo of the tank.

Best surprise ever. Thank you!!! 🎬 ♥.

As much as I will miss the girls at Clapham, I'm relieved that I left when I did. I love Nina, but it would be too weird if she was my boss. I still find it mind-blowing that she's Josh's boss.

Josh and I haven't spoken since March, and that was only a cold text exchange to split the remaining bills. We unfollowed each other a month after breaking up. He unfollowed me first. So, I did the usual, *well, screw you*, and unfollowed him too. It's for the best; we don't need to see a magazine of each other's lives. That's not to say I don't have the occasional stalk session with Abi. I am only human.

He's even more into the gym now. He even changed his name to @GymJoshGym. All he posts are Reels of him planking and lifting weights, and the occasional selfie without his top, with captions like 'PROGRESS!' It's strange how we spent our twenties together and have barely anything in common at the end. I wouldn't know what we would talk about now.

Two months after we broke up, Josh posted a video of him squatting with Tony. The caption read, #CouplesWhoSquat. It stung, but not as much as I thought it would. It was a dick move for Josh to move on so quickly, but what is there to say? I don't want to be squatting on Instagram with him. Tony does.

I may drink wine and laugh at his gym selfies with Abi, but I'm happy that Josh is being exactly who he is, just like I'm being exactly who I am – something that wasn't possible when we were together.

My desk is a blank space, ready to be made mine. I unpack my laptop and tiny globe. It's only then I spot the red garment cover hanging on the peg by the door. *How on EARTH?*

I yank down the zip to reveal a pristine white lab coat, on the pocket, sewn in red is my name – Miss Elman. There is no note, but it's not needed. I try it on and use the reflection of the fish tank. I look great. I feel great. White has always been my colour. I take a selfie and send it.

Olivia. YOU ARE WILD! 😂 x

She instantly sends one back.

You've got this Doll! Xxxxx

I write my name on the board, but I'm so nervous it comes out wobbly, so I rub it out and do it again. I've been doing private tutoring sessions to pay the bills, but it's been seven months since I've been in front of a class. It feels like I'm about to do it for the first time all over again. I clear my throat and stand up straight.

'Good morning, I'm Miss Elman, your new physics teacher. Miss Elman. Miss El . . . man.'

The bell rings. The door swings open, and a pile of boys come in. They are swinging their bags, yelling and shoving each other. Some of them say hi to me. Others walk by as if I'm as invisible as gravity. They each find their stools, and suddenly 14 sets of eyes stare at me, waiting for me to speak. I take a breath and smile, tap the space bar and capital letters fill the screen. SPACE.

'Good morning, Year 10. I'm Miss Elman – your new physics teacher.'

Acknowledgements

Writing your first book is always awkward because you have no idea if it's going to go anywhere. I pinch myself every day that it did, but it wouldn't have been possible without these lovely people.

To Mum, Julia, who has always encouraged and valued creativity, and let me go on and on and on about this book for the last three years. My eccentric Dad, Eric, who taught me to grab life by the horns, and for letting me know he's proud. To my big brothers, Jack and Joe, who always have my back. Richard Nott for his mentorship. He taught me that if you want to create something, you must show up to it every day.

To my editor, Audrey Linton, who has been a dream to work with and has made this story what it is. And the team at Hodder for all their hard work in bringing the book to life.

My fantastic agent, Elizabeth Counsell, for believing in me and for her hard work in getting this book out there. Also, to Diane Banks, Martin Jensen and the rest of the Northbank team for their continuous support

Thanks to Morag Joss and the Oxford Brookes MA programme, who helped get the story off the ground. Also, a nod to Sally Bayley, who gave a truly inspiring lecture. To the people who were kind enough to give their time and feedback along the way: Ed Roffe, Elizabeth Cleland, Etan Ilfeld, Eleanor Teasdale, Julia Newnham, and Catherine Atkinson.

My friends, who made me laugh and encouraged me from start to finish. A special thanks to Amy Clifford, Hermione Stanley, Ed Roffe, Sian King, Tom Robinson and Trevor Pomeroy. A shout-out to JP for his workout tips and to Hermione for the photos of her lab, as well as for answering my questions about her life as a teacher. And finally, to Susie Kumah, my best friend for over twenty years, who yelled across Dulles Airport, 'Finish that book or you'll embarrass yourself!'

RAISING READERS
Books Build Bright Futures

Dear Reader,

We'd love your attention for one more page to tell you about the crisis in children's reading, and what we can all do.

Studies have shown that reading for fun is the **single biggest predictor of a child's future life chances** – more than family circumstance, parents' educational background or income. It improves academic results, mental health, wealth, communication skills, ambition and happiness.[1]

The number of children reading for fun is in rapid decline. Young people have a lot of competition for their time. In 2024, 1 in 10 children and young people in the UK aged 5 to 18 did not own a single book at home.[2]

Hachette works extensively with schools, libraries and literacy charities, but here are some ways we can all raise more readers:

- Reading to children for just 10 minutes a day makes a difference
- Don't give up if children aren't regular readers – there will be books for them!
- Visit bookshops and libraries to get recommendations
- Encourage them to listen to audiobooks
- Support school libraries
- Give books as gifts

There's a lot more information about how to encourage children to read on our website: **www.RaisingReaders.co.uk**

Thank you for reading.

hachette UK

---

[1] OECD, '21st-Century Readers: Developing Literacy Skills in a Digital World', 2021, https://www.oecd.org/en/publications/21st-century-readers_a83d84cb-en.html

[2] National Literacy Trust, 'Book Ownership in 2024', November 2024, https://literacytrust.org.uk/research-services/research-reports/book-ownership-in-2024